# WHISPER

Michael Bray

First published in 2013 by
Horrific Tales Publishing
**http://www.horrifictales.co.uk**
Copyright © 2013 Michael Bray
**http://www.michaelbrayauthor.com**

A CIP catalogue record for this book is available from the British Library

ISBN: 0-9570103-8-9
ISBN-13: 978-0-9570103-8-3

## ACKNOWLEDGMENTS

As always, this wouldn't have been possible without the unwavering and unconditional support of my family and friends. Huge thanks go out to Sylvia Kerslake and Garret Cook for helping me with the edits on the first version of Whisper and suggesting some vital rewrites that helped the flow of the story. Their dedication and hard work were hugely appreciated. Also, I can't thank Simon Marshall Jones enough for the fantastic job that he did of polishing the manuscript, cutting away the excess fat until the book was as good as it could possibly be. Also, to Stu Smith from Graviton Creations, for designing a cover that really showed what the book was about. The level of detail that he put into those trees was astonishing. Finally, special thanks to everyone who offered advice and beta read the manuscript. To name a few, Joe Jenkins, Paul Levas, Bruce Blanchard and Albert Kwak were instrumental in helping me to shape the book and get it ready for release.

Lastly, a major thank you to my wife Vikki and daughter Abi, who support my passion and enable me to keep doing this thing that I love.

# Prologue

*1513*

THE SMELL OF DEATH hung heavy in the morning air. The child ran through the forest, snatching quick glances over her shoulder as the Gogoku Elder followed, crashing through the undergrowth in pursuit. She veered to the left, ducking under a gnarled, overhanging branch and hopped over a protruding root as she tried to put some distance between herself and the Elder. Her bare feet were bleeding, but in her fear, she barely noticed. Her only concern was her pursuer and ensuring that he didn't catch her. She angled back, heading to the village, her instincts driving her back to her home, even though she knew it had become a place for the dead. The Elder was closer now. She could hear him grunting as he drew near her. The girl snatched another quick look over her shoulder, and as she did, her foot twisted and sent her sprawling to the ground. The pain from her ankle was explosive, and although she struggled to get to her feet, it was too late.

He had found her.

The Gogoku Elder stood above her, breathing heavily and streaked with the blood of his fellow people. His eyes glared with fury from behind his painted face. The frightened child scrambled backwards, the agonising pain in her ankle forgotten for the time being. Her eyes were instead fixed on the spiked club held in the muscular Elder's hand, thickly matted with sinewy clumps of flesh and slick with blood.

He followed her gaze and unleashed a bloody grin, his yellowed teeth filed to points as was customary for Gogoku Elders. They were supposed to be the village protectors, the guardians and hunters, but something had gone horribly, horribly wrong. A shallow breeze pushed through the trees and the Elder blinked, casting his eyes to the dense canopy, his brow furrowed as he listened.

The child also looked, the fear within her replaced by a brief curiosity at the absolute silence which had fallen over the forest. She glanced back to the Elder, her brown eyes filled once more with fear, horror and betrayal. The Elder looked back, and smiled.

He had done as they had asked of him, and now all, apart from this one child, were dead. Another breeze moved the trees, and this time, both child and Elder heard it. The trembling child closed her eyes and waited, as the Elder reared back and brought the club down hard with a guttural roar of rage.

# 1. HOPE

THE HOUSE WAS CALLED Hope, and Melody loved it as soon as she saw it. She threw her arms around Steve's neck in the way she always did when there was something she really, really wanted. He smiled awkwardly as she released her grip and grinned at him.

"It's perfect. It's exactly what we were looking for," she said, turning back towards the building.

Steve was not convinced. He wrinkled his nose, and gave the place a cautious once-over. The agents had said the house was early eighteenth century, and to Steve, it appeared that it hadn't been repaired or renovated since. It stood like a faded white slab against a backdrop of orange and brown autumn leaves, leaving the surrounding trees looking bare and gnarled. The house looked tired and grubby, and Steve wondered when it had last been given a bit of TLC.

The single-lane private road which led to the house snaked through the trees, and as it wound its way deeper into the depths of Oakwell Forest, it narrowed so that eventually the overhanging canopy was close enough to brush against the roof of their blue Passat.

As they neared their destination, the road had opened up onto a driveway of sorts, which then turned into the front yard area of the property.

The house was set a little further back behind an overgrown garden abundant with weeds which, like the house itself, looked tired, unloved, and in some way forgotten. At the periphery of where the forest and the property boundaries began stood a rickety awning that was miraculously still standing despite its dilapidated appearance. A sign hung limply from its underside: it bore just a single word, carved in an old, swirling script.

*Hope.*

Steve's hope—as he eyed the sagging, patchy roof and rotten window frames—was that it wouldn't cost a fortune to repair or to keep the place warm in the winter months— *if* they decided to make an offer on it at all. He supposed he could do a lot of the work himself, but by the obvious state of disrepair (evident even from some distance away), he could see it being more trouble than it was worth and now understood why the asking price had been so low.

A gust of wind made the trees whisper in unison, making him shudder involuntarily. It was certainly a unique selling point— a house in the middle of the forest— but as a city boy through and through he wasn't quite sure that he was ready to make the huge leap from the concrete jungle to the literal one. The trees continued to sway, leaving mottles of diffused mid-morning sunlight shimmering across the ground. Melody turned to Steve and grinned, and he knew then by the excitement which shone in her eyes that he would be fighting an uphill battle to talk her out of making an offer on the place right there on the spot. He felt a pang of discomfort, a strange unease that stirred him as he looked beyond the house to the dense tangle of oaks and birches, seemingly stretching ever upwards in their quest for sunlight. He suddenly felt very small and insignificant.

The estate agent, a greasy, bird-like fellow by the name of Donovan, saw Steve's discomfort and with the graceful ease of a serpent slithered his way over and leaned in close, invading Steve's personal space.

7

"Don't worry about the trees. They just take a bit of getting used to," he said, nodding towards where Steve was staring, "The last couple who lived here were in this house for many happy years before they decided to sell up and move to Australia." He flashed his wide, salesman grin.

Steve didn't like Donovan, and only hid his contempt for the horrible little man for the sake of Melody, who he loved more than anything. He chose not to respond for fear of putting the gangly idiot in his place, and without missing a beat, Donovan saw this as his signal to continue his pitch.

"It has everything a young couple could need, Mr. Samson. And of course, needless to say you won't have any noise from the neighbours"

Donovan said it with a chuckle, which he quickly killed when he saw that Steve wasn't joining in. He cleared his throat and reverted to what he knew, which appeared to be grinning at Steve with a mouth that appeared to contain too many teeth. Melody called out from behind the house, her disembodied voice carrying on the wind towards them.

"Steve, come take a look at this!" she yelled excitedly.

Donovan rolled his eyes in a clumsy attempt to build some rapport. Two guys together, best pals to the end. Steve's disdain for the man moved up a notch as he walked around to the back of the house to look for his wife.

The rear of the property was bathed in blazing sunshine, causing him to squint as he rounded a corner. Donovan had produced some cheap-looking sunglasses from the pocket of his even cheaper-looking suit, which only served to add to the general ridiculousness of his appearance. Steve saw the reason for Melody's excitement and felt a dull

8

gnawing in his gut he couldn't quite explain. Maybe it was just anxiety or the fact that he was out of his comfort zone, but he couldn't quite put his finger on what it was. Melody would have laughed at him and called it the *heebie jeebies*, which was as good a description as any he could muster. Although he hadn't been able to tell when they'd approached the impenetrable density of the trees by car, it was now clear that Hope House sat on the lip of a gentle sloping hill. The back of the house led on to a long, narrow garden, at the end of which was a wide, slowly flowing river which cut directly across the bottom of the boundary to the property. The view from the house was stunning, giving the three of them a beautiful panorama of the immense forest that seemed to have swallowed the house some years ago as it had spread outwards. Steve was not one to be easily impressed, but even he couldn't help but draw breath at the view.

"Beautiful isn't it?" Donovan said as he removed his idiotic sunglasses and slipped them into his breast pocket. Steve chose not to reply, but Melody could barely contain herself.

"I love it!" she said, as Donovan flashed his salesman's grin at her. Steve also noticed that their slimy host helped himself to a quick glance at her chest before continuing with his pitch.

"Your wife has impeccable taste Mr. Samson," Donovan said around the grin that seemed glued to his face.

*And lovely tits!*

Steve imagined the smarmy salesman adding, but Donovan kept quiet. Instead, the man helped himself to a second lingering glance at Melody's tight t-shirt.

"We haven't even seen the inside of the house yet," Steve said, content to ignore Donovan's ogling for now.

"It will be perfect, I just know it!" Melody exclaimed over her shoulder as she walked down the garden to the river for a closer look.

"You hear that Steve?" said Donovan, clapping his hands together. "It seems your lovely wife approves."

Steve nodded, noting that Donovan seemed to think they had now switched to first-name terms.

*He smells the sale,* Steve thought, watching his wife explore the garden. He had a sudden desire to take her in his arms and hold her close. To protect her from—what exactly? Donovan? No. Donovan was an asshole all right, but he was harmless and certainly not Melody's type. He couldn't place it but something bristled: he wanted to shield her, to keep her safe. Steve studied her as she brushed her hair away from her face, and he knew without doubt that she wanted the house, and if that was the case, he would go with it. Not because she would kick up a fuss if he didn't— he knew that she wouldn't force him into the decision —he would agree to it because she wanted it badly, and if he could give her something that made her so happy, then he would do it without question. As if reading Steve's thoughts, Donovan leaned close.

"How about we go and see the rest of the house and fill out some paperwork?" he said smugly, walking away before Steve could protest.

Steve glanced up at the house and couldn't shake the feeling that it was scrutinising him. Shrugging it off, he waited for Melody to join him. Then, arm in arm, they followed Donovan as he led them to see the inside of the property.

## 2. A FRESH START

THE NEW YORK APARTMENT that Steve and Melody shared was in disarray. Boxes of their belongings were half-packed, the taped containers marked with Melody's hand-written instructions about their eventual destination.

Steve lay in bed watching the news. He had grown increasingly concerned over the last couple of days at how certain Melody was that the offer they had made for Hope House would be accepted. Donovan's asking price was ninety-seven thousand, which was already at the very top end of their budget. Steve had put in an offer of eighty-eight, arguing that they would need to earmark some funds for the repair work that was needed. Donovan had squirmed around behind his slimy salesman smile, but in the end had agreed to submit their offer to the so-far anonymous owners.

The reason for the low-ball offer was twofold. Firstly, the house did indeed need extensive work. The window frames were old and rotten, definitely needing replacement, and in the oval sitting room, a huge, ugly crack ran down the full length of the chimney breast, exposing the wooden slats beneath. There were other issues too. The roof had a hole in it, leaking water into the upstairs bedroom, and the kitchen plumbing was rusted and barely operating.

There was another, deeper reason too. One that he had no intention of telling Melody.

Part of him, deep down, hoped that their offer would be rejected. Not only because of the work needed to make the house habitable, but also because of how Melody was behaving.

She was always so thoughtful and considered every action before she did anything, yet had seemingly fallen completely in love with the tired old house and made no efforts to hide it from Donovan, who saw her enthusiasm as an excuse to try to push the price up.

Steve stared at the television screen without really watching, and as much as he hated himself for it, he couldn't wait to get the call saying that their offer had been rejected, so they could move on and look for something a little less —

*Creepy.*

He could hear Melody singing to herself in the kitchen as she made breakfast. Even though it had been almost a week since they'd made the offer, and had so far received no word from Donovan, Melody was convinced that it would be accepted and that Hope House would be theirs.

He tried to warn her that it was far from a done deal, but she had been adamant and had insisted on starting to pack everything. He had initially refused, and they'd had a rare argument. He'd later backed down, but there was still something that he didn't like about the place. He surmised it might have been because it was in the middle of nowhere, and he was used to the concrete comforts of city living, or maybe it was just the change in personality that he'd seen in Melody since they'd gone to view it, but whatever it was, he wasn't feeling entirely comfortable.

He was broken from his train of thought by the sound of Melody running down the hallway to the bedroom. She burst into the room, a vision of long hair and ecstatic grin as she leapt on the bed and kissed him hard which, although surprising, was very welcome.

"We got it Steve. We got the house!" she said as she came up for air.

"We don't know that for sure we—"

"—I just got off the phone with Donovan. They accepted our offer. Baby it's ours!"

Steve smiled, even as his stomach sank a little. He tried his best to hide the disappointment.

"That's great news!"

The lie wasn't that good, but in her excitement, he hoped she hadn't noticed.

"He said we can move in anytime from the end of the month, so we'd better hurry up and pack the rest of our stuff."

He nodded behind his not quite sincere smile as he chewed over the finality of the situation.

"Remember we can't move in until all the repair work has been done," he said cautiously.

She frowned, her smile briefly fading, and then reverted to its glowing glory.

"We can sort all that stuff out later, come on lazy, get up! We can drive out there and have another look at the place."

He didn't want to see it again, not really, but he saw how excited she was and couldn't think up a plausible excuse to get out of it. Besides, he decided that he had better get used to the place since he was going to be living there.

"Okay, point taken. I'll get up. Who needs sleep anyway?"

She smiled and kissed him again, and he returned the gesture, pulling her towards him. She playfully pushed him away, and grinned.

"Plenty of time for that later," she said, kissing him once more softly on the lips before leaping off the bed. She grabbed the covers off Steve and tossed them to the floor.

Michael Bray

"Hey!" he complained, breaking into a grin.

"Now get up, we have a lot to do!" she said with a grin of her own before disappearing out of the room.

He lay there for a moment, his smile as false as the realtor's had been now fading from his lips. He knew that he should be happy that they were finally buying a house together, somewhere to hopefully start a family of their own, and yet his stomach still churned with that subtle anxious uncertainty. He wondered if perhaps it was simply fear of the unknown, or even fear of change. Both of which were perfectly normal emotions ahead of such a huge life-changing step. But deep down he wasn't so sure. He had a problem with the house itself. Something about it bothered him, something in its atmosphere. Either way he was now committed to the move, and would do it without complaint for Melody's sake. He was sure it was nothing anyway, and the least he could do was give it a chance and see if his second impression was different from the first. With a sigh, he climbed out of bed and dressed.

# 3. IN THE BEGINNING

*June 14th 1809*

JONES WATCHED THE HOUSE being built, the Negro slaves' wiry bodies slick with sweat as they toiled in the intense summer heat. They in turn watched Jones through nervous and fearful eyes as they worked, making sure to give that little extra effort when his steely gaze fell upon them.

Jones was Michael Jones, and he owned a reasonably successful construction company along with his brother Francis and their business partner Alfonse Schuster. He was a large man, with huge jowly cheeks and sandy hair. He didn't care much for the Negroes. They worked hard only under constant supervision, and he was sure that if he were to turn his back, they would put down their tools and rest, and that was something he would not allow in spite of the oppressive, burning heat of what was turning out to be a scorching summer day; the kind of day when just standing still would bring sweat to the brow, the kind of day where the air felt hot and sticky.

As he looked at the house from his vantage point by the river, he could see a thick, wispy heat haze shimmering off the ground. Despite this, he would not allow the workers to rest. Four of them had already passed out from exhaustion, and had been quickly revived and set back to work. His company was known for delivering on time, and he was prepared to do whatever it took to finish the house as soon as possible — especially with Alfonse looking for any possible way to pull the plug.

He sighed and squinted at the sun which continued to burn without mercy. With a grunt, he walked towards the construction, angry and not really knowing why. The workers saw him and increased their efforts. Jones stood and watched, glaring at them even as they did all they could to ignore his stares. One of them stood and approached him, his eyes half-lidded and skin drenched with sweat.

"Mr. Jones suh," said the worker in his deep southern drawl, lowering his gaze.

Jones said nothing. He simply glared and waited. Hesitantly, the worker went on.

"Mr. Jones suh, we are tired, and would very much like some watah."

Jones shook his head slowly. "That's the trouble with you niggers. Just plain lazy."

"Please suh, we workin' hard."

"Really?" said Jones with a mocking smile. "How about you run back on over there and tell them they can stop working when the job is done and not a second sooner. You are here to work, not drink and take breaks."

"Yes suh," said the worker, about to head back to his duties when Jones spoke to him.

"Do you have a name?"

"Isaac, suh."

"Isaac? A typical nigger name. Well, Isaac you see that tree over there?"

Jones jabbed his thumb over his shoulder to the immense willow overhanging the road.

"Yessuh."

"I want you to cut that down and then make me a sign. A sign in honour of my easily frightened partner."

Jones nodded towards the awning where the dirt track opened onto the boundary of the land. Isaac looked from the awning and then to Jones, who was watching him intently.

"I uhh, don't like the heights suh."

"That is no concern of mine, I want you to do it, and do it now."

Isaac opened his mouth as if he wanted to say something else, and then closed it. He could see the venom in Jones' eyes and knew better than to push his luck.

"Yessuh. Right away suh."

Jones dismissed Isaac and watched as he hurried to the tree and picked up an axe. He shook his head, wishing he could get out of the heat and wondering why he was suddenly in such a foul mood. He supposed it could be the pressure he was under. The project had been one problem after another, and even though he would never admit it, he would be glad to see the back of it. He turned back to the house and the on-going construction, ignoring the aggrieved and fearful glances of the workers.

He deliberately took a long drink from his water bottle, enjoying the desperate, thirsty glances of his workforce. He didn't care. He wasn't there to be liked, but to get the job done, and as soon as possible. He had learned that in order to obtain results, he had to be seen as a harsh man, a man to be feared. He couldn't let them see that he was different away from the pressures of work. Even so, it was more than that.

*It was this place.*

He didn't like to think that Alfonse might be right, but there was definitely something in the air, some unpleasant flavour to the atmosphere that made Jones' skin crawl. As much as he hated to admit it, the place disturbed him, and that alone made him want to get the job finished quickly. If that meant treating his workforce with cruelty to ensure it, then so be it.

A gentle breath of wind touched him, causing the treetop to sway and sing. He half-imagined that the trees themselves were speaking to him, calling his

17

name, but he dismissed it. He was just tired. The good news was that, based on the current rate of work, he could expect the job to be completed in another week or two. Another delicate breeze moved through the trees, and again, he almost believed that he'd heard his name buried somewhere amid the natural sounds of the forest. The warning words of his business partner reverberated in his skull, and he found that despite the heat he shivered and felt the gooseflesh pop up on his massive forearms. It was as if he was being watched, prompting him to look nervously about him.

All he could see were the trees, and the dark spaces in-between. He licked his lips and stared deeper into those twisted, darkened places, hoping to see what was making him so afraid. He watched intently, for the moment the worries of the on-going assembly forgotten. Time passed. He wasn't sure how much. Seconds, minutes, hours: it all seemed insignificant. He shook his head and, unable to see anything, he slowly turned back to the building and tried to concentrate on the work at hand. He knew it was stupid, but he still couldn't shake the feeling that he was being observed. It was difficult to ignore, but he managed to force himself not to turn around and look into the trees. Partly because he didn't want to show that he had been spooked, but more because he was afraid of what he might see.

# 4. THE PURGE

*1513*

THE GOGOKU VILLIAGE WAS silent, its wooden huts now deserted shells. The blood-drenched Elder walked to the mound of bodies assembled in the centre of the village, and tossed the escapee child onto it, pausing to admire his handiwork. The earth beneath his feet was soft, mired with the blood of his people.

The trees surrounding the village swayed, and the words came to him in subtly devious tones. He saw the bodies of his children and his wife, their skulls broken and destroyed, their glassy eyes staring into oblivion. A brief sorrow overcame him, but the voices immediately drowned it out, guiding him and telling him what to do.

He walked through the blood-soaked earth to drier ground, and stood by the pile of kindling he'd collected earlier. He took a double armful and returned to the bodies, stuffing the branches and grasses deep into the tangle of corpses. The task took many hours, and whenever his strength waned, or he recognised a broken, misshapen face amid the dead, the voices in the trees would urge him on. The encouragement had long since become a warning, a fear-inducing threat which drove the frightened Elder to complete his task. He took the tree sap which he had collected under instruction from the spirits and poured it amid the huts, over the bodies and finally onto himself.

They told him what must be done, and the Gogoku smiled, for his mind was already broken. He crouched and struck a fire, using flint and dry grasses to light the torch. In the near dark, its glow made shadows dance and flicker on the his face as he touched the torch to the hovels, the flammable tree sap helping the fire to consume the homes greedily. The circle of land where the village stood was soon a raging inferno, and the Gogoku man watched as the bodies of his kin burned, their fats bubbling and popping as the flames continued to devour. The Elder stared at the flaming village from its edge, ignoring the heat which singed his skin and made breathing difficult.

Even though there was little wind, the trees moved, and the branches still spoke to him. The Elder knew it was time. The spirits that the Gogoku had wronged for so many years had finally taken their vengeance. The Elder closed his eyes and uttered an oath, cursing the lands and any who ever tried to inhabit them again.

He hoped the words would frighten the spirits, but they simply waited, silent until he did as they demanded. The Gogoku Elder grinned, and walked into the raging inferno, not even flinching as he began to burn, his flesh shearing away from bone as he lay on the mound of the dead with his kin.

The trees shook and swayed their approval, as the burning Gogoku Elder's laughter finally turned into pained screams.

# 5. HOMECOMING

DONOVAN'S OFFICE WAS A small glass-fronted building tucked between a grocery store and an antiques dealer. The sign on the front was as gaudy and cheap as the man himself. *'Donovan's Estates'* it proclaimed in blue on yellow. The windows were filled with properties for sale or rent in the area, as well as a laughable life-sized cut-out of Donovan, smiling his salesman grin, and a pasted-on speech bubble proclaiming:

*"Welcome to Donovan's! Oakwell's number one for new homes!"*

Despite his distaste for the man, Steve had to admire his work ethic. He was either brilliantly creative or ridiculously out of tune with how comically bad he actually was. Steve would have expected by the laughably high opinion that their realtor had of himself that he was an agent for a thriving and sprawling metropolis, but Oakwell was about as far from that as it was possible to get.

It was one of those tree-lined, leafy one-street towns, with the major needs of all residents within a stone's throw of each other. The corporate machine which had taken over the cities of the world, had so far not encroached onto the clean and tidy streets of Oakwell. Rather than a McDonald's you had a quaint diner that served real burgers made from real meat. Forget Starbucks too. Here it was Lou's—a charming café where the waitresses poured the coffee for you from a pot and service with a smile was something that actually existed. It was one of those places where everybody knew everyone by first-name terms, and nobody's business was sacred—or private.

Steve looked up and down the length of the street

(*aptly named Main Street. What else could it have been?*) There was the townhouse, police station, and library all within spitting distance of the other. A little way down the road was the quaint Lou's café, a couple of tables outside for those who wanted to enjoy a little sunshine with their coffee whilst they read the morning papers.

Over the road from Donovan's office was what looked to be a new store under construction, its plate-glass windows whitewashed to stop curious townsfolk from peering inside before work had been finished. Steve glanced up to the swirling red sign above the door.

*Grueber's World of Food,* it proclaimed. And then underneath *Big city quality at small-town prices.*

He could imagine that this place wouldn't be popular with the locals, as it took away some of the small-town feel to the area. It was a little too much glass and steel and not enough red brick and picket fence.

Steve had already psyched himself up for another encounter with their sleaze ball realtor, but was relieved to discover that the man himself was out of the office when they arrived. Steve assumed he was probably out hawking one of his properties, or more likely ogling somebody's wife or girlfriend, but their trip had not been in vain, as Donovan's assistant was on hand to pass them the keys to the house and wish them good luck. The key itself was like something out of an old Hammer Horror movie. It was long and made of iron with an intricate head. Melody loved it. Steve felt just a little uncomfortable even holding the damned thing.

As they drove towards the house, the pleasant, lazy stores and businesses of Oakwell gave way to rolling fields of green and yellow, and that ever-present cow shit smell that told you that the urban world had been replaced by the rural.

Steve had been watching Melody carefully and, truth be known, he did so with more than a little concern. She was smiling to herself as she turned the ugly house key over in her hands, apparently lost in its finely crafted detail. Although he loved the childlike wonder on her face, he couldn't shake his unease which, rather than fade as the day passed, had only grown. He turned his full attention back to the road and almost missed the turnoff to the narrow, single private lane, which led through the forest towards Hope House. Beside the lane's entrance, and underlined in red, there was a sign which simply said:

**PRIVATE PROPERTY - NO ACCESS**

He smiled at the thought that the sign applied to everyone but he and Melody, driving the car carefully off the gloriously smooth asphalt and onto the bumpy dirt track. A small wave of claustrophobia overcame him as the overhanging trees swallowed the light of the day and cast them into a dusky half-light.

"I'm so excited Steve. I can't wait to see the place again."

He said nothing, instead concentrating on the uneven and pitted road. Melody frowned, and set the house key down on her knees.

"What's the matter with you?" she asked.

"Nothing. Just keeping my eyes on the road," he mumbled as he glanced at her and flashed a fake smile which she saw through straight away.

"No, there's something else. You haven't been yourself since this morning."

"Honestly, I'm fine. I'm just tired, and this is a big step for us. I want it to go well that's all."

She seemed satisfied with his lie, and relaxed a little. They drove in silence for a while, Steve trying to keep the car on course and at the same time avoid ripping off vital parts of its anatomy. The narrow lane went on, and they delved deeper into the overarching trees of Oakwell Forest before eventually arriving at the house.

It looked surreal as they approached. The dense trees suddenly opened up and, as they passed under the wooden sign on to what was officially their property, a perfect, golden shaft of sunlight illuminated the house, which looked even more stunning now that they had escaped the gloom of the tree canopy. Melody grinned and leapt out of the car before it had come to a complete halt. Steve hung back.

The building was a large Colonial style property with a low, shallow roof. Since their last visit, the grass had been trimmed and a half-hearted attempt made to make the place look a little less dilapidated. Steve climbed out of the car and looked at the building, expecting to feel uneasy, but he was surprised to find that he was indifferent.

"Hey, didn't you forget something?" he called to Melody, holding the key up to her. She smiled sheepishly and came to him, kissing him gently on the lips.

"Deliberate mistake. Come on, let's go take a look around."

They started to walk towards the house, when Melody stopped.

"I left my phone in the car and want to take a few photos. Go ahead and open up," she said as she handed Steve the key.

He nodded and walked on, trying to ignore the feel of the iron key against his skin as he neared the front door. The wood looked to be warped slightly; its lines were not quite as straight as they should be, and he thought that it would probably need to be replaced before too long, adding yet more expense to his already growing mental list of 'shit that needed to be fixed.'

The door had a brass knocker in the centre which had turned green with age and exposure to the elements. Steve ran his fingers over the ornate detailing as Melody caught up to him.

"Beautiful isn't it?" she said, leaning her head on his shoulder.

He couldn't disagree. It was obviously hand-crafted, and the workmanship was amazing. It was a lion's head, with an ornate swirling letter 'J' carved on either side of the roaring face.

"I wonder what the letters stand for?" he said aloud, not really expecting an answer.

"Jones I expect. After the man who built the place," Melody said absently as she looked at the house.

Steve turned towards her and flashed a grin.

"I'm sure you just made that up."

"No," she said with an embarrassed smile. "I did some research. There wasn't a whole lot of info on the place to be found, but I remember reading about the company that built it, and I'm sure one of them was called Jones... I think."

"And where was I when all this sleuthing was going on Mrs. Samson?" he said playfully.

"Knowing you, Mr. Samson, you were probably either watching TV or had your nose buried in a book."

He laughed and turned to the door, inserting the key.

"Well, here we go," he said with a smile.

He tried to turn it, but it would only move an inch or so.

"Damn thing is stuck."

"It opened fine last time. Try turning it the other way."

He tried a little harder, pushing his shoulder into the door for leverage as he shook the key back and forth.

"My guess is that the wood is swollen, it happens when the temperature changes."

"How do you know that?" Melody asked as he flashed a quick grin.

"I saw it on TV whilst you were busy sleuthing on the internet."

She poked her tongue out at him and watched as he again shook the key back and forth in the door. After some effort, he gave up.

"It's stuck, I think the lock might be broken."

"So what do we do now?"

"Well, we could come back later, or I could break in. I mean it's our house, I suppose."

"No, you can't break it," Melody said a little too forcefully. She blushed and lowered her voice. "I mean it's so old."

"We may need to replace this door anyway, so it doesn't really make a difference, although now that I think about it, if I break it down the place will probably become a halfway house for the local wildlife."

Melody grinned. "That wouldn't bother me. I love animals."

"Maybe not so much when they are shitting all over our floors," Steve said, crossing his eyes and screwing up his face. Melody laughed, the sound carrying a long way in the stillness of the day.

"Maybe we could call Donovan, see if he can get a locksmith out here?"

As much as Steve wanted to avoid dealing with

Donovan at all costs, he had to concede that it was a good idea.

"I can try, although reception here is awful." He waved his mobile phone at her to illustrate the point, and Melody took hers out and checked it.

"I see what you mean, I have no reception either. It must be the trees."

"Probably -- either that or we are so far into the boonies we just went ahead and fell off the grid."

"Try walking around, see if you can find a spot where you can get a few signal bars."

Steve did a mock-theatrical bow, jogged down the three porch steps, and began to walk around aimlessly, holding his phone out in front of him.

"This isn't going to be practical if I ever want a pizza," he complained, shooting her a doe-eyed look.

"We can get a landline installed. For now keep circling," she winked at him.

"Yes, mein fuhrer!" he replied in a mock German accent as he began to march around in big clumsy circles.

Melody smiled and approached the door. She went to retrieve the key, and even though she knew it was stuck, tried to turn it anyway. The key turned smoothly without resistance, and the door clicked open. She turned to Steve, who was still marching obliviously.

"Hey Adolf!" she called, causing him to stop mid-march. He looked towards her, and she pointed to the now open door.

"How did you? —"

"Seems I'm stronger than I look. Come on," she said, heading inside. Steve followed, slipping his phone back into his pocket.

"I must have loosened it or something..." he mumbled as he followed her inside.

They stood in the entrance to the large circular main room. The staircase to the upper floor was directly in front of them; the kitchen opened up off a passageway to the left, and the study and dining room to the right. Dust swirled lazily in the shafts of golden sunlight filtering through the windows. Steve wrinkled his nose. The room smelled stale, like sweet wood and dry rot with a mouldering, mildewed undercurrent.

"This place could do with a good airing," he said, and was about to add more when his eyes fell upon the chimney breast. He walked to it slowly, running his hand across its surface.

"What is it?" Melody asked.

"This wall, there was a huge crack here last time we came, remember?"

"You sure?"

"Positive, I remember thinking how expensive it would be to repair."

"Maybe Donovan had it fixed?"

Steve leaned closer and examined the wall.

"I can't see any sign of a recent repair; in fact, I can't see any sign of a repair at all."

"You're comparing it to your own shoddy D.I.Y skills though," she grinned.

Steve didn't see the funny side, if anything he was decidedly uncomfortable.

"I'm serious. This is like new."

"They probably had it done for us. We did complain about the general state of the place when we first looked around."

"True," Steve replied absently, still looking for any evidence of restoration. "Well, either way, it's done now," he said quietly.

He wasn't at all satisfied with the explanation, but didn't want to ruin the day by getting into an argument, so let it slide.

"I suppose it's one less thing for us to pay for," she added, sensing his dissatisfaction.

"Yeah, I suppose so..."

"What is it?"

"You don't find this even the slightest bit odd Mel?"

"Odd? No. Just because you can't see it, doesn't mean that there hasn't been any work done. Come on, relax and let's take a look around. This is a good thing. Any saving here is money we can spend elsewhere on fixing the place up."

He hesitated, pushing away the horrible gnawing in his stomach. Instead, he followed Melody into the kitchen. He half expected to find that the previously rusted water-pipes were also now miraculously fixed, but when he turned the tap, the same deep groan emitted from the rotten pipework, and a small trickle of slightly muddy water dribbled weakly from the taps.

"Drink?" he asked pleasantly, trying to break the tension.

Melody didn't answer. She was over by what looked to be the pantry door. It was painted white and had an old fashioned latch handle. She pulled at it and, although it rocked in the frame, it wouldn't open.

"Steve —" she started to say, but he was already crossing the room.

She moved aside, rubbing her hands as he grasped the handle and gave it an almighty pull. The door popped open, and a dusty breeze hit his face. The pantry was unremarkable, a narrow room with shelves built into the walls. A huge network of spider webs criss-crossed the wooden shelves, some of its residents long dead while others were alive and well, waiting like large black olives as they sat in their webs. Steve shuddered. He didn't care for spiders. Melody grinned and nudged him aside. They had both seen what was in there and, unlike him, she had no fear of retrieving it.

"Wow, let me take a closer look at it," she said as she brushed the webbing aside and dragged the items out onto the kitchen floor.

There were two things. One of them was a rocking chair. The wood was almost black with age, and sat across its seat was the second object— an old woodcutter's axe. A few spiders disturbed by the intrusion scurried across the floor looking for a new place to set up home, but Steve barely noticed. He was looking at the chair.

"How old do you think it is?" Melody asked, looking at Steve with bright, inquisitive eyes. He ran his hands over the wood. It was obviously old, *really* old, and hand-carved. Despite its age, it was still sturdy, a shining example of the difference between good-quality handmade furniture, and the flimsy flat pack stuff that you could buy in any IKEA in the world.

"I wouldn't be surprised if it were as old as the house," he said as he ran his fingers lightly over the surface of the seat.

"Do you think we could clean it up and keep it?"

*No.*

He almost blurted it out before he could stop himself, and wasn't sure why. He looked at it rationally and told himself it was just a chair that somebody in the past had tucked away and that had been long forgotten. Instead of the truth, he chose an answer that he knew she would want to hear.

"I don't see why not. It's too nice to throw away," Steve said simply, and with some effort he even managed a warm smile.

"Come on, let's take a look around the rest of the house," he added.

They explored, and the entire experience was infinitely more enjoyable without Donovan's leering presence. They had become separated as they wandered, each finding their own way around the shell of their home.

After spending some time looking for places to store all of his 'man-crap' as Melody so eloquently put it, Steve found himself upstairs. Melody was in the circular room overlooking the forest. Sunlight streamed through the windows, illuminating the room in a stunning, golden glow.

"Just look at this view," she said softly as he approached, standing behind her and putting his arms around her waist.

She leaned into him, and the pair looked out of the huge windows. Despite his misgivings, Steve couldn't deny the sheer beauty of the view. He bent and kissed her neck, and she turned to face him.

"I think this place will be good for us. I can feel it," she said softly.

Steve nodded, declining to tell her that his own feelings of the place were anything but good. He pushed it aside and took her face gently in his hands.

"We will make it perfect."

She looked at him, searching for the right words to say then, unable to locate them, put her head on his shoulder and looked out of the window.

"Do you love me?" she asked softly without looking at him.

"Of course I do," he replied, kissing her on the head. She pulled back and looked at him, her eyes moist with tears.

"What is it? What's wrong?"

"Nothing," she said, struggling to keep her

composure, "it's just that I'm so happy, and I can't believe how lucky we are."

He pulled her to him and stroked her hair, and thought that although he was still on edge, he was determined to learn how to love the quirky house. He hadn't realised just how much it had meant to Melody, but now, as the pair stood with the warmth of the sun on their faces, he made a promise that he would do whatever it took to make sure she was happy.

# 6. ISAAC

IT WAS ALMOST DARK when Isaac had finished making the sign. Cutting down the tree had been hard work, and more than once he thought he was going to pass out, but he somehow managed to keep going. He pushed through the nagging, agonizing pain in his back and the fire in his shoulders, and the shredded, aching calluses that covered the palms of his hands. It was easier going now that the heat of the sun had faded, and the dusk had brought with it a chill which, although pleasant, would soon become uncomfortably cold. A wonderful breeze made the trees whistle and sing as it cooled his body and his thoughts turned to his employer.

Isaac didn't like him, hated him in fact, but forced himself to keep his temper in check, if only for the sake of his family. Since Isaac had been sent to cut down the tree, he had seen another four of his colleagues pass out due to being overworked in the heat, and had seen Jones treat them with the same indifference. He desperately wanted to do something, to stand up for himself, but he knew to do so would have terrible consequences, and with his family at the forefront of his mind, he somehow managed to keep his emotions under control.

Although he didn't mind working alone, especially now that the night was cool and Jones had gone home, he still couldn't shake the feeling of being watched, and neither could he ignore the stories of the things that were said to inhabit the lands there.

Another stiff breeze caressed his body, making him shiver. He paused to pull on his over-shirt, and then cast his weary eyes on the sign. He ran his fingers over the chiselled letters. Despite his

33

exhaustion, it truly was a thing of beauty. He allowed himself a smile, broad and white and proud of his workmanship.

The wind was picking up now, making the trees sway and sigh. Carefully setting aside the sign, he stood and positioned the ladder below the wooden awning and climbed carefully and slowly. Although he was only around twelve feet off the ground, still his legs trembled, and his heart raced as he positioned the heavy rope, tying it to the post and looping it back over in preparation for the mounting of the sign. The wind rushed through the trees again, and he froze, his eyes glaring into the near darkness.

He was certain he had heard his name.

It was just a murmur before it was snatched away by the bluster. Isaac listened, but this time when the wind came it was just that — the sound of thousands of branches moving together. He chuckled to himself —more to hear a human sound in the isolation than anything, but still he found it hard to take his eyes from the dense tree-line. With some effort, he turned and went back to work, tying off the thick rope in preparation for erecting the sign.

*Issssaaaacccccc...*

It was clearer this time, and he spun his head in the direction from which he thought that it had come. His eyes went wide as he stared into the darkness between the trees, but the natural sound of the forest around him made it hard to pinpoint.

Deciding it was simply the oncoming night frightening him and nothing else, he turned back to finish his work as fast as he could, so he could leave as sooner. It was fully dark now and the forest was starting to come alive, its nocturnal residents setting out to hunt and feed. With trembling hands he grabbed the rope, and knotted it.

The sound was loud and came without warning, and when it spoke his name, he could feel its hot breath in his ear, only inches from his face. He reared back and screamed, his feet kicking the ladder from under him. His head slipped through the large loop of rope as he fell and Isaac was silenced as it pulled taut around his neck. For a moment there was only silence, and then the wind came again and pushed through the trees, making the body of Isaac swing gently back and forth. He was already dead, but had he been alive, he may have heard the sound of the wind in the trees and the mocking sound of laughter.

# 7. MOVING DAY

THE DAY OF THE move brought with it all the usual chaos. They hadn't realised just how much clutter they'd both accumulated over the last few years until it was all packed up and moved into the new house, which now resembled a maze of cardboard boxes bearing Melody's careful handwritten script. Steve had ducked out for a much-needed break from Melody bellowing instructions to the removal men who, much to his amusement, seemed intimidated into following her every command to the letter.

He walked away from the house, lighting a cigarette and satisfying the gnawing need for nicotine, which had been tugging at his nerve endings all morning. He walked to the river at the bottom of the garden, flowing sedately along oblivious to the chaos of moving day for the Samsons.

There was a handy stool-sized tree stump by the edge of the water, and he sat down heavily. He felt tired, the toil of the last week or so as they'd made the final arrangements for the move beginning to wear him down.

Following the day they'd picked up the keys, he had expected that it would be at least another month before they would be ready to make the move, giving him time to make arrangements for the repair work to be done. However, Melody had been like a woman possessed, pushing preparations through at a breakneck speed, a practice with which he wasn't entirely comfortable. He was by nature a thinker, and liked to slowly and methodically work things out one step at a time. However, as far as Hope House went, Melody would have none of it, relying on her instincts and acting on them without questioning the consequences that may or may not happen as a result. It frustrated and impressed in equal measure, but like it or not he had to admit that it was quite a sight watching his five-foot-four wife order burly construction workers around as she oversaw the roof and plumbing repairs. He inhaled deeply on his cigarette, enjoying the calm.

He had tried to rein Melody in, to slow her down and explain to her that he felt like he was caught in a whirlwind of activity that he couldn't control. But she'd been unable to see it from his point of view, which had led to their first real honest to god argument since they'd met. It had blown over of course, but he still felt bad about it.

He looked towards the opposite bank of the river, into the dense trees that had twisted and slithered around each other at some indeterminate time in the past in their never-ending quest to reach for sunlight and sustenance. He noticed an anomaly, a break in the tangle of branches, and with his curiosity piqued, stood to take a closer look. He shaded his eyes against the sun, which glistened off the surface of the water and hurt his eyes. He couldn't be sure, but there was what looked like a path winding through the trunks. Absently flicking his half-smoked cigarette into the water, he inched as close to the edge as he dared, knowing that he would be a lot less bold if the water was any deeper, as he had never learned to swim.

The more he looked at it, the more he was sure it *was* a path. The ground was bare and well-trodden, the leaves and branches pushed aside. He wasn't sure what had troubled him at first and then, as he scanned the river from left to right, it dawned on him. There seemed to be no way across to the other side in order to use the track. He frowned and double-checked the full visible length of the stream, looking for any sign of a way to cross, but saw none. Grabbing a good-sized stone from the bank, he dropped it into the water but even so, it gave no indication as to how deep it went. He wasn't even sure why it bothered him. Maybe there had been a bridge once, but it had since been swept away. He could imagine that after a period of heavy rainfall, the river could easily become a frothing, white torrent of power threatening to burst its banks. Indeed, he could imagine it sweeping away even the strongest of bridges with ease.

A voice deep in his mind asked him why there were no signs of any such structure on the land, even just a few rotten and splintered timbers left safely out of reach of the surging waters, but it was a question he had no answer for. All he knew was that it bothered him—probably a lot more than something so trivial should have done. Not only because he wanted to know why the previous occupiers hadn't had the bridge replaced (if indeed it had fallen victim to the power of Mother Nature) but he also wanted to know where the path in the woods led.

He stepped away from the water's edge, and sat back on the tree stump. The sky had begun to grow a glorious shade of pre-dusk purple-blue, and already the familiar constellations were beginning to appear. He tried to forget the path in the woods and turned his back on it, looking back at the house instead.

The yellow glow from the windows was warm and inviting, and yet somehow he still felt more comfortable sitting outside on the tree stump. He wasn't sure if that said more about him, or his bad feelings about the house, which had grown considerably despite his determination to try and like the place. He dismissed it and lit another cigarette, making a mental note to cut down his intake of the dreaded cancer sticks.

He heard the steady rumble of the removal trucks as they made their way slowly down the rutted lane to their property, listening as everything faded to silence. It seemed that his wife had finally released the poor men from their duties. He took another drag, the orange glow of the cigarette now vibrant and bright as full night crept ever closer. Melody poked her head out of the door, waving to him and beckoning him.

"Could you come and help me with some of the boxes?"

He waved back and held up the cigarette. "Give me a second. I'll just finish this smoke."

Melody waved her acknowledgement and went back inside, leaving Steve alone with his thoughts. He found his mind drifting towards the path in the woods and, again, he forced himself to shut it out. He had enough concerns with sorting through the teething problems of the move without worrying about missing bridges and mysterious forest tracks. He grinned at his stupidity, flicked the remains of his cigarette into the water, and headed back to the house to help Melody.

A few hours later, they flopped down on the large plush sofa in the sitting room. The house was starting to take shape, although there were still a few boxes scattered here and there waiting to be unpacked. Melody had poured them both a large glass of wine, and then snuggled close to him.

"What a day," she said as she kicked off her shoes.

"Tell me about it. You would make someone a good dictator," Steve teased.

"You're lucky I'm not so strict, or I would have been out there kicking your ass for slinking off to smoke instead of helping."

"Promises, promises," he said with a grin. "And besides I wasn't skiving I was... overseeing the move."

Melody leapt up and straddled Steve, hooking her hands around his neck.

"Overseeing the move, huh?" she said, kissing him gently on the lips.

"Of course, I was making sure everything had its proper—"

She kissed him passionately, her tongue probing into his mouth. She pulled back, and he marvelled at how beautiful she looked in the soft glow of the corner lamp. Her eyes locked onto his, and her next words were almost a whisper.

"And how would Mr. Samson like to spend his first night in his new house?"

She kissed him again, and took her t-shirt off over her head.

"Well, I was going to suggest a quiet night and a movie, but now..."

She grinned and leaned close, and they fell greedily on each other, before stumbling to the bedroom. Neither of them noticed the old rocking chair in the corner of the room as it slowly swayed back and forth of its own accord, nor the sound of the wind as it shook the trees, making them shake and whisper.

# 8. THE RAGE

THE DOG HAD BEEN barking for over two hours. Donovan kicked at his covers and pulled the pillow over his head, but still he could hear it. He threw the pillow across the bedroom and glanced at the clock. He would need to be up in around three hours, and the little sleep he had managed had been disturbed by the incessant barking. The rage bubbled and stirred within, a feeling which both frightened and exhilarated him. For so long it had remained dormant, but on occasion, it would make itself known and he knew well enough that when that happened, it would need to be satisfied.

He climbed out of bed and walked to the closet, pushing past his array of cheap business suits to the hanger at the back, and took the clothing from it to the bed. Faded jeans, white t-shirt, dark grey hoodie, black gloves. He laid them out carefully, and his heart rate increased, beautifully complimenting the giddy butterfly feeling in his stomach. He dressed slowly, allowing the rage to bubble and build and swell. It always went this way.

Still the dog barked, a monotonous *yap yap yap*, but it no longer concerned Donovan, because the rage was now in control. Once dressed, he walked to the window and looked out into next door's garden. There it was, the scruffy terrier that had kept him from his sleep, barking at the house and pleading for its owners to open the door. He wondered how they—the Parsons—could sleep through such noise, and why they didn't just let the animal in, but whatever the reason, it didn't matter. Not anymore.

Donovan went downstairs, pausing only to grab the steak out of the fridge that he had planned to eat

Michael Bray

later in the week, but this was more important. The
rage was growing, and it was almost to that
frightening point of no return. He opened the door
and went outside.

Donovan's back-yard was small and grubby,
surrounded by a small fence which offered neither
privacy nor protection. But it was late, and he didn't
think it would matter. Sensing his presence, the dog
jumped up at the fence, growling at him and showing
its teeth. Donovan approached, holding out the steak
to the dog. The growling stopped, as the skinny
wretch of an animal drooled at the potential meal.

Donovan smiled, the expression cold and alien,
and one which, if flashed at a human, would give them
a glimpse of who he really was beneath the exterior
he chose to show people. But the dog cared only for
the meat, and so it trusted the human without
question.

"Here boy," Donovan whispered pleasantly as he
held the cut of meat towards the dog.

The animal responded, its nose twitching in
anticipation. As it licked its lips, thick strands of drool
began to ooze from the edges of its mouth. Donovan
could see the creature's name tag on its collar.

Spike.

He smiled at the irony as he reached the fence,
allowing the dog to take one edge of the meat in its
mouth. Spike tried to wrestle it away, but Donovan's
grip was firm, and the rage was flowing through him.
Spike had given up on trying to take the meat, and
was content to perch there on the fence on his front
paws and try to bite a chunk to take away.

Donovan smiled as he brought the knife up and
plunged it into the animal's neck.

It uttered a whimper and tried to pull away, but
Donovan had already grabbed it by the collar and

pulled it over the fence. He pushed the blade deeper as the dog whined and scrabbled to get away, but the rage was strong, and Donovan easily overpowered it. He sat astride the terrier and watched as its whimpers faded to shallow breaths, then eventually to silence.

The sky was starting to brighten, and the first birdsong of pre-dawn was coming. Donovan paused to savour the moment, then stood, brushing dirt from his knees as he picked the lifeless animal up, tucking it under one arm. He retrieved the partially chewed steak and walked back to the house.

He was happy.

Happy because for now, the rage was satisfied but, as always, it would only be a matter of time before it came back. He tossed the dead dog on the kitchen floor, mesmerised by the bloody streak it left behind as it slid to a halt. The knife went in the sink, the chewed up steak in the bin. Even though it had been sated, the rage was still talking to him, telling him what he had to do. And as always, he would obey it without question.

*A little while later*

Mrs Parsons stood at the door, looking into her empty back-yard, a frown etched on her portly face.

"Spike, come on Spike," she called, wondering if the stupid dog had managed to escape again. She took a slipper-clad step out into the yard, pulling her dressing gown closer to her.

"Spike!" she called again. "Stupid fucking dog," she muttered as an afterthought.

"Excuse me, Mrs Parsons."

Startled, the obese woman flicked her head toward the voice.

"Oh, good morning Mr Donovan."

"Good morning. Beautiful day, isn't it?" he said warmly, glancing up at the sky, which was a brilliant blue. "Is everything okay ma'am? Anything I can help with?"

She waddled to the fence, pausing to light a cigarette, and watched Donovan as he hosed his yard down.

"It's my dog, it's gone missing again," she said with a sigh.

"Oh, I'm sorry to hear that," Donovan said sincerely. "What breed is it?"

"It's a terrier, but he isn't house trained, so I have to leave him outside."

"Oh, I see," Donovan said as he turned the hose off and gave his neighbour his full attention.

"Well, I've been up for a while, and I did see a terrier out front in the street. Light blue collar if I remember rightly," he said with a perfectly manufactured look of concern.

"Oh, that's him. How the hell did he get out there?"

"Well ma'am, I suppose he must have escaped through the gap in the fence there."

"What gap?" Mrs Parsons said as she blew smoke out of her nostrils.

Donovan pointed to the fence panel in Mrs Parsons' garden which he had broken away earlier.

"Uh, that one over there ma'am" Donovan said apologetically, pointing to his handiwork.

"That damn dog!" Mrs Parsons said, rolling her eyes and taking another great drag of her cigarette.

Donovan smiled pleasantly, at the same time wondering how such a fat, disgusting mass of flesh was still alive. He wondered what it would be like to cut her throat, how glorious it would be to see someone so immense bleed out.

The rage stirred within him.

"Are you okay, Mr. Donovan?"

"Oh, I'm fine Mrs. Parsons. I'm just wishing I had more information to help you with."

"It's okay, it's my fault." She sighed. "I better get dressed and go look for him."

"Good idea, I doubt he would have got far." Donovan replied.

He spotted some blood by the fence that he had missed.

"Well, I'd better get back to work," he said, turning on the hose and spraying away the blood.

"Yes, yes of course. Thank you Mr Donovan," she said as she waddled back inside the house. Donovan watched her go, and then turned back to hosing down his yard.

He smiled.

It really was a beautiful day.

# 9. THE WOODCUTTER

*November 12th 1816*

THE WOODCUTTER PAUSED, wiping a grubby forearm against his brow. He had been working hard all morning, and had almost cut enough wood to see his family through the winter, which even now threatened to unleash its fury from snow-laden skies. The surrounding trees were bare and wiry, and around his feet the ground was a golden orange and brown carpet of fallen leaves. His breath plumed in the chilly early-morning air, and he returned to his work, rearing back with the huge axe and driving it down hard, expertly splintering the slab of wood and tossing it onto the pile with the others.

He had been ignoring the voices speaking to him all morning.

He hoped that by not acknowledging their existence, he would not have to deal with the possibility that he might be insane. He paused again and set another chunk of wood on the tree stump, then heard it clearly—his name buried under the breath of the wind.

He looked into the trees, green eyes staring intently as he surveyed the land. Water rolled past the house slowly under the footbridge which he had built in order to cross to the other side of the river— although now that he thought about it, he couldn't remember the reason *why*. He had neither business nor desire to go that way, and yet felt compelled to build the bridge anyway. He had half an idea that there was something over there, something powerful and important, but what it was, he couldn't remember.

Setting his axe down, he walked slowly to the bridge and looked across the water. His instinct screamed at him to turn back, but he disregarded the warning and crossed. The opposite bank was cooler, the brush overgrown and wild. He heard the chorus of the trees as they were pushed around by the wind, and held his breath and listened.

*Yes.*

The voices were clearer now, beckoning him closer, deeper into the forest. He walked towards the sounds, his work forgotten, and he ignored the sharp pain as overgrown branches and thorny bushes grabbed at his clothes as he pushed his way through the tangled foliage.

The source of the sound was hard to pinpoint, seeming to come from every direction at once, but over on this side of the water, they were no longer sweet and encouraging. Now they said things that horrified him. He covered his ears, trying to ignore the terrible, frightening things they said to him, and what they were telling him to do. He grimaced, gritting his gappy, uneven teeth. Nausea swept over him as his senses became overwhelmed. He no longer knew which way he had come, or which way he was heading. He was lost and all he could see around him were immense roots and moss-covered trees swaying and dancing and singing and speaking.

Screaming with rage, the woodcutter fell to his knees, covering his ears to try to keep the awful horrors of those words at bay, but to no avail. The voices were in his head, infecting his brain and polluting his thoughts. He reached up and grabbed the silver crucifix which he wore around his neck and began to pray for his soul, but still the words came, mocking and taunting, and as they spoke, the most atrocious ideas began to fill his mind.

*A short time later.*

He lay on his side, eyes glassy and vacant, mouth turned into a twisted grin. There was merciful silence, and even though he lay on the cold earth and was stiff and damp, he didn't mind, because he could barely hear them anymore. Those appalling, dark voices were silent at last.

The sky above him was white, and the wind jabbed at his body like thousands of tiny daggers, yet he still couldn't move or stop smiling. The first lazy snowflakes of winter fell, and one touched his cheek with its soft caress. Still the woodcutter did not stir. He was afraid that if he did, they would know, and if they knew he was sure that they would start to speak to him again. He would do anything to avoid having to listen to those abhorrent words.

He had managed to shut them out, that much was true, but he had gone to extreme lengths to do so. He knew somewhere in the back of his mind that if they should start talking to him again, he would not be able to stop them. So he would stay where he was and wait until they went away. The snow began to fall more heavily, and it had already started to cover the ground and the woodcutter himself. He closed his eyes and imagined that the snow on his cheeks was the tender kiss of his wife, or the loving embrace of his children. The wind rose and he swallowed a scream, for he was certain that he heard them again, barely audible on the very edge of the breeze, somehow spoken by the trees themselves as they swayed.

He wondered how it could be, how it was possible. He shouldn't be able to hear much. After all, he'd already cut off his ears, and that had seemed to diminish the voices—for a while at least. He began to shiver, but was still too afraid to move. He couldn't risk listening to their words again, of the things they told him to do to his wife and child, as they were things that would surely give any man nightmares for the rest of his life.

No.

He would wait. Wait until they went away. Surely, they couldn't talk forever. He was a patient man. As soon as they were quiet, he would return to the house and tell his wife all about the horrible things that the voices had said to him. It all made sense now, the inexplicable things that had been happening. Just small things, not enough on their own to cause too many concerns—things that he knew he'd put in a certain place appearing somewhere else without him or his wife moving them—or the way things would get somehow burned at the edges with no explanation. But now it made sense, because the voices had told him that it was them all along.

The snow lay against his bloated, engorged body in great drifts which reached up to his waist, and despite the intense cold, he managed a dirty, vacant smile. The voices weren't so bad once you got used to them, he thought as he forced a fistful of dirt into his mouth with blue and unfeeling hands. And if you listened to them long enough they made sense. The snow continued to fall, and he continued to eat.

It took eleven hours for the hypothermia to kill the woodcutter, but by then he was already quite mad. He had stuffed as many leaves and stones into the bloody remains of his ears as he could, in order to blot out the frightening and disturbing words that the trees whispered, and because they told him to, had continued eating the earth itself, shovelling great handfuls of rotten leaves, dirt and worms into his mouth as he gibbered and cackled.

The trees were still talking to him as he lost consciousness.

# 10. ACROSS THE RIVER

DESPITE HIS RESERVATIONS, Steve had grown accustomed to living in Hope House. Seven weeks had passed since that first night, and with the majority of the repair work done, he found himself more and more at ease with the solitude of the countryside. He lay on the sofa in the small annex off the kitchen reading his newspaper, the house now pretty much organized and tidy.

He was enjoying the benefits of working from home, and as a session musician for TV and film, combined with the wonder of high speed internet, it meant that he could work when he wanted on his own terms. He had been toying with the idea of installing a studio in the house but Melody wasn't keen, saying that it would go against the traditional feel of the building. He supposed that she was right, and instead he had managed to free up enough money to build one as a separate building out back.

He glanced up from his newspaper and could see it out of the window; it was only small, no more than a medium-sized walk-in building about the same dimensions as a greenhouse or shed, but it was his and, once the soundproofing was done and the rest of his equipment installed, it would give him a place to work without the two hour-plus commutes to the recording studios that he would have to otherwise make in order to deliver on time. It also meant that he could work whenever his creative spark switched itself on, and not be forced to try to produce something when the ideas just weren't there. It gave him a good reason to spend a little time outside the house itself, too.

Although it was true that he had got used to it,

there were still aspects that bothered him. Just silly things, like when he had come home and put his car keys in the dish on the end table by the door, and couldn't find them when he next went to get them. Melody had insisted that she hadn't moved them, and a frustrating search later, he found them in the kitchen drawer. He was certain that he hadn't put them there (before then he had never even opened that particular drawer at all) but it wasn't worth stressing over and so he hadn't worried too much about it.

There were other things as well. Even though neither of them smoked in the house (a joint agreement to avoid the ingrained stench and yellowed nicotine stains from appearing on walls and ceilings) sometimes he would walk into a room and find that he could smell nicotine fumes. Not just normal aroma from cigarettes either, but thick, heavy smoke like the stuff that used to tumble off the end of the huge brown cigars that his grandfather had been partial to.

Even worse than that was the atmosphere. Mostly It was fine, but on occasion, especially if he were in the house alone, he felt a subtle change. A horrible, skin-crawling sensation that he was being watched would creep over him. He supposed that he might still be adjusting to his new surroundings, but whatever it was he didn't like it.

A couple of times he'd considered speaking to Melody about it, but she was either oblivious or, like him, was just putting on a show of ignoring it. She still seemed perfectly content and happy, and if anything the house had soothed her just as much as it had made him feel increasingly uncomfortable. Building the studio had seemed like the best solution, especially as it meant that he wouldn't have to leave Melody alone in the house and would always be on hand if something went wrong.

He yawned, and realised that as far as days go, this was a particularly unproductive and lazy one. He heard the door open and the familiar sound of Melody tossing her car keys into the bowl on the table by the front door.

*I wonder whether they will stay there?* he thought as she called out to him.

"In the annex," he replied as he dismissed his depressing train of thought.

She came into the room, and he couldn't help but notice how good she looked in her grey pinstripe suit.

"Hey baby. How was your day?"

"Same old, same old," she replied. "You?"

"Lazy," he said, stifling a yawn. "I haven't done anything at all today."

She walked over and kissed him, then perched herself on the arm of the sofa.

"That's no good. I'm going to change and then go for a walk in the woods if you want to come along."

The mysterious footpath fluttered back into his mind for the first time since the day of the move, and he sat up, suddenly reluctant.

"Not much out there but the dirt road leading to Oakwell."

She grinned. "I meant the woods out back. We have all that land, and we haven't even given it a look."

He ignored the heavy churning in his stomach and forced a smile.

"I don't think we can get over there. I didn't notice if there's a bridge or anything," he said, trying not to sound too relieved.

"Oh, I forgot to tell you, there isn't a bridge anymore, but there is a place to cross. Come on, lazy, pour some coffee down your neck, and I'll go change, then I'll show you."

She kissed him again and then was gone. Safe from her knowing eyes, he let his smile melt and tried to ignore his overwhelming sense of uneasiness.

He spent a few moments chewing over plausible excuses to get out of the impending ramble but, unable to think of a good one, he stood and walked to the kitchen, looking out of the window, past his studio, and past the flowing water of the river to the thick band of trees on the opposite bank. From here, the impression of the path in the woods wasn't so obvious, but he knew it was there.

He thought he could see the spot where it began, and knew for sure that if he were to stand up by the old tree stump at the water's edge, he would be able to see the vague signs of a thoroughfare, although for who or what he couldn't even hazard a guess. He felt a hand touch him and he whirled around, not sure what to expect, but relaxed instantly when he saw Melody, who for her part was in hysterics.

"Sorry babe, I didn't mean to spook you," she said between snorted gasps of laughter.

His embarrassment faded to humour, and then appreciation of how good she looked in her faded ripped-at-the-knee jeans and tight blue t-shirt, which showed a teasing amount of her midriff.

"Are you trying to scare me to death?" he said with a smile as she hugged him.

"Accidental or not, that was funny. You should have seen your face," she said as she wiped her eyes.

He offered his best sheepish grin, and she pulled him close and kissed him.

"How about we forget the exploration and go upstairs," he whispered in her ear.

She kissed him again, and he thought he was going to get his way when she pulled away and grinned at him.

"Later, first let's get out of here for a while and explore."

"I'd rather explore you," he said playfully as he nuzzled her neck and ran his hands under her t-shirt. She grasped his wrists and pushed them to his sides.

"When we get back okay?" she said with a smile. He nodded, and she kissed him on the cheek.

"Come on, let's go," she said, opening the kitchen door that led on to the back garden.

They walked, neither of them feeling compelled to speak, content to enjoy the peace. They passed Steve's almost-finished recording studio, and then were standing by the edge of the water.

"See, I told you, no way across," he said as he glanced to the hidden path on the opposite bank.

Melody laughed and lowered herself to a sitting position on the grass banking at the water's edge.

"Hey, be careful okay?" Steve warned, his eyes flicking from Melody to the path in the woods on the opposite bank.

"I know what I'm doing," she said, then slid off the edge.

He expected her to disappear into the water, and had to do a quick double-take, as it appeared to him that she was standing on the surface. It looked like some kind of bizarre illusion. Melody saw the confusion on his face and laughed.

"Come over here, it's not a big secret," she teased as he walked over to her.

As he neared he could see the reason for his confusion. The water where Melody stood looked to be only a few inches deep. As he looked closer he could see how the riverbed banked upwards almost to the surface, and then down to its normal depth, making a natural bridge across the water.

"How did you know about that?" Steve asked.

"I noticed there was no bridge, and remembered Donovan saying that the woods were ours to explore. I called his office to ask about it this morning, and he told me about this natural pass."

"You should be careful."

"It's not deep, and even if I fall in it isn't flowing too fast. Come on down, it's pretty stable underfoot."

"No thanks. You know water and me don't mix."

She smiled and shook her head as she walked further out.

"Come on, you promised you would explore with me. You wouldn't leave me over there on my own, would you?"

Steve fidgeted, moving from one foot to the other as he looked from Melody to the water and back again. It was the proverbial rock and the hard place. He told himself he was overreacting, but he genuinely didn't want her over the other side of the water alone.

Out of options or acceptable reasons to refuse, he slowly and carefully lowered himself down to the sandy half-hidden water bridge. His canvas trainers soaked up water like a greedy sponge, and he grimaced as Melody teased him.

"Stop making faces and come on, the quicker we cross, the quicker you can get out."

She hurried to the other side, making him ever more aware of his own careful, lumbering steps as he followed. She watched in mild amusement as he pulled himself up onto the opposite bank, then the pair peered into the woods.

"It looks dense," Melody said, suddenly less enthusiastic.

"I think there's a path down here."

The words had left his mouth before he could stop them, and he instantly regretted it. He didn't particularly want to be over here, and wanted even less to walk down the mystery path in the woods. And yet his curiosity tugged at him and at least now that they were investigating, he might finally be able to put it to bed.

"How do you know that?" asked Melody with genuine curiosity.

"I'm not sure if I'm right, but I noticed the other day when I was sitting on the tree-stump that some of the trees look displaced a little way down there."

"Well let's go take a look," she said.

They walked along the edge of the water, Melody in front and fearless, Steve behind and keeping a wary eye on the water. The trees grew wild and overhung on this side of the river, casting the couple into shade as they carefully made their way down the edge of the riverbank.

Even before they arrived level with the tree stump on the opposite bank he could tell that the path had been no illusion. The ground was worn away by the unmistakable signs of footfall. He expected to feel trepidation as they reached the path, but now seeing it up close and with the mystery gone, he didn't. It was just a simple track leading deeper into the woods.

"Wow, it looks like it goes deep," said Melody, putting her hands on her hips.

"Do you still wanna go take a look?" he asked, half hoping that she'd say no.

"Yeah, as long as we don't go getting ourselves lost."

"I should have brought some breadcrumbs," Steve mumbled, and they peeled away from the water's edge and into the forest.

The path dipped gently downhill, and Steve noticed that the overhanging tree canopy was so dense that it kept out much of the light of the day.

The pair walked in silence, content to take in the peaceful sounds of nature as they went deeper. Bird song accompanied them as they followed the twisting trail, stepping over roots, and pushing aside branches as they went.

"This is beautiful," Melody said quietly.

Steve couldn't help but agree. Spectacularly vibrant greens stood out sharply against the dark browns of tree trunks, and even as a lifelong city dweller, he appreciated the raw, unspoiled beauty of nature.

"Hey come up here and look at this," said Melody.

Steve caught up to where she stood, having been trailing a little way behind. Although it was only mid-day, the shadows were long and the light poor, giving an eerie feel rather than a spectacular one.

Melody was standing by a huge tree. It was long dead and no more than a partially rotten shell covered on one side by spongy looking brown mushrooms. A huge cavity had been carved out of the middle of the trunk and inside, resting against the back of the hollow, was a wooden crucifix surrounded by long dead flower petals.

Melody reached into the hollow to retrieve it, and Steve almost grabbed at her hand to stop her, but didn't, and she picked it up and turned it over in her hands.

"How old do you think it is?"

She handed the cross to him, and although he didn't want to touch it, he reached out and took it from her. It was rough to the touch, and although it had obviously been made by hand, there was no pride apparent in the workmanship. It was an object that looked to have been created not from love of the craft or the joy of creation, but out of need or necessity. There was no reason for it, but some deep part of him wanted to set it down and wash his hands.

"Do you think it might be valuable?" Melody asked, her eyes bright and inquisitive as she watched his reactions, mistaking his horror for curious appreciation.

"Could be. It's a strange thing to leave out here, don't you think?"

"You think somebody could have lost it?"

Steve looked around, unable to shake his anxiety and the feeling that they were both being watched.

"That was my first thought, but it doesn't add up. This path is well walked. I mean sure enough, not recently, but it seems that somebody has been down here at least over the last couple of years. And this—"

He wanted to say shrine, but decided to choose a different word. He could already see the concern growing on Melody's face.

"This thing would be plainly visible to anyone passing. Hell, it would be hard to miss."

"Any ideas as to what it could be for?"

Steve looked at the cross, then at the tree.

"I'm not sure."

A shadow of uncertainty passed over Melody's face, and when she spoke Steve could hear the tension in her voice.

"You know what my first thought was?"

"Go on."

"That it was some kind of memorial."

Steve nodded. He thought that she'd hit the nail right on the head, and even though it didn't occur to him then, he was sure that was it.

"You think someone died here?" he asked quietly, looking up at the gnarled remains of the tree.

"It's possible. I mean it's not much now, but I would imagine back when it was younger..."

She trailed off and shrugged, and he knew her

well enough to know what she meant. He could see it too. This old tree back when it was strong and true, a desperate man, perhaps high within the upper branches, tying a rope around one of the thick limbs, and then slipping the other end already fashioned into a noose around his neck before stepping into oblivion.

"Maybe it belonged to someone who used to own the house," Melody said, and the idea made him feel like a grave robber.

"Look, I say we put it back and not mess with it," he said, looking Melody in the eye.

"Aren't you curious to find out more?"

"I am, but I would feel pretty shitty taking it away from here. I mean you know me; I'm not easily spooked, but this is giving me the creeps."

"It's just an object. A thing in the world. It's nothing to be afraid of," she said with a touch of disdain.

"I didn't say I was afraid. I said it gives me the creeps. Let's just put it back okay?" he said, sounding way more irritable than he'd intended.

"But what if whoever owned that cross has family? Imagine if we could get it back to them. I know if it were me it would mean a lot. And it's doing no good to anyone hanging out here in the trees."

"I hate to sound like an ass, but I just think it's a bad idea."

"Come on Steve, please. Let's just have it checked out. If nothing comes of it, we will bring it back and never touch it again, I promise."

He didn't want to. Something deep inside him told him that what they were doing was wrong, but as was often the case, he ignored the small voice in his head and handed the cross to his eager wife.

"Okay, but as long as we are clear. We can go and have it checked out and then if it doesn't lead to anything we bring it straight back here."

"Understood," she said absently, taking the cross and slipping it into her bag. Steve felt better having it out of his hands. He didn't like the way it had felt. His hands felt dirty, and he found himself involuntarily rubbing them on his trouser legs. His throat was dry and the charm of getting back to nature was starting to lose its hold on him.

"Shall we head back?" he asked hopefully.

"We just got here. Come on, let's go on a little further," she replied, setting off down the path before he could argue. Reluctantly, he followed.

They walked in silence for a while, Melody lost in the wonders of the forest while Steve was troubled by thoughts of the strange crucifix. It surprised them both when they found themselves suddenly cast out of the shadows and into blazing sunshine. They looked to each other and shared a smile at the unexpected turn of events. They were in a perfect circle of grass. It was as if someone had sliced a huge circular chunk out of the forest.

"This place is full of surprises," Melody said quietly, turning slowly on the spot.

"You're telling me. What is this?"

"Who knows? Could it just be a natural formation?"

Steve shook his head. "I don't think so. It's too circular, too perfect. Besides, look at the way nothing grows in here, the forest all around the edge just... stops dead."

"Then what is it?" she asked, and now he could sense fear in her too.

"I don't know," he said quietly as he wrinkled his nose. "Do you smell that?"

Melody nodded. "Smoke. Maybe someone had a camp fire here recently?"

Steve looked at the ground, but saw no evidence of a recent fire. In fact, the place had a vibe to it which made him uncomfortable. Gooseflesh prickled on his arms, and he felt as if there were thousands of pairs of unseen eyes watching them. Something was bothering him and as he was thinking what it could be, the answer came to him.

"Mel, listen."

She cocked her head and did as he asked, then shrugged.

"I don't hear anything," she said quietly.

"Exactly. Where are the birds? It shouldn't be so quiet."

The pair listened again, and indeed there was a thick, complete silence which hung in the air ominously. Where before the forest had been filled with the sounds of nature going through its daily cycles, here in the circle there was only silence.

"I don't think I like it here," Melody said softly, which to Steve's reckoning was the first negative remark she had made about the place since they'd first come to see it.

"That makes two of us. I'm not sure what it is, but this place feels so…"

He was going to say 'dead', but Melody finished the sentence for him, and her word summed it up better.

"Sterile," she said simply.

Steve nodded. "Does it give you that feeling, like we're being watched?"

Melody nodded, but didn't answer. He decided that they'd spent long enough exploring, and that it was time to leave.

"Let's go home. I think we've seen enough for one day, don't you?"

Steve expected an argument, or at least a protest,

but Melody gave neither, and he took her by the hand and led her back the way they'd come. As soon as they were under cover of the trees, they heard the world as it was intended, birds singing, unseen creatures moving through the undergrowth as they looked for either a mate or food. Neither of them spoke, Steve simply led them home, past the gnarled dead tree, and over the narrow water bridge to their side of the river. It wasn't until they were safely back inside the house and sipping a mug of hot coffee that their mood began to lighten. Neither of them wanted to make a big deal of it, but both Steve and Melody sat preoccupied. Darkness came, and for the first time since they'd moved in, Steve closed all the curtains and locked the doors before settling down to a night in front of the TV, hopeful of forgetting the afternoon's expedition.

*During the evening.*
Melody had fallen asleep curled up on the sofa. Steve gently moved her legs lying across his own, set them on the seat, then switched off the TV set and walked quietly to the kitchen. He stood there in the dark, looking out of the window into the night. He could see neither the river nor the trees, but he could still sense the presence of the circle out there beyond the waterline and wondered how the place must look under cover of darkness. It was bad enough during the day, but to imagine it at night, illuminated by the milky glow of the moon, perhaps with a light mist hanging just above the ground... he felt a shiver caress his neck and the feeling of being observed washed over him again. A strong gust of wind rocked the house and rustled the trees. He shook his head and thought that the events of the day had begun to play tricks on his mind. He was sure that he'd heard

his name whispered on the wind, and even though he knew it was quite impossible, it still gave him the creeps. He decided that he'd stared out into the darkness for long enough, so he pulled the curtains closed and went back to the sitting room.

# 11. THE DREAM

STEVE RACED THROUGH the trees, heart pounding thickly in his chest as he tried to shrug away the grasping pull of the branches. He was exhausted, but knew he had to push on. It was hard to see where he was going, as the night was dark and the woods were inky black and treacherous. However, he was not entirely unaided: there was a pale yellow moon that gave just enough light for him to keep heading in the right direction. His foot snagged on an old root, and he was certain that he was about to fall, but he pin-wheeled his arms and somehow managed to remain upright. He knew that he was almost out of time and, lowering his head, he increased his speed, driving through the sharp branches and the pained protests of his lungs.

He arrived at the dead tree, its hollowed-out trunk resembling a ghastly maw in the faint moonlight. He saw her, and stifled a scream. Melody was sitting high on a long, thick branch, her petite legs swinging back and forth as she slipped the noose around her neck. He tried to call out to her, but the efforts of running through the trees had rendered him breathless, so he could only watch, his breath coming in ragged gasping wheezes, as she stood in his oversized shirt billowing and flapping against her bare legs as she tottered for balance. He reached out for the tree, wanting to climb up to her, but he could see no way to do so, or any handholds on the smooth surface of the trunk to aid his ascent. He craned his neck and saw her smile at him, her eyes dreamy and vacant as she stepped off the edge. He felt the scream launch itself hoarsely from his mouth as the rope pulled taut and her tiny body snapped to a halt.

He woke with a start.

For a moment, he thought he was still there at the tree, but the familiarity of his surroundings found him, and he quelled the scream in his throat, instead letting out a disgruntled sigh at another night's sleep disturbed by nightmares. They'd begun the day after they'd gone to the woodland circle and had plagued him almost every night since. Often it would be the dream with Melody high up in the dead branches, but on other occasions it was he himself who was up there with the noose around his neck, powerless to stop himself from stepping to his death as Melody watched from below. He glanced over to her, checking that she was okay and still safe, relaxing a little as he watched the rhythmic breathing of untroubled sleep. With the horror of his nightmare fading, he glanced at the luminescent display of the digital alarm clock. It told him that it was just after four in the morning. As if to confirm what it said, he heard the birds outside in the trees heralding the dawn of a new day with their intrusive songs. Armed with the knowledge that his night's sleep was over with, he climbed quietly out of bed and went downstairs.

The nightly imaginings worried him. Until he and Melody had moved into Hope House, he would rarely ever remember his dreams, something which he would gladly take back if it would mean an end to experiencing them now in such horrific clarity. His mother took great pleasure in telling and re-telling the same story about how, as a boy, he had slept through a small earthquake that had shaken the house he'd grown up in hard enough to knock the pictures off the walls and send the huge silver chest freezer in the pantry sliding all the way to the opposite side of the room. She would recall with joy how he hadn't stirred, even as the other residents of the neighbourhood were charging around in panic.

He smiled to himself as he poured a glass of milk, not bothering to turn on the light—the hazy early dawn offered enough for him to be able to see what he was doing. He walked to the window and looked out over the back garden and the river. A low mist was rolling gently just above the ground, and the sky was white and cloudless. He thought there was a good chance of snow later, and as he watched he saw the treetops swaying as they were tossed around by the wind. He finished his drink then walked to the sitting room, skirting around the plush leather sofa and sitting instead in the rocker they'd rescued, now positioned by the fireplace. It was odd, as he had never had the desire to sit in it before, but as he began to sway gently back and forth, he found himself smiling contentedly. It felt right to him.

Comfortable.

*Back and forth, back and forth.*

It was as if it had been made for him, as if the hundred-year-old wood was crafted for the exact shape of his body.

*Back and forth. Back and forth.*

He thought that all the world's troubles could be solved by sitting in the quiet and just relaxing. He imagined a huge table filled with the leaders of the world, all in matching rockers, as they made peace and forgot their petty squabbles over oil, land borders and political agendas.

*Back and forth, back and forth.*

He could hear the sound of the wind rustling in the treetops, finding it soothing. It reminded him of the ocean, as well as that secret childhood sound found inside seashells. *How old were the trees?* he wondered as he closed his eyes. *How long had they stood? How deep did their roots go? What travesties of humanity had they witnessed over the years?*

*Back and forth, back and forth.*

He allowed his mind and body to rest. He liked the sound from outside. The trees sounded like they were talking among themselves, holding secret conversations not meant for human ears. Perhaps they didn't know that he was up and awake, thinking that their long, slow words went unheard. But, from his new favourite chair, he could hear everything. As he sat in the dark, listening to the branches as they were tugged this way and that, he could almost imagine that they spoke to him alone. And if they were, then it was okay. Because he thought he could, with time, learn to understand what they were saying.

His mobile phone vibrated on the coffee table, snapping him from his musings. Because the reception at Hope House was so spotty, both he and Melody had already grown used to a world away from the constant assault of text messages and the reading of social networking websites on the go, which to him wasn't such a bad thing. Curious, he scooped up the phone and looked at the display.

**1 NEW MESSAGE**

He hesitated, unsure why he was so reluctant, then swept aside his own stupidity and clicked the button to open the message.

*Hi Steve.* ☺

Even though there was nothing sinister in the content, it still made the flesh on his arms prickle, causing him to glance around the shadow-draped room. He read it again, asking himself if it was just a combination of his tiredness and the tension he felt around the house making him misread the situation, or something altogether more sinister, when the phone vibrated again, two quick pulses. His heart began to thump a little faster, and he licked his lips as he looked at the screen.

**2 NEW MESSAGES**

Both appeared to be from the same sender, although the display listed the number as unknown. He clicked into his inbox, and selected the first message.

*It's only us.* ☺

Again, on the surface there was nothing sinister about the text, but as he looked at it, the surer he was that whoever had sent it was mocking him in some way. Despite his every instinct screaming at him not to, he opened the second one. This one contained no smiley, no jovial tone of the previous communications. The content of this one was to the point, and even though he was a twenty-nine year-old man, Steve was afraid.

*We see you.*

It was simple, to the point. And raised more questions than he thought he would be able to find answers for. He toyed with what to do, or if he should take the messages seriously. He asked himself if it was a matter for the police, then almost immediately dismissed it. No crime had been committed, and he could almost guarantee he would be looked at by the local constabulary as the out of town new guy who got spooked by living in his old house in the woods.

And then there was Melody. She loved the house, and he didn't want to bother her with something as trivial as someone trying to pull a tasteless prank on the new family in town. He decided that he wouldn't give them the satisfaction and, with his decision made, he deleted the messages and switched off the phone. Not wanting Melody to be alone, and feeling a little too isolated and exposed, he went upstairs and climbed into bed. He was certain that he wouldn't sleep, and for a while he had simply lain there watching the sky through the bedroom window as it slowly and subtly grew lighter. The clock by the bedside said it was almost six, and he was just toying with the idea of giving up on sleep and getting up again, when he drifted off into a deep and dreamless sleep. Outside, the wind blustered and spoke, and the house creaked and groaned in answer.

# 12. DRINKS AT THE OAK

THE OLD OAK PUBLIC house was around a five-mile drive from Hope House and sat on the edge of Oakville. Following the stress of the last few weeks, setting up house and attending to the niggling little issues which plague a move into a new property, they decided to take a much needed break and to pay a visit to the local—in fact, the only—watering hole.

"Looks quiet," Steve mumbled as he brought their trusty Passat to a halt and looked around the almost empty car park.

"I love it," Melody said excitedly.

Steve nodded in agreement. It looked inviting, not like the snooty, modern wine bars of the city which were usually both devoid of atmosphere and filled with arrogant idiots in business suits who drank too much and got rowdy far too easily.

"I bet it's like in those movies," Steve said with a grin.

"What movies?"

"The old Westerns. You know, we walk in and everyone stops talking and look at us like we're a couple of aliens or something."

"You think the locals won't like us being here?"

Steve turned to her in his seat, and put on an awful hillbilly voice. "We don't take kindly to strangers here in these parts."

"Cut it out," she said, slapping him lightly on the arm, but still unable to mask her smile. "Come on, let's go in. I'll let you buy me a drink."

"Lucky me," he said, climbing out of the car.

They headed for the entrance, and just before they went inside, Steve leaned over and whispered in her ear.

"I bet they have one of those pictures on the wall with eyes that follow you..."

She nudged him in the ribs as they went inside.

There *was* a picture on the wall—an imposing oil painting of a heavy set man standing arms folded in front of a construction site—but as far as they could tell its eyes didn't follow them as they approached the bar, nor did the locals stop and stare at them as Steve had suggested. Instead their presence went mostly unnoticed as they took in their surroundings. It was exactly as they'd imagined it would be from outside. As with everything in Oakville, the modern world seemed to have bypassed the Old Oak almost entirely, and apart from the modern heaters and light fittings, it was the very embodiment of the word traditional. Melody grinned at Steve, and he couldn't help but return the gesture. They were greeted by the bartender, a huge, broad shouldered man with long, jet black hair and friendly eyes.

"What can I get you?" he said, leaning on the bar and watching them carefully.

"Hi. Pint of the house beer for me please and..." Steve glanced over to Melody with eyebrows raised.

"Just an orange juice for me."

The man nodded and started to prepare the drinks as Steve sat on a vacant stool.

"You two new around here?" the man asked, setting the orange juice down.

"Yeah, we just bought a place a few miles down the road."

The man held out his hand.

"In that case let me be the first to welcome you. I'm Will Jones."

Steve shook the man's hand, which felt like a block of rough granite.

"Thanks. I'm Steve. This is my wife, Melody."

"Pleased to meet you both," he said as he started to pull Steve's pint of beer. "So, where is this place of yours?"

"It's a little place in the woods called Hope House," Steve said.

Will did not pause as such, but there was a definite reaction, just a flicker of something in his facial expression, which was there and gone almost immediately. He set the drink before Steve.

"Aye, I know Hope House. My great, great grandfather built it," said Will, rolling his eyes to the portrait behind him.

Melody stepped back and, now that it had been pointed out to her, she could see a striking resemblance—Will and the man in the painting had the same eyes and jaw line.

"That's amazing," she said with a smile. "Why is it that you don't live there?"

Will flashed a small smile and shook his head. "I would never live in Hope House," Will said with a dry chuckle.

"Why not?" Melody said defensively.

*We see you.*

Melody, relax," Steve said with a nervous smile and trying to push away the memories of the strange text messages that he still hadn't told her about.

Will licked his lips nervously. "No offence of course, it's just not for me, that's all. Besides, this is my place, here at the Oak. I'm sure the two of you will be very happy there. Now if you would excuse me, I have another customer."

Without waiting for a response he headed off to the opposite side of the bar, leaving Steve and Melody alone.

"Jesus Mel, hell of a way to make an impression."

"I thought he was going to badmouth our new

house."

"Did you see the size of the guy's arms? He can badmouth anything he wants to. Besides, I don't think he meant anything by it."

"I don't know," she said, watching Will as he served one of the regulars. "What did you think about his reaction when we told him where we lived?"

"I think maybe you should just leave it alone for now, don't you?" Steve said. "We don't want to get ourselves barred from the only pub for miles because you offended the owner."

Melody knew Steve was teasing, and elbowed him lightly in the ribs. "Cut it out. I'm sure he's not offended."

"Yeah? I can imagine it now, him telling the locals about the arrogant new people who have just moved in to Hope House—all short-tempered and full of beans."

He was messing with her, and she was playing along, even though she did wonder if she had, in fact, hurt Will's feelings. She took a sip of her drink then looked at Steve with a mock scowl.

"I'll show you, Steven Samson. You just watch."

He mock grimaced, playing on the fact that she knew full well how much he hated being called by his first name.

"Mrs. Samson, I'm offended."

Melody poked her tongue out and then called across the bar.

"Mr. Jones, could I ask you a question please?"

Melody flicked a teasing glance towards Steve as the burly barman approached. For his part, Steve kept his face neutral.

"What can I do for you?" Will asked standing and folding his immense forearms. Steve couldn't help but feel intimidated.

"I'm sorry to bother you, but I wondered if you knew anything of the history of Hope House?"

Will's brow furrowed, and again Steve had the distinct impression that their host was choosing his words carefully.

*We see you.*

"Well I don't know much myself. I was never really all that interested in the past, only in what is yet to be."

"Makes sense" Steve said around a gentle sip of his beer. He tried his best not to grimace at the less than savoury taste.

"I appreciate that Mr. Jones, I just wondered if there was anything at all you could tell me," Melody pressed.

"You two bought Hope House without checking its history?"

The way he'd said it made it sound more like a statement than a question, the surprise in his voice noticed by both of them.

"What do you mean by history?" Melody asked, all joking forgotten.

Even though the immense man dwarfed her, she held his gaze, and Steve was surprised to see that it was him who seemed uncomfortable.

"I really don't know much. But a place as old as Hope House is bound to have some stories attached to it. One thing that never changes in this world is that people talk and stories are told."

"What do you mean by stories?"

"Like I said, I don't really know."

"Well, is there anyone locally who might be able to tell us more?"

Will licked his lips and looked incredibly uncomfortable. As much as Steve wanted to help get him off the hook and tell Melody to back off, he was also curious to know what Will was hiding that might explain some of the things that had been happening in and around the house.

"Mrs. Briggs over there in the corner," Will said, gesturing across the room, "She's something of an amateur historian. If anyone knows anything it's her."

Melody and Steve turned around to see a grizzled old lady sitting in the corner. She was with two other equally ancient companions and, even from across the room, the sound of their cackling was grating on the ears. Steve had a vision of the opening scene of Macbeth, and could quite imagine Mrs. Briggs and her coven cackling and stirring a huge iron cauldron, rather than sipping vodka and tonic.

"She seems... colourful..." Steve said around a small smile.

"Aye, colourful is one word for it. In fairness to them, I'd probably be long out of business if not for those three."

"They loaned you money?" Steve said, glancing again to the coven in the corner. Melody elbowed him in the ribs playfully.

"He means because they are always in here drinking."

Steve looked at her in confusion, then to Will and the three of them shared a laugh. Despite feeling a little sheepish at missing the joke, Steve was a good enough sport not to take it to heart.

"Of course he did. I'm not stupid Mel," he said, sticking out his bottom lip and giving the puppy-dog eyes.

"Like hell you did," Melody shot back, glancing over to Will, who was smiling at the pair of them.

"Come on now, let's not have a lover's tiff in front of the locals," Steve said, winking knowingly at Will.

"No offence taken, we locals have thick skin you

know."

"Glad to hear it," Steve said, fumbling for his wallet in the back pocket of his jeans. "How much do we owe you for the drinks?"

Will shook his head. "No, please, put that away, these are on the house. Think of it as a welcome to Oakwell."

"Thank you, that's really kind," Melody said.

Steve could see that she was soaking up the atmosphere of the place, and loving every minute of it. He had to admit that he was kind of enjoying it too, and for the first time since they had made the move he felt truly relaxed.

"We'll come here again," said Steve grinning and knowing that it was the only pub for miles in any direction. Will flashed a slab of white teeth through his jet-black beard and folded his arms.

"Glad to hear it, although next time I won't stop you from getting the wallet out."

"Moths and all!" Melody said, not quite under her breath causing another round of laughter. Will looked at the pair, and leaned closer.

"Seriously though, all joking aside, Mrs. Briggs may like a drink, and she may seem a bit out there and smell like those damn cats that she keeps, but if you really want to know about the history of that house of yours, she's the one to ask."

"Thanks. We appreciate the advice," Melody said, hopping off her bar stool. "Shall we go and sit down?" she said, looking at Steve.

"Yeah, let's go grab a table."

Melody walked on ahead, and Steve picked up his drink and was about to follow when Will spoke again, his tone hushed.

"About Hope House..."

Steve paused and watched the huge barman

struggle to find words. His humorous demeanour was now gone, and his features were taut and serious. Steve was intrigued.

"What about it?" he asked, wondering why part of him was already dreading the answer.

"Has everything been... okay since you moved in?"

*We see you.*

"Yeah, fine, why do you ask?" Steve said quietly, in spite the light tingle of fear starting to build in his gut.

Will's eyes flicked from side to side, and one corner of his mouth twitched nervously.

"It's nothing, forget I said anything."

"Hey come on, you can't ask a question like that and then clam up. It's obvious there's something you want to tell me, although I get the feeling I'm not going to like what I hear."

***

Melody sat at the table and sipped her orange juice. She had chosen a seat which gave her the best view of the room as a whole, and couldn't help but smile as she took it all in. She glanced over to the bar, and could see Steve and Will deep in conversation. She considered calling out to Steve to hurry him along, but she could see that whatever they were talking about was apparently important. In fact, as she watched she realised that Will that was doing most of the talking. Steve was simply watching, nodding or saying the occasional word which Melody had no hope of hearing above the general din of the pub. She decided not to disturb him, and was glad that Steve was making friends.

She'd been concerned that he was becoming isolated; he had seemed tense and withdrawn of late.

The two looked over at Melody, who smiled warmly, but neither husband nor bartender smiled back, and she saw a frown on her husband's brow that concerned her. She was about to get up and see what the delay was when Steve walked to their table and sat down.

"What was all that about?"

"Nothing, just small-talk."

"You looked to be pretty deep in conversation to me."

"Yeah, we were talking sports, nothing that would interest you, sadly."

She took a sip of her drink and left the line of questioning there, even though she knew him well enough to know he was lying, as he wasn't enough of a sports fan to engage in such a lengthy conversation about it.

They sat in silence for a while, watching their fellow patrons drink. Every so often, a bray of laughter—or more accurately cackles—filled the room, but it seemed everyone was so used to Mrs. Briggs that they barely seemed to notice.

"So, what do we think about the old battle-axe then?" Steve asked, nodding towards the witches sat at the corner table.

"I'm not sure."

She didn't really care about Mrs. Briggs in the corner anymore, or even how quaint the pub was. She was concerned about Steve and the lie on his face that she was still able to read despite his best attempts to hide it.

"Might be worth asking her for some info, get a bit of local flavour of the house," he suggested, trying just a little too hard to be normal and conversational.

Melody nodded, looking across to the corner but not really seeing. She felt nauseous and couldn't imagine why Steve would lie to her. For his part, he seemed oblivious, and it was clear that he was trying just a little too hard to act like there was nothing wrong. She sipped her drink and began to tear nervously at the cardboard beer-mat.

"What's wrong?" Steve asked quietly.

"Nothing," she responded with a shrug. "I'm just taking in the ambience."

"I quite like this place," he said, trying his best to force conversation.

"I do, too. It's nice."

Again, their conversation fizzled out until Melody spoke up. "Why are you lying to me?" she asked suddenly.

"I have no idea what you mean, I—"

"What did Will say to you over by the bar?"

He could see that she was angry, and because he didn't feel the time was right to share the information given to him by Will, he was forced to continue with the lie. "I told you, we were talking sports. Jesus Melody, don't you think you are overreacting?"

"I can tell when you're lying. It's all over your face."

"Well go ahead and ask him yourself since you obviously don't believe me!"

He was also angry now, and noticed that the argument they were on the verge of was already attracting unwanted glances from neighbouring tables. He leaned forward and took her petite hands in his. "Look, I don't know what you think you saw but really, there's nothing to tell."

She pulled her hands away, cupped her half-empty glass and lowered her gaze. "I'm sorry. I... I don't know what's wrong with me tonight. I'm... just tired I suppose."

Steve drained his glass and set it down. "Let's not

argue, okay? I hate it when we fight."

"Me too."

They were silent again, and the awkwardness drifted back.

"Look, I need to go to the bathroom, then I'll get us another drink okay?" Steve said suddenly.

"Yeah, why not."

She smiled, but the gesture felt fraudulent, however it must have been enough because Steve seemed satisfied, kissing her on the head as he passed her.

"Back in five. Love you."

"Love you, too," she said as he went.

# 13. MRS. BRIGGS

STEVE RETURNED FROM THE bathroom to find their table empty. He knew that Melody was pissed at him, and although she knew he wasn't telling her the truth, he had to stick to his guns, for the time being at least, until he had a chance to consider the new information that had been presented to him. With Will's words swimming around his brain and the chilling text messages still plaguing him, he was sure he had made the right decision. However, as he looked towards their recently vacated table, he considered the very real possibility that she had walked out and left him here.

He was about to move casually towards the door and try to catch up with her when he heard her voice calling him from across the room. He turned towards the sound of her voice, and had to force himself not to wince.

She was sitting with the witches, and was smiling at him, the teasing tone unmistakable, or at least to him it was. To anyone else she was just a wife smiling at a husband.

His eyes flicked to the witches—who glared at him as if he had sprouted a second head, or was a notorious love cheat. Melody was waving him over and to his horror saw that she had made a space for him to sit, and a fresh drink was waiting for him. Realising that there was no escape, he forced a smile, weaved his way towards their table, and squeezed in next to his wife.

He looked at the three women in turn, his eyes finally coming to rest on Mrs. Briggs. There was no nice way to put it, but the old lady really was a hag. Her massive head was perched on her shoulders, her chin (if she possessed one) seemed to be forever lost among folds of flab, which threatened to spill over her mustard-coloured blouse. She had tiny, yellowed eyes with brown irises—a sure sign that the old girl's liver was close to giving up the fight. Her mouth was thin and harsh, her crimson painted lips turned into a humourless smile. All of this paled in comparison to her two most dominant features: her nose was a huge, red-tipped bulbous lump hanging off her face, and her hair was ridiculous: an immensely tall, badly-dyed, purple perm. She held out a flabby hand, her cheap gold jewellery jingling as he shook it.

"You must be Steve. I'm Annie Briggs," she croaked.

Her hand was warm and sweaty, and he was more than a little relieved when she released her grip and gave it back.

"Pleased to meet you," Steve mumbled.

"I have already introduced your wife to the rest of the girls, but for your benefit, I suppose I'll do it again."

He wanted to tell her not to bother, that he had no desire to speak to them, but he could feel Melody's eyes on him, and even without looking, he knew she would be wearing that secret smile on her face, the one reserved for them when they want to share an unspoken joke.

"This is Molly," she said, pointing to the woman beside Melody.

She appeared to be the polar opposite of Mrs. Briggs, stick thin with features which seemed too small for her face. Her hair was pulled back into a tight black bun, and like Mrs. Briggs was trying desperately to hang on to a youth that had last been seen sometime in the fifties.

Steve smiled and nodded, and was met with an icy

stare and a barely perceptible nod. She reminded him of the grandma from Roald Dahl's *George's Marvellous Medicine*, and in his mind saw her growing, shooting up through the pub roof and into the night air. He suppressed another smile, and turned to the third member of Mrs. Briggs' coven.

"And this is Petunia."

Steve turned to the woman nearest him, and offered a smile. She, at least, responded in kind — offering a wide grin that showed her numerous but somewhat odd-looking teeth. They seemed like baby teeth—way too small for the rest of her face. It was as if they had stopped growing with the rest of her when she'd been a child.

"Pleased to meet you young man," she said, flicking her ridiculously fake eyelashes at him. He either smiled or grimaced, not quite sure which as he shook her oily hand.

Introductions done, Steve sat back and took a long sip of his beer. Melody reached out under the table and gave him a reassuring squeeze of the thigh—or at least he hoped it was Melody. His mind's eye filled up with a bizarre image of Molly reaching her marvellous medicine elongated hand under the table to cop a feel of his leg, and couldn't help but smile into his glass as he took a drink. The rest of his laughter he swallowed with the beer, but he glanced over to Melody, and he knew she had seen it.

He desperately wanted to leave, but he reasoned that Melody no longer seemed to be angry, and at least here he wouldn't be in her bad books. So he battened down the hatches, took a deep breath and prepared for what would come.

\*\*\*

The hags could drink, of that there was no doubt. For the last hour, Steve and Melody had endured the cackling and the increasingly slurred conversations which seemed to increase in volume with their intake of alcohol. Steve had only drunk a couple of beers, Melody sticking to the orange juice, but the trio of witches drank as if their lives depended on it. It would be kind to say they were 'merry' or ' three sheets to the wind', but the fact was, as Steve listened to them bitch and moan about another community controversy featuring people that neither of them knew, that they were well on their way to being shit-faced.

Steve had been making the 'let's go home' eyes at Melody for the last twenty minutes, but she seemed to be thoroughly enjoying the show and his own discomfort in equal measure. She sipped her orange juice as she listened to the old women debate and bicker and argue. There was a lull in the conversation, and Melody decided to speak up.

"Will said you might know some history of the house we just bought."

"Who?" slurred Annie, who was now visibly swaying in her seat.

"Will. Behind the bar."

"Ohhhh, you mean young William!"

Melody nodded, a huge grin filling her petite face.

"Oh, I know young William. Not as well as I'd like to though, eh?" the old woman said as she laughed a little too loudly.

"It's Annie you want to talk to if it's about history isn't it, Annie?" Petunia interjected.

Mrs. Briggs nodded pleasantly.

"I know a little about a lot, and sometimes a lot about a little. I'm something of a historian, you know," she said, draining the rest of the vodka from her glass as Steve tried to make sense at her ridiculous attempt at a rhyme.

"Yes, Will said as much. We just wondered what you know about our house." Melody pressed.

Mrs. Briggs shrugged, again causing her tacky gold jewellery to rattle.

"Depends where it is you live, I know a little about everywhere, and a lot about a few places,"

she repeated, and chuckled to herself as Steve's mind conjured images of Tolkien's *Hobbit*, imagining Mrs. Briggs sitting in Gollum's dark underground cave, playing word-games and clutching her precious booze to her chest. He smiled to himself, but nobody noticed. Melody was now the focus of attention.

"We live a few miles down the road in Hope House."

*Silence.*

Where Steve had earlier jokingly suggested that everyone would freeze as they walked through the door and stare at the strangers, it had now actually happened. Not in the entire room of course—the rest of the pub carried on, oblivious to their conversation. People chatted and laughed and drank. However, around their table—the one Steve thought simply as *'the witches table'*—there was a deep and somewhat disturbing silence.

Mrs. Briggs leaned close, the smell of her breath almost enough to get them both drunk.

"You live in Hope House?" she repeated, as she cast her glassy gaze on them.

Steve and Melody exchanged puzzled glances.

"Yes. We moved in a few weeks ago."

She was watching them both carefully, and Steve was sure he could feel her probing around in his mind somehow.

"Has everything gone well since you moved in?" she asked.

He felt Melody grasp his hand under the table, and as he glanced at her he saw a flicker of uncertainty in her eyes.

*We see you.*

"Everything's fine," Steve said flatly.

Mrs. Briggs swayed in her chair and leaned even closer, her words slurring together as she looked at them both. "Good. The moment that changes, make sure you leave. Leave and don't go back..."

"That's enough, Annie."

Steve looked up to see Will standing beside the table. He glared at the drunken woman in the mustard blouse.

"I'll decide when I've had enough, William Jones. Don't you talk down to me."

"Whilst my name is listed as landlord, I'll be the one deciding who does and who doesn't drink here, and when they've had enough."

"Away with you," she said, waving a flabby hand at him. "I'll not be bullied. These lovely young people need to know the truth, and if nobody else will tell them, I will."

"Anne I think it's time to leave," said Petunia, looking flustered and apologetic at the same time.

"No I won't have it, I won't be silenced!"

Mrs. Briggs was now causing quite the scene, and their corner table had the full attention of all the other patrons.

"I won't ask you again," Will hissed between gritted teeth.

"You won't stop me, not like last time!"

"That's enough!" Will said, grabbing Mrs. Briggs roughly by the arm as she was half-walked half-dragged to the door.

"'Ware the woods! Hear me now! 'Waaaaare the woods!" she wailed dramatically.

"'Ware em yourself," came a single voice from the other side of the pub, followed by a short bray of laughter.

Steve didn't find it funny though and, by the look on her face, neither did Melody. Mrs. Briggs was unceremoniously bundled outside, and her cronies quickly followed, keeping their heads low and eyes down. Steve and Melody sat awkwardly at the now empty table, not enjoying the unwanted attention. They could feel the eyes of the locals burning into them, and did the best job that they could to ignore it and act as if all was well.

"I'm sorry about that. She doesn't know when to stop," Will said as he returned to their table.

"It's okay, it's not your fault."

"Still, it's my pub, and I don't want my customers having to see that. Please, let me clear these glasses and get you another drink, on the house of course."

"You don't need to do that," Steve said.

"I want to. It's not the welcome we wanted to give you. Please, accept my apologies."

He began to gather the plethora of empty glasses and bottles when Melody reached out and put a hand on his arm.

"The things that she said... what did she mean?"

"Nothing," Will said, smiling warmly and picking up more glasses, "just the drunken ramblings of a crazy old fool. Forget about her."

With arms laden with more glasses than Steve thought humanly possible to carry, Will straightened and grinned again.

"Just sit tight, I'll bring your drinks over straight away."

"Thanks," Melody said absently as she leaned back in her seat.

"He's a nice guy. Good of him to give us free

drinks, too," Steve said, offering a warm smile to Melody, who managed to flash one back despite the icy feeling in her gut.

She had seen it, the quick glance between Will and Steve when she'd questioned Mrs. Briggs's ramblings. A furtive, knowing glance which confirmed that the two of them knew something she didn't. She absently spun her silver wedding ring around on her finger. For whatever reason, her husband had chosen to hide whatever had been said to him by a man he had only just met, and that alone disturbed her immensely. She wouldn't make a fuss of it, however; she decided to be quite the opposite, and would act as if all was well, but one thing was for certain. She was determined to find out what was going on.

# 14. THE SEARCH FOR ANSWERS

HE KNEW HE WAS dreaming again. The woods were cast in the milky, ethereal glow he'd become accustomed to during his non-waking hours. It was always the same. The sky was cloudless, the moon full and bright, and the shadows deep and opaque. Silence hung as thickly and heavily as the ground mist clinging clammily to his ankles as he walked the dirt path snaking through the woods.

He no longer ran in his dreams, as he knew it made no difference. He would always arrive at the same time, and would invariably be too late to stop Melody's death. Suddenly, it was upon him—the giant, gnarled tree where his dreams came to an end. And there as always was Melody, standing atop the branch, a noose around her neck, eyes staring vacantly ahead. He heard himself shout to her, expecting his cries to be unheard as they always were just before she stepped off the edge of the branch, but this time, she blinked, and looked at him, and he in turn grew afraid for what would happen now that the normal routine had changed.

He could see that she was crying, and as he watched, a wispy, translucent figure appeared beside her. It was a man, African-American and wearing tattered trouser bottoms. He was so painfully thin that he resembled the classic horror movie ghoul. The milky figure whispered in Melody's ear, and Steve watched in horror as she listened, nodding in places. As he watched, other figures appeared, men, women, even children, surrounding Melody on her high perch, moving through each other as they took turns to whisper at her. Steve had seen enough, and began to climb, pulling himself up the rough, cold trunk. He recalled the skills he'd had as a boy, willing the dexterity to be as nimble as it had been then as he climbed, ignoring the vertigo-induced dizziness as he moved ever closer to his wife. The branch where she perched was just ahead and, as he looked at her, pale and fragile in the moonlight, he saw that she was once again alone: her ghostly visitors had disappeared back into the ether.

As he clambered onto the branch, he was astounded at how incredibly vivid the dream was. He could feel everything in minute detail, a slight breeze ruffling his hair, the thick, heavy pounding of his heart racing in his chest, and even the stinging pain in his palms from the effort of climbing.

"Melody!" he said, his words coming out listlessly as she looked towards him.

"I don't want to do it Steve, but they say I have to."

"You don't have to do anything, just stay there; I'm coming to get you."

He said the words with conviction, but his own abject terror and the fear of heights he'd had since childhood left him unable to release his grip on the safety of the tree trunk. He willed himself to do it, but it was taking too much time, and he knew he would be too late. Inching across the sturdy bough, he somehow kept his eyes fixed ahead, ignoring the sick feeling in his stomach every time the tree rocked and swayed. She was close now—he could smell the perfume that he'd bought her for her birthday as the breeze blew around them both.

His eyes drifted to the noose and to her thin, fragile neck. He reached out, their fingertips touched, but then he was yanked backwards by painful fingers that dug deep into his shoulder. Screaming in rage he spun around to face his attacker, ignoring the precarious drop below him. He came face to face with himself, his mirror image naked and its face twisted into an ugly, glaring grimace. He whirled back to face Melody, but she wasn't alone. Donovan stood beside her, naked and aroused and, unlike the milky ghosts, was quite solid and real. Steve watched as he put a hand around her shoulder, cupping one of her petite breasts in his hand.

*And lovely tits!*

Steve could do no more than watch as Donovan leaned close to whisper unheard words in her ear, keeping one eye on Steve as he did so.

"They have a message for you," she said softly. "They said to tell you they can see you."

It was all she said before she stepped off the edge. Steve's screams were lost in the gibbering cackles of Donovan and his own grimacing alter-ego.

There were no screams when he snapped awake, no cold sweats or panic, only confusion, as he was not in his bed. He was standing by the kitchen window staring out at the black tops of the trees swaying in the darkness.

*'How long have I been here?'* he asked the empty room, suspecting that it may have been a while, as his back and legs ached, and his throat was dry. His confusion increased as he looked to the floor. His bare feet were filthy and scratched and, as he held his shaking hands up to his face, he could see that they too were covered in scratches and matted with dirt. He felt sick, and hurried to the mirror above the fireplace, praying that he wouldn't see what he knew would be there.

The bruises formed a perfect circle, and were shaped like fingertips on his collarbone. Ice replaced his blood, and he felt its chilly fingers brushing his spine with cold fingers. His dream came back to him in all-too-stark clarity. He glanced at the clock on the mantle, and saw that it was just after five in the morning. Melody probably wouldn't be up for another couple of hours, and he made the difficult decision to keep this latest turn of events from her. He didn't want to shatter the illusion of this being the perfect place for them to live and grow old in.

He thought he knew a way.

He washed, dressed and made himself a coffee, and although he tried to convince himself otherwise, was still shaken as he sat at the kitchen table and booted up the laptop. He took a sip of the drink as he waited for the computer to rattle into life, then clicked on the search engine icon. Fingers poised over the keys, he hesitated. There were many questions that he needed answers to, and he knew that the best way would be to form some kind of order.

He keyed in '*haunted houses*' and waited for the computer to spit back the results. The six million plus hits told him that he would need to reduce his parameters slightly, or face wading through pages of irrelevant bullshit. He searched instead for '*genuine paranormal evidence*' and cycled through a few pages detailing reports of poltergeists, demonic possessions and all things in between.

The magnitude of the task ahead dawned on him, as each link he clicked seemed to lead to dozens of other potential branches of investigation. Soon enough, the notepad by the computer was filled with hand-scrawled notes, and he felt no further along than when he'd started.

He leaned away from the computer, drained his coffee and rubbed his eyes. Outside the wind shook the house. He glanced out the window, but was unable to see anything. He got that horrible, skin-crawling feeling of being watched again, and took a peek over his shoulder towards the sitting room, still shrouded in darkness. For a split second, he thought he saw a movement. He stared down the hallway, forcing his eyes to penetrate the gloom, finally telling himself that he was being stupid, although he wasn't convinced enough to actually go and take a look. With some effort, he turned his back on the darkened passageway and his attention to the computer screen. He paused, then typed in *'dreams causing physical pain'*, and pushed the search button.

He was about to give up when he stumbled on an entry on the third page. He clicked through to the website that, although sloppy in construction, had some interesting information about a young girl who'd experienced cuts, scratches and bruises from her dreams. He read the entry, the similarity to his own situation disturbing.

*Laura exhibited signs of bruising and scratches from her dreams, which were at first thought to have been self-inflicted during sleep. Laura, who claimed she could never recall her dreams in any great detail, was so terrified by her ordeal that she began to suffer from bouts of insomnia, caused not by the inability to sleep, but by unwillingness to risk being hurt.*

*Her parents convinced her to undergo evaluation at a dream clinic, which recorded and observed her sleep patterns for three consecutive nights. The first two nights passed without incident, but on the third evening, Laura experienced quite a violent nightmare and, to the surprise of the doctors present, woke with bruises on her upper arms which resembled a human hand.*

*Any suggestion that she had done them herself was dispelled, as the bruises, on her right arm, clearly showed finger and thumb patterns from a right hand, meaning that it would have been impossible for her to self-inflict the injury. Although unresolved, Laura's nightmares stopped as immediately as they began, and although the suggestion of whatever Laura had dreamt about causing her pain, the experts at the dream clinic suggested that it was possible, however unlikely, that the dreams could, if vivid enough, trick the brain into thinking that physical pain had been caused, and as a result show evidence of this on the body.*

Steve rubbed the bruises under his shirt absently as he read then, looking for something a little more specific, returned to his search engine and typed his next query.

'*Genuine hauntings*' brought up too many results, so he went back and refined his search to '*Hope House haunting, Oakwell*." He pressed search and waited, but there was nothing related to their house. One link did catch his eye though, and he clicked through to the article.

*Although the physical presence of spirits cannot always be detected, it is possible to record them in audio format. EVP - or electronic voice phenomena - is a mysterious event in which human-sounding voices from an unknown source are heard on recording tape, in radio station noise and other electronic media. Most often, EVPs have been captured on audiotape. The mysterious voices are not heard at the time of recording; it is only when the tape is played back that they are heard. Sometimes amplification and noise filtering is required to hear them clearly. Some EVP is more easily heard and understood than others. And they vary in gender (men and women), age (women and children), tone and emotion. They usually speak in single-words, phrases or short sentences. Sometimes they are just grunts, groans, growling or other vocal noises. EVP has been recorded speaking in various languages.*

Steve searched out a few samples which were linked at the bottom of the page, and although many were indistinct, there were a few which were genuinely creepy in their clarity. He had the start of an idea, one which might help him to find out what was happening in their house, but he needed a few things before he could proceed. There was one more link that interested him:

*Every culture over all time periods possess stories of the spirits that roam the earth. This constant inhuman civilization leaves no room for doubt on the presence of spirits of the dead coming back to the human plane as an ethereal existence. According to the stories, folklore, and witness testimonies, the world is full of spirits. Their method of interacting with the human world differs from spirit to spirit as well as their intentions, however. Some are evil. Some are benign. Some are indifferent. The manifestation of a spirit who wishes to do harm to the living or is intentionally being a bother to living humans does happen from time to time. At the worst it can lead to outrageous fear and trouble, or at the least annoyance to the humans the spirit chooses to haunt. Here is a list on how to get rid of any spirits that you wish to leave you alone.*

He skimmed down the list, dismissing the more unlikely entries such as holy water and healing herbs, and his attention was grabbed by an entry labelled 'Banishing Ritual'. He read on:

*The idea of a banishing ritual is seen throughout history and across the globe. Any culture that has a strong belief in malicious spirits and their ability to interact and affect the living has a type of banishing ritual. However, modern Western culture has designated most banishing rituals as a pagan custom.*

*Spells that banish can vary greatly even from person to person. Yet, they can be relatively simple. The easiest way is to write down the problem on a piece of paper, being as concise and specific as possible. After focusing deeply on the problem written on the paper, you must burn it. Most people prefer to burn using a white candle or by lighting the paper and placing it in a white bowl to allow it to burn in a controlled setting.*

It seemed plausible, and definitely something worth considering if his suspicions about the house proved correct. He yawned and stretched, and mused on the irony that now that it was almost morning, his inability to sleep had left him, and he wished he could lie down for a few hours. But as he glanced out of the kitchen window, the first pinkish hues of the new day were just starting to creep over the horizon, and knowing that Melody would soon be awake, wanted to make an early start and get the things he needed before she asked too many questions. He shut down the laptop, hid his notes in one of the kitchen drawers and prepared to leave the house.

Michael Bray

# 15. MESSAGES

STEVE WAS GONE WHEN Melody woke up. He had left a note in the kitchen saying that he was heading into town to pick up a few things, and that he would be back as soon as he could. It was the first time she'd been in the house by herself since they'd moved in, and following her obligatory morning routine, she was now sitting in the living room in her favourite dressing gown -- the pink one that Steve had bought her for Christmas -- and was cradling her mug of tea as she leafed through the telephone directory. There were only three listings under the name Briggs, and of those only one was initialled with the letter A.

Melody had been staring at the phone for a good twenty minutes, and was still undecided whether she should call or not. She found the old woman to be something of an enigma—on one hand she was plainly a little eccentric to say the least, but on the other she did seem to be very sure in her conviction that there was something that Steve and Melody ought to be told about their new home.

She chewed on her bottom lip, torn between what she thought was right, and what her impulse told her to do. Her main stumbling block was that she didn't think that Steve would approve. In fact, she got the impression that he already knew some part of the secret that everyone else but her seemed to be aware of.

As crazy as the old woman appeared, Mrs. Briggs did seem to be knowledgeable about the history of the house and whatever deep dark secret that seemed to be all so vital for her to get off her chest. Melody looked around the room, its circular design complimented by its original fittings. The old stone surround of the mantelpiece, the bare wooden beams holding up the ceiling, the large windows (unfortunately not the original frames; they were in too poor a condition and had to be replaced), and she sighed, content and happy, warm and safe. She listened to the house, cocking her head to the side and holding her breath, straining her senses and listening for anything that might seem untoward or out of the ordinary.

*Utter silence*

The old house made sounds of course, but what house didn't? The wood creaked and groaned; the wind pushed and probed in search of a way in, and when a particularly large gust hit, its sound would whoop and whistle as it plunged down the chimney and into the living room. As if on cue, one such gust came now, a sudden, powerful prod of wind, which caused her fringe to ruffle as it blew through the room. Steve had been meaning to block off the fireplace permanently, but she had convinced him not to. He had argued about how cold it would be in winter, and in the end, they'd decided to leave it open. The idea of a natural, open fire was just too hard to resist. Just then her mobile phone vibrated, and she fished it out of her pocket, surprised to see that she had received a text message. It was unexpected, as they had been unable to receive them since moving here. She didn't recognize the sender, and opened the message anyway.

*Hi Melody.* ☺

She thought it must be from one of their friends from the city, someone who assumed that Melody would know who it was. She could think of no other way to identify the sender, so bit the bullet and typed a reply.

*Who is this?*

She waited, inexplicably on edge and her stomach knotting with anxiety. The phone vibrated, and she hesitated before clicking on the envelope icon.

*It's us. We see you.*

At that she felt a surge of panic, and glanced nervously out of the window, but saw nothing unusual. Her mind told her to stop interacting with whoever it was, but she felt instinctively that perhaps it had something to do with whatever Steve had been hiding from her. She composed a new message, unsure if she were more afraid or angry at the invasion of her privacy.

*Do I know you?*

She sent it, keeping it short and snappy, hoping that the recipient would grasp her annoyance. The reply came almost immediately.

*Not yet. But you will.*

She felt sick and light-headed, and genuinely afraid now. Why somebody would choose to threaten her and how had they managed to get her number in the first place were things she was spared from thinking about for long, as the next message was even more terrifying in its simplicity.

*You look good in pink.* ☺

*Terror*

It overcame her with alarming speed, and this time she walked to the window directly and looked out. Everything seemed normal, but she felt her eyes drawn to the dense stand of trees and the fact that not only could anyone be watching her from within its tangled branches, but if they chose to try to get into the house, she was isolated and alone. She hurried to the door and locked it, her hands shaking as she went around the house, checking that all windows and doors were secure and then realising that it didn't make her feel even the slightest bit safer. Her phone vibrated again, and even though she didn't want to, she couldn't help but read it.

*Lol. Lock lock.*

She felt exposed, and the atmosphere had changed. It now felt oppressive and heavy. She tried to compose herself, deciding that whoever this prankster was needed to see that she wouldn't be intimidated. She walked to the window, putting herself in full view as she replied to the message.

*You don't scare me. I'm going to call the police.*

She waited and watched, looking for any sign of movement outside, saw none and then wondered if perhaps she had managed to scare off whoever had decided to try to trick her. The reply came in, and she looked at her handset.

*If you do, we will kill Steve. DON'T tell anyone.*

That changed things, and the simple prank had taken a sinister turn. She opened a new message and hovered over the keypad, unsure what to say, then decided against it and turned the phone off, not even wanting to touch it. Even though it was only mid-morning, she closed the curtains in every room of the house. Then, unsure what else to do, sat back down at the kitchen table, waiting for both her heart-rate to slow and her hands to stop shaking. She wanted to call Steve, but didn't want to turn on her phone for fear of what might await her. Instead, she stood and threw it in the bin. It felt spoiled now, and she knew she would never be able to use it again without feeling that horrible twist in her stomach.

An hour passed, and then another. Steve still hadn't returned, but she already felt better. She thought that anyone who had serious intentions of harming her would have tried to come into the house by now, and although she was still shaken, she thought that she'd be okay.

Michael Bray

She decided not to let it ruin her day, and turned her attention back to the telephone directory on the table. Mrs. Briggs's number seemed to glare at her from the page and she hesitantly picked up the handset for the landline phone and punched in the number, still not even sure what she would say to Mrs. Briggs if she answered. She waited as the line connected, and felt a flash of both excitement and dread as she waited for the call to be picked up. She waited for ten rings, and then reluctantly hung up , not sure whether she were more relieved or deflated that her investigation had come to such a sudden stop.

She wondered if it might be possible that she was making too much of nothing, and the huge conspiracy she had crafted in her mind was, in fact, non-existent. Still, it niggled at her, in spite of her best efforts to ignore both it and the threatening anonymous messages. It dawned on her that moping around the house and dwelling on it wasn't going to help anyone. She decided that she would wait until Steve came back and they would go and visit Mrs. Briggs in person at her home.

She finished her drink and showered, during which she heard Steve's return from wherever he'd gone to. She dressed and went downstairs, expecting to find him in the living room or kitchen, but was surprised to find the house empty. A fresh wave of panic overcame her. She walked to the window and looked outside and sure enough, there was the car, parked in the maddening not-quite-straight way that he always insisted on leaving it.

She hurried to the kitchen, and found him there with two large plastic bags. "What have you got there?" she asked, surprised how calm her voice sounded.

"Just a few odds and ends for the recording studio, mostly boring wires and plugs.."

"I hope you didn't overspend."

"Would I?" he said, flashing his best winning grin. "I didn't think you were here. The door was locked."

"I didn't want to leave it open while I was in the shower."

He didn't pursue it, but he did look around at the windows still covered by the curtains. "Dare I ask?" he said with a smile.

"Headache," she said simply, wanting to tell him all about the the threatening texts but not daring to.

"Ah, okay. Well lucky for you, I'm gonna get out of your hair for a while and do some work on the studio. Will you be all right?"

"I'll be fine. Actually, I'm heading out myself now. I'm going to go to the shops and buy us some actual food, unless you fancy cooking up some of your wires and cables tonight."

"I could," he grinned, "we both know I make a mean cable stew."

Melody groaned and shook her head, then gave him a peck on the cheek and picked up the car keys. "I won't be long. Can I trust you not to burn down the house while I'm out?"

"I think so," he joked as he picked up his bags of purchases.

"Okay. Do you want anything specific to eat tonight?"

"I'm easy. Whatever suits you."

*How about the truth?*

She almost said it, and for a split second was sure the words would come before she could stop them, but realised that she was doing a fair amount of lying herself now. Instead she managed to flash a warm smile. "I'll pick something up. I won't be long."

Steve nodded absently as he sorted through the contents of his plastic bags. Taking the opportunity to slip away, Melody left, picking up the telephone directory on her way out the door.

He waited until he heard the car pull away from the house before he hurried outside. He didn't want to have to explain to Melody what was happening, not yet at least. The wind rocked him as he made his way down the garden, which was now flecked with golden-brown autumn leaves.

The recording studio looked like nothing more than an oversized, windowless shed from outside. Steve set his bags down and fished in his pocket for the key, letting himself into what would be (when finished) his office. The studio was furnished in red, with a large multi-track mixing desk dominating the room which was split down the middle by a soundproof window leading to the as-yet unfinished live room. Several cables and half installed recording equipment units littered the floor. Steve set down his bags, flicked on the overhead strip light and closed the door, plunging the room into silence and dampening the sounds of the increasingly blustery weather.

He crossed to the large leather chair in front of the mixing desk and sat down, switching on the power. Bright red and green lights greeted him, the myriad of controls at his fingertips, which would be daunting to most, were as familiar to him as his own reflection. He assessed the situation, and thought that with his new purchases he could have everything up and running within an hour or so, two maybe? He switched on the computer, and whilst it coaxed itself into life, he began to empty the bags and sort the contents as he prepared to go to work. He felt suddenly cold, a vicious gust of winter wind rocking the little shed. Steve thought it was as if nature itself knew what his intentions were, and was keen to deter him.

He now wished that the soundproofing had been fully installed. For some reason, the sound of the wind was bothering him more than he allowed himself to think about. As he unpacked his bags, he could hear its incessant rage, and for every new gust and shake of the treetops, he was more certain that his theory was right, and that he would be able to prove it to Melody. The feeling of being watched crept over him, a slow and stealthy thing, and he had to force himself not to look over his shoulder as he connected jack to plug, male to female, wire to board. A heavy, ominous atmosphere had begun to descend, and even though he tried to ignore it, there was no denying that it was there. Something yet nothing, palpable but non-existent.

*We see you.*

Icy-cold shivers danced down his spine, and the hairs on his forearms stood to attention. He heard a distant rumble of thunder, and he toyed with the idea of running back to the house and forgetting the entire idea. He told himself that focus was the key, focus and concentration. The rain that had threatened since mid-morning had come, and he could hear the gentle probing tap of its fingers on the roof and walls. He ignored it as best he could and set about what he needed to do.

# 16. SEEKING PROOF

MRS. BRIGGS'S HOME WAS a semi-detached white-painted cottage with a thatched roof and a small, tidy garden which smelled of cut grass and roses. Melody walked slowly down the narrow path, and despite the rain which fell heavily from leaden skies, she couldn't help but appreciate the beauty of the place. The combination of birdsong and the rain was somehow comforting and, for a split second, she forgot the reason for her visit.

She paused by the door, blood red with an ornate floral brass knocker set in the centre. She reached out to knock, then withdrew her hand, asking herself for the umpteenth time if she really wanted to know whatever it was that was being kept from her. She couldn't possibly fathom whatever it may be that Steve deemed so important as to keep from her. A wave of giddy uncertainty swept over her. She told herself not to be silly, and knocked on the door. There was no response and she was about to leave when the door to the neighbouring house opened, and a familiar head poked out. Melody struggled for her name, only remembering her as one of Mrs. Briggs's drinking buddies. It came to her just before it became awkward.

*Petunia.*

The one who'd kept making eyes at Steve.

"She's not in," said the plump, floating head as it peered around the door.

"Oh, I was hoping to speak to her, do you know how long she might be?"

"She's usually out most of the day on a Thursday. I would expect it will be late. Can I help with anything?"

"Oh, it's nothing really, I just wanted to ask some questions about our new house."

Petunia nodded, and stepped outside. Melody saw that she was wearing an oversized floral dressing gown and faded pink slippers, and looked infinitely more attached to her sobriety than the last time they'd met.

"Yes, Anne said that you might drop by, if you were curious enough."

"She did?"

"Yes, although she says a lot when she is a little the worse for drink."

Melody nodded, and looked hopefully at Mrs. Briggs's red door, then back to Petunia. "I don't suppose you know why she expected me? I mean I didn't know I was coming over myself until I got here."

"I couldn't say," Petunia said with an exaggerated shrug. "Whatever it was she didn't share it with me."

"Any idea where I might find her?"

"Hmm, you could try the greengrocer's on Mercer Street, or failing that she might be in the café over by the green. To be perfectly frank, she really could be anywhere. Would you like me to take a message?"

Melody shook her head. "No, no it's fine. I was just passing and thought I would stop by."

Petunia nodded, even though they both knew it was a lie. "Well, I'm sorry I couldn't be of more help. You should get out of this rain before you catch your death dear."

"I will. Thanks for your help."

Petunia opened her mouth to speak, and then closed it. Melody watched as a troubled frown crossed her brow, and the old woman looked at her with an expression which was one part sympathetic, two parts concerned.

"You take care," she said simply, stepping inside again and closing the door.

***

She chased all over town in search of the elusive Mrs. Briggs. For such a small community Melody had discovered that tracking down even such a distinctive person was proving difficult. Drenched and frustrated, she had given up and now, making her way carefully down the dirt road back towards Hope House, she found that she had more questions than answers. She pulled in and was surprised to see the house in darkness. There were no lights on and, in the half-gloom brought on by the storm, it looked like an abandoned shell and more than a little unsettling considering the day's events. She hurried to the house and found the door open and unlocked.

"Steve?"

Her enquiry went unanswered, and she made her way through the rooms, switching lights on as she went, not really sure why. She remembered that he'd been planning to do some work in the studio, going to the kitchen window and looked out she saw a crack of golden light shining from under the studio door. Unsure why her nerves were so frayed but remembering that they had every right to be, she relaxed, went outside and headed down the garden.

He came out to meet her as she approached, and Melody instantly disliked the expression on his face. His eyes were wide, and he was wearing a grin which looked to be more afraid than happy.

"I wondered where you were—"

He cut her off by holding a finger to his lips. "Shh. I've been waiting for you to get back."

"Why are you whispering?" she asked, trying to

hide how afraid she was.

"I'll show you. Come on inside," he said, opening the studio door and ushering her over the threshold.

She entered, and couldn't help but glance at the door as it closed and shut them both into the tiny room.

Melody had only been inside the studio a couple of times during its construction, but if Steve had done any work then she wasn't able to tell. The place was in the same chaotic disarray as when she'd last seen it. Steve turned over a plastic crate and set it beside his chair by the computer.

"Come on in and take a seat. I have something to show you."

She sat down, watching him carefully. His eyes darted nervously, and he kept licking his lips. She saw a notepad on the desk in front of him filled with scruffy longhand. "Steve what's going on here?"

"You'll see," he said, flashing a grin which was more reminiscent of the husband that she'd had left in the house just a few hours ago.

"Are you okay?" she asked, genuinely concerned.

"I'm fine. I'm just... I don't know. Excited, nervous... I can't really explain," he grinned and turned back to the computer, moving sliders and adjusting controls.

"What's going on?"

"Just wait, and listen," he said without looking at her.

He clicked an icon on the screen and pushed the faders on the mixing desk up. The sounds of the wind that had been previously blocked out by the soundproofed studio filled the room. Steve adjusted a couple of settings on his console and turned the volume down a touch.

"Steve -- I don't understand, I..."

"Shh, just listen," he said as he adjusted a few more settings then turned towards her. "I set up some microphones in the woods."

She didn't like the way his eyes were wide and showing too much white, or the self-important grin etched onto his face.

"Steve, are you drunk?"

"Of course not. I know this seems bizarre but please, just humour me, okay?"

Melody nodded silently. She was frightened and worried, not only for her husband, but also for her own safety, which was crazy as he wasn't the type to ever hurt anybody. "Why would you want to record the woods?"

"Just listen," he said as he turned the volume up higher.

The room was filled with the stereo sounds of the bluster of the weather conditions outside, the angry roar of raging wind, the rustle of the trees swaying in unison.

"There!" Steve barked, making Melody's heart leap into her throat. "Did you hear it?"

"Steve…"

"You must have heard it. Keep listening!"

She had never seen him like this. He was wild and manic, and she felt very afraid of him. She watched him hunched over the computer, eyes staring at the screen and body taut as he waited for whatever it was that she was supposed to be hearing.

"There it was again!" he said as he emitted a short stab of laughter. "Can you believe this?"

"Steve, this is freaking me out. I don't hear anything."

"What? Are you deaf? Open your damn ears!"

Melody inhaled sharply, and Steve looked at her as the horrific grin melted from his face.

"Baby... I'm sorry... I just got carried away."

"Well it would help if you told me what the hell I'm meant to be listening to."

"The voices in the woods," he said simply.

She smiled, and then realised that he was serious. She looked at him, trying to ignore her instinctive fear.

"Steve," she said, taking his hands in hers. They felt the same as always, soft and smooth. "This is really freaking me out. There are no voices."

"I know you love this place, and I know how insane this sounds but ask yourself. Have I ever done wrong by you before? Have I ever done anything to hurt you?"

Her lip was trembling as she shook her head "Of course you haven't but..."

"Then please, just listen."

Even though she was still afraid, she decided to give him the benefit of the doubt. "I don't hear anything."

"Let me play you something I recorded earlier. It's clear and—well I don't know what it is. I don't normally believe in this stuff."

She wanted to stop him, to hold him close and tell him his mind was playing tricks on him, that whatever he thought he could hear was no more than the sounds of the natural world, sounds that he'd never heard before having most of his life in the city. However, she knew him well enough to let him play it out, because once he had an idea in his head, she knew he wouldn't rest until he'd seen it through to the finish. Although it was a trait she loved, it also worked against him because it made him too stubborn to see any opinion apart from his own.

She sat and waited as he searched through the files on the computer. He turned back towards her and was wearing that wide grin again which looked so out of place that it gave her the chills.

"Here it is. Just listen."

Steve played the audio, and the room was filled with the sweeping, whooshing sounds of wind shaking trees. Melody strained her ears, listening for anything that might sound out of the ordinary. Not because she believed it — she didn't buy into the idea of the supernatural. She believed in evolution, in science and cold, hard facts. But in this instance, she half hoped that she was wrong, because the alternative meant that Steve had some possible issues with his mental state, and to consider that at a time when they were just about to start their lives together frightened her more than any mysterious woodland voices ever could. He was watching her with an expectant grin, waiting for her to register that she had heard the same things he had, but try as she might, the only sounds that Melody could hear were natural ones — trees being barraged by the elements. She shook her head slowly, and was pained by the hurt, confused expression on her husband's face.

"I'm sorry... I don't hear anything."

"But it... it's right there."

She stood and crossed the room, unsure how she felt. Hot tears stung her cheeks as she opened the door and turned back to face him. "I want you to see a doctor."

"I don't need to see a doctor. I'm not crazy!"

"Then do it to humour me. I'm worried about you."

"I'm fine...I..." he trailed off and looked at the floor. "You were supposed to understand..."

"Don't put this on me," she said, unsure why she was so angry. "What did you expect, sneaking around and talking about voices in the damn woods?"

She was surprised at the venom in her voice, and

although she felt guilty, she was also genuinely angry at him.

"Are you surprised that I kept it quiet?" he asked, standing and pointing at her. "I knew you'd be like this. Let me tell you something Mel, the world isn't all cold, hard facts and science and black and white. Maybe, there are things out there that we don't understand."

"Oh, so it's my fault for being rational? You can be really pig-headed sometimes."

"And you can be so fucking naïve sometimes," he roared, slamming his fist down on the table.

She could feel the heat flush in her cheeks, and wanted to walk away before things escalated, but something in her wanted to make a point, and so she stood her ground.

"Naïve? Try realistic. This was supposed to be a fresh start away from our old lives, and here you are making up stories about voices in the trees. Do you know how insane it sounds? Just listen to yourself."

"You think I don't know that? Why do you think I didn't just say it outright? Why do you think I knew I would have to prove it for you to even entertain it?"

"Prove what? I didn't hear anything unusual."

"I played you the damn audio," he screamed, eyes wide and tendons bulging out of his neck.

"You did," she said softly. "And I didn't hear anything."

She turned away, stepping out into the cold.

"I'm going to bed. I want you to sleep on the sofa tonight, and then go to see a doctor tomorrow," she said from the doorway.

He shook his head. "I don't need to see a doctor. I need you to believe me. I'm trying to protect you here."

"Either see a doctor, or this is over," she said, and

Michael Bray

then closed the door before he had time to respond. She walked quickly to the house, hugging herself against the cold and trying to make some sense of the life that seemed to be slowly unravelling around them.

# 17. WAKING THE DEAD

SHE WOKE WITH A start, confused and disorientated, surprised that she had actually been able to fall asleep in the first place. The content of her dream was enough to tell her that the earlier spat with Steve was still very much on her mind. After the two of them had argued, she had come straight to bed, but found that she was too upset to sleep and had lain awake for what felt like an eternity, staring at the ceiling and half hoping that he would come upstairs to make up with her.

She remembered how her mother used to tell her never go to sleep on an unresolved argument, and in the past had always abided by that advice, but this was bigger than a standard argument. This could be a relationship changer. She wondered what could be wrong with Steve. Could it be schizophrenia? Or could it be nothing more sinister than her initial guess – that his years of city living had left him unprepared for country life and the natural sounds that came with it? She had heard him come into the house just after midnight, but he hadn't come upstairs. She tried to stay awake in the hope that he would come up to see her, but despite her best efforts she had fallen asleep.

The dream had been disturbing.

In it, she was naked in the grass circle in the woods, the trees rocking and swaying, but this time, she could hear their voices, mocking her, teasing her, making despicable, lewd suggestions at her. She had tried to run, but her movements felt sluggish. The whispers had grown louder, and the circle began to close in, the ancient, thick trunks pulling themselves out of the ground and dragging themselves closer on filthy, black roots. The branches reached out and

115

were suddenly the groping arms of people that she knew.

She saw Donovan, her sister and her father, all grabbing at her, clawing and tearing at her flesh. No matter how much she tried to distance herself, their arms seemed able to reach. They surrounded her, closing in and grabbing, groping, tearing. She screamed, and one of the gnarled roots went into her mouth. She gagged on it, feeling it crawl down her throat, making its way into her stomach as she breathed raggedly through her nose. The arms were now too many to count, stroking and grabbing, tearing muscle away from bone. As one clawed away a handful of her flesh, it was replaced by another. She could feel it all in agonising detail, and would have screamed if not for the slick, wet root which filled her mouth and was now probing around inside her. Her skin started to rupture, and just when the agony had seemed too much to bear, they disappeared, leaving her standing alone.

Panting and crying, she looked around. She was standing on the edge of a forest clearing. In front of her was a village comprised of simple wooden huts. At its centre,, a huge mountain of corpses burned and sizzled. She knew they were dead, as nothing could possibly survive such an ordeal, but still she heard them screaming. The heat of the fire was fierce, and as she watched, a lone figure walked out of the flames. It was Steve. He was silent, watching her. His naked body showed his arousal as he looked at her, and when he grinned, his teeth were filed into sharp points. He pointed at her, and then, as she continued watching, he walked back into the flames and climbed onto the mountain of bodies. She screamed, because although he was burning and his skin was melting and bubbling, falling from his face like hot wax dripping from a candle, still he smiled, and observed her with that sharp-toothed, manic grin. The wind howled, yet it still wasn't enough to mask her husband's horrible laughter.

That was when she'd jolted awake, sweating and confused. She noticed that Steve still hadn't come to bed. It was almost three in the morning and, with a sigh, she lay back down and closed her eyes, trying not to think about the nightmare. She was in that place—the hazy no-man's-land between full sleep and consciousness when she felt an icy breeze touch her body. She sat upright, imagining Donovan's grinning face as he reached out to caress her skin, but the bedroom was the same as it always was. She relaxed and told herself it was just her nerves making her imagine things that weren't there when she felt it again, a cool caress which chilled the sweat on her skin and made her shiver. She sat up, straining her eyes as she stared into the darkness, trying to locate its source.

The windows were all closed and locked, as she had made sure before turning in for the night, but she climbed out of bed and checked again anyway, looking for the tell-tale sign of the curtains moving in the breeze, but they were still. And yet she could still feel the steady touch of cool air on her skin.

"Steve?" she called out, her voice sounding incredibly tiny and insignificant as she stared at the open door to the shadow-draped hallway beyond.

She felt like secretive eyes were inspecting her, and she pulled the sheet off the bed and wrapped it around her body.

"Steve?" she called out again, straining her ears for any response.

She waited, but was met only with heavy silence and the feel of that inexplicable chill on her skin. Even

117

with her eyes now accustomed to the gloom, she couldn't force herself to step outside the safety of the bedroom.

She could see the ghostly shape of the bannister and the closed door to the circular room above the lounge, which they'd not decided on a use for yet and was, for now, storage for some of the things that they hadn't got around to unpacking. Everything looked normal and as it should except—

She held her breath and listened, straining her ears. She heard the occasional muted gust of the wind battening against the house, although it was now considerably less violent than earlier in the evening. Beyond that she could hear a steady dripping coming from the bathroom—the tap in need of repair, which was on their ever growing 'to-do' list. She also heard the hum of the water boiler in the cupboard next to the bathroom and—there.

Something else.

A sound from downstairs. A small secretive thud, so quiet it was almost inaudible. She exhaled slowly and walked quietly on to the hallway carpet, leaning over the bannister rail and looking over them, hoping to see the glow of the downstairs lights that Steve had a habit of leaving on when they came to bed. However it was still dark down there, and Melody felt an awful feeling trill up and down her spine as she tried to see what the source of that subtle but definite sound was. Downstairs could have been a hellish, deep pit for all she could tell, and memories of the threatening text messages buzzed and darted around her brain. She wanted to call Steve's name again, but her throat was dry, and she could muster neither the courage nor the willpower to make a sound, afraid of what might answer.

She heard it again. A dull *tap-tap* sound.

She crept to the top of the stairs, every footfall feeling deafeningly loud in the overpowering silence of the house. The steps loomed in front of her, an opaque void leading to whatever was making that stealthy sound. She willed herself to go and find out what it was, but was afraid, and it had rooted her to the spot, reducing her to peering into the darkness and imagining monstrous eyes crawling over her body.

*Tap tap*

She wished now that they'd replaced the upstairs light bulb in the hallway, as its presence would have surely shooed away the terror surging through her body at the thought of walking into the dark. However, the bulb had blown the day they'd moved in, and because they hadn't really seen it as a high-priority fix, it had been pushed down the list and forgotten about it completely. But now, as terror clung like a physical thing to her body, she'd have given anything to have been able to reach out and turn it on, knowing that its light would make everything seem a little less frightening, and to feel a lot less isolated.

*Fourteen steps.*

Just fourteen steps and then she'd be able to reach around the corner of the living room door and flick on the light. She took a deep breath and slowly began to descend, counting the steps as she went. Halfway down she heard it again, that out of place, stealthy tapping sound. It was sharper now and much clearer. She stood and listened, one hand on the wall, the other clutching her dressing gown across her chest as she forced herself to calm down, to slow her breathing and be rational. She attempted to push herself to continue, to make it down the steps and flood the shadows with warm, artificial light, but her thoughts were interrupted by other ideas, and instead of the comfort of light, she imagined reaching around the corner and groping for the switch only to have something cold and wet grab her wrist and pull her into the shadows.

*Tap tap*

She held her breath, the cold chill sweeping through her body, raising gooseflesh on her skin. She continued her descent, acutely aware of every creak of the old wood, every groan of the house as she made her way down. She reached the bottom of the steps and peered into the dark living room, her furniture so familiar during daylight hours now vague, threatening forms. They played tricks on her mind and she saw them as gnarled and twisted humanoid figures, horrendously out of proportion, with long, reaching fingers which were spread across the walls, instantly bringing back vivid memories of her nightmare and the groping hands which had tried to tear her apart. She reached into the room, and ran her fingers across the wallpaper in search of the light switch.

*This is when it's going to happen*, she thought. *This is when whatever is making the sound is going to grab me and drag me away, and I'll never be seen again.*

*Tap tap*

She whirled around, her eyes staring at the entrance to the kitchen. The sound had definitely come from there and now, nearing it, the cool breeze was more intense, ruffling her hair as she stood at the threshold. She glared into the gloom, and it happened, the same sound, but sharp and loud. It was close.

*Tap tap*

She instantly saw the source of the sound and was both alarmed and somehow relieved that it wasn't some otherworldly thing formed in her mind by Steve's rambling talk of voices in the woods. The kitchen door leading to the garden banging against its frame, pushing more of the cool outside breeze towards her.

*Tap tap*

Her initial fear was replaced by anger at Steve, who had not only left the house in the middle of the night, but had left the door open and scared her half to death. She hoped for his sake that he wasn't in his studio recording more pointless weather sounds to try and 'prove' something to her, as she didn't know whether she could handle any more stress. She crossed to the door and was about to walk over to the studio and give him hell when she saw him. He was standing by the edge of the river in his shorts and the old t-shirt that he usually wore for bed. She opened the door and was hit by an icy blast of wind which drove her back against the door frame.

"Steve!" she shouted, but the wind rose, snatching the words out of her mouth and carried them away. He was tottering on the edge of the bank, his bare feet struggling to grip the wet grass. She started to run towards him, but the wind fought against her, pushing with tremendous force and slowing her progress. Its pure ferocity was frightening, and as the black husks of trees swayed and billowed, and the autumn leaves skittered and rolled, she could almost believe that they *were* talking.

The rhythmic sound could almost be interpreted as words, or more specifically one word, and the word chilled her more than the icy bite of the weather.

It sounded like they were saying '*jump*'.

A loose length of branch was picked up by an exceptionally violent gust, skittered across the ground and slapped her painfully in the face, and now the sound of the trees was like slow, mocking laughter. Stumbling back, she saw Steve being buffeted by the wind, and yet somehow he didn't fall. She yelled out to him again, so loudly that it made the back of her throat raw, but he remained unresponsive as the violent wind continued its barrage. The grass was wet underfoot, making her slip, and she'd almost regained her balance when a second gust pushed her in the back sending her to her hands and knees, against the direction of the wind that was keeping her away from Steve.

She looked up from her hands and knees, and knew that she was too late. She could only watch as Steve casually stepped off the edge and into the water. She screamed and scrambled towards the riverbank, trying to ignore the deep rumbling laughter which surrounded her. She peered into the swollen, raging water but could see no sign of him. She wondered how deep it was and as she processed the thought she saw him, floating face down and being carried away by the current. She scrambled to her feet and raced along the bank, trying to get alongside him. She wasn't sure when, but at some point she had started to cry. She was alongside him now and, without thinking, leapt into the water, its icy shock sucking the breath from her body.

For a few seconds, she couldn't move, and was sure she was going to drown, but her feet kicked at the sandy bottom as she struggled to regain control. She swam towards Steve, closing the distance more quickly than she imagined possible. She grabbed him and turned him over so that he was face up, not quite sure what to do or even how to get them both back onto dry land. Hooking her arms under his, she kicked hard towards the edge, hoping to find something to grab on to in order to stop them from being dragged along, but her strength was dwindling, and with it she felt herself tiring. She wanted to close her eyes, just for a second, to regain some strength before the final push, but knew that if she did, then they would both die, and so forced herself to keep kicking and stay awake. The riverbank was close now, but it was downstream from the house and the edge loomed over them, too high to climb. She grabbed at the loose roots and long grass, hoping to slow their motion, but she overcompensated, and her head slipped under the water.

She coughed and spluttered as the cold water tried to fill her lungs and weigh her down. She kicked harder, but it was no good. She had no strength left. She held onto Steve, who looked blue and lifeless under the moonlight, and closed her eyes and prepared to accept her death when her back scraped across the sandy bottom. They were suddenly motionless, sobbing and coughing. She got to her feet and dragged Steve up the smooth incline, laying him flat on the grass. He wasn't breathing, and his eyes stared with glassy indifference towards the heavens.

"Don't you die on me," she sobbed, as she began chest compressions in an effort to revive him.

The wind roared, and still it sounded like laughter. She ignored it and continued the compressions, hoping and praying for a miracle. Steve gasped and coughed up a great gout of water, and Melody held him, kissing his head. The trees rocked and swayed, a violent cacophony of branches whipping and snapping, thrown around by the elements which continued to assault Melody and Steve where they lay shivering on the grass. Although she knew it was quite impossible, she couldn't help but notice the noise of the trees as they shook fiercely.

They sounded furious.

# 18. REVELATIONS

MRS. BRIGGS WALKED UP the gravel car park to the Old Oak, panting as she breathed in the fresh, invigorating autumn air. It was a Sunday, and as had been the case for the last hundred years, the pub was closed all day. Pulling her fur coat tighter around her neck, she waddled past the main customer entrance to the recessed door at the rear of the building and knocked sharply twice. She waited, breathing heavily and peering out from under her wool hat. The door opened and Will stared at her as he stood, arms folded and a half-smoked cigarette hanging limply from his bottom lip.

"I wondered when you might show up," he said, regarding her coldly and without welcome.

"You and I need to have words young William. We knew this would happen again eventually."

Will shook his head. "I told you last time, and I'll say it again. Keep me out of it."

"I would rather we discussed this inside."

"You aren't welcome here, Anne. Please, just go home."

She didn't reply, or make any effort to leave. She simply waited and watched him with a small half smile etched onto her wrinkled lips.

"You'd better come in," Will said with a sigh as he stepped aside.

"Thank you," she said, sweeping past him and leaving the spicy, overpowering scent of her perfume behind as he closed the door.

"You remember the way. Straight up the steps," he said as he closed the door.

Mrs. Briggs nodded curtly, and began to ascend slowly, dragging her massive frame while the floorboards groaned in protest.

"Do be a dear and fix me a drink," she said over her shoulder.

"The bar is closed."

She paused on the steps, and half-turned towards him. "I think under the circumstances, we can forget the old traditions. Come on, William. Your father never begrudged me the odd tipple."

He sighed and shook his head slowly. " It's only ten in the morning. Isn't it a little early?"

"Not for what we have to discuss it isn't."

Will looked at her, and she met his gaze.

"Go on up. I'll bring the drinks," he sighed.

"There's a good lad. Make mine a double will you?"

He glared at her but she only smiled. He broke eye contact, and headed through to the bar.

"Good lad," she said, continuing breathlessly on her way.

\*\*\*

Burbain Hospital was in stark contrast to the rest of the sleepy town of Oakwell. A modern building of steel and glass it serviced not only Oakwell and Westland, but also the city of Blackhill. At any one time, it could house over six hundred patients and boasted some of the best healthcare in the country.

Steve was in a private room and Melody sat beside him holding his hand. Wires and electrodes snaked out of his body to a vast array of machinery, constantly monitoring his condition. His heart had stopped three times on the way to the hospital and, combined with his severe hypothermia, he was lucky to be alive. His condition was now stable, but he was sleeping, and Melody knew that for her part she had been incredibly lucky, somehow escaping injury-free.

She looked at her sleeping husband and stroked his hair, realising just how close they had both come to dying. The door opened softly and a slim, blonde-haired doctor walked into the room. He set his clipboard down on the small table by the door and checked the monitoring equipment.

"You should be resting," he said, looking at Melody kindly. She offered a weak smile.

"I can't sleep. I'm too worried. I thought he was dead."

The doctor smiled; the expression looked slick and well-practiced.

"Well let me reassure you that the worst of this is over. I'm Doctor Davies. And don't worry, he's in safe hands. He actually has you to thank for saving his life."

Melody shrugged and stroked Steve's hair. "I still don't know why he was out there."

"Does your husband have a history of sleepwalking?" the doctor asked.

Melody shook her head. "No. Not for as long as I've known him. I can't imagine him walking out there in the cold without waking up."

"Oh you might be surprised. People do all kinds of things when they sleepwalk. We had a case once where a man drove his car whilst somnambulant and crashed into a tree. On another occasion, a woman didn't know why she was gaining weight. She had been cooking and eating in her sleep."

"Really? Is that true or are you just telling me this to stop me from worrying?"

"It's all absolutely true. It's actually fairly common. Don't be so alarmed, you did a fantastic job, and even though all the machinery hooked up to him looks intimidating, he's over the worst now. He just needs some rest."

"I was worried about brain damage."

Davies shook his head and offered another reassuring smile.

"No danger of that. His neurological signs are as expected. We'll keep him under observation for a few days, and then he can go home."

"That's great. Thank you, doctor."

"That's why we're here," he said with a smile. "How are you feeling?"

"I'm okay, just a little tired."

"Well maybe you should get some rest, especially under the circumstances."

"What do you mean?" Melody frowned.

The doctor's smile slightly and he picked up his clipboard.

"I'll have one of my colleagues come and speak to you soon."

"No," Melody said, standing and looking him in the eye. "What is it? What's wrong with me?"

"I'm sorry, it's not my place to discuss this with you."

"I'm giving you permission to tell me. What is it? What's wrong?"

"Nothing's wrong with you," he said softly, "you're pregnant."

It was a rare occasion that Melody was left speechless. However, as the magnitude of Davies' words sunk in, she sat back slowly in the chair.

"I'm sorry you found out this way. We picked it up during your examination."

"Are you certain? Could it be a mistake?"

Davies shook his head.

" No. It's confirmed."

"But... how could I have not known?"

"It happens," he shrugged. "Morning sickness and

cravings aren't an exact science. Not everybody gets them."

She frowned and shook her head.

"Are you okay?" he asked, waiting patiently in the way only those who practice medicine seem able to do.

"Yes... no. I don't really know."

"We have people you can speak to. I could have one of the nurses come by and make an appointment if you like?"

"No, no that's okay. I just need some time to process this, that's all."

"I understand. I'm sorry for breaking it to you in such a ham-fisted way."

"No that's okay. It's not your fault."

He smiled, but she could still see how awkward and uncomfortable his error had made him. He crossed to the door, opening it softly.

"Well, I'll leave you two alone."

"Wait," Melody blurted, wishing she didn't sound so sharp and desperate.

"Yes?"

"When I jumped into the water... is there any chance that I might have done any damage...?"

"No, none at all," he said, giving her a reassuring smile. "The paramedics said you were in remarkable shape considering the time exposed and the temperature of the water. You were lucky. Both of you."

She glanced at Steve, who was still blissfully sleeping.

"I don't feel so lucky."

"You've been through a trauma, and it's been a long night. Try to get some rest. Things will feel better later, once you and your husband have had time to talk."

She nodded. He was right, and now that she thought about it, she *was* tired. Exhausted, in fact.

"I guess so. Is it okay if I sleep here?"

The doctor shifted awkwardly. "I'm afraid you can't. Hospital policy."

"Oh," she said, unable to hide her disappointment.

"Why don't you go home and get some sleep? Tomorrow you can come back refreshed."

"Yes, I suppose that makes sense. Thank you, Doctor Davies."

"No thanks needed. You take care, okay?"

"Yes. Yes, I will. Thank you."

The doctor left and closed the door, leaving Melody alone with her thoughts. She held her hands to her stomach, unable to see any evidence that she was carrying a child. Her skin was still flat and smooth. She realised that had she known she was pregnant before the accident, then she was quite sure she wouldn't have leapt so haphazardly into the water after Steve, and if that had happened, she would now be a widow. The weight of the stress that had been building over the last few weeks suddenly hit her. She felt isolated and alone, regretting her impatience with Steve and her narrow-minded stubbornness.

They had discussed the idea of having children but hadn't made a decision either way on it, and so for the duration of their relationship had been careful. However, she knew that contraception wasn't absolutely foolproof, and it seemed that they'd been part of that tiny percentage of couples where despite the care they'd taken, had found themselves with a child on the way. That alone was a huge life-changing event, but combined with her concerns over her husband's mental well-being, the strange harassment messages and her suspicions about some of the local townsfolk, made any decision all the more important.

It was all too much to think about, and with a shallow sigh, she stood and crossed the room, pausing by the door to look at Steve. Despite everything, she loved him, and that was enough to make her determined to get through whatever issues would come from recent events. She closed the door softly and headed home.

# 19. SECRETS

WILL'S APARTMENT SCREAMED BACHELOR. He had lived above The Old Oak for over twenty years, and although he'd had short-term relationships with a few women, things had never quite worked out for him. The signs were everywhere, from the single coaster on the table, to the tray containing last night's microwave meal for one, discarded on the floor beside the armchair that showed significantly more wear and tear than the rest of the furniture.

Mrs. Briggs sat on the sofa, hands placed palms-down on her knees. She watched Will coolly, and then took a sip of her gin and tonic. "You know why I'm here, don't you, William?"

Will sat in his chair; he looked awkward and uncomfortable and couldn't help but fidget. "I can guess," he said gruffly, "but I told you last time that I wouldn't be a part of it. Not anymore."

"That's not for you to decide, William. You know that."

"I can't do this anymore. It's already ruined my life. I'm done."

Mrs. Briggs took another sip of her drink, and then sat back and offered a narrow smile. "Must we always go through this? Do you think any of us wanted this?"

"They seem like nice people," he spat, quickly composing himself and repeating the statement with deliberate calm. "They seem like nice people."

"I agree, and I'm sure they are. However, you know as well as I do that we cannot interfere."

The old woman looked at William, her eyes bright with ancient knowledge. She leaned close and the light shifted on her face, giving her features a ghastly sunken appearance.

"They will be fine, as long as they leave it in place," she said, the smile growing on her face, yet still without humour.

"And what if they don't? How much more do I have to sacrifice? Hasn't my family name suffered enough?"

"Whatever it takes. Just like your father did. He knew the consequences of the mess your grandfather made. You should, too."

Will shook his head slowly. "Don't you think I've suffered enough?"

"Ah, haven't we all?" Mrs. Briggs said, shrugging her shoulders for emphasis. "But the fact remains that we have to hold our silence."

"I don't see why I should pick up the pieces for the actions of my ancestors yet again!"

"It's the way it has to be William."

"Keep your preaching to yourself. You have as much blood on your hands as I do."

"William, I don't like it, but this is the way it's always been. We took precautions this time; they'll be fine..."

"Only if it works!"he said, glaring at his guest. "What if you're wrong?"

"I... I don't know..."

Mrs. Briggs looked flustered, and greedily gulped down the rest of her drink. She exhaled and there was a heavy silence before she spoke again. "I understand that this makes you uncomfortable William. I really do, but we've been here before. We can't blame ourselves for this. You would do well to keep that in mind."

"Oh, I think we can," Will said sharply. "I think we are as much to blame as anyone. And every time someone moves into that damn house, and we don't do anything about it...." He trailed off and lowered his gaze to the floor.

"Things will be different this time. We took precautions; they are protected."

Will looked up at Mrs. Briggs, his eyes pleading as he nervously chewed his lip.

"And the question still stands. What if it doesn't work?"

"It will," Mrs. Briggs said, but she sounded uncertain, and Will straightened in his chair.

"You don't know either way what will happen, do you?"

She said nothing, and was condemned by her silence.

"Can't we at least warn them, give them half a chance if they should decide to... interact with them?"

"It's not our place. Besides which, it's too risky, not just for us but for the community. That's the important thing here."

Will stood quickly, pointing an accusatory finger at Mrs. Briggs. "I refuse to live like this anymore. If you won't say anything to them, then I will."

"You can't!" she shrieked, lurching to her feet and nudging the table, sending her empty glass onto its side where it rolled in a lazy circle.

"You can't do that," she repeated softly.

"Annie," Will said calmly "listen to you, listen to us. How long can we keep this up? Eventually word will get out and you, me and everyone else involved is going to pay for what we've done."

"I know," sighed Mrs. Briggs, and she suddenly seemed tired and drained as she flopped down onto the sofa. She eyed the spilled glass wistfully and then picked it up and set it right. Will watched her carefully, but remained silent.

"William, I understand how you feel, and perhaps

you are right, but we can't tell them too much. Let me speak to the girl, I can at least tell her about the cross in the tree, and how important it is to leave it there."

"No. Giving them some old wives' tale about something that may not even work isn't good enough. We need to do what's right and tell them to go, to leave whilst they still can."

"As long as the cross isn't removed, then they'll be safe."

"So you keep saying. But let's assume you're right about it protecting them. It still doesn't answer the question of what happens if they find it? Worse than that, what happens if they move it?"

"I don't know," she said softly. "I just don't know."

"And that's exactly why we have to tell them."

"William," Mrs. Briggs said, suddenly looking old and exhausted, "that's exactly why we can't."

\*\*\*

Melody drove down the narrow, single lane road in silence. She had watched the sky grow from dark purple to a pale, hazy blue as the night became day and, as she neared Hope House, she realised just how tired she was. The car rocked and bounced over the uneven road surface, but she barely noticed. She glanced to the empty passenger seat, the seat where Steve should have been sitting.

She wished he was there with her, but at the same time reminded herself that at least he was alive, that the outcome could have been much worse. She brought the car to a halt outside her home, and looked out of the window.

The building looked ominous and intimidating, and for the first time saw beyond her initial sense of wonder and amazement. She rested her head on the steering wheel, Steve's manic ramblings about the voices in the woods reverberating and swirling in her mind. She hadn't believed it, but for some reason, it nagged at her. Steve was normally so level-headed and down to earth, that for him to be convinced there was something out of the ordinary was strange enough, but there were also the very real things that had been happening to them, too.

The dreams, the threatening text messages, and the way that things she had put in a specific place moved to somewhere else of their own accord, and although it was possible that she could have moved them without realising, she was pretty sure she hadn't. On top of that, there was the inexplicable terror as she'd stood at the top of the stairs, certain that there was something in the dark below watching her. It had bothered her so much, that she had almost convinced herself that there *was* some kind of presence in the house and had felt compelled to run, or go back and lock herself in the bedroom. Of course if she'd done so, then Steve would have drowned in the river, leaving Melody widowed instead of simply tired and cranky. None of it made sense to her.

She got out of the car and walked slowly to the house, struck by how cold and uninviting it appeared now. Perhaps it was just a trick of the light, or her own admittedly high-stress levels, but something felt *different* to her, but she didn't know what it was.

Fumbling for her keys, she was about to unlock the door when the wind dragged at the trees, and her heart leapt into her throat. She whirled on the spot and pressed her back to the door, staring wide-eyed into the swaying canopy of birch, cedar and oak.

She was sure she'd heard her name.

It was subtle, perhaps no more than her exhausted brain playing with the thoughts plaguing her.

Nevertheless, she was sure enough to be spooked, and as she listened, she heard it again, a low, secretive whisper almost completely hidden beneath the rustle of the leaves. Her stomach somersaulted, the heady cocktail of fear and excitement attuning her senses as she stared into the dense foliage surrounding the property.

Just like the previous morning when she'd received the anonymous text messages, she was struck by that horrible, overwhelming sense of being watched from the shadowy recesses of the woodland. She was suddenly acutely aware of everything around her.

The feel of the chipped wood of the door where her fingertips pressed against it, the bite of the cold as the wind probed at her clothes, and above all else she was aware of just how vulnerable and alone she was.

She strained her ears, and almost simultaneously realised just what was wrong. Other than the wind, there was complete silence.

Usually the land surrounding Hope House was alive with birdsong, but now nature was silent, leaving just the wind. The atmosphere had taken on a decidedly dark, sterile tone. She drew breath, the crisp freshness of the air doing little to clear the terror that rippled within her like a living thing. It threatened to overwhelm her and send her running from the house never to return, and she asked herself if that were such a bad thing, to just get into the car and go to the hospital to collect Steve, and then from there back to New York. Away from the house, and whoever or whatever was trying to frighten them away.

The wind hit her, flapping her long coat against her legs in a series of persistent taps. She barely noticed. She was listening for the sound of her name. This time, however, she couldn't decipher anything other than the natural sounds of the environment, and the charged atmosphere in the air suddenly diffused.

She relaxed then, not realising how hard she'd been pushing herself back against the door and immediately took a step forward, allowing herself a small embarrassed smile. She had given herself the *heebie jeebies*, and hated the fact that she had allowed the situation to get on top of her. Turning back to the door, she unlocked it and let herself in.

She wasn't sure if she would even be able to sleep after everything that had happened, but within a half-hour and after a quick shower, she lay down and fell into a deep and much-needed slumber.

## 20. THE VISITOR

SHE KNEW IT WAS a dream. It held that ethereal, hazy quality that dreams always had. Hope House loomed in front of her, and yet it was different. Its paint was fresh and its wooden beams strong. The sun had almost set, and the grounds were bathed in a fiery orange glow which did nothing to stop the chill of the wind biting at her arms and legs. As she watched, a milky ground mist began to form in the dark reaches of the tangled forest. The vivid nature of the dream made her uncomfortable, as she looked around the familiar yet strange grounds, she felt the distressing sensation of being watched.

Her eyes fell on the sign which hung above the dirt road leading away from the house. Here in her dream, however, the wood was new and the sign only half erected, tied at one end to the huge overhead beam. The main section of the sign proclaiming the house name swayed gently in the breeze and at the opposite side, a rickety looking ladder was propped against the wood.

She was suddenly standing at its base having no recollection of walking to it. The sign towered above her, the thin mist she saw earlier clinging to her ankles.

"Be careful, missus."

Startled, she whirled around and faced the source of the voice.

She didn't recognise the man.

From his appearance, she could see that he was some kind of slave-worker. He was wearing tattered brown trousers, and his cocoa-skinned frame was painfully thin. She only noticed these things for a split second. However, her eyes were drawn to his neck,

138

which bore the horrifying purple-blue ligature marks of strangulation. She should have been afraid, but the man's eyes were kind and friendly.

"Who are you?" she asked, unsure if she was ready for anything that this man had to say.

He smiled, the expression knowing yet sorrowful. "Don't be afraid, I aint' gonna hurt you, missus," the man replied in a deep, Southern accent.

Even though she wanted to believe him, she took a cautious step backwards. Her foot clattered into the wooden leg of the ladder. "What do you want?"

The man looked pained, and his eyes were filled with sorrow. "I come to warn you," he said softly.

"Warn me about what?"

He smiled gently and looked around him, holding his arms to his sides as if showing the fruits of his labour. "This place, missus. This place and its whisperin'."

"I don't hear anything."

"You will if you stay here, course by then it'll be too late."

"Are you somebody who died here?"

He smiled, and it was enough of an answer.

She opened her mouth to enquire further, but no words came. The wind rustled the treetops, and the man cocked his head to one side, and nodded.

"They're angry with you. They say you messin' wit' their plans."

"Who? What are you saying?"

The man simply smiled. "Listen and you will hear, but not for too long, or they will get in yo' head, like they did with your husband."

As if in direct response, the wind pushed and pulled at the treetops, and this time Melody *did* listen, trying to stretch her senses out into the forest which was now in heavy shadows as the last of the daylight faded.

"I can't hear anything; it's just the trees."

"You have to listen past them. Listen to what's *under* the wind."

"I tried I..."

"Shhhhhh!" he said, putting a thin finger to his lips. "Jus' listen."

She listened again, but could hear little more than the high tempo drum of her heart and the constant *shhhhhhhhhhh* sound of the trees. "This is stupid. I can't hear anything."

The man nodded, and gave a thin smile. "Then could be that it ain't too late for you."

He turned and walked towards the tree line, his arms folded behind his back. She noticed that nothing was disturbed as he moved—neither mist nor the grass underfoot.

"Wait! Who are you?" she called to him.

The man turned and set his gaze on her, and again offered his warm smile. "I ain't nothin' no more," he said simply, and then walked into the woods.

"Wait! Wait!" she called after him, but he didn't answer, and was soon lost in shadows.

She chased after him, her insatiable curiosity piqued. She wanted—*needed*—to know more, to extract more information from this man who had visited her in a dream that was infinitely more real and vivid than any she had ever experienced. She tried to push through the woods, but it felt as if it were trying to stop her, its sharp thorny branches clawing at her clothes and skin.

"Please, wait!" she called breathlessly, but the man neither turned, nor did he deviate from his course.

It seemed to Melody that as much as the trees were trying to stop her progression, they seemed to be opening up in front of the man, who didn't have to duck, or change direction for a stubborn root, or overhanging branch.

"Please!" she gasped, but the man walked on, and she fought against the dense woodland.

She was suddenly in free air, and realised that she'd entered the vast open circle carved out of the forest. The man was standing in its centre, watching her. The circle was bathed in moonlight, and the man no longer looked friendly. His eyes were wide and filled with fear.

"You shouldn't have come here," he said, his eyes flicking towards the trees that surrounded them.

She wanted to tell him she wanted answers, but she didn't have time to ask, because all rational thoughts were replaced with terror. The circle was drawing in, closing around them.

"What's happening?" she stammered.

"You need to wake up. This is the bad place," the man said softly.

The air was charged with static, and the earth shook as the trees dragged themselves closer, their gnarled limbs slithering and swaying, resembling long-fingered talons stretching for her.

"I don't understand!" she sobbed.

The man stood motionless, watching her with the same pleading look on his face.

"No mo' questions missus, you need to wake up!" he ordered, and she saw that he was as afraid as she was.

The trees were touching her, cold and dry against her skin, probing at her clothes with sharp fingers.

"Please!" she bellowed.

"I... I cain't help yo'."

The trees grasped at her, and she saw that they were now thickly muscled claws, long and knotted.

One of them grabbed her arm, and she pulled away, tearing the skin from her wrist. She continued to scream as the trees smothered her, and then she was awake, sweating and panting, desperately wishing that she was not alone.

It was daylight outside and bright bars of sunlight streamed through the window, pushing away the horrors of her nightmare. However, even awake, she was afraid to be alone in the house. But all paled in comparison to the fear that overcame her as she looked at her arm, and the narrow scratches across her wrist, which were still weeping blood.

# 21. HOUSE CALL

SHE WASHED AND DRESSED in a daze, unable to find the will to think about what had happened. The silence in the house was heavy and although Melody did her best to ignore it, she couldn't help but feel discomfited. She sat at the kitchen table, sipping her third coffee of the morning, staring out of the window at the slate-grey skies and trying her best to ignore the house's creaking and groaning as the wintry conditions pulled it this way and that.

The house that was meant to be her sanctuary now felt as cold and desolate as a tomb. She marvelled at how, in such a short space of time, everything that had felt so right had become hopelessly derailed. She had been so preoccupied with the move and Steve's increasingly erratic and irrational behaviour that she had neglected to consider how she was coping herself.

She looked inward, testing the waters, trying to gauge just how she felt inside. The prognosis wasn't great. She felt frayed and overstretched, sick with worry. *And why not?* she asked as she glanced at the scratches on her arm and ran her fingers lightly across them. She was determined not to get carried away with the situation. Besides, she supposed she could have done the scratches herself in the midst of the vivid nightmare, but even the thought of that was dismissed when she looked at her fingers—more so the lack of nails, which had been chewed down to the skin—an old habit from childhood gained in the midst of the never-ending arguments eventually leading to her parents' divorce, which had now seemingly returned.

She watched through the window as the treetops

were wrenched in every direction, the hypnotic manner in which they moved making her eyes feel heavy. It reminded her of the ocean, ebbing and flowing, lulling her to sleep. She wondered how old those trees actually were? How ancient? How many people had they seen live in Hope House? How many had they seen move away or die here?

Just to imagine such things made her aware of her own insignificance in the grand scheme of things. She didn't want to look at them anymore, and turned her gaze away and saw the letter on the floor behind the front door.

It was a plain brown envelope, unsealed and with no writing or other markings. She walked to the door, picked it and opened the flap, removing the folded slip of paper from inside.

*We need to talk.*

*See me as soon as you can.*

*Annie Briggs.*

Melody's heart-rate increased as she threw the door open and stepped outside, but Mrs. Briggs was nowhere to be seen. The wind buffeted and teased her with droplets of rain. She clutched her arms to her body, shielding herself against the cold as she scanned the green and brown foliage and the exit road for her unannounced visitor.

Immediately, she felt exposed and observed, and the sight of the wooden awning over the road leading away from Hope House brought back horrible, disturbing memories of the previous night's dream. As much as being in the house made her feel uneasy, outside was somehow more frightening.

She went back inside and closed the door, and, without really thinking about it, locked it. It was still too early to go and visit Steve at the hospital, plus she needed to think about what to do about the Mrs.

Briggs situation.

"Hell with it," she muttered under her breath, then went upstairs and began to fill the bath.

\*\*\*

For the first time in what felt like an age, Melody felt relaxed. Basking in the silence, she lay in the deep white bathtub, her head back and eyes closed as she tried to soak away her troubles. The house was silent, and it seemed that even the endless blustery gusts weren't able to penetrate her steam-filled sanctuary.

She had found that rare place—the middle ground between sleeping and consciousness—and there her worries seemed distant and detached. She put her hands on the flat of her belly under the water and realised that, soon, everything was going to change. Since finding out that she was pregnant, she had managed to avoid thinking about it. However, now in her relaxed state the fear and doubts about not only her ability to be a mother, but also the current state of affairs with the house, Steve and even herself, tried to push their way to the fore.

She felt as if someone were inside her head and picking away at the seams of her sanity. She was surer than ever that something was being kept from her. Mrs. Briggs certainly knew more than she was letting on, and she suspected that Will at the bar knew something too. Even Steve had appeared troubled when they were in the pub, but was fine before his secret conversation with the barman. And so, despite everything she was still in the same place and as unsure of anything as ever—which in turn made her more determined to find out.

She still wasn't sure how to proceed with the Mrs. Briggs situation, and was swaying towards leaving that particular can of worms unopened, but at the same time she *did* want answers.

*And what if those answers only raised more questions?*

Well then, she would just deal with that as and when. Either way, she knew that lying around feeling sorry for herself wasn't going to help.

As if somebody had listened in on her thoughts, there was a knock at the door. Sure that it was Mrs. Briggs, she quickly got out of the bath and wrapped a towel around her, then hurried downstairs.

"Just a second," she called as she walked as quickly as she dared with wet feet across the wooden floor.

She opened the door.

"I'm sorry I was... "

She stopped, losing her train of thought. Instead of Mrs. Briggs, it was Donovan, who was barely able to hide his delight at her wet, half-naked appearance. He flashed his sleazy, wide grin as she shielded herself with her arms.

"Mrs. Samson, apologies for the intrusion," he said with apparent sincerity, which was betrayed by the sleazy way in which he openly stared at her body.

"I hope I didn't get you at a bad time," he said, leaning on the door frame and giving what she supposed was his best flirtatious smile.

"Actually it is, I'm a little busy right..."

"Oh, I'm just checking in. I heard about the incident with Mr. Samson and wanted to make sure everything was okay."

She felt exposed and vulnerable and even a little afraid of the leering realtor, but tried her best to hide it.

"Oh, we're fine. Thank you for stopping by, though."

"I love what you've done with this place," Donovan replied, walking past her uninvited into the house and looking around the sitting room.

"Mr. Donovan, this isn't the best time..." she said, unable to fully hide her anger.

"Don't worry Mrs. Samson... or may I call you Melody?"

He waited for a response with his head slightly tilted to one side, and she could feel him willing the towel which was just about covering her modesty to fall down.

"Mrs. Samson will be fine," she replied sharply, closing the door as Donovan walked around the large sitting room, looking at ornaments and photographs in between leering glances in her direction.

"Understood. Some clients prefer the more... personal touch," he said, shooting her towel another hungry look.

"Look, no offence Mr. Donovan, but this isn't the best time. I have a lot to do today."

"Oh, I won't keep you. I'm also busy today. This is just a courtesy call. How is Mr. Samson?"

She couldn't shake the ominous vibe which radiated off Donovan in waves. Her state of undress made his leering even more uncomfortable than ever.

"He's fine. He should be home today or tomorrow."

Donovan paused in his inspection of the photograph of Steve and Melody on their wedding day, and half turned toward her.

"Oh, is Mr. Samson still in the hospital? I was under the impression that he was here."

A tiny voice of warning began to speak in Melody's head, and she realised that she was half-naked and alone in the middle of nowhere with a man she didn't know. She wanted to be rid of him, not only because he had no business calling, but because she was nervous and more than a little afraid to be with him without Steve.

"He could be home any minute," she lied, forcing herself to smile. It was no more than an empty gesture, a manipulation of the facial muscles that she hoped showed more confidence than she felt.

"Would you like a drink?" she heard herself say, because that was what people did when guests called, even ones as unwanted as Donovan.

"Coffee would be fantastic, thank you," said her slimy guest, who for the umpteenth time undressed her with his eyes. "It's a little brisk out there."

She nodded, walking as casually as she could towards the kitchen even though every fibre in her body told her to run. "Take a seat, I'll put the kettle on and go get dressed."

She half expected some suggestive remark from Donovan, but he simply nodded.

"Thank you, Mrs. Samson," he said as he sat in the rocker beside the fireplace. "I'll be fine here. You take as long as you need."

He flashed his grin at her again, but she did her best to ignore it and walked into the sanctuary of the kitchen.

Although she immediately felt better away from Donovan's leering gaze, her hands still shook as she filled the kettle and set it to boil. She walked back to the sitting room and made sure just to poke her head around the corner so that Donovan couldn't get another look at her.

"I'll just be a few minutes."

"No rush," Donovan replied. She thought that he was going to say something else, but instead he turned his gaze to the window and set the rocking chair swinging back and forth.

Something about that image, of Donovan sitting in that chair by the window alarmed and frightened her, enough to make her skin prickle and for the warnings in her head to go all the way up to eleven. Without waiting, she hurried upstairs to dress.

***

Donovan continued rocking back and forth, his eyes fixed on the tree line. His brow furrowed into a frown as he listened to the house. He knew of course that all houses made sounds. Wood contracted and expanded according to temperature, foundations settled, even more so with a house as old as this one. Even though he had received an unexpected look at the woman, enough at least that he could imagine the rest, he was keen to be on his way. He knew the history of this place and what had happened here.

He supposed he should feel guilt for hiding it from the Samsons, but like everyone else he had a job to do., bills to pay, ends to meet, and even though he had to be nice to people even when they were rude and arrogant, or pushed him around because they knew that as the agent who was desperate for his commission, he would take it.

He had always considered himself thick-skinned, able to roll with the punches and take whatever life threw at him. But deep down—when he went home alone to his apartment full of luxurious furnishings which meant nothing to him, where he was finally able to drop the act and be himself—he would find himself miserable and unfulfilled.

He'd continued to rock and listen to the strange groans and creaks of the building, and the subtle whispering rustle of the trees outside. He smiled. He could easily understand why the house had such a myth around it. If a person were to listen for long enough, Donovan surmised that they could easily interpret the house sounds as the voices and whispers that previous occupants always insisted that they heard here.

*And what would they say?* Donovan asked himself. Would they recognise him as the insecure, miserable waste of a man that he knew hid below his flashy exterior? Would they tell him to take control of his life and stop being so pathetic?

*Probably.*

The wind whistled and the trees shook, and he closed his eyes. As he listened, he thought that he could hear voices, subtle and secretive whispers buried under the wind. They were hard to make out, but the more he concentrated the clearer they became. The things they said, the things they told him to do were disturbing, and yet they made sense.

He needed to make an example. He needed to show the world that he wasn't just a pushover, that he was a man to be taken seriously.

*That was the problem,* he mused as he stared out of the window. People never really took him seriously. Women were the worst, pushing him away when he tried to be nice or to get to know them—even when they were flirtatious bitches like this one, answering the door half-naked and then looking offended when he happened to take a quick look at what she had to offer.

He shook his head slowly as the rage stirred within him.

And why shouldn't he look? After all if she's willing to flaunt it, then surely she can't blame him for looking. The voices listened, whispering and coaxing him to continue.

Women like her—the ones who used their

sexuality to get what they wanted—were the worst kind. They would give out all the signals, and then the second he would go in and make his move, they would shut up shop and look at him like he was wrong, like he was some kind of perverted monster.

*Sluts.*

All of them the same. He thought he must have the patience of a saint to put up with them, to cope with their incessant overuse of their bodies to get what they wanted. The house creaked its agreement to his unspoken thoughts.

How was a red-blooded eligible bachelor like him supposed to know when they were up for a little bit of action? How could he tell the difference between the willing, and those who would turn their nose up and look at him as if he were some vile piece of shit that they'd just stepped in and couldn't get off their shoe?

Over time, he'd taught himself to learn their patterns, but unfortunately, it wasn't an exact science. On the occasions when he got it wrong it would often only end with a slap across the face, or a torrent of unwarranted abuse hurled in his direction, but sometimes they wouldn't let it go.

The intern drifter that had come to work for him back in 2007 (strictly off the books of course) had seemed willing enough, responding to his flirtatious and suggestive comments in kind, but when he crept up to her in the office one night when they'd been working late and put his hand up her skirt, she didn't seem to see the funny side. He'd apologised even though he was raging inside—after all that was what society would demand—but she wouldn't listen. She was one of those independent stubborn bitches that thought they were going to change the world. He offered her money, but despite his noble efforts to smooth it all over, she kept threatening to report him to the police, and he knew he couldn't have that. He had a job, a business—a respected position in the local community—all worth more than some stuck-up drifter bitch that had somehow got the wrong end of the stick and was accusing him of being some sort of vile sex pervert.

In the end, the choice was taken out of his hands, and the rage forced him to silence her.

The house creaked, and the wind whistled.

He'd tried to tell himself that he hadn't wanted to kill her, but he didn't believe it. Not really. He knew how messy it could become if word started to spread that he was some sort of sexual deviant. He wouldn't be able to walk down the street without people calling him a pervert, never mind the impact on his business.

So he'd strangled her. She'd stared at him and died with open eyes; he'd wept for them both, because it was his first human kill. For a time, he hadn't known what he would do with the body, and had left it in the trunk of his car for five days, rotting and stinking whilst he struggled to decide one way or the other. The funny thing was that nobody asked. The locals had seen her kind before, drifters who stay in a place just long enough to save up the cash to move on to the next town, or the next city.

He'd taken her body out into the hills, a vast open range of rolling green. During the summer time, the various nature trails were frequented by walkers—ramblers keen on getting back to nature—but this was January and the hills were icy cold, and they were shrouded in a low-lying mist which hung in the air and made the grass slick with dew.

With some effort, he'd found what he was looking for: a stinking peat bog. The stagnant water looked dark and ominous and yet entirely suitable for his needs. He'd parked the car—a rental taken out in her name—by the edge of the track and had carried her corpse across a mile and half of rough terrain to the black, festering waters and had thrown her in, watching as she slowly sank into untraceable oblivion, and with her, any problems that she may have otherwise have caused.

He had half-expected to feel different because he had moved on from animals to humans, perhaps guilt or sorrow, but found that his life went on for him as if nothing had ever happened. On the few occasions when people did ask about his former employee, he would shrug and say she had moved on to pastures new, and they would nod knowingly and move on to talking about the weather or whatever small-talk came to mind.

As far as he knew nobody had ever even filed a missing persons report. Some might say he got away with murder, but his defence was that she'd left him no choice.

*What else could I have done?*

He asked the room, and listened to the soothing creaks and groans, which drifted in and out of his mind.

Exactly.

*Nothing at all. I did what I had to.*

He nodded, folding his arms across his chest.

*Did what I had to in order to survive. Did what anyone else would do because...*

He paused, listening intently.

*Really? Do you really think so?*

It began to rain, the droplets tapping on the window and giving him his answer.

*But she seems so nice, so accommodating and helpful.*

The house shook, the wind gusted, and Donovan frowned.

*Surely not, she's married after-all. But then again... she did answer the door half naked. Surely, she wouldn't do that unless... unless she wanted me to see her like that...*

He waited and listened to the old house's symphony of tiny noises.

"Tell me what to do," he muttered under his breath.

## 22. ATTACK

DRESSED IN HER OLD jeans and a grey t-shirt, Melody felt a little more in control and a lot less exposed. She came downstairs, went into the kitchen and grabbed two cups from the draining board. "Do you take sugar?" she called over her shoulder as she added a large scoop of instant coffee into her own cup.

Donovan didn't reply.

"Mr. Donovan, do you take sug...?"

She almost screamed outright as she turned around. He was standing behind her, his brow furrowed and eyes glaring. She wasn't sure what to say or how to react, but she knew she was in danger a split second before he slapped her across the face.

She staggered back into the counter, dropping the mugs, only distantly aware of them smashing on the kitchen floor.

"You cock-teasing bitch!" he spat, grabbing her by the hair and throwing her roughly to the ground. She landed hard on her knees amid the shards of the cups, and somewhere in her head, she wasn't quite able to acknowledge that it was really happening to her.

Donovan loomed over her and although her brain was screaming at her to get to her feet and run, she found that she was frozen in place, her face stinging from the slap.

"You think you can get away with flaunting yourself? I won't have it, they won't have it!"

He grabbed her by the hair and pulled her to her feet, slamming her into the side of the refrigerator. The impact itself didn't hurt her, but the shock of the situation filled her with terror unlike anything she'd ever felt before. She looked at the snarling, glaring

155

Donovan and tried to make sense of what was happening. Donovan paused and tilted his head, then nodded.

"Yes," he said to the empty room, and struck her again, this time it brought her back to reality, and she lunged towards the kitchen door. However, Donovan was too quick. He grabbed at her shoulder, lost his grip then snatched a handful of her t-shirt. She squirmed and twisted, but Donovan's grip was tight.

"You know what they want! Why can't you keep out of their business?"

Her throat was dry, and she squirmed and twisted as she attempted to free herself. He took a quick step forward, and shoved her hard in the back. Combined with her own momentum, she smashed face- and chest-first into the door-frame, spinning around and landing on her back in the short hallway between kitchen and living room.

White spots danced in front of her eyes and she tasted blood in her mouth. She wanted to run, but couldn't convince her body to co-operate. Instead, she gawped at Donovan, who stood over her.

"They want me to show you, they want me to teach you a lesson," he said calmly, as if they were discussing the weather.

She watched as he unbuckled his belt, and flashed his grin, which was now more manic than sleazy.

"You had this coming, don't try to deny it."

*Rape.*

The word was the only one that filled her mind—filled her life—as the beastly Donovan stalked towards her. In an ideal world—where people react like they do in the movies and fight off their attacker—she would be okay. However, here in the real world, she was too terrified to do anything but lie there and wait as Donovan knelt beside her and tried to push her legs apart.

"You know this has to happen," he said as she fought against him.

He was crazy, or at least now he was. He had seemed fine when she had first let him into the house, but now he was changed and he was going to rape her right there in her own hallway.

It was then that another word sprang to mind. One which also comprised of four letters but with only one vowel, although the power it had on her ability to react surprised even her. That word was baby, and as she thought of her unborn child, a sudden rage at this man's attempt to defile her overwhelmed her, and she screamed out, driving her knee as hard as she could into Donovan's groin.

He let out a grunt and rolled to the side, and even though her limbs felt as if they wouldn't be able to sustain her weight, she lurched to her feet and charged into the living room, heading for the door. She opened it so hard that it bounced off the wall, almost slamming closed again, but she grabbed it and squeezed through and then was outside.

She ran, the cold air needling her skin and wet hair with the same sharp intensity as the slap administered by Donovan. She didn't look back but heard the door slam again, and knew he was chasing her. She veered off to the right, towards the side of the house, hoping to make it to Steve's studio, where she would at least be able to barricade herself away from Donovan.

She stole a quick glance over her shoulder, and saw him charging towards her in an odd, loping run. She charged around the side of the house, the white roof of the studio visible now as she headed for it.

Donovan was catching up, closing the ground quickly between them. She reached the studio door and wrenched at the handle, but it was locked, and in terror, she realised that Donovan must be close by now. Without looking back, she headed towards the water at the end of the garden, to the place where in seemingly another lifetime, she'd seen her husband almost throw himself to his death in an out of character sleepwalk.

She knew the safe route across, hoping that Donovan didn't, and if she could buy herself enough time then she prayed she might be able to hide from him under cover of the trees. She reached the swirling water, and spared its grey depths only a glance as she made for the place where she knew it was shallow enough to cross to the other side. She risked another quick glance behind, seeing that Donovan was now no more than ten feet away, eyes wild and arms outstretched towards her.

She angled away from her pursuer and aimed for the part of the water that she knew was shallow. Doubt overcame her, as the water looked deeper—no doubt due to the amount of rainfall over the last few days—and which was now swollen and churning.

She knew that there was no time for caution, and half-fell, half-slid down the banking. Her foot lost purchase, and she had a horrific image of it twisting under her and rendering her immobile, but somehow she made it into the water. She drew breath as the cold hit her. Unlike the first time she crossed, the water went almost to her knees, and she felt the intense cold pulling at her limbs and trying to drag her away downstream.

The memory of Steve's accident was fresh in her mind as she moved quickly against the freezing currents. She heard Donovan's splash in after her, risking a quick glance, she saw that he was neither put off nor dissuaded by the cold of the water enough to abandon his pursuit.

She reached the other side, her jeans now heavy with water below the knee. Donovan was close behind; his eyes fixed on her and a horrible wide grin on his face. She turned and plunged into the woods.

Everything seemed unreal. Her breath came in ragged, gasping heaves as the cocktail of fear and adrenaline coarsed through her body. She knew that Donovan would easily catch her here on the path, plus she was already feeling her stamina ebb as she grew tired. She plunged into the dense forest, zigzagging in the hope of losing her pursuer. However, ever determined, Donovan followed, pushing branches aside as he crashed through the trees.

She felt something snarl her hair, and knew it was him, that he had grabbed her and was about to finish what he started, but a quick look told her that it was only a branch, its thorns stubbornly clinging on to her. She didn't slow, and winced as she pulled free, leaving the thorny branch with some prize strands of hair as she plunged deeper into the undergrowth.

Somehow the trees themselves seemed denser and more tightly packed, which slowed her progress. For every root that snagged her foot, every branch that scratched at her arms and face, and every pothole she stumbled over, she was certain she was going to fall, but nevertheless she somehow managed to stay on the razor's edge of balance and keep upright.

Frightened and disorientated, she charged blindly ahead, hoping to put some distance between her and Donovan, but he was still there, only a few steps behind. She could hear him bulldozing his way through the branches. Sudden bright light filled her eyes, and that was all it took to finally make her stumble. She thought that she was going to recover, and took another few steps as she tried desperately to regain her balance, but her momentum sent her to the hard ground on her hands and knees with a grunt. She scrambled to her feet and charged forwards, certain that Donovan was inches away from grabbing her hair and pulling her back. She flicked a quick gaze over her shoulder, but discovered her pursuer wasn't following.

He stood just outside the edge of the circle, panting and watching her with a horrible, wide grimace. Melody waited, separated from her attacker by only twenty feet of open ground.

*Silence.*

Utter and complete silence apart from the sound of her own exertion. The atmosphere in the circle seemed somehow wrong. The air tasted sharp, and the sick-looking yellowed grass swayed soundlessly and clung to her wet jeans legs. Even the wind had died off completely. Donovan's eyes showed too much white as he glared at her, and yet he made no attempt to come into the circle. Instead, he stood and panted, his skin covered in a light film of sweat.

She couldn't fathom what reason Donovan could have for not following her, but whatever it was she was grateful, because she knew her energy was spent, plus now that she was standing still and, having time to acknowledge her surroundings, she was aware of the cold air on her skin.

She looked carefully around her, all the time keeping a cautious eye on Donovan. The circle was as unremarkable as ever, and yet for its apparent blandness, she imagined that she could sense something in the atmosphere, a depth or...

*It feels dead.*

The thought frightened her, but was accurate in its starkness. Dead was a good term. The grass at her feet was pale and lifeless. She looked at the trees circling her, and noticed that even their limbs didn't encroach into the perfect circle of grass. Their roots turned away at its edge and grew back on themselves in a way that was as disturbing as it was unnatural.

She noted that like the last time she'd come, the usual ceaseless forest chorus of birdsong was strangely absent here, as if, like her, they too could sense the change in atmosphere.

She shivered, and cast her eyes back to Donovan. He hadn't moved, still rooted to the spot on the very edge of the circle, no more than a single stride away from joining her in its sun-bathed emptiness. He licked his lips, and slicked his blonde side parting back into place.

"Fighting only makes it worse. Give them what they want."

He'd said it in a whisper, and yet she'd heard it, his words echoing around her as if coming from every direction at once. She realised instantly that all the fight had gone out of her. She was both physically and mentally exhausted, unsure of how much more energy she'd have if she needed to run again. There was an overwhelming urge to just sit down and rest, regardless of what would happen to her.

*But it's not just you is it?* she heard herself ask in her head. *There's another one to consider, remember?*

Of course there was. There was the baby. As yet, it was nothing more than a tiny cluster of cells, but before too much more time passed it would be another living, breathing human being. One that in spite of the horror of the situation and her own fragile state, she was prepared to do anything to protect. Defiance replaced fear, and she glared at Donovan. "What are you waiting for?" she screamed, her words seeming to fall flat in the heavy atmosphere of the circle.

"Are you just going to stand there or come and finish what you started?"

Her temples throbbed with rage, and even though she didn't know what she would do if she did manage to goad Donovan into the circle, part of her—a rarely seen darkness that lived deep within—wanted him to do it. She saw herself tearing out his eyes, or straddling his cowering body, rock in hand and shattering his fragile skull as she rained down blow after blow.

But Donovan didn't enter the circle. Like a caged animal, he paced back and forth at its edge as if there were some kind of physical barrier keeping him from doing so. His grin was now replaced with a scowling mask of frustration and indignation.

"Come on you prick. Come on in here and see what happens, I'm not running anymore."

She waited, praying for him to respond and at the same time clueless as to what she would actually do if he did. Donovan for his part looked as if he wanted to, but was still physically unable to transgress into the circle.

*This is what they call a Mexican stand-off,* Melody thought distantly, more aware than ever that nobody was likely to come to her aid. Her options were limited, and she had just about managed to convince herself to head back into the woods in the hope that she could evade Donovan for long enough to get help, when he spoke to her.

"If you know what's good for you, you will keep this to yourself."

He was slick with sweat and, combined with his wide-mouthed grin, it gave him the look of a tall, venomous ventriloquist's dummy. He gave a last glaring look at Melody and then turned smartly on his heels and walked away into the trees.

Somehow, being alone felt worse. She waited, holding her breath and peering into the trees. The rational side of her was certain he'd gone, having slunk away to whichever rock he lived under, but the frightened, overstretched side of her said it was a trick, and that he would either be lying in wait, hiding in the trees for her to leave or, worse still, the idea that Donovan couldn't enter the circle was a ploy and he would come bursting out of the woods from behind her, grimacing and leering as he closed the distance between them and....

She pushed the thought aside, trying her best to be rational, to think like the Melody of even a few days ago—before the world which she thought she knew and understood had shown her a darkness which she was struggling to comprehend.

She looked around the circle, trying to get her bearings and perhaps figure out what to do. It felt as if a lifetime had passed since Donovan had called unannounced to the house, but she was shocked when she checked her wristwatch to see that it had only been twenty minutes. Either way, she knew that she would have to make her move soon. She could just about make out the path that she and Steve had followed when they first stumbled across the bizarre and out of place circle of dead grass in the middle of the otherwise thriving woodland.

She walked towards it, slowly and controlled at first, but soon the oppressive silence and the thought of Donovan lurking out there in the trees forced her to speed up and then break into a run. The second she left the sanctuary of the circle, the woodland exploded to life around her. Birds chattered, animals trampled through the undergrowth, and the wind tugged at her and pushed her, its whistling voice laughing at and mocking her feeble efforts.

She broke into a sprint, ignoring the painful slap of branches and leaves on her face or the sharp jolt when her ankles twisted or snagged the uneven ground. She realised as she ran that it wasn't even Donovan that she feared anymore, but the woods themselves. She felt cold eyes watching her from the deep, shadowed places buried under the greens and browns of the foliage. And she feared the wind, whistling and gusting, shaking the trees into an almighty rumbling din, which seemed to push against her, slowing her progress as she stumbled on.

Time seemed to lose all sense of meaning and she wasn't even sure if she was even heading in the right direction. Her luck didn't last however, and her foot twisted painfully under her, making her stumble. She almost regained her balance and grabbed wildly at a wispy cluster of branches, but they were old and rotten and pulled free, and she fell heavily to the ground, hitting her head hard. She felt darkness envelop her, and as her consciousness faded, she imagined for a moment that she was by the ocean, hearing the ebb and flow of the tide. She realised as she lost rational thought that it wasn't the ocean, but the trees, swaying and hissing their silent conversations.

She was certain that they were laughing at her.

# 23. CONFESSIONS

*Cold.*

IT WAS MELODY'S FIRST thought as she began to regain consciousness. She lifted her head slowly, great waves of nausea washing over her. Gingerly, she pushed herself up to her knees and looked around. She couldn't even begin to imagine how long she'd been unconscious. It felt like only seconds, but she saw that the shadows had elongated and deepened, telling her that she had been there for some time.

She was shivering, and looked at her grazed palms and filthy clothes. She got painfully to her feet and began to trudge down the snaking, tree-lined path leading back to the house.

Her head throbbed with the intensity of a rotten tooth in need of removal, and it occurred to her that she may well have suffered a concussion. She was on familiar territory now, hearing the steady gurgle of the stream as it made its endless journey past the bottom of her garden. Clenching her jaw to try to stop her teeth from chattering, she carefully picked her way through the undergrowth, taking her time and favouring her twisted ankle, which seemed to be throbbing in sympathy with her head.

Golden sunlight enveloped her as she exited the woods and, exhausted and cold, she crossed the water as quickly as she could and hauled herself onto the opposite bank. It seemed whatever spell had overcome her was broken now that she was out of the trees, and it was then that the true horror of Donovan's attempted rape hit home.

She wanted to change and take a bath that she knew would be far too hot, but necessary if she were

Michael Bray

to try to wash the oily feel of his hands from her body. She supposed that the next course of action would be to call the police and tell them what happened. She could see it now. Donovan flashing that grin, the one that said

*'Trust me, I'm really a nice guy, and this is all a big misunderstanding.'*

And when she would protest and scream rape at him, she knew what would happen. He would flash that confident, smug grin at the police officer who was questioning him and say *'Rape? Oh no, not at all. Mrs. Samson actually tried to instigate things. I wouldn't dream of doing anything so vile.'*

And when she told them about him chasing her through the woods, shedding his clothes as he went, that manic, sadistic grin still plastered to his face, she knew how it would play out. He would roll his eyes at the police officer, perhaps a second or third generation who had lived in Oakwell all his life, and then shake his head slowly and say *'Oh no, that's not how it was. I was just trying to explain that I wasn't interested when she ran. I was concerned for her safety. If you ask me, it's her fault. City folk coming here and mistaking our friendly nature for something it isn't. They seemed like such nice people.'*

And then their lives would be ruined. They would be shunned, branded as liars and troublemakers.

*No!*

She wouldn't do that to Steve. Not after everything that he'd sacrificed to make the move. She would keep it from him, because she knew that if he found out, it would change things forever between them. Either way there was a lot for her to think about, but sitting cold and wet on the grass wasn't going to help anything. She would think about it later, after she had bathed and changed. Melody got to her feet, brushed the grass off her knees, and walked towards the house.

The kitchen door was open.

*Donovan.*

She felt her stomach lurch violently, and knew beyond doubt that he was in there watching from the shadows, waiting for her to go inside and lock the doors so that he could finish what he'd started. She looked at the windows, hoping to see a flash of movement, a flicker of a clue that might alert her as to where he might be hiding, but the building betrayed nothing. It stood there, a huge, aged and brooding slab of white against a backdrop of browns and greens, its windows like black sightless eyes, the open kitchen door a mouth frozen in a never ending wail of terror.

*Maybe you just left the door open?*

She paused to consider it and, even though she had received a pretty nasty bump on the head and was still groggy, she was almost certain that she hadn't. She distinctly remembered leaving via the front door, and hearing it bounce against its frame as Donovan followed her. The back door had been closed.

*Just run.*

The idea seemed sound enough, but at the same time redundant. Where would she go? They'd deliberately bought the house in such an isolated area so they wouldn't be disturbed. But now, she would give just about anything for a neighbour to call on, someone whose door she could pound on and beg to be let in, so that at least she could feel safe. But the reality was that the only sanctuary was the house, and she would have to go back inside if she intended to call for help.

She'd always looked upon Hope House as a

beautiful period property, a rare glimpse into an age of gorgeous architecture and a refreshing change from the concrete jungle she'd become accustomed to. However she now saw it in a different light. It was a hulking sentinel, a sinister thing harbouring whatever had let itself in through the back door. She thought of all the dark places where somebody might hide, all the places where—if a person were so inclined—could wait and then cut her off with no means of escape.

The urge to run was strong, but she was drawn to the house by an invisible bond that pulled her forward. She was now standing in it's shadow, and found that her feet were refusing to carry her any further.

She peered through the open kitchen door, but everything inside looked normal. She could see the counter-tops, the walk-in pantry and the edge of the dining table but still couldn't move. Her self-preservation instincts had kicked in, stopping her going any closer.

*Well, you can't just stand out here all day.*

Her mind agreed in principle, but her body remained rooted to the spot. She might well have stayed there forever, if she hadn't spotted the knife block on the kitchen counter. Thoughts of running metamorphosed into thoughts of revenge, and before she'd realised she'd done it, she'd already stridden across the threshold, and grabbed the huge stainless steel carving knife.

It was quite amazing, the way that just having an equalizer made her feel confident, and although she wasn't about to go running around the house like some stupid bitch in a B-movie horror flick, she felt better.

The plan was simple. She was going to walk

quietly upstairs, grab her phone (replaced after telling Steve her original one was lost), come back down for her car keys and then get the hell out of there.

*Forget the phone! Just get the keys and get the fuck out of here!*

Now that it had found its voice, her inner monologue was desperate to make itself heard, and in this instance, she decided it was right. Forget the needless risk of a diversion upstairs, she would drive to the village and call for help from there. It was stupid to be in the house any longer than she had to be. She...

She heard a stealthy thud.

Her brain told her it could be any number of things. The house settling, perhaps an unbalanced book falling over or a million other perfectly normal things. However, that had been before Donovan had tried to rape her.

She thought the sound had come from upstairs, but she couldn't be certain. All she knew was that she wasn't alone. She wasn't sure how she knew--she just did. Maybe it was some kind of untapped sixth sense, or possibly those self-preservation skills making themselves useful. Whatever it was, she knew that she would be a fool to ignore it. That was how people got themselves killed.

She inched forwards, eyes focused on the sitting room at the end of the hall. She could just see the edge of the small table by the front door where her car keys were kept, but to get there meant possibly revealing herself to anybody lying in wait.

She heard it again, an almost inaudible noise. A subtle, dragging thump, which could have been anything or nothing. Tightening her grip on the knife, she walked quickly, keeping her eyes focused on the front door.

She saw a figure out of the corner of her eye as she passed the staircase. It was on its way down, and almost clattered into her as she passed. She screamed and lunged out with the knife, registering that she had made contact even as she made to run.

She stumbled, banging her shoulder painfully on the door jamb and by chance finding herself in the same position as she'd been during Donovan's first attack. She would have screamed, but there was nobody around to hear her. Instead, she closed her eyes where she cowered and waited for the attack to come.

"Melody?"

The voice, however shocked, was familiar. She looked up, and her relief was immediate.

"Steve!" she blurted, launching to her feet and hugging him tight.

"What the hell's going on here? I..."

He held her at arm's length, seeing immediately that something was wrong. She couldn't even begin to imagine how she must look. If it was even half as bad as she felt, then she knew it must be pretty awful.

"What happened? Who did this to you?"

She didn't answer, and could only sob as he held her awkwardly by one arm, his other one cut across the palm where she'd lashed out with the knife.

"Melody, talk to me. What's going on?"

Although she'd already decided not to tell him what had happened, the words were out before she could stop them.

"I thought you were him, I ...he. He tried to rape me!"

He cupped her swelling face gently in his one good hand, and looked her in the eye.

"Who did this?"

"Donovan," she said softly, and buried her head in his chest. He stroked her hair gently.

"Let's get you cleaned up, and then I want to know everything."

It wasn't a request, but a demand. She could tell that although he was trying as best he could to keep calm, the fury was burning and simmering just below the surface. She knew then that she had to tell him what had happened, tell him everything.

*Even about the baby?*

Maybe not everything. She decided that her pregnancy was one little nugget best left for a different conversation. For now, there was plenty for them to contend with.

# 24. OUIJA

ALTHOUGH SHE'D SHOWERED twice and scrubbed her body so hard it was pink and stung to touch it, she still felt dirty. She had expected to be the owner of a couple of black eyes from the force of Donovan's blows, but it seemed that in that respect at least she had been lucky and, apart from a small swelling on her right cheek and a nasty bruise on her head where she'd hit it when she'd fallen in the forest, she was okay. Under the circumstances, she reckoned she'd got off lightly.

She was now sitting in the living room opposite Steve. He had lit the natural fire in the hearth, making the room cosy and warm. Even though he'd assured her that he had checked the house from top to bottom and had locked all the doors and windows, she'd made him check a further three times. She took a small sip of tea, while looking over at Steve, who was observing her intently.

"How's the hand?" she asked him softly, trying her best to offer a smile and not quite succeeding.

"It's fine, just a scratch," he replied, showing her the bandage.

"I'm sorry... I... didn't think it was you."

"Melody, my hand is the least of our troubles. Now I need you to talk to me. What happened here today?"

She lowered her eyes, staring into her cup. "I was supposed to come and pick you up. You shouldn't have had to come home by yourself, I..."

"Melody," he said sternly, and then gave her a reassuring smile that was only marginally more successful than hers. "It's okay. Now please, tell me what happened."

She set her cup on the table, and looked him in

the eye. "Promise me something first."

"Okay."

"Promise me that when I tell you, you won't go and do anything stupid. We've just moved here, and I don't want this to ruin things for us. Can you promise?"

"I can't, not before I know what happened. The best I can give you is that I'll try to do what you ask."

"You always do. God, I'm so stupid." She would have wept, but didn't think she had any tears left. Instead, she held them back and wiped her eyes with the sleeve of her sweater.

"Melody, please, this is killing me. What the hell happened here?"

She told him.

About Donovan, about how he chased her through the woods as well as his unwillingness to follow her into the circle. All the time she was speaking, he watched her in stony silence. She had hoped for a reaction, and would have settled for any kind of emotion at all, but he simply watched. She had reached the part of the story that on some level, she was more reluctant to discuss than the Donovan situation.

"Steve, there's something else."

*Silence*

Shadows licked at his face from the glow of the firelight, and there was something about it that troubled her.

"Go on," he said softly.

"It's about the things you said... the things you said about this house."

He waited patiently for her to elaborate. It occurred to her absently that this must be how therapy was. The patient rambling on to a silent and overpaid listener.

Michael Bray

"There *is* something... off about it. I know that now," she blurted, watching carefully for his reaction.

He licked his lips and leaned forward slightly.

"Did you hear them? The whispers?"

"I'm not sure... maybe I... everything is like a huge blur right now. But if you are asking me if I think that there's something off about this house, then yes, I would agree."

It felt good to get it off her chest. She waited for Steve's inevitable leap into action, but instead he simply nodded, sat back in his chair and took a sip of his coffee.

The silence seemed to last an age, and for what seemed like an eternity the only sound was the spit and crackle of the fire and the dull bluster of the conditions outside. He looked at her, his eyes impossible for her to read.

"What do you think we ought to do about it?"

"I don't know," she shrugged. "I mean I'm not even sure what '*it*' actually is. All I know is that there is something here, an essence, a... I don't know."

"Let's call it what it is. An entity. A spirit. A fucking ghost."

His smile seemed to shimmer in the shifting light of the fire, and despite the heat of the room, she shivered.

"I think we should speak to the old woman from the bar."

"Mrs. Briggs? I don't see how she can help us."

"She knows the history of this place."

She was going to mention about the note that Mrs. Briggs had left, but that might lead to questions she didn't want to answer, so skimmed over it. Steve didn't seem to notice. He set his cup down and perched himself on the edge of the chair.

"I think I know a better way. Wait here."

174

He stood and walked into the kitchen. She had no idea what he was up to, but could hear him rummaging around in the pantry. He came back with an unmarked cardboard box. He had a strange half-smile on his lips as he sat opposite her again and set the box on the coffee table.

"I picked this up the other day when I went for my studio stuff. I didn't want to mention it to you until I was sure you believed me."

"What is it?"

He opened the box and set the contents on the table, and as soon as she saw it, she felt a wave of dizzy, nauseating terror.

It was a Ouija Board. It looked to be incredibly old, and the wood had a smoky hue. Its smooth front had the letters of the alphabet arranged neatly, and underneath were the numbers zero to nine, and below that a large YES and NO. At the bottom of the board was the word 'goodbye'

Steve grinned and pulled a small, smooth heart-shaped piece of wood from the box and set it beside the board. "That's the planchette. You use it to communicate."

Melody felt her throat tighten as she looked from the board to Steve.

"A fucking Ouija Board? Are you insane?"

She wasn't sure if she were more angry or scared.

"It's okay; they're perfectly safe. They actually sell these in toy shops. I read about them," he said, realising that she obviously wasn't as thrilled as he was.

"Oh well if Google says its safe, then I suppose it must be. Jesus Christ Steve, do you really want to screw with... well with whatever it is that's here?"

"Look there's no need to be afraid okay? All I want to do is try to see if we can communicate with it, try

Michael Bray

to find out what it wants. I can then read about a way
to get rid of it. Have a ritual!"

"Ritual or no ritual, I want it out of the house. And
I don't mean tomorrow. I want it gone right now."

"Don't you think you're overreacting?"

"No I don't. The idea of using that thing scares the
hell out of me, and I won't have it in this house!"

"You could at least have an open mind about this!
Jesus what made you so uptight?" Steve yelled,
putting the wooden board back in its box.

"I was almost fucking raped earlier, and you dare
to ask me why I'm uptight?"

"Look I didn't mean that... I was just making the
point that..."

"Get it out of here!"

"Look I'm sorry okay, I thought you understood!"

"No!" she screamed, throwing her cup across the
room. It smashed off the wall, splashing hot tea all
over the paintwork. "No Steve I don't understand. I
don't understand anything. I don't understand how
our fucking lives have gone down the toilet ever since
we moved out here. I'm scared, and I'm confused, and
I feel like I'm going it alone whilst you're obsessed
with looking for ghosts!"

She was breathing in ragged, short breaths and
found that she was crying again. Steve stood, his face
serious and twisted into a determined grimace.

"You're right. What sort of man am I? Some prick
tried to rape you, and I almost let you talk me into
doing nothing about it."

"Steve you promised, you said you wouldn't do
anything."

"No, I said I would try not to. I didn't promise
anything."

He stood and strode across the room, and put on
his jacket.

"What are you doing? Where are you going?" she said, hurrying after him.

"I'm going to do what I should have done when you first told me about this."

She had never seen him so angry, and that alone scared her.

"I don't want you to leave me here alone!"

"Someone has to teach him a lesson."

"Steve! Please!" she screamed, grabbing onto his arm. He shook her loose and opened the door.

The wind drove through the house, whistling and moaning. Steve looked at her then, his eyes dark and filled with jealous rage, which looked so alien on him that he almost resembled a stranger.

"What are you going to do?"

He smiled at her, and she wished she hadn't seen it. That simple gesture drove home the fact that whatever happened, things between them would never be the same. He'd given her a glimpse of something dark, something that had been hidden below the surface all the time she'd known him and which had now risen to the surface.

"I'm going to give him what he deserves."

"I'm scared to be alone!" she pleaded, as he stood framed in the door, the wind billowing around him.

"Lock the door behind me. I'll be back as soon as I can."

"Please, stay here with me," she begged, but he wasn't listening.

He closed the door, and she watched him jog to the car. He gunned the engine, spun around in the soft, leaf-covered dirt, and raced away from the house. He either didn't hear or had ignored her pleas to stay.

Michael Bray

# 25. CONFRONTATION

DONOVAN SAT IN HIS office working on finishing the bottle of scotch he'd been saving for a special occasion. He'd closed early, knowing that before long he might be living his life behind bars. He still couldn't fully remember the details of the incident with the Samson woman—it was hazy like the fragmented memories of a night out where there were way too many drinks and drugs available. It had taken him a while, but he'd put most of the pieces in place apart from one.

*Why?*

He took a long slug of the sour mash whiskey, wincing as it burned away a little more of his sobriety. He realised that the *why* of the situation wasn't the real issue, not if he wanted to save his own skin.

*So, what to do?*

The options were limited. His first thought was to blame her, accuse her of making it all up like most bitches were prone to do, but he suspected that there was more than enough DNA evidence to cast reasonable doubt. He could offer to pay them off, but he suspected that it too was a no-go. It would imply that he was guilty, and with a reputation as stellar as his, even if it was as part of a little inbred and backwards village like Oakwell, it was important to his business. With no reputation, there was no business, and with no business, what else was there but plain old Donovan?

He reached into his desk drawer and pulled out the handgun. He held it up in front of his face, marvelling at how such a simple, primitive instrument could both cause and solve so many of the world's problems. He had already half-fleshed out the idea in his mind. He would make it look like a home invasion. He nodded and set the gun on his desk.

Yes, he thought that it would make a very neat, tidy solution. Of course, he couldn't be sure that they hadn't already called the police, but that was a loose end he could do nothing about. Either way, he knew that if he waited there for long enough, someone would come knocking on his office door. If it was the husband, out looking for some kind of macho way of reasserting his superiority, marking the boundaries of his territory, then he would let him have it. At least that way, he would have the proper time to work out the details of his plan.

And if it's the police? Well, that was a different story. Although he was almost certain that he'd be able to talk his way out of any immediate arrest, he still had a lot of skeletons in his closet that he definitely didn't want dug up. Sure enough, he had done a reasonable job of hiding them, but any amount of professional scrutiny could link him to any number of things, which would see him living the rest of his days behind bars.

He would never accept that. He took another long drink, picking up the gun again from the desk and looking at it.

*No!*

If the police came knocking, he knew exactly what he'd do.

He put the barrel in his mouth and bit down. He tasted the steel where it pressed his tongue onto the floor of his mouth, and was surprised to find that he was completely unafraid. He flicked the safety off, then on, then off again. *It was amazing*, he thought, looking down the topmost edge of the weapon. Just a few pounds of pressure to the trigger and it would be lights out. Game over. End of the road. He wondered

179

if it would hurt, if he would feel it when his skull exploded, and his brains became part of the décor.

*Probably not.*

And either way, by then it would be too late to do anything about it. He heard a car pull into the car park, and removed the gun from his mouth. He waited, listening and wondering what his fate would be.

Pounding on the door, and yes, shouting too. He recognized the voice, and with a smile, put the gun back into the desk drawer and stood. He paused long enough to smooth down his suit, and prepare the Donovan mask that he wore in public, and then walked from the office. He could see the Samson woman's husband beating his fist on the glass and demanding to be let in. Although Donovan could tell just by his demeanour that there was only one reason why he would be here, he intended to let him in and get it out of his system. He knew what he was going to say, how he would at least try to smooth things over and appease Steve, even though he didn't expect to be successful, he was confident that he could sow a few seeds of doubt.

He fished his keys out of his pocket, and unlocked the glass-fronted door.

"Steve, I'm glad you came I..."

*Pain.*

Steve hadn't given Donovan time, and had hit him hard in the face. It was unexpected, sending him staggering back to slam into his receptionist's desk, paperwork cascading to the floor. The bitter sting of blood filled his mouth as he tried to regain his senses. It seemed that he had underestimated just how aggressive Steve would be, because before Donovan could even begin to reorganise his thoughts, Steve was upon him with two quick strides.

He dragged Donovan upright by the collars of his cheap suit, and hit him again, this time mashing his fist into Donovan's nose and sending him sprawling to the floor on his hands and knees.

"Wait! Let me explain..." Donovan blurted, spitting out blood as he crawled on all fours.

Steve was only half a step behind him. He grabbed Donovan by the head and hauled him roughly to his feet, then threw him into his office. Donovan clattered painfully into his desk, and more by instinct than conscious thought, hurried behind it, putting some distance between him and Steve, who had stalked after him and slammed the door shut.

"Stevey listen, this is a misunderstanding... just sit down and listen."

"What? Not so brave now, are you, you little fuck?" Steve hurried around the desk, and although Donovan did the best he could to keep his distance, he couldn't move in time. He felt vice-like fingers grab his throat, then a fresh explosion of pain as Steve head-butted him hard in the face. Donovan fell into his plush leather chair, his ears ringing, and his nose throbbing angrily. Donovan thought that he might have misjudged the situation, and his eyes drifted to the desk drawer containing the gun.

"You son of a bitch!" Steve roared, hitting Donovan hard again. He managed to flinch away a little, and his neck took most of the impact.

"Steve, please... it's not what you think..."

"Shut up!" Steve raged, and grabbed Donovan again by the lapels of his jacket and hauled him to his feet.

"Let me make this crystal clear you son of a bitch. You should be behind bars for what you did, but my wife doesn't want to cause a fuss."

"Please... let me..."

Michael Bray

"....SHUT UP!" Steve bellowed as he shoved Donovan back into his seat.

"Now I'm a reasonable man Mr. Donovan, and for that you can think yourself lucky. Otherwise I might not have shown such restraint."

Steve was shaking, his fists balled as he glowered at Donovan, cowering in his chair.

"Now, in my book, a slimy rapist like you doesn't deserve to walk free, but I happen to love my wife, and so will do as she asks."

"Mr. Samson, be reasonable I..."

"Open your mouth again, and I swear to God I'll break your jaw."

Donovan snapped his bloody mouth shut. Steve leaned close.

"If I ever... and I *mean* ever... see you anywhere near my house, anywhere near my wife again... if I even see you look at her from across the street, then I swear, with God as my witness, I will kill you, Donovan. Do I make myself clear?"

Donovan nodded enthusiastically. Steve grinned and leaned close, whispering in Donovan's ear.

"I do as my wife asks, Donovan. But there's nothing to say that the police won't receive an anonymous tip off as to your rapist exploits. Something tells me that a slimy, disgusting freak like you has done this before. If I hear even the slightest whisper that you've said anything to anyone... well I think you can guess what will happen. Understood?"

He leaned back, and Donovan nodded.

"I said is that understood?"

"Yes, yes. I understand!"

Steve walked back around the desk. He paused at the door to Donovan's office and looked over his shoulder.

"Don't make me come back here, Donovan. Keep

182

your mouth shut."

Donovan could hear Steve but was barely listening. He was looking at his desk drawer, and thinking about the gun nestled inside. The rage stirred, and it took all of his willpower not to snatch it up and shoot this pathetic little man in the face, but he convinced himself that he would only enjoy that in the short term. He wanted to make his revenge meaningful. He watched as Steve left the office and slammed the door behind him.

For a few moments, Donovan sat in silence, allowing the pain in his throbbing face to settle, and the rage to swell and grow. With a shaking hand, he picked up the overturned bottle of whiskey from the floor, and took a long, bitter swig. He set it down, and considered his options.

He had been embarrassed, made a fool out of by some out-of-town prick that thought a couple of black eyes would be enough to frighten him off. Donovan opened the drawer and took out the gun. He held it in his hands, the weight familiar and reassuring. He removed the full ammunition clip, then pointed the weapon at the open door, holding it with practised assurance, closing one swelling eye as he looked down the sights.

"Mr. Samson...." he said as he pulled the trigger, the unloaded weapon clicking harmlessly. "You don't know what you just got yourself into."

Despite the throbbing pain in his face, Donovan managed a bloody smile.

# 26. FAIR WARNING

*December 22nd 1808*

THE OFFICES OF JONES & Schuster were nestled in the busy district of Whitechapel, London. Although just a stone's throw away from the poverty-ridden streets of the capital's East End, it stood majestic and proud, the building standing shoulder to shoulder with doctors' offices and high class legal firms. Inside, Michael Jones was in the second hour of his meeting with his business partner, which so far had gone anything but smoothly.

Schuster sat in his chair, huge stomach stretching out in front of him as he looked at Jones contemptuously. He filled and lit his pipe with his tiny, chubby hands, and offered a thin smile across the desk.

"You can't build there," Schuster said sternly, taking a huge pull of his pipe and leaning back.

Jones was furious, but kept his expression neutral as he took a sip of his brandy. "I see no reason not to. The land is not yet owned as far as I can tell."

"Aye, and with good reason. Come on, Michael, You know the reasons."

"I'm sorry, Alfonse, but I don't believe in ghost stories. Francis is in agreement. It's just you who's holding this deal up."

Schuster shrugged and took another pull on his pipe. He stared into the flames of the fire for a moment, and then leaned forward, turning his dark gaze on Jones. "Michael, do we really need this? Why not build over in Burwell or Greenwood, why does it have to be there?"

"I would have thought that would be obvious. The

land is unclaimed. What starts as one could grow into many. It could be the start of a huge, and dare I say, lucrative business for us."

"It is also difficult terrain. The entire area is forest. Perhaps this is more trouble than it's worth."

"It's a calculated risk. Besides, just imagine it. A small-town cut out of the forest, an idyllic retreat. A beautiful amalgamation between the craft of man, and the subtlety of nature."

"It's just too big. Far too risky I'm afraid."

"Then let me start with one. Just one build, one house to prove that it can be done."

"And, if you fail? What happens to our money?"

"Alfonse, if I thought that there was even the slightest chance that I would fail, then I wouldn't have suggested it. Not only can I do this, but I can make it work."

"And who will you get to work there? Who will be your foreman when so many are afraid?"

"I have a friend who can provide me with the workforce. They are Negroes, but they work hard. As to overseeing the build, I will attend to it personally if need be."

"You?"

"If need be, yes."

Schuster shook his head, his jowls trembling as he exhaled another great plume of smoke.

"Let me be sure that I am clear here. You are personally willing to oversee the build in order to see this project progress?"

"Indeed I am. Think of it as a measure of how confident I am in its certain success."

"I'm not going to be able to convince you otherwise am I?"

Schuster's wry smile made Michael break into a grin of his own, and he sensed that at last he was close to a breakthrough.

"No. As you can see I am determined to get you to open that dusty old cheque book of yours Alfonse."

Even though he smiled as he said it, Schuster seemingly wasn't amused, and only frowned as he prepared to write the cheque. He sighed as he filled it in.

"I want you to know that, for the record, I don't like this, not one bit. You know how superstitious the locals are, and it could damage our reputation."

Now it was Jones's turn to be contemptuous. He sneered at Schuster and flashed a confident grin.

"I never took you as the superstitious type Alfonse. Especially when there's money to be made."

"There's more to life than money, something that you and your brother might do well to learn. Besides I never said that I was superstitious. I just think it pays to be cautious."

Jones set his glass down and leaned close, looking his flabby partner in the eye.

"Look, I know the stories. I know what's said of the land there. However, I also know that we are a business, and if we are to continue to grow then we cannot afford to pay attention to such things as idle gossip."

"Idle you say?" Schuster responded, his eyebrows arched. "Evidence suggests that perhaps this is more than mere idle gossip my friend. I for one would be uncomfortable working on such a project."

"Evidence you say? And what evidence might that be? Please indulge a cynic if you would be so kind."

Schuster knew that Jones was mocking him, but was too concerned to care. He licked his thin lips and folded his hands neatly on the desk.

"They say the woods are haunted. They say there are voices that can drive a man mad."

"Ah!" exclaimed Jones, clapping his hands together and giving Schuster a fright.

"The proverbial *'they.'* And who are *they*? Who do *they* represent? How do *they* know these things?"

Colour flushed in Schuster's cheeks, and he grew serious.

"I don't appreciate you mocking me, Michael. I'm only trying to warn you."

"Oh I'm not mocking you my friend; however, I am finding much amusement in the morbid nature of your tone. The collective *'they'* amounts to nothing more than rampant speculation of over-active minds! Why, I could this instant go down into the streets of London and tell a tale of ghouls in the shadows or strange creatures lurking in the darkness! It wouldn't make it so. Alfonse, it seems that you have paid too much attention to speculation and fantasy!"

"It might serve you to do the same," Schuster warned. "The spirit world is not one to be taken lightly."

"That, my friend, depends on what you happen to believe in. I am a firm believer of the here and now, the things that inhabit the real world. Do we not after all have enough monsters of our own, without worrying about whispering trees and haunted woodland?"

"Michael...."

"Oh Alfonse! How you do amuse me! However, I will mock no more. A man is entitled to his own opinion, and although ours differ greatly in this matter, please rest assured, that you need not leave the comfort of your office, the warmth of your fire, or endure the whispers of the dead. All I need from you my friend is the funds to proceed."

Schuster frowned, and looked at his business partner in the eye.

"It seems that you are determined to go ahead with or without my approval."

Jones grew serious, and poured them both another drink.

"All jest aside. I believe this to be the start of an exciting period for us. I will build the grandest, most beautiful of homes, and when you lay eyes on it, you will forget all about haunted trees and other such nonsense."

"Under ordinary circumstances, I would outright refuse to entertain this. As much as you find amusement in my beliefs, I am deeply concerned. However, I must give you the benefit of the doubt. You have always made the right decisions in the past Michael, especially when it comes to making a profit. So with that said I will give you your money on the understanding that you will take the greatest of care, and even if you do not believe it, heed what I say."

Jones smiled, and looked about to mock his partner further when Schuster pointed at him.

"You might think my feelings towards this particular project unconventional, and perhaps even a little irrational. However, I have always been a very spiritual man, and I have both a healthy fear and respect for forces outside of our knowledge. But, it is true that I also like money. After all, show me a rich man who doesn't. If you think that building this property could be the start of the next great project for us, then I'm prepared to go along with it despite my misgivings."

"You won't regret it Alfonse, that I promise."

"That remains to be seen. I will wait and hope that you complete the task without any incident, spiritual or otherwise."

Jones grinned, and reached over the desk, shaking Schuster's hand vigorously.

"My friend, you will not regret this! A year henceforth, you and I will share laughter at this very evening! As a matter of fact, you have just given me an idea for the name of the property. I shall call it Hope. Hope House in honour of you, Francis Schuster, the most superstitious of men!"

Jones was elated, but Schuster couldn't quite shake his own sense of unease. He licked his lips and spoke quietly, and even Jones felt a small shiver brush his spine.

"And what if it's true? What if we don't heed the warnings and the stories come to pass?" Schuster said quietly.

"Fortunately I do not believe old wives' tales and folklore. Let me answer your question with one of my own. Are we to grow our business and go where nobody dares to go before us? Or do we shy from driving forth into the unknown?"

Schuster shifted in his seat, and set his pipe down on the desk.

"Michael. You and I have been business partners for, what, four years now?"

"Five."

"Five years. And in all that time, have I ever doubted you, or stood in your way?"

"No. No you have not."

"Then not as a business partner but as a friend, please... please promise me one thing. If only to ease my own discomfort."

"What would you ask of me?"

"If at any time you do encounter anything... otherworldly, anything at all that might lead you to believe that your life is in danger, then promise me that you will stop. Down tools and leave, money or no money, build or no build."

Jones grinned, and drained his glass.

"If that eases your worry, then yes my friend. You have my word. At the first sign of ghoul, ghost or demon, I shall return here in haste and tell you that you were right, and buy you a drink by way of apology."

Jones stood and held out his hand.

"Until next time Alfonse."

Schuster pushed his oversized frame out of his chair with some effort, and shook hands with Jones.

"Please be careful Michael. Even if you think me a naïve fool, just... be on your guard."

"I always am. I shall see you soon, and when I do, you can buy me a drink!"

The pair shook hands again, and Jones walked to the door and opened it. He paused at the threshold and turned back to Schuster, who was watching and wringing his hands nervously.

"I wonder," Jones said with a half-smile. "What will happen if you are right, and I do experience some kind of phenomena?"

He looked at Schuster for a response, but instead his partner topped up his glass and drank the bitter scotch down in a single great mouthful.

"I only hope you never find out. Good luck Michael."

Jones nodded and left Schuster alone in his office. They would never see each other again.

# 27. RECONCILIATION

EARLY MORNING SUNLIGHT BLAZED through the windows of Hope House, leaving shafts of golden warmth across the tile floor. Steve sat at the table nursing his coffee in one hand and moving his other around the bowl of ice water in an effort to reduce the swelling from his previous night's altercation with Donovan. Melody was busy transforming bacon into unrecognisable charred slabs. They'd barely spoken since the previous night's events, and Steve had spent a miserable and uncomfortable night on the sofa.

He removed his hand from the water and flexed it gently, wincing at the pain. His knuckles were now a landscape of blue-purple bruises, but even though he expected to wake up with regret, he found that beating the shit out of Donovan was one of the few actions recently that he was reasonably sure was the right one. He dipped his hand back into the cooling water, as Melody arrived with his sandwich.

"Thanks," he said softly as he eyed the blackened substance stuffed between the bread.

Melody gave no reply, and returned to the stove, opening a window as she passed to let out some of the smoke. She turned off the hob and then sat opposite him with her own black-stuff sandwich.

The couple ate in silence. A million miles away from happily sharing breakfasts in bed, or snuggling on the sofa in front of the morning news. Steve took a bite of his sandwich, doing his best to grind up the bacon-flavoured coal while taking another look at his knuckles.

There was so much that he wanted to say, so much that he wanted to ask, but it seemed the woman opposite him, the one who he'd thought he could

191

never see himself arguing with, or hurting, was now a pale-faced shell. She pushed her dishevelled morning hair aside and ate, staring off to somewhere between infinity and oblivion.

Steve supposed it wouldn't matter where it was, as long as it wasn't in his direction. There was a saying that came to mind, something about approaching a large trunked animal in a room, when he noticed her looking at him.

"How's the bacon?" she asked, watching carefully for his reaction.

Several responses came to mind, but none that would help him get back in her good books. As he pondered the best way to tell her it was awful without hurting her feelings, she cracked a smile, which quickly grew into a grin. The gesture was simple, and one that he had for a time taken for granted, but now he saw it as if for the first time and couldn't help but smile himself.

"It's uh..." was the best he could manage. Melody tried to revert to her serious face, and although she got the frown, she couldn't wipe off the grin.

"Awful isn't it?" she said, tossing her own on to the plate.

"It's... cooked," he mumbled.

The couple broke into laughter, and like the flick of a switch, the tension in the air dispersed. It was the kind of relief Steve imagined a mother might feel when their child who's late home from school walks through the door safe, or when the test results for brain cancer come back clear.

"How's the hand?"

"Not too bad. Actually that's a lie, it hurts... a lot."

"You shouldn't have gone over there. If he tells anyone..."

"He won't. He understands the situation."

"So what do we do now?"

"We carry on. Try to get our lives back on track."

"And this place?"

He looked into her eyes, hoping that his own gaze reassured her or at least took the edge off some of the fear that was all too easy to see.

"Like I said. We carry on."

"You want to stay?"

"It's not that. It's just..."

"What is it?"

He didn't want to say it for fear of another argument, or shattering the fragile peace, but she had asked the question, and he owed it to her to be honest about the situation.

"Well, we can't afford to. The house was cheap enough, but with the repair work and cost of building the studio... we're pretty much broke, Mel. Leaving here isn't an option."

"What if we sell?"

"I thought you loved this place?"

"I did... I *do*... it's just.... I don't know, it seems off somehow."

"Spoiled," Steve said, and Melody nodded as she sipped her drink. He was going to say cursed, but thought that, for now, they could both do without the melodrama, even if it was a more accurate expression.

"Besides," he added. "Donovan is the only agent for miles in any direction, and I don't think he'll be so willing to bend over backwards to help us this time."

"So if we can't sell, what happens next?"

She was looking to him for an answer, and his stomach quivered for the simple reason that he didn't have one to give her—at least not one that she would accept as viable. He still wanted to use the Ouija board to try to communicate with whatever presence was in or around the house, but he didn't think that

Melody was ready to entertain that notion just yet. He was desperately trying to think of something to get him off the hook when Melody bailed him out.

"I think we should go and see Mrs. Briggs."

"I don't see anything that crazy old crow could tell us that would help in any way."

"Didn't the barkeeper at the Oak say she knew the history of this area? Maybe she could give us a few answers."

"Maybe she's as crazy as a brush, too."

He'd meant it as a joke, but he saw that his words had hurt. It was just the briefest flicker of a reaction, one so small that anyone other than him might have missed it, but he knew her well, as well as it was possible to know another human being at least, and he immediately felt bad.

"Look, don't get me wrong, I'm all for finding out more about this place. In fact, it's driving me crazy. I'm just not sure that talking to some senile drunk is going to do anything other than cause more confusion and uncertainty."

"I'm not saying we should take what she says as gospel, but it might not harm to get a little background."

"And what if she's wrong?"

"Then she's wrong. We waste an afternoon and look into other options. Everybody is wrong sometimes. That's how life is."

*Even a stopped clock is right twice a day.*

The saying came to him out of nowhere. It was something his mother had used to say, but it must have been fifteen years or more since he'd last heard it. Why it had come to him now he was at a loss to say. He took a long draught of coffee. It was a little cold, but still drinkable, and helped a little in washing the chalky bacon taste out of his mouth. "Okay then, let's go see the old fruitcake," he said with a shrug.

She seemed pleased, and they sat in silence, both looking out of the window at the garden, now covered in an early morning dusting of frost. Although the view was picturesque, both Steve and Melody were thinking about their respective nightmares—for Steve, the dip at the end of the garden, where he knew that the stream that had almost killed him flowed relentlessly. For Melody it was the trees on the opposite bank: she stared into the tangle and re-lived every vile second of her ordeal.

"So, for argument's sake, we go see the old girl and she can't help us, what then?"

She shrugged, letting out a deep sigh.

"I really don't know. The internet I guess, see what we can dig up."

Steve shook his head.

"Already looked into it. There's nothing at all that I could find about this place being out of the ordinary. Hell, there's no information full stop. It's as if the place doesn't exist. There *is* one other thing that's been bothering me for the last couple of days."

"What's that?"

"The cross we took from the big tree out there," he said, nodding towards the woods. "I'm starting to wonder if we should have left it where it was."

Melody stood and walked to the pantry, grabbing the cross from the shelf and bringing it to the table. They both looked at it, its simplicity of design and the rough nature of its construction giving it an authenticity which made it appear all the more sinister and out of place sitting on their kitchen table.

Steve didn't like it. The cross seemed to hum with a life of its own. There was an energy about it, something ominous and knowing. He thought it could be the key to their troubles, but how, he didn't know.

"You think we might have caused all this by taking the cross?" Melody asked, her eyes frightened and her words spooking Steve in their closeness to his own train of thought.

"Not caused. I think whatever is happening here was always going to manifest itself regardless. I just keep thinking that this thing was out there for a reason. And it might be in our interest to put it back, that's all."

"I don't want to go back over there."

She knew that she'd said it too quickly, too sharply. He looked at her across the table, and saw the true depth of her terror. He saw that, no matter what, Hope House was spoiled for her. It had gone from a quirky, unique property that could have been a place to raise a family, and live out their lives, to a place of constant fear and misery. It was hard to believe that in such a short time things had changed so quickly.

"I wouldn't ask you to go back over. Not under the circumstances. I'll take it okay?"

He smiled reassuringly, and was sure that he'd just about managed to hide his own trepidation—and yes, fear—because he was afraid, afraid of the house, afraid of the woods, afraid of the tree from his dreams where he always saw Melody dead or dying, and afraid of the circle where nothing grew and the creatures of the woods never ventured. However, his own fear was secondary, because whatever had happened or would happen, he would do anything to give Melody back even a little of the magic that she'd once seen in Hope House. She seemed relieved, and yet still troubled.

"Maybe we should ask Mrs. Briggs if she knows anything about it?" she said, glancing from the cross to Steve.

"Good idea."

She looked surprised at his willingness to comply, not knowing that he had only done so in order to delay having to make the journey to put the cross back where it came from.

"I thought you would have objected."

"Hell, we may as well get our money's worth out of the old hag. I just want some answers. The sooner the better."

"Steve... do you still love me?"

It came out of the blue, and it both surprised and saddened him.

"Of course I do...I can't believe you even asked me that."

"I just... I don't want this situation to ruin what we have that's all," she said, fighting and just about managing to keep the tears at bay.

"Look Mel, no matter what this place throws at us, we will stick together. Just like always, it'll be you and me against the world, okay?"

"Okay, I'm sorry--I just needed to know."

He grabbed her hand across the table and gave it a reassuring squeeze.

"Look, there's no time like the present. Let's get dressed and go pay Mrs. Briggs a visit. Best to get her early whist she's sober I suppose."

He tipped her a wink as he said it, which brought out a grin on her despite how upset she was.

"We will be okay won't we?"

"Whatever it takes," he said, giving her hand another squeeze, "whatever it takes."

She appeared satisfied with his response, and he was certain she hadn't seen his own worry that things wouldn't be okay, or his own suspicions that things were likely to get worse before they got better.

# 28. LOOKING FOR ANSWERS

MRS BRIGGS WAS A hoarder. That much was apparent as Steve and Melody perched on the end of the sofa, surrounded by huge piles of magazines and newspapers. The walls were filled with family photos, seemingly from an era before Mrs. Briggs had become a slave to alcohol or collecting everything she could lay her hands on.

Steve looked around the room trying to conjure some kind of sense of order from the chaos, but he realised that a man could only look for so long at such a mishmash of trinkets and ornaments before any attempt became pointless.

Instead, he concentrated on keeping his facial expression neutral as one of the old girl's many cats snaked its way past his leg and slipped between a haphazard stack of yellowed newspapers to whatever lay beyond. Steve glanced at Melody, who flicked a small semi-smile at him that said more than words would ever be able to. It was one of those shared moments that only extremely close couples had when a thought was transferred with just a single look, and this one was clear.

*This old girl is crazy.*

Mrs. Briggs waddled her way back into the room, somehow managing not to spill the tray carrying their cups of coffee. She was wearing a garish tangerine jumpsuit with purple trim, and was panting so hard when she set the tray on the table (or, more accurately, on one of the mountains of papers) that she looked and sounded more like someone who'd just run a marathon rather than slipped into the kitchen to make drinks. Steve noted that she hadn't made herself one, and he would have bet that she'd be sipping something a little stronger just as soon as they were out of the door.

She scooped the ginger tomcat out of her chair with one podgy hand, disregarding its inconvenienced wail as she flopped down hard in the creaking seat. She looked at them both, her eyes as sharp as her skin was waxy. "I wondered when you were going to come. I expected you yesterday."

"We... couldn't make it."

Mrs. Briggs looked at Steve as if he had spoken out of turn. "I wasn't expecting you at all, young man."

"What do you mean?"

The old woman locked eyes with Melody, and even though Steve wasn't sure what it could possibly be, some unspoken message passed between them. She cast her blue makeup-daubed eyes back to Steve and smiled politely. "I mean simply that I didn't think that two women chatting would be your idea of a fun afternoon, that's all."

The explanation was almost as weak as the delivery, but he let it go. Whatever it was could wait. They had bigger issues to deal with. "I was interested in the information you might have. I—rather, *we* hoped that you might be able to tell us a little about Hope House."

"I can tell you both a little or a lot young man. It depends upon how much you are willing to hear."

The answer baffled Steve, and seeing that he was about to say something which could end the meeting before it began, Melody interjected, smiling warmly at Mrs. Briggs and giving Steve's hand a squeeze.

"Anything that you can tell us would be great. We're interested in the history, the previous occupants. Anything really."

With some effort, Mrs. Briggs sat back in her

chair, and folded her hands over her pendulous bosom. She smiled warmly, as the displaced ginger tomcat that she'd so rudely ejected, leapt onto her knee and settled down to sleep. She stroked it gently, then turned her attention back to her visitors.

"Well, there's much that I could tell you. As you may know, I'm something of an expert on local history, and have learned over the years almost all that there is to know. However, even I don't know every secret. And there are many secrets."

She sounded like a cheap horror cliché, and delivered the line with such cheese, that Steve couldn't help but laugh.

"Something funny?" she asked him sharply.

"No. Look, no offence but we don't need the doom and gloom routine. All we want to know are the facts."

She smiled thinly. "You seem afraid."

"I'm not."

"So you say. However, the tiredness in your faces says otherwise."

She glared at him, and he stared back. A battle of wills which, for the time being, didn't include Melody.

"Mrs. Briggs, it's obvious there's something that you want us to know, so let's cut the Hammer House of Horror crap and get to it."

"Steve!" Melody chastised, looking apologetically towards Mrs. Briggs, but for her part she only smiled and continued to stroke the ginger tomcat's head as he purred appreciatively.

"It's okay; it's obvious that your husband is only here under protest. However, it doesn't matter, because you both need to hear what I have to say, whether you like it or not."

Steve started to answer, but Melody interjected.

"Look, Mrs. Briggs, we came to you because we thought you might be willing to help us."

"Perhaps I can. That depends on you."

"Forget it. This was a bad idea," Steve said, standing up quickly and scaring the cat from Mrs. Briggs's leg.

"Steve please..." Melody said as she grabbed at his arm.

"No, this is pointless. It's a waste of our time."

"We haven't even given it a try please..."

"What did the voices in the trees say to you Mr. Samson, before you jumped into the water?"

Her words were like a sledgehammer blow, bringing Steve and Melody to a crushing silence. They looked at her open-mouthed as she watched them expressionlessly.

"Please," she said, "sit down."

# 29. A WARNING TOO LATE

*June 15th 1809*

"SON OF A BITCH."

Jones stood with his hands planted on his hips, one eye shut against the morning sun. Isaac's body was hanging from the awning, his bloated tongue protruding from his mouth, his dead eyes open and staring. The rope had embedded itself deep into his neck, and already the drone of curious flies could be heard.

"What do we do?"

Jones glanced to his brother Francis, who was still staring at the body.

"Well we can hardly leave him there can we?"

"Who found him?"

"I did. Nobody else knows about it."

Francis nodded, and the two brothers watched the body in silence for a few seconds. Francis had a more elegant facial structure than his brother. His high cheekbones and piercing blue eyes gave him an intimidating appearance, and it was well deserved, for he had a cruel streak which had become somewhat legendary in the local community.

"This could shut us down, as if we haven't had enough setbacks with this project," Jones said with a sigh.

"Setbacks? If by setbacks you mean the never-ending catalogue of disasters since this bastard project began, then yes, setbacks we have had."

"Don't be so dramatic Francis, it isn't that bad."

"Really?" Francis replied, flashing a grin that reminded Michael all too well of their abusive father "How exactly do you come to such a conclusion?"

"What I mean is..."

"...We are already seven weeks overdue. Alfonse is breathing down our necks for progress, and that's not to mention the other... issues."

"You sound as superstitious as the locals! This is nothing more than circumstances not working in our favour."

Francis turned to his brother, his brow furrowed.

"Michael, why don't we just stop? Let's give this up as an experiment that went wrong and move on. There's a superb plot over in Ridgefield that we can..."

"No, I won't give up. Not when we're so close."

Francis turned to look at the shell of Hope House, complete apart from the roof, a black skeleton against the pale morning sky.

"I don't think it's in our hands anymore. Once word spreads about this... situation then we can forget any hope of them ever setting foot on these grounds again. They're already afraid."

"Afraid!" Jones snorted, giving his brother a disgusted sneer. "They're lazy. Nothing more, nothing less."

"Perhaps. Perhaps not."

"What are you suggesting Francis, that our workers make slow progress because of the voices in the trees or the blood in the earth? You sound just like mother with your superstitious talk."

"And you sound just like father with your pig-headed refusal to see in anything other than black and white."

"I trust what my own eyes see, and my own ears hear, nothing more, nothing less. If you prefer to listen to gossip and hearsay then that, I'm afraid, is your own burden to bear."

Francis frowned, and looked ready to continue the

discussion, but decided against it, and instead nodded towards Isaac's body.

"Either way we're losing sight of the issue at hand. What are we going to do about this?"

"Well," Jones said as he turned towards his brother, "we could cut him down and hide the body."

The two brothers were locked in eye contact, and when Francis realised that his sibling was serious, he shook his head.

"No, absolutely not. Just the fact that you have suggested such a thing is disturbing to say the least. Does this project really mean so much that you would deny a man a decent burial?"

"Decent burial? He's not worth the trouble or delay. And yes. This project means everything to me. I've invested more than any man should to make this happen."

"And you would do anything, even break the law in order to see your precious project completed?"

"I would. However, not just for me but also for us, and our business. You're quick to call my judgement into doubt, and yet here you are believing the rambling gossip of apparitions and disembodied voices within the trees."

"And you might do well not to be so quick to disbelieve that which you do not understand."

Jones shook his head, and spoke quietly.

"Are you going to help me to cut him down or not?"

"No. I'll have no part of it."

"Nobody need ever know. The rest of the workers won't be here for an hour or more. We can..."

"No. This is too much. We need to do the right thing," Francis said, flashing a quick glance to the woods.

"I agree. And the right thing now is for us to move

the body and complete this project."

Jones searched his brother's eyes, hoping for his acquiescence, but found only a hard, cool gaze.

"No," he said, shaking his head, "I want nothing more to do with this project. Consider my involvement over. If you are determined to ruin both your reputation and your life then you will do so without me."

"Francis please..."

"No. This is madness!"

"Then I'll do it alone. At least help me to cut him down."

"No. If you insist on doing this, then you will do it alone. I want no part of it."

Francis turned and walked away, not looking back at his brother, or up at the still-hanging body as he passed it and made his way away up to the forest road. He would never see his sibling again.

*** 

Jones didn't have much of a head for heights. As he teetered on the ladder, struggling to cut through the rope on which suspended his former employee's body was suspended, he could barely contain his fury. Fury at his brother, fury at the thought of another day of construction wasted because of one man's selfish decision to take his own life.

The sun had begun to creep over the treetops, and he felt its warmth on his back as he continued cutting through the rope—simultaneously managing to maintain his balance. The virtually severed rope creaked and then, with a sharp snap, gave way, sending the body tumbling to the ground and almost taking Jones with it as it clattered into the ladder. He grabbed at the sign, noting that at least the Negro had had the decency to erect it before he hung himself. Jones cut away the remaining length of rope from the awning, and carefully descended.

It was a cold morning, Jones's breath pluming in the chill air as he struggled with the corpse. He hesitated, and wondered exactly where he could deposit it. The trees stretched upwards around him, and he was aware of a heavy stillness that made him feel more than a little uncomfortable. He shook it off, thinking it was just nerves and perhaps a little fear at what he was about to do.

He glanced at the tree line behind the house, and knowing there was a river which cut across the land that eventually emptied out into the ocean some miles away. It would be perfect. He was sure that the corpse would be lost forever, and even if it was found, nobody would know where it had come from. At least, when it was done, he could at last return to his work and get back on schedule.

Grabbing the body under the arms, he dragged it, the effort making him acutely aware of his poor physical condition. Despite the chill, it didn't take long for a sweat to form on his brow, and his breathing to become laboured. He cursed silently and quickly realised that it was a job for two, and because Francis had lost his nerve, he was now being forced to do it alone.

The terrain was difficult, and his arms burned with the effort of dragging the body. He wasn't sure how long he had toiled, but by the time he reached the water's edge he was drenched with sweat, and he could barely feel his arms. The sliver of sun which had just been creeping over the horizon when he'd begun, now burned fiercely down from almost directly above him.

Exhausted, Jones sat on the grass bank then lay

back, enjoying the relief on his shoulders and spine. He closed his eyes, allowing his complaining body the luxury of rest. The silence was total, apart from the steady flow of water and the occasional rustle of the trees as the wind breezed through them. He thought about the development, and how it would be when completed. A community carved out of the forest, a thriving self-contained town set against a beautiful natural backdrop. A world away from the filth and noise of the city and its streets overcrowded with—

He opened his eyes and sat up quickly, staring into the woods.

He had heard someone speak his name.

"Francis?" he said, his voice sounding flat and somehow lifeless in the still air.

He looked into the tangle of trees, the shadows cast by the sun playing tricks on him.

"I'm not amused, Francis. This is not the time for..."

He heard it again, this time from behind him. He scrambled to his feet and looked towards the sound, but there was nothing but the trees and the unfinished structure of Hope House.

"Hello?" he called, unsure if he was angry or afraid.

There was no answer, and he looked down at the bug-eyed corpse of Isaac, as if he had perhaps decided to call out to his former employer. The wind pushed through the trees, and within the resulting *shhhhhhhhhh* of thousands of branches moving together, he heard it again, only now it seemed to come from across the water. He whirled around, the house at his back, and stared wide eyed into the shadowy undergrowth on the opposite bank.

There was nothing there—not that he could see, at least, but he was sure that he could sense something watching him, staring back at him with an intensity that matched his own gaze.

*"MICHAEL!"*

His own name was shouted impossibly loudly into his ear, despite being alone. He heard himself shriek as he spun to face it, but his feet caught on Isaac's body, and he pitched over into the water.

The cold hit him hard, and he involuntarily took a deep breath, taking in great mouthfuls of water. Choking and spluttering, he came to the surface, thrashing his arms and legs wildly, because for all of his business skills and determination, Michael Jones had never learned to swim.

He thrashed and kicked and somehow just about managed to keep his head floating above the surface.

He reached for a tangle of overhanging grass on the edge of the bank, which seemed to be impossibly high, even though he knew in reality it was less than two feet. The wind raged, and water swirled around his body and pulled at him, trying to take him into its chill embrace as it ebbed his strength. He snatched and panicked but his fingers found purchase, the strong grass enough to keep him in place.

He could now clearly hear the terrible sounds, the voices that were everywhere but nowhere, all around him and at the same time faint and distant. They were laughing as he tried to haul himself on to the safety of the riverbank. He put his arm over the side onto blessed dry land, grabbing a handful of Isaac's shirt, distantly aware of the cold chill of his dead flesh against his own skin.

He pulled himself up, the water reluctantly releasing its death grip. He was going to make it, and as soon as he did, he would down tools, march into their shared office in London and tell Alfonse that he was sorry and had made a huge error in judgement, and that he should have listened to the warning given by his friend.

His elbows were out on the edge, and he quickly released his grip on the overhanging grass and grabbed another handful of Isaac's shirt, trying to haul himself to safety. His strength was waning, and the wind bit into his wet body with ferocious, razor-sharp teeth.

*I'm going to make it.*

The thought entered his head but was replaced almost instantaneously with panic, as Isaac's body shifted slightly and then, just as it appeared it would hold still, slid towards the edge, sending Jones plunging back into the water and pulling the dead weight of Isaac's corpse with him.

He thought he had known fear but now, pinned under the water with the hanged man's dead stare looking into his eyes, Jones knew the real meaning of true terror at its most primal. He kicked and thrashed, his lungs burning and screaming in their desperation for air.

But he couldn't move, and was acutely aware of everything happening to him. He could feel the sandy gravel digging into his back and the heavy pressure of Isaac's body on top of him.

He drew breath but was unable to hold the air in his lungs any longer, and instead took in a huge mouthful of water. He started to choke, but with every gagging inhale, more and more water filled his lungs. Soon enough, the pain faded, as did the light from the world.

The last thing that Jones was aware of as life was torn from him was the sound of the water as it pulled its two-person cargo towards the ocean. Beyond that he could still hear the voices in the trees.

They were laughing.

## 30. FAMILY TIES

SOMETHING STRANGE HAD happened to Mrs. Briggs since she had gained Steve and Melody's full attention. When they'd arrived, she'd seemed every bit the harmless old, eccentric, alcoholic busybody that they'd expected. But now, with Steve and Melody perched and holding hands opposite, waiting for her to speak, a subtle transformation had occurred. Where her happy-go-lucky smile had been, there was now a thin, serious line of pursed lips. Her eyes that were so placid and calm, now carried a depth, seriousness and wisdom that had perhaps always been there, but until now had been unnoticeable. Now —far from taking anything she said with a pinch of salt—Steve was sure that he would believe whatever she was about to tell them.

She licked her lips, and when she spoke it was assured and confident, a far cry from the previous shrill whine from their first encounter at the pub.

"Are you both prepared to listen with an open mind to what I am about to tell you?"

Melody glanced at Steve, and then nodded. "Yes."

"What about you, Mr. Samson?"

"Look, I just want to know what's going on... I'm struggling to make sense of this."

"Some things don't make sense Mr. Samson. Some things just happen."

"I just want to know what to do so that I can put this right."

The old woman frowned, and then with some effort, leaned her huge frame forwards.

"How much do you know already about the history of Hope House?"

"Nothing," Melody said, grabbing Steve's hand for

reassurance, "we just liked the look of it and put in an offer."

"I'm starting to wish we hadn't," Steve grumbled.

"Don't be too hard on yourself, Mr. Samson. Hope House chose you. There was nothing that you could have done."

"Forgive me if I don't agree, but I don't really believe in any of this stuff. It's... difficult for me."

The old woman nodded, and sat back. She stroked the ginger cat on her lap, and then looked Steve in the eye.

"Do you know how many people have lived in Hope House since its construction?"

"No," he said.

"Forty-one," she replied. "Of that forty-one do you know how many passed away on or around the property?"

Steve and Melody looked back blankly, and Mrs. Briggs continued.

"Twenty-nine."

The number was mind-bogglingly large, and both Steve and Melody were struggling to put it into perspective.

"Twenty-nine deaths. All of them were under unusual circumstances. Murders. Suicides. In some cases, the inhabitants would just disappear, leaving their possessions behind. The ones who didn't die had the good sense to leave. Either way, nobody stays there for long."

"So you're telling us that everyone who lives in Hope House dies. I get it. Ghost story 101. Well, let me tell you that I don't appreciate you trying to frighten my wife and scare us away from our home," Steve spat.

He was angry, and could feel himself shaking, yet Mrs. Briggs took the tirade in her stride, and waited for him to calm.

*This old goat is tougher than she looks.*

Steve suddenly felt foolish for losing his temper so quickly. He calmed, and spoke softly. "I'm sorry... it's just... I'm struggling here."

Melody gave his hand a reassuring squeeze. "Look, Mrs. Briggs, it was my idea to come here. I... I just thought you might be able to tell us what we're dealing with."

"I can tell you what I know, although the story is, as you might expect, a bleak one. Hope House is special, and its history is one that we as a community have gone to great pains to hide. The last thing we want is to be bothered by paranormal investigators and souvenir hunters."

"But why let us move in? Somebody could have warned us," Steve said.

The old woman smiled, and it was friendly and wise.

"Would you have listened? What if you had, what then? You would have gone back to wherever you came from and told of the small town with the haunted house that everyone was deterred from owning. And that in turn would bring exactly the kind of attention that we are desperate to avoid."

"But people died... you knew that and yet you still let people move in..." Melody was just about managing to hang on to her emotions. She felt hot, salty tears reach the corners of her mouth and wiped them away.

"It wasn't quite as inhumane as you think, if that makes a difference. It didn't always seem to affect everyone. Some people moved in to Hope House and were unaffected, although nobody ever really stayed there for long. The couple that owned the house before you lived there for over ten years, and as far as

I know never experienced anything. We thought we had made it safe."

"Safe? How the hell did you think you could make it safe?" Steve had found his voice, and was glaring at Mrs. Briggs with contempt. Melody held his hand in both of hers. Sensing that things were about to get heated, the ginger cat on Mrs. Brigg's knee vacated the room, leaving the bad-tempered humans to their own devices.

"We did what we thought was right. We thought it was over, that the house was protected."

"Protected by what?" Steve said as he struggled to comprehend.

"By this," Melody said, placing the carved crucifix that they had taken from the woods. For the first time since they'd arrived, Mrs. Briggs looked flustered—in fact she looked horrified.

"You moved it from the tree?"

"What is it? I don't understand..."

"You should have left it alone. You would have been safe...."

Mrs. Briggs was wringing her hands nervously and looking from the cross to Melody and back again. She hauled herself out of her chair, and waddled over to the drinks cabinet wedged in the corner of the room. She poured herself a large scotch, and then immediately drained the glass, before refilling it and making her way back to her seat.

Steve and Melody looked on perplexed as Mrs. Briggs swirled the golden liquid in her glass and then looked directly at Melody.

"When is the child due?"

Steve started to laugh and then saw the horrified expression on Melody's face and knew that it was true. Words failed him; all he could do was look at her.

"I... I'm sorry," Melody stammered, as she looked him in the eye, then she stood and rushed from the room. Steve followed, as Mrs. Briggs called after them.

"Wait, there's more, you need to hear it all. Come back!"

Melody charged out of the door, blinking through the hazy tears as she reached the front gate. She felt sick, angry and afraid. Steve walked out behind her. She didn't turn towards him, but could feel his eyes on her back.

"When were you going to tell me?" he asked softly.

She didn't answer, not out of cruelty, but because she didn't know what to say. A thousand explanations swirled around her head, and yet she wasn't able to pin down a single one.

"Mel please... I deserve to know what's going on here."

"I'm sorry... I wanted to tell you, I just didn't know how."

He put a hand on her shoulder to comfort her, but she flinched away, embarrassed.

"No, please... I don't think I can look at you right now. I don't want to see how much I've hurt you."

Steve withdrew his hand, and was unsure what to do. He looked around Mrs. Briggs's garden, and tried to come to terms with the life-changing news. He focused on the cherry blossom tree, at how delicate and natural it looked. But the tree wasn't the issue. If only he could find the words, if he could know what he was supposed to say, or even how he was supposed to feel about it.

"Are you angry?" she asked, still not able to face him.

He knew he should say no, that he should comfort her in some way, but he realised that part of him *was* angry at her for keeping it from him, and also angry at himself for not realising that something was amiss. And he was angry with the house, which seemed for better or worse to be the centre of all of their problems.

She turned to him and, when he saw the expression on her face, be it dejection, shame, or fear, he found his anger slip and his affection for her take over. He cleared his throat, if only to say something, anything to break his involuntary silence.

"No... I'm not angry," he managed. "It's a shock, that much I can't deny. And I'm upset that you didn't feel you could tell me, but I'm not angry."

"I think we need to talk," she said quietly.

"Agreed, but not here, not with this crazy old witch hovering around."

He glanced over his shoulder at Mrs. Briggs's badly hidden silhouette as she peered through the edge of the curtains.

"We could go back to the house."

A tremor of dread seemed to hit him all at once, but he managed to hide it and shook his head casually.

"No! No, not there. Somewhere else. Somewhere..." He wanted to say safe, but at the same time didn't want to cause any more alarm or distress. "... neutral."

It was as good a word as any, and he searched Melody's face for any hint that she had read his thought process, something which she seemed to have a real knack of doing the more time they spent together. However, it seemed that she had bigger things on her mind, and simply nodded.

"Where then?" she asked softly.

"How about the pub?"

"When?"

Steve checked his watch. "No time like the present. We really need to talk this through."

"I'm sorry. Please don't hold this against me."

Part of him wanted to hold her and say it would be okay, but he was surprised to find that a small voice telling him that she should suffer for her deception. As much as he tried, he couldn't offer the comfort she needed, and wondered if a fundamental part of their relationship had already been irreparably broken.

"Let's just take one step at a time okay?"

She nodded, and he saw the hurt in her face. He was surprised to find that the new darkness within him gloated.

\*\*\*

Mrs. Briggs watched them through the gap in the curtains as they walked to their car, and chewed nervously on her bottom lip as she contemplated what to do. She walked to the table and picked up the rough handmade cross and ran her fingers over its uneven surface, then set it back down. Her body screamed that it needed alcohol, and to continue building the slight buzz started by the whiskey she'd already consumed. She'd learned many years ago, that even if she could resist for a short time, eventually the craving would win and she would fall to its bitter embrace. She decided that today it would get its way without a fight, and if that was to be the case she would at least give it the good stuff, not the cheap brand reserved for guests.

She walked with some effort to the kitchenette, past the mountain of unwashed dishes in the sink and squeezed her massive frame into the breakfast bar. She opened the fresh bottle of Jim Beam that she'd been saving for her birthday and, unable to see a glass, she took a huge drink direct from the bottle and wondered what she was going to do about the situation. She had already said too much, and didn't know what to do. But she knew someone who would. Her piggy eyes landed on the photograph frame on the wall. She reached up and took it down, looked at the picture and ran her fingers lightly over the glass.

Struggling to her feet, she went back to the sitting room, taking the photograph with her and headed for the telephone in the corner. It was thick with dust as she hardly ever used it, but kept it connected because like today, she never knew when she needed to make an emergency call. She snatched up the handset and pressed 1 on the speed dial, waiting for the line to connect. Whilst she waited, she looked back at the picture.

It was of a much younger, less alcohol-dependent version of the woman she'd become. She was smiling broadly, and she mused that it was a long time since she'd been able to produce such a carefree smile. The boy in the picture was also smiling, a wide grin that was all teeth. Even though he was just a boy, Donovan was easily recognisable, as he had barely changed. The line connected.

"Hello?" Donovan said, sounding somewhat irritated.

"It's me."

"Who?"

"Your mother."

"I'm a little busy right now, can it wait?"

"Not really. What are you doing that's so important?"

"I'm just... busy. What is it?" Donovan said evasively.

"It's about those people that you sold Hope House to."

There was a brief silence on the line before Donovan responded.

"What about them?"

"They're starting to ask questions about the... activity."

"Don't worry about it."

"Freddy, look...."

"Donovan. It's Donovan now."

"Regardless of what you choose to call yourself, you are still my son."

"That's debatable...but anyway, I don't have time to get into this right now. Like I said, I'm busy."

"I need your help. Talk to them. Smooth it over. And more importantly, don't let them go to the authorities."

"Authorities?"

"Yes! The authorities. The two of them are close to breaking point. We can't have them digging..."

There was a moment of silence, and then Donovan spoke.

"Don't worry about the Samsons. I'll take care of it."

The line disconnected before she had a chance to reply, and Mrs. Briggs set the handset back in its cradle. She watched one of the cats, a black-and-white tabby with mismatched eyes, as it tucked into its food from the blue bowl by the fridge. The cat was missing half its tail, a war-wound from a vicious attack by a dog when it had been a stray. Mrs. Briggs had taken it in, nurtured it back to health and had named it Stump.

"Well Stump," she said as she took another long drag of the whiskey, "I think the shit has really hit the fan this time, don't you agree?"

# 31. VOYEUR

DONOVAN SLIPPED THE PHONE into his pocket, put on his black leather driving gloves and turned his attention back to Hope House. He knew that the Samsons were out, as he'd been watching and had seen them go. He peered through the trees, wishing he'd been able to bring the car a little closer to the house, if only to avoid having to walk cross country for the last mile and a half.

He was dressed in the khaki army fatigues that he'd bought from a charity shop the year before, and had spent the night in the green army tent that he kept especially for occasions like this. Usually, he just liked to watch. He had a stressful job, and whereas some chose to unwind by going drinking or playing sports, he watched people. He liked to imagine being in their lives, living in their homes. It aroused him, and sometimes he couldn't help but touch himself as he watched them going about their lives with no knowledge of his presence.

This was different, however, and it was one of those occasions where he would be forced to get a little more 'hands on' than normal. Even so, the thought of what he was about to do excited him, and he had to force himself to be patient.

He didn't worry about getting caught. He was good, *really* good. He realised long ago that it was the little things that would throw off any police investigation.

The little things that the average psychopath might overlook, like the boots. They were regulation army shoes, picked up at a yard sale in Portland some years ago. Donovan only wore a size nine, but deliberately bought his boots in a twelve and padded the toes with rolled-up socks, so that if he were ever questioned, he would have the perfect reason to be eliminated from any enquiry when the footprints didn't match the size of his feet.

His night in the tent had been uncomfortable, and the little sleep that he had been able to manage was plagued with dreams of malevolent, shadowy presences telling him to do things that even he would never consider. They were dreams of violence, and murder and rape. Rather than repulse him, as he would have expected, they had instead filled him with a restless sense of expectation that had fuelled the rage in ways that he'd never experienced. He cast his eyes back to the house, and went through the plan in his mind.

Today would just be a dry run. He of course knew the layout of the property, as he'd seen it prior to the Samsons moving in, but he hadn't seen it furnished, and later when he went ahead with his plan, he didn't want something as trivial as tripping on something unseen in the dark to ruin things.

So he would do as he always did. Go and examine the house, check the layout of the rooms. He had his camera, one of the best money could buy, so that he could photograph the rooms and study them. Forming a mental picture of the place so that later, under cover of darkness, he'd have no trouble getting around unseen and unheard.

He wished that he'd purchased some night-vision goggles, for they would make his life infinitely easier. One of his favourite movies was *Silence Of The Lambs*, and he'd often fantasised of stalking around in the dark like Ted Levine's Jame Gumb in the movie's finale.

How sweet it would be to do such a thing for real. He made a promise to himself to make more of an effort to find some just as soon as he could do so anonymously and without tying anything back to him.

He moved through the trees on the grounds of the property, walking quickly towards the front door. This, he always found, was the most exciting part. The anticipation of doing something forbidden, something that he knew he shouldn't. He reached the door, checking over his shoulder and listening for any sounds of approaching vehicles, but the only noises were those of nature, so he fished the spare house key out of his pocket and opened the door.

It was a perk of the job. He found it unusual that people rarely, if ever, changed the locks when they moved into a new property. He had keys for hundreds of homes, and on those occasions when he chose to visit when the occupants were out, he was always amazed at how many hadn't bothered to upgrade security. He didn't complain, for it made things go a lot more smoothly. He couldn't imagine something as crude as breaking the door, although he would do so on his way out when the job was done for real if only to sell the illusion of a home invasion.

After all, he'd learned from experience that in order to get away with murder, one must know how the police think and be one step ahead at all times.

Safely inside, he closed the door and held his breath, basking in the silence of the house. There was a faint smell of old wood and lemon polish; he looked around the room, taking it all in, and then took out his camera and began to take pictures. It never got old, which was the beauty of it. No matter how many times he did this, it was always fresh and exciting.

He walked through to the kitchen, snapping pictures and looking at the possessions the Samsons had collected. He wasn't impressed. Assorted crap, creature comforts which brought nothing but hollow joy. It was as pointless and unfulfilling as he suspected most people's lives were.

But not him.

Even when he was a boy, he'd known he was different. However, that was a different lifetime. That was when he'd still been known as Freddy Briggs, before his mother had sent him to that place. She'd promised that they just wanted to check his brain, to make sure it was working fine, and that he would come right home after. But his mother had lied.

Apparently, the quacks were concerned at little Freddy's penchant for torturing and killing the local wildlife. He didn't see the big deal. As if the world was going to miss the odd fox or rabbit or cat or dog. They had it in their heads that he might decide to do the same to humans. And even though he cried and screamed and begged to go home, his mother let them keep him at the hospital, and for months that was all he knew. They'd given him pills, and asked their questions, and when he had no more answers to give, they would ask again anyway.

Donovan was upstairs now, and took a quick snapshot of the bathroom, paying attention to where things such as the light switches were. It would pay him to know the little details for when he cut the power, as he knew it was in human nature to make for the nearest switch and try it anyway. It would help him to know where to hide. He crossed the hall to the bedroom, and saw what he presumed to be the real Steve and Melody Samson.

Here, there was no evidence of the pristine showroom style of the house on display downstairs. It was more... lived in. Clothes were strewn on the bed and on the floor, and the covers were turned back and the bed unmade. Donovan lay down on it, inhaling the sweet smell of Melody's perfume. He picked up one of her screwed-up vests from the floor beside him, and inhaled deeply, revelling in her scent as he cast his mind back to those early years in the hospital.

For what seemed like a never-ending cycle, they'd questioned him, made him take their stupid pills, and mingle with the crazy people. What kind of ten-year-old could cope with such an ordeal and worse, deal with it alone? Because his mother, the woman who claimed to love him, who, on those occasions where he screamed and pleaded to come home, told him she was only doing what was best and that he had to stay. Eventually, she stopped coming to visit him altogether. So he went through it alone. He'd started to wet the bed and, even now on occasion, he would wake from nightmares of that frightening place only to find his bladder had let go. It appeared he would never be free, so was prepared for life as a permanent resident of Creasefield Institution when he happened to speak to Joey.

Joey was older by three years, and had spent his life in and out of institutions. He had multiple personalities and Tourette's to boot, but as a boy Donovan didn't know that. He just thought that Joey was incredibly cool. He remembered his words well, even after all these years:

*"If you wanna get out of here, you have to start playing their game. Don't tell them what you actually feel: these fuckers will never let you out. Start telling them what they want to hear. You'll be out in no time."*

As a lonely direction-less child looking for someone to look up to, he'd done as Joey had said.

*Yes, I feel fine.*

*No, I don't like hurting things.*

*Yes. I feel bad for what I did.*

*No, I won't do it again. Even thinking about it*

*makes me feel sick.*

Days became weeks, weeks became months. And all the time he waited. Waited and lived with his lies. He smiled when they spoke, even though he wanted only to tear out their tongues, and he thanked them for the medication, when inside he saw them lying in steaming pools of their own innards, their dead eyes glassy and staring.

Eventually, they told him he was ready to go back into the world and live his life, and he smiled and thanked them. But his smile was not one of gratitude for being allowed to go home: it was a smile because he'd fooled them. Because despite their best efforts, he felt no different inside after their *'treatment'* to how he had felt before.

He got off the bed, and tossed Melody's vest back where he'd got it from, crossed the room, and looked out the window. He could see the spot from where he'd been watching the house, and smiled. Everyone always underestimated him. They saw only what he chose to show them, which was just the way he liked it. He preferred to be the anonymous face in the crowd, the nice guy nobody paid much attention to.

He absently opened the dresser drawer, and pulled out a skimpy pair of Melody's pink underwear. He rubbed it against his cheek and his bruised eyes, to his mouth and nose. He inhaled deeply, hoping for a secret sniff of her womanhood, but instead got only the fresh smell of washed clothes. Even though he was disappointed, he stuffed the lacy underwear into his pocket as he walked out of the bedroom and into the large, circular room on the opposite side of the hall.

It seemed that they had not allocated a purpose for this space yet. It was filled with boxes and other miscellaneous crap that they either hadn't had a chance, or hadn't bothered, to unpack. A smile found its way to his lips, and he knew that this was the room. This was the room where he would hide and wait until the time to strike was right.

But! Not now.

Now was all about the planning. Preparation was the key, preparation and planning. Donovan took out his camera again to snap pictures, making sure to get every conceivable angle. As he took them, his thoughts went back to the resurfaced memories of his childhood .

He had gone into hospital as a slightly disturbed child, and had come out a confused and bitter fourteen-year-old knowing nothing of love, or remorse or compassion. His mother had met him at the gates, and he was shocked at how much she'd let herself go. She'd gained weight and, although he didn't know it at the time, was already a hopeless slave to the alcohol she poured into her system just to get through the day.

He had fully expected to go home, to return to his normal life (whatever the hell that was) but was met with news, which only served to deepen his isolation.

"You can't come home with me Freddy," his mother had said as she'd wrung her hands nervously by the waiting car.

"I have a reputation... the family name would suffer too much, and I don't think I can cope with you."

He nodded, wondering if feeling nothing whatsoever was a normal reaction.

"Don't worry, I've arranged for you to go and live with your Uncle Donovan in Baskerville. It's for the best."

He had simply looked at her, and couldn't help but think she would look a whole lot better if her insides were on the outside.

"I'm sorry okay? It's just... it's best this way. They'll look after you."

And that was the end of the conversation. He went from one place where he felt isolated and alone to another.

He had moved in with his Uncle and Aunt Donovan, but they were far from nice people. Uncle Donovan was a lazy drunk, and his wife was so out of it on drugs that she appeared to drift through the days with a goofy, half-asleep expression planted on her ugly face.

He became a live-in slave. He would cook, and he would clean. And sometimes when Uncle D was really, really shitfaced he would be unlucky enough to find himself touched up. He would lie impassively in his bed whilst his red-faced, booze-smelling uncle tried in vain to get him hard: even though his uncle's own excitement was obvious, Donovan never responded in the same way and the abuse stopped almost as soon as it began.

He coped during this time by reverting to his secret hobby. He killed things, mostly rats, or if he was patient, he might snag a large bullfrog down by the pond, but sometimes he'd get lucky.

He found a badger once, and although it had put up a pretty good fight, he'd won. And when it was subdued, he'd made it suffer. He made it suffer like no living creature ever had deserved, because although he felt barren and empty inside, there was always the hate. And the hate brought anger, and the anger fed the rage. They went together like ham and eggs, salt and pepper, sea and sand. And, because it was all he had, he embraced it.

So his seventeenth birthday came, and his Uncle Donovan had decided that perhaps with age, he would have developed a liking for his own brand of sweaty palmed 'affection' and had tried his usual trick. But this time Donovan didn't just lie there. He waited, waited until his uncle's hand was just about to slip under the waistband of his shorts, and then he struck. The frustration poured out of him, and with the rage flowing through him, he quickly overpowered the old man. As he sat astride his terrified abuser, he took great pleasure in slowly, deliberately snapping every single finger on his disgusting, fondling hand. Every delicious snap, every whimper for mercy made him feel complete, made him feel powerful. It made him into something other than the anonymous boy who had been kicked and beaten by the world.

He left the house that night, taking only the name, by which he would be known from then on with him.

*Donovan.*

He moved back to Oakville, and although his mother kicked and screamed and complained, they had agreed to live with no acknowledgement of each other. As far as the town knew, Mrs. Briggs's son, Freddy, was dead. And in a sense he was, because the creature than was now known only as Donovan was a different breed.

Over time, the lie had grown easier to live with. They moved in the same circles, after all in such a small community it was almost impossible not to. And yet in any capacity other than privately they didn't acknowledge each other's existence.

Donovan often wondered if she knew of his secret activities. He suspected that she did, however, with secrets of her own to keep; she either turned a blind eye or was too afraid of exactly which skeletons would crawl out of the closet if she made her suspicions public. At the very least, he thought she suspected what had happened to the drifter who used to work with him. She'd never mentioned it, which in itself was as good as admitting her suspicion. After all, wouldn't a normal reaction be to ask where the flirtatious slut who used to lead him on was these days? It would certainly have been a more natural reaction that the cold, icy stare that she'd give him. He hated that stare. Every time she flashed it at him, he wanted to pluck out her eyeballs and crush them in his fist.

He snapped more photos, making sure to get every angle that he could. It was perfect, it...

Someone walked past the door.

He was certain of it. He'd only noticed it with his peripheral vision, but he had definitely seen it. Could they possibly have come back, and he had been so distracted with reminiscing about his history that he just hadn't noticed?

It was possible, but unlikely. He remembered that shit-box car of theirs and the tired spluttering sound of its pained engine.

No, he would certainly have heard them. However, at the same time, he knew that he *had* seen somebody walk across the hall outside the door. The entire terrible history of the house tried to infiltrate his mind, and it took some effort to push it away. He was suddenly very aware of the absolute silence of the house.

He walked to the edge of the door, and looked out. Steve & Melody's bedroom was directly opposite, and he could see that it was exactly as he'd left it. To his left was a short length of hallway, leading to the staircase. To the right, the corridor ran all the way to the bathroom door, which was closed. There was no sign of anybody, although he could feel something.

Maybe it was no more than a subtle shift in the atmosphere, but it was noticeable nonetheless.

Whatever he saw had walked towards the bathroom. Part of him wanted to run, but he feared that if he was driven out of the house by something as simple as a trick of the light, then he might not be able to find the courage to come back later and do what needed to be done.

He walked down the hall, trying to ignore the hairs standing up on the back of his neck, and the over-speeding rhythm of his heart as it drummed against his ribcage.

*Do I even believe in ghosts?*

He wasn't sure. He supposed he'd learned that anything was possible. But he'd also had the privilege of seeing death first-hand and up close. He'd watched the life leave the body, and was pretty convinced there was no soul, no lingering life-force that went to whatever the individual perceived as heaven. However, he was always prepared to believe that there could be a first time.

He reached the bathroom door, and was surprised to find that it took a supreme effort of will to force himself to reach out and grab the handle.

*It 'll be empty. Stop being such a pussy.*

He took a deep breath, then in a quick, fluid motion swung the door open.

*Sink.*

*Bath.*

*Toilet.*

*Mirror.*

*Empty*

He looked at his bug-eyed reflection in the mirror directly in front of him, and couldn't help but smile.

"Donovan, you stupid shit," he said to his reflection, letting the tension out of his body.

"The only force here capable of anything is you my friend," he said, flashing his very best, oozing grin at his mirror image.

It was then as Donovan was smiling that the door to the round room slammed closed.

He spun round, knowing that nobody was out there this time as he would have seen them in the mirror. This time it wasn't fear, but anger that surged through him. It was the most basic of human reactions. Something was encroaching on what he considered to be his territory, and he wasn't prepared to accept it. He strode down the hallway, ready to confront whatever was waiting for him in the round room. Images of spectral beings and formless mists filled his mind, but still it didn't deter him. He grabbed the door handle and threw it open, not quite sure what to expect.

Empty

Now that the initial burst of adrenaline had run its course, he felt the sick feeling of fear spreading up his spine. It was akin to a cold embrace pulling him close, and he was suddenly very aware of everything around him. There was a great sense of dread, a negativity in the air that he was certain hadn't been there before. The only comparison he could make was the way the air got just before a particularly bad storm. The way you could almost taste the electricity.

He cocked his head slightly and listened, but all he could hear was the muted sounds of the wind and the natural creaking and groaning of the house.

*Had it been so noisy before?*

He wasn't sure. He certainly wasn't as aware of it, but now it seemed to be all that he could hear. The rational side of him said it was normal, especially in a house as old as this one. Wood became swollen and then contracted; timbers creaked and settled; foundations rocked. It was normal, and yet the more he listened, the more it sounded like...

*Words*

Or more specifically, a single word.

Whatever it was filled the cold, remorseless Donovan with an emotion that he hadn't felt for quite some time.

*Fear.*

He left the room, quickly walking down the steps, trying as best he could to ignore that creaking, moaning, old house sound. The more he tried to tell himself that it was simply his imagination, the clearer that single word sounded, and the more that supercharged, thunderstorm atmosphere seemed to increase in intensity.

He walked rapidly through the sitting room, banging his shin painfully on the coffee table and opening the door with hands that were shaking more than he would ever have expected. He hoped that just to be out of the house would be enough, but it seemed that somehow, the creaking house noises had transferred onto the very wind itself, and as it rushed through the trees, he heard it again—that same word spoken with such venom that he wondered if he had, on some level, gone insane.

He started to jog, then broke into a run, forgetting the tent that he'd set up in the trees, and forgetting, for the time being, all about exacting his revenge on Steve and Melody. He just wanted to be away from that house and away from that word. Because he knew that it was a warning, as clear and concise as any could be. He ran, ignoring the slap of branches on his skin and the pull of thorns on his clothes. All that mattered was outrunning that word. That one single word that made him re-assesses his plan. Just one word, but it was enough. He could still hear it as he finally reached his car and drove, leaving a great wad of dirt and leaves behind as he streaked away from the house.

He wondered if he would ever be able to forget that word.

That one simple word.

*Mine.*

# 32. BREAKTHROUGH

THE OLD OAK WAS busier than they'd expected, and although it wasn't the ideal place to talk, they decided to take their chances over the lunchtime chatter rather than return home, which for now was something that appealed to neither of them. At first, they'd sat close to the big-screen TV, but quickly realised that due to the football match being cheered on enthusiastically by the locals, they would be better to relocate. They settled on the furthest corner away from the noise.

"It's not quite as... quaint as I remember," Steve said as he tried his best to offer a grin, but couldn't quite manage it. Instead, he took a long drink of his beer, and weighed up the pros and cons of getting absolutely shitfaced.

His wife sat opposite, lost in thought as she methodically pulled the cardboard beer mat to pieces.

"So, when were you going to tell me?" he asked.

"I don't know. Everything all happened at once and...." she trailed off, and looked at the table.

"Look Melody, I've been giving this some thought, and I think we should go home."

"I don't think I can, not just yet."

"No, I don't mean here. I mean home, back to the city."

She looked at him, and he couldn't quite tell if it was with relief or sadness.

"We can't let this beat us. We made a commitment to make this move."

"Come on, Mel, that was before. I mean look at what's happened since we came here."

"You said so yourself, we can't afford to buy a new place."

"Then we can rent. All I know is that I don't want to stay there anymore. It was different when it was just us, but now with a baby on the way I..."

He was going to say he was afraid, but Melody already looked close to the edge, so he decided to be a little less blunt.

"I just don't want anything to affect the pregnancy that's all."

He watched her, the woman he loved, as she tried to stop herself from crying. He thought she had just about managed it when the flood came, and she lowered her head. He reached across the table and held her hands.

"Hey, come on. Whatever happens, we will get through this."

"I hate myself for feeling this way, for feeling so weak. I'm scared Steve. Scared of what's happening to us, scared for the baby. I'm... I'm scared of Donovan."

"I took care of that. He won't be back."

"It's a small village. We can't avoid him forever, and our house is way out in the middle of nowhere... it just scares me, that's all."

Steve knew what he wanted to say, but was wary, because even in his head it sounded ridiculous. He drained his beer, hoping for a little Dutch courage, and then spat out the words that he'd been chewing over.

"What about the house and the things that are happening?"

"I've been thinking about that," Melody said as she wiped her eyes with the sleeve of her sweater in an unconsciously childlike way.

"What if it's just our imagination?"

"I don't think..."

"No, no, just hear me out okay?"

"Okay, go ahead," Steve said.

"So let's be logical. We—two people who have spent their entire lives living in the city - buy a house in the country. Not just a house, but a big old house in the middle of the woods. Now this house seems charming and quaint and beautiful, right?"

Steve nodded, half wanting to add creepy and evil to Melody's list of things describing Hope House, but deciding against it. Instead, he glanced into his empty glass and realised that a slug of alcohol would go down a treat. Melody went on, not realising how obvious it was that she didn't even believe the words she was saying.

"And like all old houses, it makes strange noises. I've read about it—you know, old wood, tired foundations. It happens. And we—as city people—get confused, thinking them to be something they aren't, and there we have it. An explanation."

"What about the circle and the stuff Mrs. Briggs said about the cross?" Steve said, watching his wife as she worked through her thought process.

"They could mean anything—or nothing. Anyone with a little imagination could make up some half-baked story. Don't try to tell me that Mrs. Briggs is someone who you see as sane and rational."

"Hey, it was you who wanted to go and see the old trout, I said she was crazy from the start."

"But the point is it can all be explained. Maybe we're just more susceptible because we're both out of our comfort zone."

Steve could feel his frustration growing, and with it, his anger. Ever since he had known Melody she'd always been a level-headed woman, but now either fear or denial had changed her. One thing was for sure, and that was that he didn't want an argument, even if she was missing some of the more obvious things. The fact that he'd tried to throw himself in the river, the way the woods grew silent when they were in the circle, or even the way the atmosphere would change in the house and make their flesh crawl for no reason.

"Look, I can't say I fully agree," he said "but it's definitely worth talking over."

He waited for a reply, but Melody said nothing. He glanced again at his empty glass.

"I could use another drink. Do you want one?"

"No—actually yes, I'll have an orange juice."

He stood and collected their empty glasses, kissed her on the head as he passed and made his way to the bar. He perched on one of the stools and watched a little of the football whilst he waited for Will to finish serving another customer. With his local armed with a fresh drink, the heavyset barman approached.

"Ah, afternoon Mr. Samson. In to see a bit of the game? You've missed a fair chunk, I'm afraid."

"Hi, Will. No, we just came in for a quiet drink that's all."

As if on cue, a large roar erupted as one of the teams scored, and Steve and Will shared a look and burst into laughter.

"Quiet drink, eh?"

"Maybe not. How's business?"

"Eh, it's as good as it ever gets, I suppose. Just about keeping my head above water."

"That doesn't sound too good."

"It's normal," Will shrugged. "What can I get you?"

He wanted something strong with a high alcohol content that would burn his throat when he drank it, but even under the circumstances, getting hammered at eleven o clock in the morning was unacceptable, however he tried to spin it.

"I'll take a beer. And an orange juice too. Fresh if you have it."

"Coming up."

Will grabbed the orange juice out of the fridge and poured it.

"So, you two settled in okay?"

"Well, it's been..."

*Horrific. Frightening. Fucking insane.*

"Eventful..."

"Eventful, eh?" Will set the glass of orange juice down on the bar and started to hand pull the beer, his huge forearms flexing as he worked the pump.

"Nothing serious I hope?"

Although he was certain it was just barkeep banter, he could see a haze of darkness in Will's face.

"No... not really. Just normal teething troubles that's all."

Will nodded, and Steve waited for him to elaborate, but instead he prepared the drink in silence. Melody approached and stood beside Steve.

"Hi, Will."

"Hello back."

"Is this one mine?" she asked, pointing to the orange juice.

"Indeed it is," Will replied as he set Steve's beer down. "Unless I can get you something stronger that is."

Melody glanced at Steve, and then smiled.

"No, no thanks I'm not drinking right now."

"On the wagon eh?"

"No—we're expecting."

Will faltered. His eyes flicked from Melody to Steve then he turned his attention back to the beer pump. It was just a flicker, but they both saw it.

"Congratulations," he said just a little too sharply as he set the glass down on the bar.

"Yeah, thanks," Steve answered as he and Melody shared a concerned glance. "We just found out ourselves."

"Well, I wish you all the best. I meant to ask, did the two of you speak to Mrs. Briggs about the house?"

"We tried," Steve said, rolling his eyes, "but that old girl is out there. We didn't get much sense out of her."

"I can't say I'm surprised. It's a shame though. Mrs. Briggs might seem like she's a little eccentric, but most of that's the booze talking. She's actually very, very knowledgeable."

"Maybe so, but I doubt we'll be rushing back to talk to her."

"Oh?"

"She just tried to spook us," Melody said, taking a sip of her orange juice. "In fact, she didn't really tell us much of anything."

"I see," Will said thoughtfully. "Tell you what. Wait right there and I might have something that will help you."

Without awaiting a response, Will left, heading out of the bar and upstairs towards his flat.

"What the hell was that all about?" Steve asked, taking a sip of his beer.

"Who knows, I have pretty much given up on trying to work things out around here."

"Tell me about it. Did you see his reaction when you mentioned the baby?"

"I saw it. I wouldn't read too much into it, though. It probably wouldn't have registered as odd if not for the conversation we'd been having."

Steve was frustrated. Despite everything, he still couldn't make Melody see that there was something badly wrong with Hope House. It wasn't even just the house anymore. It was the entire village. Everything seemed off to him. He supposed it was possible that a lot of it could be down to him and his difficulty getting used to country life, but on the flip side, until things had started going askew, he was enjoying the new lifestyle. So what was it? What was it that gnawed at his guts and wouldn't allow him to relax?

"Steve?"

He came back to the present, for the time being pushing aside his worries.

"Sorry, I was miles away there."

"So I noticed," she said with more than a little irritation.

"Sorry, I'm just trying to put all of this into perspective, that's all."

"I don't think it's as bad as you think. I mean I know we've both been spooked for various reasons, but I think we need to look at this rationally and think about our baby."

"That's all well and good," Steve said as he took a long drink of the bitter brew, "but what if we're wrong?"

"About what?"

"About the house. About this damn village, about everything. Doesn't it seem a little odd to you?"

She was about to respond when Will returned. He was carrying an old scrapbook, which looked to be only a stiff breeze away from falling apart. He set the book on the bar in front of them. This time the fear in him was plain to see.

"This book contains lots of history. More specifically, the history of Hope House."

Steve had questions, but before he could fire off even a single one, Will held up a huge hand to stop him.

"Please, just let me finish."

Steve closed his mouth, allowing Will to continue.

"When my great-grandfather had the idea to build Hope House, he could never have comprehended what it would lead to. Over the years, the community here have hidden the truth, tried as best we could to keep this place free of attention from the outside world. My great-grandfather was a good man by all accounts, and although he was hard working, he was also stubborn. Even back then there were legends, stories of some... presence inhabiting the woods. But he never paid attention to stories, and in the end, it cost him his life."

"Everything that has happened since the house was built is in this folder. There are no newspaper articles. As I said we kept it quiet. But these written notes are a chronicle of events as we know them to have happened."

Will looked at the pair, and a small humourless smile formed on his lips.

"Despite what Mrs. Briggs said, I urge you to take this seriously. I'm taking a huge risk here in showing you this."

"Then why do it?" Melody asked quietly.

"Because as I get older, I'm becoming afraid that I've already gone beyond redemption. But I have to try. I have to try and at least help."

"Are you saying that the house is unsafe?"

Will shook his head. "It's not my place to tell you anything. All I can do is give you what no other owner of Hope House has had. I can give you the facts. What you choose to do with them is up to you. All I will tell you is this, read with an open mind, and do whatever your instincts tell you."

Steve was unsure how to react. He was part afraid, part excited. His stomach was in a tight knot, and he had trouble finding the appropriate words.

"Can we borrow this?"

"No, it's got too much sentimental value, but you're welcome to read it here."

Steve looked around at the general racket from the football game. As if reading his mind, Will fished his keys out of his pocket and handed them to Steve.

"Go on up to the flat if you like. It's not the tidiest place in the world, but at least it'll be better than listening to this lot screaming at the TV."

Steve looked to Melody, and she nodded her approval. Steve took the key.

"Thanks, Will, we really appreciate this."

The huge bartender nodded, his face dark and unreadable.

"Go on up. Take as long as you need."

Steve picked up the folder and led Melody through the bar and upstairs. They settled down in Will's bachelor flat, opened the book and began to read.

# 33. LETTERS

*September 12th 1807*

*Dear Michael,*

*I grow concerned at the increasingly desperate and vigorous nature of your recent letters. As I have stated several times during our previous correspondence, I am deeply troubled by your unwillingness to acknowledge what is, in essence, a very real issue with the proposed location of your building project.*

*It is my suggestion that you seek an alternative site, one which is perhaps a little less inclined to cause the issues outlined in my last letter to you and your staff.*

*As you know, my interest is only in ensuring your safety, and as governor of Oakville, it is my responsibility to ensure the safety of all residents.*

*I'm sure you will agree that the last thing that the town needs is to be embroiled in controversy such as your building project could potentially bring about. In anticipation of your veto, I have taken the liberty of conducting the assessment of several alternative locations, as outlined on the reverse of this letter. I hope you will have the good grace to see that this idea, as ambitious as it is, can only lead to problems for Oakville and its residents.*

*Sincerely,*

*Governor Thomas Hume.*

20th September.

Thomas,

I read your letter with great interest and must confess that although I greatly appreciate the sentiment, I find the theatrical tone somewhat amusing. Indeed, if I didn't know any better, I would have been certain that you had already been whispering in the ear of my business partners, who are so far reluctant to proceed.
Let me assure you, Governor that not only am I unconcerned with local folklore, but somewhat surprised that such idle gossip has you in such a state of agitation!

However, I did you the courtesy of reviewing the alternative sites on the reverse of your previous letter, and although some would indeed make for interesting opportunities, I must decline. Perhaps it is my inherent inflexibility or more likely my desire to prove wrong you naysayers and doom merchants!

Although I do appreciate your concerns for my safety, I must reiterate that I hold you in no way responsible for any harm that comes to me during the build. I only hope that the concern shown isn't a sign of your intention to withdraw permission for the project. I do believe that our assigned agreement will be upheld should we need to involve the courts. I truly hope that this is not the case.

I do sometimes wonder how all of this talk of phantoms began, and why nobody seems to know the ultimate truth.

I would suggest it is because it is simply no more than fantasy designed to scaremonger. Fortunately, the Jones family are not easily alarmed by such stories.

Sincerely,

Michael.

\*\*\*

*October 3rd*

*Dear Michael,*

*It seems that I must concede that you are determined to go ahead with this venture no matter what I or anyone else says. As to the idea that I might try to stop the project from going ahead, then I must confess that the thought had occurred to me. However, it seems that my own lack of foresight in signing the agreement to allow the build before checking the location thoroughly means it would be a long and expensive battle, which I have neither the desire nor energy to undertake.*

*As it seems that you are so determined to proceed, I took the liberty of researching the source of the legend or 'scaremongering fantasy' as you so quaintly put it.*

*I spoke to a gentlemen well versed in local legend, who said with great conviction that in the year 1556, there was a vicious tribe of flesh eating savages called the Gogoku, who inhabited the woodland. They would raid entire villages and abduct the local children, who they would murder and feast upon.*

*Legend says that the earth became dark with their blood, and over time, the spirits of the dead began to whisper to the villagers, which in turn drove them to insanity.*

*The men of the tribe, if the story is to be believed, slaughtered their kin and then set fire to the village. When it was a towering inferno, they walked into the flames, and they themselves were burned alive.*

*Oddly, there is a circle where nothing grows close to where you plan to build. I am told that this is the location where the village used to be, and where the damned souls of the restless tribesmen are said to roam, forever in search of blood and in protection of their lands.*

*It seems that even the souls of their victims were unable to find their rest, and so are said to inhabit the trees, whispering to each other and waiting for their chance to leave purgatory.*

*I wonder if knowing this will change your mind, but I suspect, if anything, it will only strengthen your resolve.*
*I can only hope that your business partners can dissuade you from proceeding. I cannot stress enough my concern.*

*Yours,*

*Thomas.*

\*\*\*

October 14th

Thomas,

Thank you for the information about the Gogoku tribe. If only such stories were true, then life would be substantially more exhilarating wouldn't you agree?

For as much as I don't believe a word of it, I was intrigued enough to make my own enquiries and was surprised to find the version of events that I received from my sources was almost identical to yours, however with a few minor embellishments which I think you will find entertaining.

In the version of events that I was told, the Gogoku were not only cannibalistic, but also inbred. Can you imagine Thomas?

Inbreeds!

What a fantastic addition to an already lavish story!

I must confess that after reading your last letter, I made a visit to the area of the wood where construction will take place and would you believe that I found the circle you spoke of.

I must acknowledge that there was indeed a heavy atmosphere there, and the silence within its borders was total. Not a bird sang, nor a leaf rustled.

Strangely, the grass didn't seem to grow there.

If I didn't know any better, I would have thought there

was somebody maintaining the grounds in that particular area in order to keep up this ridiculous legend.

I'm afraid that's where my experience ended. No ghost children or phantom inbred cannibals I'm afraid, just acres of green land ripe for development. This will be my last letter for a while, as I have a business trip, which cannot be rearranged. I will be meeting with my business partner upon my return and fully expect to get authorisation and funding to proceed. I hope to begin construction next year.

Do not worry my friend. Soon enough you will see that your worries were for nothing, even if your concern is appreciated.

Sincerely,

Michael.

***

*November 20th*

*Michael,*

*I understand that there is no stopping you, and also that no matter how often I ask you to be cautious, you will not listen.*

*As much as I would like to wish you luck, I can only be truthful and hope that your business partner refuses to fund the project.*

*This is not something I say out of cruelty, but out of*

*concern for your safety.*

*I wonder if you would keep writing to me as often as you can so that I can at least know that you are safe and well.*

*Until next time my friend,*

*Thomas.*

\*\*\*

January 2nd 1808

Thomas,

First let me wish you a Happy New Year and apologise for the delay in getting back to you.

I appreciate your concern, and take no ill feeling at your desire to see the project fail. However, I must inform you to your probable displeasure, that the project was approved!

Bless Alfonse, he is as jittery as you my friend, and also tried to warn me away from proceeding. How any of you lead a civilised life I'll never know!

Work will be commencing shortly, and truth be told I cannot wait. This is now a personal mission to prove that there is nothing out in those trees but prime land waiting to be developed.

Apologies for the brisk nature of this letter, however, there is much to do in preparation, as I'm sure you can appreciate!

I will update you just as soon as I can.

Your friend,

Michael.

\*\*\*

May 14th 1808

Thomas!

Construction is underway! I write this to you now from the very place which seems to strike fear into your heart! The solitude of this circle is a good place to come and think and to pen my letters. I have a solid crew of workers, Negroes mostly, but they have strong backs and work hard. If only you could see it Thomas!

It even has a name. I have christened it Hope House, and I'm sure that when you see the completed project, you will understand my determination to push forward. Perhaps one day you will have a home of your own here?

As for the Gogoku, I'm sorry to say that I have seen or heard nothing of them and their kind. The only sounds are of construction and the heavy breathing of exertion.
If all goes to plan, we should be complete in August.

Sincerely,

Michael.

***

*May 22nd.*

*Michael.*

*Despite my misgivings, I am happy for you that things are progressing well, and even more so that work goes on without incident.*

*I do not know if you are interested or not, but I couldn't help but do a little more research on the Gogoku, and although I know you do not believe any of the stories, I thought that you might be interested to know what I discovered.*

*It seems that the Gogoku was a very spiritual tribe. They practised the dark arts, Michael, black magic. The tale here becomes a little vague, but by all accounts the Gogoku men, after killing the rest of their tribe, decided that no child shall ever be born on their lands again, and cursed the very earth with the blood of their people.*

*The ground became sodden with blood from the slaughter, which in turn was taken in by the trees.*

*Can you imagine?*

*The living forest fed by the inbred, insane blood of the Gogoku tribe. I only hope that you are correct, and that it is just a story, for could you imagine what would happen if it were true?*

*Although I doubt that this story will give you any kind of caution, but I ask you again anyway to be careful, and do not linger any longer than you have to amid the trees.*

*Thomas.*

***

May 30th

Thomas.

I think I heard it. It said my name.

Michael.

***

June 8

*Michael.*

*I sincerely hope that your last letter was in jest, and if so, I find it in extremely poor taste considering my very real concerns for your safety. Please reply at your earliest convenience if only to put my mind at rest.*

*Yours,*

*Thomas.*

***

*June 24th*

*Michael,*

*I had hoped to hear from you by now, and with each passing day my concern grows. Please let me know you are safe and well at your earliest convenience.*

*Thomas.*

***

July 9th

Dear Governor Hume,

I write to you with regret to announce the passing of my brother, Michael.

As executor of his estate, I felt it my duty to write to you to inform you of this dreadful news, and to advise that upon reading of his correspondence to you, must share in your concern that all is not well with Hope House and its surroundings.

Although I haven't witnessed anything myself, I have often experienced a bone-deep chill and the uneasy feeling that I was being observed. I don't wish to speculate or cause alarm, but I have my own personal suspicion that perhaps that place had something to do with his passing. The official line is that Michael drowned; however, I know that he was deathly afraid of the water and had been wary of it ever since we were children.

There was an incident on the day I last saw him, which I was reluctant to include; however, I suppose it matters little now and I believe I can trust you.

A man hanged himself on site the night before I last saw my brother, and although I pleaded with Michael to call the police, he in his stubbornness refused, and we had words.

I left him there and our parting was sour, and his last words to me were that he would deal with the body himself. I wonder if he might have been trying to dispose of the body in the river when he saw or heard something that shocked him enough to frighten him into the water. I only hope that death found him quickly, and he has at last found peace.

I must go now to that god-forsaken place and continue his work, although my heart tells me to stay away, the loyalty to my brother forces my hand. I can only hope that the work can be completed swiftly so that I might be able to at last mourn, and put this terrible ordeal behind me.

Sincerely,

Francis Jones.

***

*July 18th*

*Dear Mr. Jones,*

*Firstly, allow me to express my deepest of sympathies for your loss. I must confess, however, that I was always concerned for Michael's safety, and although a shock, the news of his death came as no great surprise, I'm afraid.*

*I am relieved that you have seen sense enough to know the forces that operate within Oakwell forest are not to be taken lightly. I do wonder why you would even go back to the site, as it is plain to see that you have personally experienced some of its power. Perhaps I might be so bold as to suggest abandoning the site and leaving it for the trees to reclaim at their leisure?*

*Kindest regards,*

*Thomas.*

\*\*\*

July 30th

Mr Hume,

Thank you for your response to my letter, and for your condolences, which are truly appreciated. I would have liked nothing better than to abandon Hope House in its unfinished state, and was quite prepared to do so. It seems my wily brother had written a will prior to the project's beginning (perhaps he had some respect for the legend surrounding the forest after all) requesting that if anything should happen to him to stop him completing the work, that I complete it for him.

I know there is no legal obligation to do so, but I have to confess to finding myself torn between listening to the fear in my heart and in completing the work of my late brother. It was with great reluctance that I chose the latter.

I have spent some time on the site of late, and although the workers are frightened, I think it shall soon be complete.

It is unusual Thomas, that even though I haven't witnessed anything I can directly say is spiritual in nature, I have imagined I have heard my name whispered by the wind as it passes through the trees.

Perhaps it is the stress of recent events, or the dreams of that infernal place that haunt my nights, but either way I will soon be free of its shackles.

Sincerely,

Francis.

*** 

*August 9th*

*Dear Francis,*

*I see the dilemma you face, and the decision must have been difficult. I must express my concern at your experiences in the woods surrounding Hope House, and hope that these have been a suitable enough warning for you to vacate with haste.*

*I can appreciate your desire to adhere to Michael's wishes, but surely he would not wish for you to put your own safety at risk in the process?*

*I can only urge you to down tools now and leave whatever resides in those grounds to its own devices.*

*Yours,*

*Thomas.*

***

Aug 20th

It is I, Michael, back from the dead!

Ha-ha!

I of course jest.

The house is almost finished and rather than stay away, I find that the solitude of the trees soothe me with their whispers.

If I listen well, I imagine I can hear my brother calling to me, reassuring me that I am doing the right thing. I wish you could experience it for yourself.

Francis.

***

*Aug 29*

*Francis,*

*I am deeply concerned by the content of your last letter.*

*I can only urge you to get as far away from Hope House as possible. I fear for not only your sanity but also your life.*

*Regards,*

*Thomas.*

***

Thomas.

It isn't all bad.

They really do make quite a lot of sense once you listen to them.

House is complete, but they are angry. I must pay the price, and it is only fair.

I was afraid at first, but they convinced me that this way is for the best. I don't suppose you and I will converse again, and for that I am sorry.

Farewell.

Francis.

P.S. Michael sends his regards.

***

Steve looked up from the book at Melody, and saw his own horror mirrored in her expression. She glanced at the open volume on the table, and his gaze followed hers in looking over the fragile old letters taped to the pages.

At last, it seemed that reality had finally hit her, and she'd gone beyond making excuses or trying to pass everything off as coincidence. She looked broken and beaten down, and far from the easy-going, carefree woman who first moved in to Hope House.

He wanted to reassure her, to tell her that everything would be okay, but how could he when the chilling letters in front of them said otherwise.

"What do we do now?" she asked quietly.

"I don't know. Let's read on a little further before we decide that."

She nodded, and the pair turned their attention back to the book.

# 34. PREPARATION

SO INVOLVED WERE THEY in the scrapbook when it was presented to them by Will, that they hadn't noticed Donovan walk into the bar and sit far enough away to just be out of earshot. And their lack of recognition was no surprise, for every time in the past that they'd dealt with him, he'd been clad in one of his cheap suits, and his hair meticulously combed over in a ridiculous side parting. But now, he was incognito, wearing his scruffy jeans, a grey hoodie and baseball cap, and well on his way to being drunk.

The events at the house earlier that day were being played in a never-ending loop in his head. At first, he was afraid—terrified, in fact. However, now that he had had time to think about it, and the alcohol had had a chance to do its magic, all he felt was the rage gnawing at his guts.

Fortunately, it was something that he'd learned to live with over the years and, more importantly, control. He reached into the front pocket of the hoodie and touched the knife. It was his favourite. Not too long, but sharp and serrated. It would do the job nicely. He had at first planned to use the gun, to make it quick and painless. But not anymore, now he wanted them to suffer, and for that, the knife was best.

He looked across at the Samsons, and had to fight to stop himself from charging over and stabbing their eyes out in front of everybody.

Patience. That was the key.

He watched as the stupid fucking bartender, Jones, gave them the keys to his flat and ushered them upstairs with their book full of secrets. He ought to have known better. He knew how important it was

259

to keep the town free from attention. He of all people couldn't afford to have people sniffing around. Who knows what they would find out?

Snapshots of his past came to him.

*A pained scream.*

*Pleading for mercy.*

*Blood soaking into the carpet.*

There was so, so much of it that it had caught him off-guard the first time. It was a mess, literally and figuratively. However, everyone had to start somewhere, and since then he'd become good at it. Efficient.

*Am I a psychopath?*

He had asked himself the question before, and as always, the answer was unclear. He supposed he was. He had killed people, felt no remorse for it. In fact, he enjoyed it. But despite all that, on some level he knew it was wrong, and if he wasn't careful, he could get caught. For a while, the fear of capture was enough, and he had managed to refrain from doing those depraved things that he so desperately wanted to do, but the rage was strong, and seven years was a long time to resist those urges. He thought he'd done a pretty good job of it, too. But whatever darkness existed in Hope House had coaxed it to the surface, telling him it wasn't wrong to feel how he felt, that if bloodshed was his release from a twisted and cruel world, then so be it. He had listened, and he'd felt a great relief, for it was all he had.

Of course, the business was fine for what it was, but it was no more than a means to an end, a way to keep a roof over his head and food in his belly. There was no joy, no real desire to be successful. It was a sham, an empty shell. Sometimes, it got so bad that he couldn't even bear to look himself in the mirror without seeing the broken ghost of a man.

But now was different. With his knife in his pocket and the anticipation of what he was about to do, he could be proud. Because he knew he was good, and he knew that the Samsons deserved what was coming to them.

He looked at Will, and wondered if he, too, deserved to be silenced. After all he had shown them things, told them secrets they had no right knowing.

He wondered if they'd shared their own secrets with him, more specifically, secrets about his visit to the house. Perhaps his name had come up in conversation, and if it had, who knows what could have been said. One thing he'd always done was to live by his instincts, and right now they were telling him that he couldn't afford any loose ends.

Donovan gauged Will as an adversary. He couldn't overpower him, that much was obvious. He was broad and strong, and in a physical confrontation Donovan would surely fail. That was okay though, there was always another way. He just had to be patient and wait for his chance.

And then, of course there was the issue of the house itself. Even though he was on his way to being drunk, it still wasn't quite enough to fully blot out the sly, whispering nature of those voices chasing him, and as much as he hated it, the expert in that particular area was the woman who'd spawned him, and as much as he wanted to avoid any and all contact with her wherever possible, this was a unique situation that warranted a visit.

He slowly got up, sliding out from behind his table and walking to the exit, keeping his head low and his eyes on the ground.

# 35. TRUTH

STEVE CLOSED THE SCRAPBOOK, leaned back in his seat and exhaled. He couldn't bear to look at Melody, not yet at least. Not until he had a grasp on things for himself. They had read the book together, and each account was depressingly similar. There had been a mixture of suicides, mysterious deaths including madness. For a short while, Steve had tried to convince himself that it was all an elaborate hoax, but the more he read, the less he could convince himself that it was anything other than truth.

It was in the way it had been written, the way it wasn't sensationalised. It was exactly as Will had said. A written history pieced together and then collated to give a harrowing history of Hope House and the surrounding land.

"What do you think?" Melody asked him. He had a bizarre urge to laugh, because it seemed that they'd traded their cramped, overpriced, noisy city apartment for their own little slice of country hell, and as much as he hated himself for thinking it, he blamed her. She was the one so taken with the charming nature of the house. He saw the dry rot and damp for what it was, but she had seen it as *'original features'* and then Donovan had chimed in to say that it could be a *'restoration project'* for them to do together.

"Steve?" she repeated, and it took all of his effort to turn towards her and force a smile.

"Sorry, it's just a hell of a lot to take in."

"Yes. Yes, it is."

He looked at her pained expression, and realised that at last she got it, she understood exactly what they were dealing with. Despite the pain that it was plainly causing her, part of him was glad that she could see things for what they were.

"So... what do we do now?" she asked him, and he realised that he had no idea. There was nothing that he could give by way of an answer that would give her any sense of safety or comfort, although as he contemplated, the ghost of an idea had begun to form in his mind.

"Well..." he began, carefully choosing his words. "This tells us a lot, but there are still gaps. I think we can agree now that we are dealing with something... out of the ordinary."

"Yeah, I can't bury my head in the sand anymore. Whatever it is, it's supernatural in nature."

"More than that, it seems to be hostile, and obviously doesn't want us or anyone else on its land."

"Agreed, but this doesn't make me feel any better."

"Well I do have one idea that might be worth considering."

"What are you thinking?"

He hesitated, unsure how his suggestion might be received.

"You know the Ouija board that I bought...?"

"No. Absolutely not!" she snapped, standing and pacing around the small apartment.

He could see that she was afraid, and struggling to hold her emotions in check.

"Look, let me explain what I mean..."

"...I can't believe you would even suggest that, especially now after everything we've just learned!"

"Mel, please, just calm down. Hear me out," he stood and tried to pull her close, but her fear had turned into anger and she swatted him away.

"Don't touch me! Why the hell are you so determined to use that god-awful thing? What do you expect to prove?"

"All I'm suggesting is that it's worth a try. Maybe... just maybe, we can communicate with it and perform the ritual I told you about to get rid of it for good."

"That's your idea? Are you fucking kidding me, Steve?"

"It's better than doing nothing! What do you suggest?"

"I don't know! But not that!"

"Look, I know the idea frightens you, but I don't see that we have many other options. We're stuck in the house for the short term at least."

"Maybe it'll just leave us alone?"

Steve shook his head and leafed through the scrapbook on the coffee table.

"Almost every account in this book either involves children being born, or kids already in the house. Here listen to this."

He turned to one of the later entries, written beside a list of the names and ages of everyone who had lived in Hope House. The text was written in an old fashioned, swirling hand and Steve read one of the entries out loud.

*Although there is nothing in the way of proof to suggest that the spirits which plague Hope House are more drawn towards families with children, my research shows that those families who do, or are expecting a child, do suffer increased activity almost without question. In point of fact, it seems that the only time activity appeared to be reduced to nothing, was in those times when the inhabitants of Hope House had no children, either by choice or by design:*

*Edith Miller 1910 – 1914*
*Edward & Molly Harris 1933 – 1935*

*James Goodwill 1936 – 1937*
*Frederick & Joan Mirfield 1955 – 1962*

*In each instance, I find it interesting that even without children, the pattern of short-term residency in Hope House has continued.*

*Unfortunately, there had not been opportunity enough to speak with all of the above householders, but both Mr. & Mrs. Harris, and Mr. Goodwill stated that they never felt comfortable in Hope House, and indeed felt compelled to move on as quickly as they arrived. I wonder if the spirits had somehow managed to sour the atmosphere, in order to make the residents of the house leave. If so then that idea begs another question:*

*Why is the activity so sporadic?*
*Could it really be that children, either born or unborn, are the key?*
*Could the spirits of Hope House feed from the energy of the young and innocent?*
*As always, my investigations raise more questions than answers.*

Steve glanced at Melody, who, for the time being, was silent. She sat beside Steve as he looked for another passage later on in the scrapbook.

"Then there was this. This relates to the people who lived in the house just before us."

*It has been three and a half years now since the Crofts moved in to Hope House, and I wonder if we have finally managed to contain the evil that lurks within those trees. I myself am too old, and will shortly pass this book to my son, William, in the hope that he will keep it safe, and more importantly, secret.*

*But I digress.*

*The Crofts are a polite, if subdued, couple. They always ask after my health when they come to drink in the pub, and even though I have tried to tease information out of them, they seem to be perfectly at ease in Hope House, which gives me the belief that the measures taken to protect the property have worked.*

*Annie Briggs, a colourful local and amateur historian who has been more than helpful during the course of my research, also professes to be some kind of 'white witch' who claims that although she couldn't do anything to rid the lands of spirits, she could protect it and its future inhabitants. This would be done by way of 'blessing' an artefact—in this case a crucifix carved by her own hand—and placing it between the circle where the Gogoku village is said to have been located and Hope House.*

*Annie's claim that this enchanted cross would form some kind of 'spiritual barrier' seems to hold some weight, especially in light of the Croft's claims that they have noticed nothing unusual since it was placed at the perimeter of the Gogoku village boundary.*

*As eccentric as she is, perhaps she does have some kind of power. Indeed, she was quite forceful in her insistence that we keep the entire operation secret, as she claims that the barrier will only last until the cross is handled and removed from its position in the woods. I only hope that this is the end of a saga that has plagued my family since my grandfather decided to build on that land which has seen so much bloodshed.*

*I pray that this is the end.*

Steve once again closed the book, and set it down on the table. He was desperate to know how Melody felt, but for the time being her expression remained neutral.

"This is all my fault," she said softly.

"No, don't say that."

His response was automatic, but that little voice in his head affirmed Melody's statement.

"But it is. I mean, I hardly gave you a chance to say no to buying the house in the first place, and it was me who picked up the cross from the tree..."

He wanted to tell her that it really wasn't her fault, but that niggling voice said otherwise, and it took some effort to push it aside.

"Don't... there's no way you could have known."

"But that doesn't change things, not really."

He pulled her close, and this time, she didn't fight him off, and buried her head in his chest. He held her there, not quite sure why he was still so angry with her.

"Look, I know it scares you, but you need to trust me. You need to let me use the Ouija board. Let me at least try."

"What if it makes things worse?"

"It won't. It's perfectly safe."

He sounded convincing, even though his stomach knotted at the thought of what he was about to do. It was a giddy feeling, the rational part of him sure that nothing would happen and yet somewhere, deep down, another part of him knew that it would. Even so, he had to come across as calm and in control. She pulled back from him and looked him in the eye.

"Promise me that if things get weird, you'll stop it right away."

"I will."

"Promise me."

"I promise."

"Okay, then I suppose it's worth a try."

He held her close to him and kissed her on the head, unsure if he was relieved or afraid. He decided it was a little of both.

"Come on," he whispered in her ear. "Let's go home."

# 36. NO LOOSE ENDS

STUMP THE CAT WAS enjoying the soft warmth of its master's chair when it was grabbed rudely under the belly and picked up. He voiced his disapproval, but that didn't deter his master as she carried Stump across the clutter-filled room.

He glared up at his misshapen owner when he felt the cold air ruffle his fur, and before Stump could cling on to protest, he had been unceremoniously dumped on the doorstep.

"Go on now Mr. Stump, back before bedtime okay?"

The cat didn't understand the strange sounds coming out of its human master, and walked gingerly into the garden, wishing that he was back inside and warm. It was contemplating its best course of action when it sensed the vibration of an approaching car.

For Stump, cars meant danger, and so it skittered across the garden and under one of the rosebushes where it would sometimes take dead birds and mice if he were lucky enough to catch them. For now, it was a safe enough haven.

Stump watched as the red sports car came to a halt outside the gate, and the other human approached his master's home. There was something familiar about this one; it had visited before, but not for a while. Stump watched, his whiskers twitching, his tail swishing slowly in the dirt.

The human jogged up the short driveway and knocked loudly on the door. Stump watched, and the human waited. The door opened, and Stump saw his master at the threshold. The two humans conversed for a few seconds, and then both went inside, leaving Stump outside in the cold alone.

He waited for a few moments to see if they would come back to let him in, and then realising that it wasn't going to happen, he climbed out from under the rosebush, hopped over the garden wall and into the night to do whatever cats do.

***

"That damn cat stinks," Donovan said as he sat on the sofa opposite his mother, barely hiding his disgust.

"They keep me company," Mrs. Briggs grumbled as she lowered herself back into her favourite seat.

"You should air the place out, and clean up some of this mess."

"I'm sure you didn't come here to talk about my living conditions."

"No, no I didn't," Donovan said, offering an oozing smile.

"You've experienced something, haven't you?"

She leaned forward as she said it, watching with wide-eyed excitement, which both repulsed and angered Donovan. He counted back from five in his head and managed to keep control.

"Yeah, you could say that. Whatever is in that damned house chased me out of there. *'Mine'* it said, over and over again."

Donovan watched his mother, and noted that she didn't seem at all surprised. He wondered absently how the fat bitch was still alive. Surely her arteries would be clogged with excess fat, her liver and kidneys destroyed by the daily alcohol abuse. He could imagine that as he watched he could see her edging towards her inevitable and deserved death.

"It's not you it wants, Freddy..."

"...Donovan. How many times do I have to tell

you?"

"You can call yourself whatever you want, but you will always be my Freddy."

He was going to tell her how he didn't seem to matter so much when she shipped him off to live with his paedophile uncle, but didn't want to become embroiled in another argument, and so let it slide.

"Look, I need your help. I'm not going back to that damn house. Not after what happened."

"They aren't interested in you. They just want the woman."

Donovan sneered and leaned back in his seat. "Oh, I see, and you know this how?"

Mrs. Briggs smiled, and it was then that any onlooker would have known they were mother and son, so similar were the expressions.

"I know more than you credit me for, son. People think I'm the crazy old woman drinking her days away, but that's not how it is. I watch, and I listen."

"That still doesn't tell me anything useful."

She reached down beside her chair, and pulled out the carved wooden cross that Steve and Melody had left there earlier. She set it on the table and looked at Donovan with a smug smile on her plump lips.

Donovan raised his eyebrows. "Am I supposed to be impressed?"

Her smile soured, and she sat back and folded her hands over her huge stomach.

"No, but if you take it with you, it'll keep you safe."

"Safe?" he said as he picked up the cross and turned it over in his hands. "Safe from what? I seem to remember you always saying that the dead can't hurt us?"

"I did, but that was before I knew any better."

Donovan looked at his mother, genuinely

interested for the first time in what she was saying.

"What do you mean by that?"

"This activity or energy or whatever it is, is more concentrated than anything I have ever experienced before. It seems I have spent my entire life with Hope House and its woods. The first half learning about it, and the second half trying to keep it a secret."

Donovan nodded. He knew all about secrets.

"What we don't need,'" she continued, "is for those two to go running and shouting from the hilltops about the things that happen here."

"Maybe it would be for the best," he said with a confident smile, playing the *'unconcerned son'* card to perfection whilst inside, he thought of the implications of any unwanted attention pointed at the town, more specifically, towards him. He looked at his mother, and was surprised to see that she too was smiling.

The rage rumbled deep in his gut.

He wondered if he had been outwardly speaking his thoughts, and that she had heard them.

"I don't think I'm the only one who would benefit from our secrets staying hidden... am I, son?"

He looked at her blankly, his face not betraying the terror inside.

*She knows.*

"Look," he said as calmly as he could manage "all of that aside, why don't we just leave the spirits or ghosts or whatever they are to do what they do?"

She shook her flabby head. "No, there won't be enough time. I saw them earlier, and they look ready to just up and leave. Maybe as early as tomorrow."

"That could be... a problem."

He smiled thinly, and the game of cat and mouse went on, both for now content to sidestep the serial killer, psychopathic-son-sized-elephant in the room.

"If something is going to happen, then really, it needs to be tonight," she said, watching him with an icy stare.

"That place isn't safe."

Mrs. Briggs leaned forward and slid the crucifix across the table.

"That will make it safe."

"Why are you giving it to me?"

She said nothing, and he was suddenly a child again waiting under the watchful gaze of his mother. Without saying a word he picked up the cross and stuffed it into the front pocket of his hoodie.

"No loose ends," she said simply, and he felt a chill caress his skin at the cold way in which she said it. He realised then that he had been wrong. He'd always assumed that he had become the monster he was because of his upbringing, but now as he looked at the obese, beastly woman opposite him, it occurred that a lot of the monster in him had been passed down from her.

He stood and pulled his hood up over his head, peering out at the evil thing that he'd always seen as a harmless old woman. He'd often wondered if she'd known about his secret past, and it was only now that he knew that she did. She had known all along.

"I'll take care of it," he said simply.

He walked around the table and bent to kiss his mother on the cheek. She smelled of soap and hairspray, just the way he used to remember. He stood, and in one smooth motion pulled the knife out of his pocket and plunged it into her chest.

She gasped, and stared at him as the blood pooled around the hilt of the knife. He applied more pressure, surprised to find himself crying as he waited for her to die. Her breath became shallow, then slowed and eventually stopped.

"No loose ends," he whispered as he stood and pulled the knife free, absently wiping it on the arm of the chair and slipping it back into his jacket.

Calmly, he crossed the room and opened the door, pausing at the threshold to make sure he hadn't forgotten anything. Stump, the displaced house cat took full advantage of the open door and hurried back inside, not liking the cold conditions. Donovan let it go past him, watching as it crossed the room and jumped up onto his dead mother's lap and curled up to sleep. Donovan smiled and quietly closed the door.

# 37. CONTACT

HOPE HOUSE BASKED IN the orange glow of late-afternoon sun. It had been a cold, crisp day, and already the grass that had spent much of its day in the shadow had a light dusting of winter frost on it. Inside the house, Steve and Melody sat at the kitchen table, the wooden Ouija board between them. Beside it was a plain white bowl, a notebook, pen and a lighter. Steve looked into his wife's eyes, and marvelled at just how quickly a life which seemed so positive and full of promise could change. There was no joy, no feeling of Hope House ever being the home that they desperately wanted. They felt like intruders, lodgers who had overstayed their welcome. For all her stubborn refusals to initially do anything to avoid the truth, Melody had been hit hard with the barrage of information they'd gleaned during the course of the day. She was pale and looked exhausted, and he supposed he shouldn't be so surprised.

When they'd first arrived back at the house, neither of them was sure what to expect, and had simply sat outside in the car with the engine running and the heat on full, just looking at the building. Somehow it seemed changed. There was a sinister, foreboding vibe about it. He thought back to that day when they'd first come out to look at the place, a time that felt to him like a whole other lifetime. He remembered feeling something then, a slight discomfort that he'd put down to a combination of the abundance of green and Donovan's blatant ogling of Melody, but maybe there was more to it and on some level he had sensed whatever was out there.

"So what do we do?" Melody asked, her eyes wide and completely trusting of him to lead the way as she

275

brought him back to the here and now.

"Well," he said, licking his lips "we write down our problem, in this case the harassment by these... spirits. Then we concentrate hard and will them away, before we burn the paper in this bowl."

"Are you sure it 'll work?"

"No, I can't be sure. But people all over the world say this is the best way to deal with situations like ours."

"Let's do it, then."

"Not yet. First, I want to try to communicate with them."

"I don't see why we have to."

"I just want to try it."

"What do we have to do?"

"Well, we each put a finger on the planchette here, and then I guess we start asking questions."

"That's it?"

"Yeah, that's it."

"I'm still not sure about this. Why don't we just go stay in a hotel or something?"

"Because this is our home."

He said it a little sharper than he'd intended, so he grabbed her hand across the table and somehow managed a reassuring smile.

"This is our home, Mel. Every penny we have is tied up here. Surely, this is worth a shot if it means we might fix this issue rather than run away from it."

"And what happens if we can't fix it?"

He had no answer to the question, instead taking the planchette and placing it on the board.

"I don't know," he said quietly. "Maybe we can learn to live with it, show it we aren't afraid."

"But I am afraid. You should be too," she said, pulling her hand free of his.

"I'm just trying to do what's best here. This is still

our damn house."

"Is it?" she said with a sick smile. "It doesn't feel like it to me, not anymore."

"What are you saying?"

"I'm saying that there's a reason why we don't feel welcome. There's a reason why all those people died here."

"Maybe it's because they didn't do anything to try to stop it."

"Maybe there was nothing they *could* do."

He didn't answer. Instead he stood, crossed to the sink, filled the kettle, set it to boil and prepared them both a cup. Melody stared at the Ouija board, and was overcome with such a feeling of absolute dread that she was certain that she was going to throw up. She concentrated on watching Steve make the drinks, and waited until he came back. He set the cups down and sat opposite her again.

"Look, we can't put this off forever," he said, picking up the planchette. "I don't know about you, but I'd rather do this now than wait until after dark."

"Yeah, me too. Okay, let's do it."

She had said it as confidently as she could, but still her voice wavered, and Steve felt her pain. He too was apprehensive, and yet still excited. He set the planchette on the board, reached over and took Melody's hands in his. They were shaking.

"Relax, it's going to be okay," he said as reassuringly as he could, at the same time trying to ignore the butterflies in his own stomach. He released her, and put his fingertip lightly on the edge of the pointer.

"Go ahead," he said to Melody. "Just lightly."

She joined him in placing her index finger on the cold wood, and looked him in the eye. "Okay. What now?" she asked.

He licked his lips, and forced himself to speak.

"We try to communicate."

"Let's do it, but promise me that if things get weird..."

"Understood," he said, flashing an encouraging smile, "we stop. I promise."

He took a deep breath and then spoke as clearly as he could.

"Is there any spirit or presence here that wishes to speak with us?"

They held their breath and waited, each of them staring at the small wooden pointer, but nothing happened. Steve licked his lips and repeated his question, but again to no avail.

"This isn't working," Melody whispered, her eyes wide and frightened.

"Give it a minute."

He hesitated and then tried again. "Is there anybody who wishes to communicate with us?"

The pair waited, and listened to the silence of the house. Steve shook his head and leaned back in his seat.

"You were right. This is stupid," he grumbled.

"To the spirit who resides here," Melody said. "Do you have a name?"

"This is pointless, Mel. You said so yourself."

"Let's just give it a chance. Please."

"Okay," he sighed, placing his finger back on the pointer. "But I think we're wasting our time."

"Maybe, but at least we'll know either way."

She waited for a further complaint, received none, so went ahead.

"Is there anything in the house or surrounding grounds that wishes to communicate with us?"

The couple waited, and Melody was about to speak again when the planchette began to move. The sensation was strange as the pointer slid slowly across the board. Steve and Melody shared a disbelieving look. The pointer had come to rest on yes, and then glided back to the centre.

"Holy shit," Steve whispered. "Tell me that's not you screwing around with me?"

"It's not me, I swear. This is hardly the time to start playing pranks on each other."

They stared at the board, still trying to process what was happening.

"What now?" she asked.

"Ask it some questions."

"Do you have a name?"

As before, the planchette slid smoothly to the word 'yes' and then back to the centre of the board.

"This is unbelievable," Steve whispered.

"-Did you die here in the house?"

The pointer slid to 'no'.

"-Did you die near here?"

'Yes'.

"-Are you a part of the Gogoku tribe?"

They watched as the planchette slid smoothly to the word 'yes', then back to the centre.

"What do we do now?" Melody said quietly.

"We find out what it wants."

The couple turned their attention back to the board as the last rays of the sun fell behind the tree line.

Michael Bray

## 38. MORE LOOSE ENDS

SINCE IT HAD FIRST opened in July 1899, the Jones family had run the Old Oak public house. Passed down through the generations, it had survived relatively unscathed, including the flood of '86 when over eleven inches of rain had fallen overnight and submerged the entire village in knee-deep water. Now in its fourth generation of ownership, Will was ushering the last of its patrons out of the door.

In what had become a tradition ever since the pub had opened its doors by his great grandfather, he was closing up for the traditional three-hour break between afternoon and the start of the evening shift at seven.

As a bachelor who ran the pub alone, it gave him a chance to get a few hours' rest and a bite to eat before he re-opened. With the last of his regulars safely ushered out, he locked the doors, basked in the silence for a few seconds and then trudged upstairs to catch some much-needed rest.

He went straight to the kitchen, pulling a microwave meal for one out of the freezer and setting it to cook. As the meal was being irradiated, he went into the sitting room, kicked off his boots and flopped into the chair. He could see the scrapbook on the table that he had let the Samsons look through, and again hoped that he had made the right call. He thought he had.

His family bloodline was already responsible for so much death over the years that he hoped his actions would break the cycle. He closed his eyes, thinking of grabbing a quick snooze after he'd eaten before the evening rush began.

He never heard Donovan creep into the room.

He'd been hiding in the bedroom for the last hour, and now his patience was about to be rewarded.

\*\*\*

Donovan had spent the time intimately learning the layout of Will's apartment. He knew all too well the consequences of stepping on an uneven floorboard or opening a creaking door and now, due to his research, he moved in a stealthy silence. The sleeves of his hoodie were still stained with his mother's drying blood as he moved to the back of Will's chair and took the length of piano wire from his pocket. He stretched it between his gloved hands and looked down at what he deemed to be another loose end that needed to be tied up.

He poised himself, enjoying the moment, the feeling of absolute power and control, which surged through him as he prepared to take Will's life. He licked his lips, and took a deep breath.

The microwave chimed to signal that it had finished blitzing Will's meal, and he opened his eyes. He only had a split second to register what was happening, as the hooded Donovan hooked the piano wire around Will's neck and pulled with all the effort he could muster.

The thin wire embedded itself into the soft flesh of Will's throat, and cut off his air supply. He kicked and squirmed, but Donovan was out of arms' reach. Will's vision began to fade, and with it, a strange peaceful euphoria swept over him as the edges of his vision dimmed. He looked up into the twisted face of the monster standing above him, and as his oxygen-starved brain finally shut down his organs, Will Jones realised that his life had come to an end. He stopped struggling, and Donovan smiled as he watched the last surviving member of the Jones family die.

Donovan released the pressure, and crouched beside Will, looking into his open eyes.

"I'm sorry I had to do that," he whispered as he folded the dead man's arms back into the confines of the seat.

"I had no choice. And I can't afford any loose ends."

He watched Will pleasantly and nodded as if listening.

"Thank you, I appreciate your understanding."

Donovan paused again, and then smiled warmly.

"No, thank you. It really means a lot to me that you support my efforts."

He stood and made to leave and then paused, and turned back towards the chair where Will's body lay.

"Say again, Mr Jones?"

He looked at the corpse and then nodded.

"Of course, I forgive you. And thanks for the reminder."

Donovan crossed back towards the chair and picked up the scrapbook. He flicked through it, and then tucked it under his arm.

"This could have caused a few problems with what I'm about to do. It has to look like an accident."

With his free hand, Donovan grabbed Will's dead one and shook it firmly.

"Thanks again Mr. Jones. You really have been more than helpful."

Donovan crossed the room and walked downstairs into the empty bar. He helped himself to a double shot of brandy, and stood looking out into the empty landscape of tables and chairs. Outside, it was almost full dark, and Donovan saw that it had begun to snow. He had always liked the snow. He finished the brandy, enjoying the warmth as it coursed through his body, and slipped the empty glass into his pocket.

Some would have just left it there on the bar, but he wasn't stupid enough to leave a huge slab of his DNA for anyone to find. He would dispose of the glass later. Right now, he had one more task to complete. He let himself out of the pub, making sure he was unobserved, and closed the door gently behind him. The snow had already left a light dusting on the ground, but he thought that it was heavy enough that it would soon mask his footprints.

He walked towards his car, which was parked some distance away. As always, he was thorough, and had taken every precaution. There were just two more loose ends to tie up, and then he could turn in for the night.

'It was a dirty job,' he thought as he walked down the street, whistling tunelessly.

But somebody had to do it.

# 39. WORDS WITH THE DEAD

STEVE AND MELODY SHARED an excited glance across the table, then turned their attention back to the planchette.

"Do you mean to harm us?" Steve asked.

They watched as the pointer slid to the word '*no*'.

Melody couldn't help but grin. "What is it that you want?" she asked, and they watched as the pointer spelled out a single word that turned their brief feeling of relief into abject horror.

*Baby!*

Melody instantly removed her hand from the pointer and stared at the old wooden board. Steve felt a wave of nausea sweep over him, and thought for a horrifying moment that he was actually going to be sick. His heart raced as the pointer moved back to the centre.

"This is our house now. You are not welcome," he tried to say confidently, but suspected that he wasn't fooling anyone. They waited for the pointer to move, but it stayed where it was.

"Did you hear me? I said you aren't welcome here," he repeated, this time managing to sound at least a little less afraid. Still, the pointer remained motionless.

"Melody, help me out here."

She shook her head. "No—you promised you would stop if it got weird."

"We need to see this through, we need to let these things know that we aren't afraid of them."

"I *am* afraid of them," she said softly.

Steve was about to speak, when the pointer started to move. It spelled a single word.

*Out!*

"Steve, I want you to stop!" She looked pleadingly at him, but she recognised the look in his eye; it was that same mixture of anger and defiance that she'd seen on only a few occasions, and she knew that even though she was pleading, he wouldn't stop until he had a resolution of some kind.

"Steve, please," she said again, and was dismayed to see him flash a confident grin.

"No. This is our house," he said defiantly. "These things aren't welcome here. Do you hear me? You aren't welcome here."

The pointer moved and spelled the word *'out'* once more. The atmosphere was charged and heavy. Melody couldn't shake the feeling of gross intrusion; she felt as if she were being leered at, as if some oozing, oily thing was looking over her shoulder. She hugged herself tightly as Steve continued to communicate with the spirits.

"I don't care what you did to the other people who lived here before us, but we won't be bullied out of our own home. Do you understand? You aren't welcome here."

He took his hand off the planchette, and saw that it still continued to spell the same word in continuous motions.

"Steve..."

"Hang on Mel, let's finish this."

He grabbed the notepad and pen, and quickly began to write.

*Spirits of Hope House.*
*We will not be terrorised by you.*
*You will not harm us or interact with us.*
*We are not afraid of you.*
*You are not welcome here.*

He folded the paper, and grabbed the lighter.

"Mel, are you ready?"

She nodded and watched as the planchette continued to move of its own accord. He flicked the lighter into life, and touched the flame to the paper. The edge blackened and then was greedily devoured by the flame. Steve set the paper into the bowl and watched as it began to burn.

"You are banished from this house," he said loudly and confidently, "you are no longer welcome. You will no longer harm us. You are not welcome here."

No sooner had the words left his mouth, than the planchette launched itself off the table and across the room, slamming into the refrigerator door hard enough to leave a small nick in the door. It was as if a switch had been flicked, and the suddenly heavy atmosphere seemed to melt away.

"Is that it? Is it over?" Melody asked. She was shaking, and Steve couldn't blame her, as his own hand trembled in sympathy.

"I... I think we did it."

"How can you be sure?"

"I'm not, but... it just feels different in here suddenly. Or is it just my imagination?"

"No," Melody agreed, visibly relaxing. "I sense it too, it's a lot less... heavy in here. Do you think it's over?"

Steve considered for a moment. He listened to the house, trying to gauge any sense of the oppressive atmosphere that had plagued the property of late, but found nothing. "I think it is," he said simply, flashing a relieved grin.

He reached over the table to grab her hands, intending to offer some reassurance, when she stood and came to him, hugging him tightly around the neck. It was such a simple gesture, and one that he realised had been sadly absent from their relationship for quite some time. He pulled her away, and looked at her, reminding himself just how lucky he was to have her.

"I'm sorry that we had to go through all this," he said softly. "I know it was your dream."

"It still is, let's not let this ruin things for us."

"Agreed. At least after this, we know that nothing can come between us that we can't overcome."

She kissed him hard, and he realised that it was something that had been missing from their relationship for almost the entire duration of the time they'd been here.

"Wow, that was unexpected," he said with a grin as she came up for air. She smiled broadly back at him, and he tried to kiss her but she pushed him away.

"That's all for now," she teased. "First I want you to throw that damn Ouija board out."

"I'd be happy to. How about we have a bite to eat and then get an early night?"

She couldn't help but laugh at the goofy way that he stood there with his eyebrows arched, and the pair burst into laughter.

"Maybe," she said playfully, "depends what you go ahead and cook me for dinner."

"Ah, I know just the thing madam," he replied in a bad, mock-French accent.

He opened the door, and grabbed the Ouija board off the table. "Damn, have you seen this snow? Pass me the thingy would you?" he said, pointing to the planchette on the floor by the fridge.

Melody did as he asked and then stood and watched as he went out to the waste bin, and dumped both inside. Her breath plumed in the frigid air, and she noted that already the ground was covered in a hefty dusting of the white stuff. Steve came back inside, brushing the snowflakes from his hair.

"Cold out there!" he said as he closed the door.

"It looks like we could be in for a bad one. I hope we don't get snowed in," Melody said, giving the skies a concerned glance.

"Nahh, the tree cover over the road should keep it mostly clear. Worst case we'll have to dig the car out before we go into town."

"We?" she said, looking at him in mock surprise.

"Sorry, my mistake. You will have to dig the car out before we go..."

She slapped him lightly on the arm, and the two embraced, him behind with his arms around her waist and on her stomach. They watched the snow fall, and Steve kissed her on the top of the head.

"Despite everything that's happened," he said softly. "I can't wait to be a father."

Melody didn't reply. Instead, she smiled and felt as if finally, after what felt like an age of panic and stress, that she could relax.

"Come on," she said, pulling free. Let's make dinner, then have that early night you mentioned."

# 40. DONOVAN'S PATIENCE

DONOVAN WAS PERCHED IN the same tree as before, watching Hope House through his binoculars. The snowfall was heavy, and had a beautiful blue hue under the cover of darkness. The cold, however, didn't touch him. He was only concerned with tying up the last of his loose ends.

He'd been watching Hope House for the last five hours. He'd barely moved, and was covered in a light dusting of snow. He worried that the combination of snow and nightfall would hinder his observations, but the golden light from inside the house made viewing easy, and he could track their movements well enough through the windows. They'd just finished eating, and were now washing the dishes together.

He looked at them, so happy and content with their lives, and felt that simmering rage begin to grow inside him. People like the Samsons sickened him. How could people live with so much devotion to another human being? Although his own life had been one of abject misery, he at least knew enough to know that he would never be able to engage in what would be termed a '*normal*' relationship. It would take too much time and effort to keep control of his moments of blind rage at the stupidity of humanity as a whole.

He wondered if it was solely him that saw the world for what it truly was—a cruel, cold place, filled with selfish beasts doing everything they could to make their existence seem even a little bit important.

Still— he thought while adjusting his position and wiping the snow from the binocular lenses— at least it made it easier for him to do what he intended.

He thought of himself as a superhero: by day a mild mannered letting and sales agent, by night, he was Donovan, top of the food chain, a peerless predator who was so intelligent that he could do what no other could. He could get away with murder. He could hide unseen in the shadows, meticulously planning his next move. He did as he pleased, and let nothing stand in his way.

Until recently, he used to think he wanted what everyone else appeared to have, but now understood that everyone else was wrong, and he was right. Like any full-blooded man, he had urges, but if he wanted the warmth of a woman, there were plenty of places where he could pay for the privilege. And if they didn't like the violent way he liked to do it, then he would make sure they disappeared. It was easy with whores. Nobody ever missed them. Even the inconvenience of disposing of them was better than engaging in the kind of sham that he was looking at right now.

*What is love?*

It was a question that had been asked through the ages, and even though man had struggled to find it, he knew the answer. Love was bullshit. Love was lies. Love was a sham.

He'd often fantasised about explaining it, picturing himself on a podium speaking to a worldwide audience, telling them how they had it wrong, and that his way of living was a much more enjoyable way in keeping with every other species in the animal kingdom.

It dawned on him, as he sat perched there in the tree, that he could actually be some kind of god. Perhaps he had transcended normal mortality to become some kind of unstoppable force of nature. He liked that idea, and smiled to himself as he checked his watch, and saw that it was almost ten o'clock. If they followed routine, it wouldn't be long now before they turned in for the night, and he could at last begin.

He had initially decided to kill the husband first, then he'd remembered the needless assault that had been made on him, and decided that he deserved to suffer. He would disable him, perhaps cut his hamstrings and tie him to a chair so that he could watch as he finished the business that he'd started with the wife just a few days before. He smiled at the thought.

No sir. He wouldn't be paying for the privilege tonight, and would be able to get as violent as he wanted.

After he had finished with the wife in every way that he could think of, he would make sure the husband was done slowly. It dawned on him then that he wouldn't have to rush. For once he would be able to take his time and really savour the moment.

His attention was drawn back to the house, and as he watched, the lights were switched off, first downstairs and then a little later in the upstairs bedroom. He couldn't help but smile as the adrenaline surged through him. He wanted to get straight to it, but understood that he had to be patient. He had to give them time to sleep. And that was fine, because it was a beautiful night, and the waiting would only serve to increase the anticipation of what was to come.

*He waited*

An hour passed and he barely even noticed. He was going through the plan in his mind, meticulously going over each step whilst coaxing the rage to the surface. He would approach the front door and quietly let himself in, remembering that the door started to creak when it was pushed two-thirds of the way open. He had that covered though. A small can of motor oil that he'd found in the dead bartender's home would suffice to lubricate the hinges enough to kill the noise.

Donovan marvelled at his own sublime genius, and was convinced more than ever that he truly was the greatest specimen of humanity that had ever lived. He felt for the weight of the protective cross given to him by his mother, and felt immortal. Not even the dead could harm him now.

He stretched, opening and closing his hands, trying to get the blood flowing again. It wouldn't be long now, and his anticipation grew. Soon enough, he would be able to remove the last threat to his own safety, and go back to his unassuming double life. The wind picked up around him, a furious, blustery gale that shook loose snow from the branches. They swayed in unison, and although Donovan was too preoccupied to hear it, it sounded like a furious roar.

# 41. WHAT IS REAL?

THEY WERE LOST IN sleep. Melody's was dreamless and deep, her face relaxed and stress-free, while Steve's were plagued with nightmares. He tossed and turned and kicked at the covers. Despite the cold outside, he was covered in a light sweat as his face contorted with the toil of his terrible visions.

He was dreaming of the circle in the woods. He stood in it alone, his hands and feet restrained by thick black tree roots curling out of the ground. He was aware of the biting cold attacking his skin, and the feeling of hundreds of pairs of unseen eyes glaring at him. There was a man before him, dark-skinned and muscular, wearing animal skins, his lean body daubed with streaks of white paint. His face was adorned with a painted skull, his eyes glowering with a ferocity that frightened him.

The man approached, and although Steve heard the man's voice, his mouth didn't move: instead it seemed to come from all around him, from the trees and earth themselves.

"You know who I am?" the man asked in his head.

Steve didn't know how, but he did. Something told him exactly who this man was and how dangerous the situation, and was about to say it when the man nodded.

"I am of the Gogoku," came the broken, whispered voices from the trees. "These lands are ours."

Steve winced away as the man leaned close. The raging winds slammed into him, impossibly appearing to emanate from the Elder. The Gogoku man smiled, and Steve saw that his teeth were filed into sharp points.

"These lands are cursed. These lands are ours."

Steve flinched at the man's words, unable to help feeling deathly afraid despite this being a dream, albeit vivid and realistic.

"We didn't know, nobody told us!" Steve shouted, his voice barely audible above the fury of the elements.

The Gogoku Elder smiled, and even though his lips remained closed, Steve heard his every word.

"You live on the land that was cursed, and cursed you shall become."

Steve shook his head, and struggled to free himself. "We didn't know, it's not our fault!"

"You must feed the earth with blood, as did those who came before."

"Go ahead," Steve said, "hurt me if you want to."

The Gogoku Elder flashed his sharp smile, and Steve heard the words he feared enter his head.

"We demand the blood of the unborn child. And to us it comes."

With that, Steve found himself back in the bedroom, the journey from the circle happening instantaneously. He was hovering near the ceiling, looking down on himself and Melody. As he watched, she climbed out of bed, her motions slow and robotic. He knew that even though he was dreaming, this was happening in the real world. He screamed at her to wake up, but knew that it was pointless, as he was only there as an observer.

As was the way with dreams, he was transported back to his restraints in the circle. The Gogoku Elder looked at him, and laughed.

\*\*\*

As Steve tossed and turned in the throes of his nightmare, Melody opened her eyes. She climbed out of bed and walked towards the bedroom door. It swung open of its own accord, allowing her to exit and move down the hallway. She was sleepwalking and heading downstairs, her subconscious mind steering her around the darkness of the house.

She walked to the kitchen, and pulled the large butchers' knife from the wooden block by the sink. With it in hand, she went to the kitchen door, which unlocked itself and opened. Icy wind and snow billowed in, blowing the oversized T- shirt that she slept in around her legs. She was oblivious to the cold as she trudged through the ankle deep snow to the bottom of the garden. Behind her, the door closed.

Seconds later, Donovan silently unlocked the front entrance, and edged his way into the house. He paused to allow his eyes to adjust to the gloom, and for the initial surge of adrenaline to pass. He took a moment to dry the soles of his boots on the towel he'd brought with him, another example of him leaving nothing to chance.

Some might not bother, but to Donovan, squelching around a dark house in wet footwear was asking for one of two things. To either be caught, or to fall and have a nasty accident. With his feet dry, he stuffed the rag back into his jeans pocket, and tested his step on the wooden floor. He was pleased. His footfalls were silent, and would go unheard.

He walked to the foot of the stairs, and peered up into the darkness, barely able to contain the excitement of what he was about to do. Slowly, remembering which floorboards were likely to make a noise when stepped on, he made his way upstairs in silence.

# 42. SURVIVAL

STILL LOCKED IN HIS dream, Steve fought to free himself. The Gogoku Elder smiled, appearing to revel in his struggles. As Steve looked around, more of the Gogoku were coming out of the trees, but unlike the Elder, they were blackened, burned things, shuffling from their hiding places in the woods. They formed a circle around the perimeter of the clearing. As Steve watched in sick fascination and whilst struggling get free, Melody entered the circle, and when he saw what she was carrying, it took the fight out of him.

She had a baby in her arms. Steve watched as she stepped to the centre of the circle and stood beside the Elder. Steve was screaming and pleading with her to run, but she paid him no attention. The Gogoku tribesman stroked the baby's tuft of back hair, and then with his free hand unsheathed a long curved knife with a serrated blade.

"Please... don't!" Steve whispered.

The Gogoku looked him in the eye and smiled, then reared back, and brought the blade crashing down towards Melody and the baby.

He awoke with a start, a pained yelp escaping from his lips before he could cut it off. He was disorientated, and for a few seconds wasn't exactly sure which part was dream, and which was reality. It was just as he had begun to calm himself that he realised Melody was no longer beside him. His stomach rolled, and he sat upright.

"Mel?" he called out, even though he knew she was gone. And he had a fair idea where she was. He quickly got out of bed, opened the bedroom door and stepped out. He was about to call Melody's name again when he registered a flash of movement out of the corner of his eye. It was only his reactions—perhaps fuelled by the adrenaline that surged through him—that allowed him to jerk away from the blade, which cut into the air where his skull had been seconds before.

He only had another split second to realise that it was Donovan who had attacked him. The knife—no more than a flash of silver in the darkness—darted towards him again, this time aimed at his throat. He stumbled backwards, and for a moment was sure that he was going to go over, but somehow managed to steady himself. There was no time to recover, as Donovan was right there.

He took two quick strides forward and slashed at Steve, this time making contact, the blade cutting deeply into his forearm. The pain brought his mind into focus, and he narrowly avoided another lunge aimed at his throat.

Questions as to the how and why of Donovan's presence in his home was quickly rendered as secondary to the idea that his own life was in mortal danger, because as he looked into Donovan's eyes in the shadowy half-light of the hallway, he saw a remorseless and aggressive beast devoid of any sense of humanity. They stood in stalemate; Donovan was swaying from side to side, and Steve was reminded of a cobra.

"You ruined how it was supposed to be!" Donovan hissed, as he flashed a waxy grin. "Mrs. Samson!" he said loudly." Why don't you come out and join us?"

In the confusion, Steve had completely forgotten about Melody, and was aware more than ever that every second wasted was vital if he were to save her.

"You're going down for this, I'll make sure of that," Steve said, hoping that he would be able to intimidate Donovan, but it quickly dawned on him that the game had changed.

The man in front of him was a million miles away from the birdlike and slightly annoying idiot who'd first shown them around Hope House. This Donovan was a monster.

"This isn't my first rodeo, Mr. Samson. Just ask my mother." As he said it, he let out a short, sharp cackle that frightened Steve more than the idea of the knife-wielding man himself.

Time seemed to slow, and all Steve could think about was Melody and where she might be.

"You tell that slut wife of yours to come out here and join us, or I'll cut you and then hunt her down anyway."

There was a chilling calmness to the way he said it. It was as if the two were in idle conversation about the weather. Steve knew he had to go for broke, and try to bluff his way out of the situation.

"She's not here. She heard you break in and has gone to call the police."

Donovan frowned, and then grinned in the murky half-light. "No she didn't. I've been in the house for a while now, and nobody's downstairs, which means she's up here somewhere. Tell me where she is, and I'll make it quick."

"I've already told you, she's not here!"

The terror in his voice was convincing, as he truly didn't know for sure where his wife was, although the sick and horrifying idea where she could be still lingered in his mind. Donovan grinned, and seemed to be enjoying the situation immensely.

"Don't screw with me. You have no idea what I'm capable of. Tell me where she is, or I swear I'll gut you and feed you your own innards."

Again, the words had been said with a cool, calm

indifference, and Steve believed every word. It was as if there was some twisted beast that had inherited the harmless man that Donovan used to be.

"I'll die before I let you hurt her."

"Yes, you will," Donovan agreed, and lunged towards Steve with the knife.

Without thinking, he grabbed Donovan's wrist, and they were locked in stalemate. However, Donovan was stronger than he looked, and forced Steve backwards down the hallway. He was slammed spine first into the bathroom door frame, and the air was driven out of him. He relaxed his grip, and in that split second, Donovan pulled his arm free and stabbed the knife at Steve's stomach.

He half-twisted away, but the blade caught him in the abdomen, slicing through skin with ease. Trying to ignore the pain, he shoved Donovan towards the steps, hoping to push his attacker down them, but at the last second Steve felt himself swung around, and before he could halt his backward momentum, felt his foot slip off the top step and gravity take over.

Instinctively, he held on to Donovan as he fell, pulling the psychotic intruder with him. The pair fell together, crashing and rolling as they tumbled down the steps. They landed hard at the bottom, Steve banging his head on the floor as they both came to rest. Steve attempted to lift his head, but nausea swept over him, and his vision began to dim at the edges. He was vaguely aware of Donovan clambering to his feet and picking up the knife. He was smiling.

# 43. ALIVE DEAD, DEAD ALIVE

MELODY MADE HER WAY through the snow, the uneven ground and freezing temperatures failing to wake her from her trance. She had passed over the water, and was now heading towards the circular clearing.

The wind raged, and the trees shook violently, pushing her onwards and guiding her to her destination. She entered the clearing and came to a halt in its centre, standing motionless, the knife at her side.

He appeared like a thin mist rolling out of the trees. As he formed, some deep part of her subconscious snapped awake, making her aware of everything and that she was in danger, yet also powerless to do anything other than observe. Her body was no longer hers to control.

The Gogoku Elder who'd appeared to the dreaming Steve stood before her. He took the knife from her and tossed it aside.

"No," he said directly into her mind, "not this way."

She nodded absently and waited.

"Let me show you," the Elder said. "Let me show you what you have done."

They came from the trees. At first they were nothing but vague mists, formless tendrils that snaked across the ground. She would have done anything to be able to turn her head away, but her body forced her to look on as they formed into the shades of the dead.

She was so preconditioned to the notion of ghosts being floating, transparent things, that it took her a moment to accept them for what they were: they appeared as solid and real as she herself was, and although she was desperate to scream and run, she was frozen—a confused prisoner in her own body. The Gogoku smiled at her, but it was humourless.

"Look upon the dead. Why do you not heed our warnings?"

"We didn't know," she said—or at least she thought she did. It was then that she realised that the conversation was taking place entirely in her head. In reality, both she and the Gogoku were silent.

"You were warned. And now you will pay with the life of the unborn."

Panic swept through her which only served to highlight her absolute helplessness and frustration.

"I need to wake up! Please let me wake up."

The Gogoku smiled, the voice in her head now just a sinister whisper.

"This is no dream."

"Just leave us alone!" she pleaded.

"Give us what grows inside you."

"Please!" she screamed in her head, even as her physical body stared into the darkness.

"Give us what grows inside you," repeated the Gogoku, and the other spirits of the dead began to repeat the mantra as they moved closer towards her.

"I won't let you hurt my baby," she roared, and in her mind's eye hugged her own stomach protectively.

"You have no choice. We are in control."

"I won't do it!" she sobbed, but the Gogoku tribesman only grinned.

"We shall see."

She was walking, and even though she fought against it, her body wasn't hers to control. The sensation was strange. She could feel the icy bite of the snow and dirt under her feet, and the sharp numbness on her skin from the cold, but it was distant, as if she were observing someone else.

The sensations of her detached body made her feel helpless and violated as she was forced towards the outer edge of the circle. She recognised the path, and knew where it led.

She had gone way beyond afraid. Her terror had risen to an all-new heights, and she struggled to break the bonds with whatever it was that governed her, but like a puppet attached to the strings of a puppeteer, the Gogoku tribesman led her out of the circle and towards the huge old hanging tree. She screamed inwardly again, begging to be set free. The blustering winds buffeted her ears, and she could clearly hear the voices of the dead as they laughed and willed her on.

\*\*\*

Consciousness came back to him slowly, and he was immediately aware of the thick throbbing in his head. He made as if to hold the suddenly heavy appendage in his hands, but found that they were bound in front of him with duct tape.

He looked up, the kitchen lights burning into his brain and bringing with it another wave of nausea and dizziness. He was pretty sure he was concussed.

Donovan was leaning on the kitchen counter, absently chewing on the tip of the knife.

"Rise and shine," he said warmly as Steve's head fell back to his chest. It was hard to hold upright, but in the brief glimpse he'd had of his assailant, he was dismayed to see that he looked completely unharmed.

"Melody..." Steve murmured.

Donovan continued to watch and chew on the tip of the knife blade.

"Funny you should mention her, Mr. Samson, or

can I call you Steve?"

He didn't respond, and instead concentrated on clearing the thick soup of confusion that clouded his mind. Donovan went on anyway, enjoying the moment.

"I think we're beyond formalities by now aren't we Steve? I think you and I are friends now aren't we?"

*Ignore him. Don't answer.*

And although the advice was sound, he didn't think he could, even if he'd wanted to. He attempted to focus on his feet, attempting to piece together what happened since the fall down the stairs. As best he could tell he was sitting on one of the kitchen table chairs, and it didn't take a genius to work out that Donovan had brought him in here and tied him to it, waiting patiently until he awoke to administer whatever kind of punishment he had in mind.

*Just focus on something. Anything.*

He did. He stared at his big toe, trying to make the three that he could see become one. As he focused, Donovan continued to goad him.

"But it seems you and I have the same question that we want answered. Where oh where is your lovely, sweet wife?"

Steve felt rage welling up inside him, and forced himself to push it aside and concentrate on his toe, to bring it into focus. Donovan crouched in front of Steve and lifted his head. Now instead of his toe, he could only see Donovan's crazy-eyed gaze.

"Let me tell you Steve. I really did try with you. But I always knew you had a problem with me. I tried to build some rapport with you. Remember, back when I first showed you this place?"

He did remember. He remembered Donovan in his tatty suit and ridiculous glasses, leering at Melody's chest, and he remembered thinking that, although an irritation, Donovan was harmless. But how wrong he'd been, because it seemed that when all of those external layers were peeled back, the Donovan underneath was a cold, brutal monster.

*He went on*

"I knew then you know, I knew that you would be trouble. You with your arrogance thinking you were better than me, and that bitch leading me on with her tight clothes and her flirting."

He leaned close and whispered in Steve's ear. "I think she will enjoy it when I fuck her."

Steve tried to lunge, but Donovan pushed him back down into his seat by the shoulder.

"No. You're staying here. Please don't make this difficult. Whatever happens, you are going to die here tonight. The only question is how quickly and how much it hurts. Now tell me where your wife is."

Steve looked Donovan in the eye, and smiled himself.

"Fuck off," he grunted, hoping that Donovan would get angry, but he didn't. He simply walked around Steve and stood behind him.

"I admire your strength. I admire you as a person in a way. I think under other circumstances, we could have been great friends. Don't you agree?"

Donovan sounded so pathetic and hopeful, that for a split second, Steve almost felt sorry for him.

"Why are you doing this?" Steve slurred, wondering just how hard he'd hit his head to feel so groggy.

Donovan began to laugh, and walked back in front of Steve so that he could at least see him.

"Oh, I suppose this is the part where you expect the long movie-style explanation of what made me a monster? If so, then you'll be disappointed. What you have to understand is that sometimes, things just happen. Sometimes people are born who are of superior intellect and who aren't afraid to take what they want. You ask why? I say there is no why. Some things just are."

Steve found that he could half understand where Donovan was coming from, and even though he was an egotistical lunatic, he at least seemed to be able to justify his actions.

"Why can't you just leave us alone?" Steve said, his voice a little less slurred and the cobwebs just a little bit clearer.

"If it was up to me, I would," said Donovan apologetically, "but there's more to this than the two of you, I'm afraid. I... well let's just say that there are a lot of skeletons in a lot of closets that I don't want found. And as I told my mother, I can't afford any loose ends."

It dawned on Steve just how pointless that fighting was. Melody wasn't in the house, and if she had, in fact, headed outside to the circle, then ghosts or not, she was probably dead or on the way, and even though he didn't want to admit it, he too was probably about to die. He looked Donovan straight in the face and spoke as clearly as he could.

"Enough talk. Just do it already. Make it quick."

"I would Steve, I really would, but you know how it is, there are two loose ends to tie up not just one."

He had partially reverted to the sleazy salesman Donovan, although the wide grin took on a different tone with the wild way in which he was glaring.

"I suppose," he went on, "I could do you here and now and wait for her to show. But something tells me you really don't know where she is."

"So do it, then," Steve grunted, "Do it fast and get it over with."

Donovan grinned then, and as scared as Steve

was, the expression took him to new heights of fear.

"Oh no. I'm going to take my time with you. I want you to experience every last cut, every moment of sweet agony."

Donovan began to approach, and Steve knew it was coming. He hoped it wouldn't be bad, that it would go numb eventually and he could drift away, but something told him Donovan meant every word, and intended for him to suffer. He had never thought about death before, but now that it was close he couldn't help but think about all the things he had never done, all of those things he had put off for another day. His eyes drifted to the knife, then to Donovan and then...

*There was a man.*

At first, Steve thought he was suffering from his suspected concussion, especially as it seemed that Donovan couldn't see him, even though the figure was right next to him. He looked to be some kind of slave. He was thin and clad in rags, his skin such a dark shade of brown that it seemed to have an almost purple sheen.

Steve looked at him and although the man didn't speak, a name popped up into his head.

*Isaac.*

"Spirit..." Steve mumbled, still not fully in control of his faculties. Donovan only widened his grin.

"Oh, let's not even go there. I know all about the things that haunt this house. Don't worry about me though, I'm protected."

He reached into the large front pocket of his hoodie, and pulled out the wooden crucifix and showed it to Steve like some hard-won trophy. Steve was barely listening. He was too busy concentrating on the man or spirit or whatever it was glaring at Donovan.

"No!" said the apparition, this time out loud instead of in Steve's head. Donovan flicked his head towards him, and this time saw him, as he recoiled and held out the knife.

"Stay back!" he blurted, waving the knife. "You can't hurt me—I'm protected!"

Steve couldn't help but be amazed at the transformation. Donovan flipped from a confident, remorseless killer into a frightened, wide-eyed and uncertain man.

"Your weapon can't hurt me."

The spirit said it calmly, speaking to Steve's would-be murderer as if chastising a child. If he'd heard him, Donovan didn't show it. Instead, he glared and waved the knife.

"Maybe not against you,'" sneered Donovan "but it will against him!"

Steve saw it coming, and tried to recoil, but was unable to move as Donovan took two quick steps towards him and drove the knife all the way to the hilt into Steve's chest.

Michael Bray

# 44. POSSESSION

MELODY STOOD AT THE base of the massive, ugly tree that had housed the protective crucifix. It looked sinister enough during the day when she'd last seen it, but now deep in the shadow with snow at its base, it looked positively terrifying. She could sense the Gogoku and the other spirits behind her, watching and waiting for her to die.

"This is our sacrificial tree," the voice of the Elder said inside her mind. "Climb it and offer yourself to us. Give us the thing that grows inside you."

Melody was crying, on the inside at least. Outwardly, she wore a blank expression of indifference. She tried to regain control of her body and force herself to mentally break the bond with the Gogoku, but she couldn't physically do it. It was impossible, as if there was a barrier between her consciousness and her own volition.

The voices of the Gogoku came to her again, their tone venomous and malign. It was a chant, which soon became a deafening symphony.

*"We are the wood and the trees, and the blood-soaked earth.*

*"We are the things that live in the dark, all seeing but unseen."*

"Please, don't..."

She was unheard or ignored, and still the chant went on.

*"We are the wood and the trees, and the blood-soaked earth.*

*"We are the things that live in the dark, all seeing but unseen.*

*"We are the wood and the trees, and the blood-soaked earth.*

*"We are the things that live in the dark, all seeing but unseen.*

*"We are the wood and the trees, and the blood-soaked earth.*

*"We are the things that live in the dark, all seeing but unseen."*

She wanted to scream, or cover her ears, anything to avoid having to hear those awful words, growing louder and more intense with each passing. But instead, her stubborn out of control body reached out to the tree and ran its fingers across the rough, cold bark.

She willed her body to stop, to listen to her, but the battle of wills was one that she couldn't win, and even though she did everything to stop it, she started to climb. The chant was with her as she ascended, mingling now with the sound of leaves as they rustled and swayed in the wind.

It was a cauldron of noise, a terrifying wall of malevolence that, for a split second, made her want to climb higher if only to get away from the terrifying mantras. But when she realised where she was going, and what the likely outcome would be, terror found her again. She was about to die, and wondered why Steve wasn't there to help her.

\*\*\*

*It doesn't hurt!*

That was Steve's first thought as he stared at the handle poking out of his chest. Donovan was just inches away, his face twisted into his maniacal grimace. As if he hadn't already done enough, he pushed the blade in deeper, but even as he did, Steve found it remarkable that he felt nothing. No pain, and certainly no white light, which in his book could only be a good thing.

He looked at Donovan with genuine bewilderment, and it seemed that Donovan was just as confused, as his twisted expression melted into one of equal confusion. He stood and pulled the knife free, and Steve immediately saw the blood well up—actually no he didn't.

His mind expected to see his life's fluid leaking out, and for a second he had, but as he looked now at the white t-shirt covering his chest there was not only no sign of blood, but no wound either. Now it was Donovan's turn to look at Steve as if he were some kind of monster.

"I don't understand...!" he mumbled as he looked at the knife in his hand.

Steve could sympathise. He didn't much understand either.

"He can't hurt you no more," Isaac said in his deep drawl.

Steve and Donovan both looked to the spirit of Isaac, who looked at Steve with kind eyes.

"I don't understand...!" Steve said, echoing Donovan.

Although he didn't say anything himself, it seemed that his attacker was still in agreement.

"He be one of us now. A part of this place."

Isaac looked towards Donovan, and offered a pleasant smile.

"No!" Donovan said, shaking his head. "I'm protected!"

He held the cross towards Isaac, who seemed unconcerned.

"Sometimes, it takes moah than words..." he said simply, and stepped aside.

Donovan's body lay in the hallway at the foot of the steps, his dead eyes gazing straight ahead. Blood pooled on the wooden floor around him, and Steve could see the bulge of the wooden crucifix where it had wedged itself into his stomach as he had fallen, Donovan's previously grey hoodie now a deep maroon in colour.

Steve looked at Donovan, and then back to his body.

"This isn't right... I'm okay!" Donovan blurted, and he looked down at his own dead body and then at Isaac.

"Steve, help me out here!" Donovan pleaded.

But Steve didn't think there was any help for Donovan. Not now, because Donovan was dead, killed as the two of them had fallen down the steps. He just didn't seem to know it yet. Now, like the ones gone before him, he would be bound to Hope House forever.

He turned his attention back to Isaac as Donovan stared at his own corpse and struggled to come to terms with what had happened.

"How did I get here, who tied me to this chair?"

Isaac smiled patiently.

"This place, it plays tricks with yo' head as well as yo' eyes. You ain't any moah tied up than this one is still livin'.'"

"But..."

"...Just look, mistah. Look and see what's real."

Steve looked at his hands and saw that Isaac was right. They *were* unbound. He stood and was now completely unconcerned with Donovan. He looked at Isaac instead.

"Melody...?"

"Go to the place across the rivuh. You may still have time. Give them what they desire moah than their thirst for blood."

"I don't understand... I..."

"Hurry mistah, you don't have much time befoah it's too late."

He gave a quick glance towards Donovan, and then pulled on his boots, opened the door and sprinted towards the woods.

Whisper

## 45. SACRIFICE

SHE HAD CLIMBED TO the long, thick branch from her dreams, and now clung to the tree trunk as the wind tried to pull her away and send her crashing to the ground twenty-five feet below.

Although she couldn't really connect to her physical body, Melody was mentally exhausted. She had almost given up trying to push the Gogoku out of her mind, and on some level had accepted the inevitability of her impending death.

A particularly vicious gust of wind almost yanked her off the immense trunk, and had she been in control, she knew that there would be no way that she would ever have the courage to be able to move out away from the relative safety afforded by the tree. However, she was the slave of another, and with dismay felt herself begin to inch across the branch.

For now, it was thick and sturdy underfoot, but she could see it would soon begin to taper away. As if foreshadowing the thought, the wind rocked her and, for a split second, she was sure she would fall. In her mind, she tried to rectify her balance, and then realised that her body was reacting to someone else's commands in order to keep itself upright. She shouted out in frustration, and immediately felt the oozing smile of the Gogoku Elder.

The branch was starting to dip underfoot with each tentative step and that alone made her feel nauseous, a feeling which increased tenfold when she saw the thick rope tied to the branch and the noose at its end, swaying with the wind. Although she knew it was fruitless, she screamed anyway.

313

***

The cold bit at him, and sharp, unseen branches clawed at his skin, but did nothing to stop his progress. He had reached the edge of the water, and as much as he was desperate to get to the other side, vivid images of his near-drowning filled his head. Thoughts of his lungs filling with the cold, black waters flooded his mind, and fear of the burning sensation of needing to breathe as he took on the icy stream,rooted him to the spot.

He stood by the water's edge, staring into the opaque depths as they raced past him, and knew that he couldn't do it. He couldn't bring himself to step into the water and cross.

"Yes you can. Yo' have-tuh."

It was Isaac. Not in physical form, but deep inside his head. Even with the encouragement, he knew that he simply couldn't do it, and had to on some level applaud the supreme planning of the malign force wanted him to be kept away from Melody, because whatever had compelled him to throw himself into the waters before was always in a win-win situation.

If he had died, then he would be completely out of the equation. However, even now after surviving his ordeal, it still made no difference, because he was afraid—no, he was terrified to set foot anywhere near the stream. Even though it was just twenty feet or so to the opposite side, it may as well have been an ocean.

"I can't..." he repeated, and this time the response came with much more conviction.

"If not for you mistah, for your unbo'n chil'."

That triggered something, some spark transcending self-preservation. He launched into the water, stumbled and fell to his hands and knees. His head momentarily went under, and the sheer shock of the freezing liquid drove the air out of his body. But it seemed that for once, luck was on his side and he regained his footing.

Gasping against the fierce cold, he waded across the water and onto the other side. The wind roared around him and, even in his half-concussed, freezing state, he could sense the fury directed at him. He lowered his head, climbed out on the opposite bank and ran towards the place where he knew that Melody would be.

***

She was sitting on the branch, legs hanging over the edge. The ground looked impossibly far away from where she was perched, and it would have been enough to terrify her on its own, but she could see and feel the noose in her hands. There was an inevitability about what was about to happen as the spirits of the dead continued their remorseless chant.

*"We are the wood and the trees, and the blood-soaked earth.*

*"We are the things that live in the dark, all seeing but unseen.*

*"We are the wood and the trees, and the blood-soaked earth.*

*"We are the things that live in the dark, all seeing but unseen.*

*"We are the wood and the trees, and the blood-soaked earth.*

*"We are the things that live in the dark, all seeing but unseen."*

"Melody!"

The sense of relief was overwhelming at hearing Steve's voice. She could see him, breath pluming in the frigid air. In her head, she called back to him, but her body simply watched him and remained still, apart from her hands toying with the noose.

Steve couldn't see the Gogoku or the rest of the dead, but he could sense their presence. The feeling was that awful, skin crawling sensation of being watched that had been a part of their lives ever since they'd moved into Hope House.

"Stay there, I'm coming up!" he shouted, not liking the vacancy in her eyes, or the familiarity of the situation.

He made for the tree and was about to lay a hand on it when he felt a tremendous force slam into his shoulder, sending him crashing painfully to the ground. The voice was incredibly crisp in his head, and familiar as that of the Gogoku Elder.

"No!"

It was just a simple word. Delivered with such venom and aggression, but serving its purpose of delivering its message. Steve climbed to his feet, brushing snow from his arms.

"Leave us alone. You can take me instead!" he bellowed into the frigid night.

"Steve, no!"

He heard her.

It was a strange sensation. He along with Melody and the Gogoku appeared to be connected mentally by a telepathic bond that allowed them to communicate.

"It's okay," he said confidently, "I'd rather they sacrifice me than you."

The Gogoku chief began to laugh, and his next words were enough to horrify them both.

"We want what grows inside. We want what is owed to us."

"Take me instead."

Something happened then. Whatever bond he had been privy to was suddenly pulled away, and his thoughts were now his own and not shared by either the Gogoku or Melody.

"Please!" he shouted into the raging wind. "Let her go!"

The wind blasted into him, and even though he thought it could just be his overtired brain imagining things, he was sure he could hear the voices of the Gogoku laughing.

He glanced up at Melody, torn between what he knew he had to do, and what he wanted to do. She watched him from her vantage point as he looked at her, and then he stood and ran back the way he'd come. She called after him, but of course, it was no more than an idea of a scream. Her body was still not cooperating.

"It is time," the Gogoku said to her.

She fought, and for a moment, her hands wavered, and then dropped the noose. She was celebrating her small victory when without missing a beat; she balled her fist and slammed it into her own face. Pain engulfed her, and for a horrifying moment, she was sure that she was going to topple backwards off the branch and plummet to the ground, but somehow she managed to retain her balance. Despite the lack of control over her physical self, it appeared that pain still registered. With dismay, she saw that she had bought herself only seconds, and was powerless to stop herself from reaching out and begin to reel in the noose from where it hung below her.

\*\*\*

He knew exactly what he was looking for. He had sprinted to the house, and this time crossing the water was no more than another part of the journey. He threw open the back door to Hope House, ran across the room and stepped over Donovan's corpse, barely registering its presence as he rummaged through the storage cupboard under the staircase.

Donovan's spirit, or energy or whatever it had been, was gone, as had Isaac. He couldn't think about such things now as he had to work quickly. He found the can of gasoline tucked away at the back underneath a box of old mouldering curtains they hadn't unpacked yet. He hoped there would be enough, and was thrilled to discover as he grabbed it that it felt reassuringly full and heavy.

He opened the can with hands that wouldn't quite stop shaking, and began to splash the gasoline all over the walls and floor. He was sure that the old wood would ignite quickly, and the blaze would take hold easily despite the wintry conditions outside. He covered their possessions in the pungent liquid, things which had seemed so important before but now held no relevance. He was acutely aware that time was against him, so much so that for all he knew he was already too late. He couldn't accept that yet though, and concentrated all of his efforts on soaking every surface.

With the can empty, he looked for something to light it with, but had neither matches nor a lighter. He ran to the kitchen, and almost slid in the semi-dried blood that had come from Donovan's stomach on the way.

He ignited the hob, which came to life with a blue-flamed *whump*. There was a magazine on the kitchen table, one of Melody's glitzy fashion ones that he'd never quite understood her reasons for reading. He tore out a few pages and rolled them into a cylinder ready to be ignited.

He paused and walked to the back door and opened it, making sure that he had a quick escape route once he set the house ablaze. The fumes burned his nostrils, and he was grateful for the blast of cold air that blew in when he pulled the door open and wedged one of the dining room chairs in front of it. He hurried back to the hob and took a deep breath, then lit the paper.

It held the flame better than he could have hoped, blackened flakes of the pages drifting to the ground as he crouched by the start of the fuel trail. Steve touched the burning paper to the liquid, and it ignited quickly, the heat causing him to screw up his face as he watched the flame snake its way across the room, around Donovan's body (he couldn't bring himself to pour the fuel over him) and into the sitting room.

The flames greedily devoured the old, dry wood and attacked the furnishings, and it was immediately obvious that it would easily take hold. Satisfied, he hurried to the door just in time to see the chair slide across the kitchen floor of its own accord and the door slam closed. He grabbed the handle and tried to open it, but it wouldn't budge. It was as if some unseen but powerful force was holding onto it from the other side.

*Panic!*

He turned to go towards the front before the fire got too out of control, and saw two things, which finally broke him and made him scream outright. The first was the fire, which had already become a raging inferno, making the option of escape completely impossible. That was secondary to the sight of Donovan, who was now standing and blocking his exit route, the cross still hanging at a nauseating angle from his bloody stomach.

Donovan's dead man's stare was unchanged, but

his crazy salesman's grin now more red than white.

He spoke, and the sound was an awful, grinding sound. It reminded him of the way his father had first spoken after his stroke, wet and slurred and barely comprehensible. However, even if the words were unclear, the rhythm was familiar, painfully so.

*"We are the wood and the trees, and the blood-soaked earth.*

*"We are the things that live in the dark, all seeing but unseen.*

*"We are the wood and the trees, and the blood-soaked earth.*

*"We are the things that live in the dark, all seeing but unseen.*

*"We are the wood and the trees, and the blood-soaked earth.*

*"We are the things that live in the dark, all seeing but unseen."*

The figure in his way looked like Donovan, but possessed the voice of the Gogoku. Steve was trapped.

\*\*\*

Back at the tree, the rhythmic drone of the chanting enveloped Melody, but that was the least of her concerns as she placed the noose around her own neck and pulled it taut. She had gone beyond frightened, and was now withdrawn and lost within herself. All the fight had gone out of her when Steve had left her alone. But alone wasn't the right word, because *he* was still there. He was the one who was pulling the strings.

"Come to us now, and give us what grows inside..." she heard his voice, coming from under the wind's breath.

She wondered if it would hurt or if it would be just a short, stomach-churning fall followed by blessed darkness and peace. After everything that had happened, she was looking forward to some rest. The Gogoku seemed to have read her entire thought process, and she felt his smile.

"Come! It is time."

She shuffled to the edge of the branch, made sure the noose was tight around her neck, and the chanting fell silent. All eyes were on the Gogoku Elder, awaiting his command to proceed.

\*\*\*

Back at the house, Steve glared at Donovan, and was surprised to find that he had reached a place that went beyond fear. He had heard about soldiers who had spoken of the same thing, where in certain situations a person could somehow become detached from emotion and do whatever was necessary to survive. It was anger that came to him, and the sight of Donovan's reanimated corpse only served to inflate it, and make it boil to the surface. Already the heat of the flames was almost unbearable, and a thick black smoke had begun to drift through the house. Without knowing he was going to do it, he charged at Donovan, grabbing him by his dead throat and driving him back into the sitting room.

They were thrust into the inferno, the heat surrounding them indescribable. Donovan wasn't fighting back, and seemed content to simply restrain Steve from reaching the front door, which looked out of reach as the flames licked at it hungrily.

He pushed anyway and tried to struggle past, but Donovan's grip was strong and vice-like, and he flashed his sick, dead grin at Steve even as his hair burst into flames.

*You won't sell many houses looking like that.*

The absurd thought came and went as quick as a flash, and Steve wondered absently if he was already mentally damaged beyond repair. It was then, as he was prepared for his coming death, that Isaac's words came back to him.

*Just look, Mistah. Look and see what is real.*

Steve stopped struggling and smiled at Donovan; whose skin was beginning to bubble and blister.

"You are dead Donovan. You can't hurt me. You can't hurt my family," he shouted above the raging sound of the fire.

A moment of uncertainty passed over the Donovan thing's melting face as Steve pulled out the protective cross from where it was embedded in its stomach. It staggered backwards, and fell to one knee.

"This House is no more. The Gogoku can rest, nobody will inhabit these grounds again," Steve gasped and coughed as the smoke began to fill his lungs, and his own skin began to peel and blister.

"Leave my family alone," he added weakly, trying to ignore the agony of his burning flesh.

It wasn't a request, but a command. And Donovan seemed to shudder, then fall to his knees and sideways into the flames, which hissed as the fatty parts of his skin were devoured by the intense fire.

Close to losing consciousness, and barely able to breathe for the thick, black smoke, he turned back towards the kitchen and half ran, half staggered as fast as he could towards the glass-panelled door. He slammed into it at full speed, the door exploding in a shower of wood and glass. He landed face first on the blissfully cool and snow covered grass. The voices on the edge of the wind screamed in fury, and he only hoped that his sacrifice had been enough to save his wife and unborn child.

He lapsed into unconsciousness, and his world became a silent, black void.

# EPILOGUE

*Eighteen months later.*

The city was alive with rush-hour traffic jockeying for position as thousands of commuters made their way home from work. For Steve and Melody though, the sound was one that always brought them great comfort.

Since the night of the fire, their lives had changed almost completely and yet, if anything, it had brought them closer together. Melody sat by the window, looking out over the concrete jungle from their seventeenth floor apartment, and smiled.

She was an older, wiser woman who, since their brief stay at Hope House, had lost a little of her happy-go-lucky exuberance. She was more careful, more considerate of her life choices. She was okay with the change, because at least she was alive.

She wasn't even really sure what had happened until later. One moment she was a powerless consciousness in a body that she was unable to command, and the next she was back in control.

Only later—after the questions and the hospital visits and the psychological evaluations — did they manage to piece it all together. It seemed that either by fate or prior design, Steve had managed to break the Gogoku curse at the exact second that her body shuffled off the edge of the branch.

If it had happened just a second or two later, she would have fallen and been unable to stop the inevitable, but as her body became hers and the vile thing was banished from her, she managed to twist and grab onto the huge branch. The fury in the wind was intense and frightening, and the white streak that now cut through her hair was testament to it.

Somehow, she had found the strength to pull herself onto the branch and remove the noose. Of the Gogoku, there was no sign. It was as if they'd been erased.

Confused and relieved, she's seen the orange glow on the horizon as their home burned to the ground, and she suspected what Steve had done. She didn't know then the magnitude of his actions, or the toll it had taken on his body.

She smiled as she looked out at the city, a place where she felt safe and, more importantly, far away from that horrible sound of trees blowing in the breeze. She was broken from her thoughts by the sound of Steve shuffling into the room.

As it always was, the sight of him filled her with both immense sorrow and gratitude, for he had sacrificed everything to make them safe.

When she'd found him, face down in the snow by the blazing shell of the house, she'd been sure he was dead, but somehow, against the odds, he'd survived; however, it was not without consequences. The skin on over half of his body was now mottled and rough from the numerous skin grafts required to fix his injuries. Almost all of his hair had been burned away, along with most of his left ear. The fingers of his left hand had been fused and melted together, and he was in almost constant pain.

He never complained though, not once, even though he now resembled a broken old man rather than the young, slightly impetuous husband who'd lived with her in Hope House.

Regardless of his appearance, she loved him more than ever because he'd saved her. Saved them all. She had tried several times to talk to him about it, but whenever she approached the subject, his eyes glazed over and he would stare into oblivion.

The doctors and psychologists seemed to think that he was imposing some kind of mental block, and that the events were just too painful to deal with, but she thought that was—to be blunt—bullshit.

She suspected that, as ever, he was trying to protect her, and whatever he'd experienced in the house that night was something that would be his and his alone until his dying day.

He held the baby in his arms.

It was a boy, and had her eyes, and his nose and jaw. It was the glue that had held them together during that awful time after their ordeal. They'd watched their son grow and marvelled at his wondrous, curious joy of life, something which had once lived in them before everything went so badly wrong.

Melody had wanted to call him after his father, but Steve had insisted on the name Isaac. He'd never told her why, only that it was something to do with what had happened that final night at Hope House.

She watched as Steve set baby Isaac down on the floor with some effort grimacing at the agonising pain in his arms and back. In the way that babies do, Isaac went off to explore the second he was released, gurgling and whooping as he examined his surroundings.

Steve went to his chair in the corner and sat slowly, wincing as he settled his ravaged body into some kind of semi-comfortable position.

*He slept.*

The nightmares hardly came anymore, which she was immensely pleased about. For the first year, they were a fairly regular occurrence, but over time had faded.

A little later, with Steve still sleeping away his

pain, Melody watched little Isaac as he explored, crawling on all fours and chewing on one sock, which he had removed for reasons known only to him. He sat on the carpet cross-legged, and stared up at his mother with the unconscious and pure love that only the very young knew how to provide. She smiled back at him, and realised that even though they'd lost all of their possessions, and almost lost their lives, they had gained so much more, because they now shared a bond, a strength that was unbreakable. No matter what life chose to throw at them from then on, she knew they would be able to cope with it.

Isaac crawled towards her and she scooped him up, holding him close and kissing his cheek.

Even though they'd lived in a house called Hope, she thought that the real hope was in Isaac, and they would do whatever they could to provide a future for him.

Her son gurgled and smiled on her lap, and in spite of everything that had happened, Melody was grateful, because they'd seen death up close, and having survived it, were determined to make sure the years they had left together were spent well.

Outside, the October wind rocked the apartment block and in spite of herself, she held her breath, listening to it, part of her expecting to hear that secret sound, that breathy, half-whispering of her name. But it was just the wind, and she smiled to herself and relaxed.

"Come on then," she said, kissing her son's cheek as she stood. "Let's get you down for your nap."

She contentedly crossed the room, and put Isaac to bed as Steve slept on dreamlessly.

Michael Bray

## **ABOUT THE AUTHOR**

Michael Bray is a Horror author based in Leeds, England. Influenced from an early age by the suspense horror of authors such as Stephen King, and the trashy pulp TV shows like *Tales From The Crypt* & *The Twilight Zone*, he started to work on his own fiction, and spent many years developing his style.

In May 2012, he signed a deal with the highly reputable Dark Hall Press to print and distribute his collection of interlinked short stories titled *Dark Corners*, which was released in September 2012. His second release was a Novella titled *MEAT* which was initially self-published before being picked up by J. Ellington Ashton Press. His first full length novel, a supernatural horror titled Whisper was also initially self-published, and following great critical acclaim, was sold to Horrific Tales publishing - his first advance paying sale.

WWW.FACEBOOK.COM/MICHAELBRAYAUTHOR

WWW.TWITTER.COM/DARKCORNERSBOOK

WWW.MICHAELBRAYAUTHOR.COM

Whisper

# ALSO FROM HORRIFIC TALES PUBLISHING

# HIGH MOOR

When John Simpson hears of a bizarre animal attack in his old home town of High Moor, it stirs memories of a long forgotten horror. John knows the truth. A werewolf stalks the town once more, and on the night of the next full moon, the killing will begin again. He should know. He survived a werewolf attack in 1986, during the worst year of his life.

It's 1986 and the town is gripped in terror after the mutilated corpse of a young boy is found in the woods. When Sergeant Steven Wilkinson begins an investigation, with the help of a specialist hunter, he soon realises that this is no ordinary animal attack. Werewolves are real, and the trail of bodies is just beginning, with young John and his friends smack in the middle of it.

Twenty years later, John returns to High Moor. The latest attack involved one of his childhood enemies, but there's more going on than meets the eye. The consequences of his past actions, the reappearance of an old flame and a dying man who will either save or damn him are the least of his problems. The night of the full moon is approaching and time is running out.

But how can he hope to stop a werewolf, when every full moon he transforms into a bloodthirsty monster himself?

If you're craving some good werewolf action with well-developed characters and a fantastic plot, skip the Hollywood films and go straight for this electrifying novel, which is far more entertaining.
- **Hellnotes.com**

Graeme Reynolds has written a captivating, action packed, this-should-be-a-movie werewolf novel in High Moor and if this is going to be a series of some sort, count me in for the ride. It should be a fun one. - **Horrortalk.com**

**http://www.horrifictales.co.uk**

329

Michael Bray

# HIGH MOOR II
# MOONSTRUCK

The people of High Moor are united in horror at the latest tragedy to befall their small town. As dawn breaks, the town is left to count the cost and mourn its dead, while breathing a collective sigh of relief. John Simpson, the apparent perpetrator of the horrific murders, is in police custody. The nightmare is over. Isn't it?

Detective Inspector Phil Fletcher and his partner, Constable Olivia Garner, have started to uncover some unsettling evidence during their investigations of John Simpson's past – evidence that supports his impossible claims: that he is a werewolf, and will transform on the next full moon to kill again.

However a new threat is now lurking in the shadows. A mysterious group have arrived in High Moor, determined to keep the existence of werewolves hidden. And they will do anything to protect their secret. Anything at all.

A reminder of why werewolves are supposed to be scary – 10/10 – **Starburst Magazine.**

A masterclass in modern action horror – **Gingernuts of Horror**

An absolute must for werewolf fans – **Hellnotes.com**

The action is explosive and relentless, the violence is gory and ferocious, yet it is far from mindless as it is underpinned by a superb and fascinating story. - **The Eloquent Page**

I don't think I can recommend this book highly enough but with the caveat that this tale is not for the faint of heart, or indeed those looking for Twilight-type lycanthropy!  - **Andy Erupts.com**

**http://www.horrifictales.co.uk**

s
,
r
a
t,
d


at
he
n,
ily
of

"quotations", the source of some of which is given in the endnotes. The multi-vocal aspect of the letters suggests Mikhail Bahktin's notion of polyphony. (…) Could we say that the Letters as a whole are called "spiritual" because they express a preoccupation with a search for meaning—making sense of human existence—both in and beyond the here and now, i.e. in terms of transcendence. Certainly the sad, tragic, violent, transitory features of human existence are very thoroughly presented, the brevity of the episodes or incidents making them that much more poignant.

Doreen Maitre, 'Creative Consciousness: The Metaphysics of Lived Experience and Its Relationship to Literature' (Greenwich Exchange)

**The textual and textural** weave of *Spiritual Letters* is quite unlike anything else published in English poetry this century. Forget concepts: it really needs reading. The poems are limestone, full of fossil patterns seemingly randomly distributed, but linked by an evolutionary poetic.

Keith Jebb

010383

Also by David Miller:

*The Caryatids*, 1975

*South London Mix*, 1975

*Malcolm Lowry and the Voyage that Never Ends*, 1976

*W.H. Hudson and the Elusive Paradise*, 1990

*Pictures of Mercy: Selected Poems*, 1991

*Stromata*, 1995

*Art and Disclosure: Seven Essays*, 1998

*The Waters of Marah*, 2005

*The Dorothy and Benno Stories*, 2005

*British Poetry Magazines 1914-2000* (with Richard Price), 2006

*In the Shop of Nothing: New and Selected Poems*, 2007

*Black, Grey and White: A Book of Visual Sonnets*, 2011

*Reassembling Still: Collected Poems*, 2014

*Matrix I & II*, 2020

*Some Other Days and Nights*, 2021

*Afterword*, 2022

*Circle Square Triangle*, 2022

*Some Other Shadows*, 2022

*An Envelope for Silence*, 2022

Edited by:

*A Curious Architecture: contemporary prose poems* (with Rupert Loydell), 1996

*The ABCs of Robert Lax* (with Nicholas Zurbrugg),1999

*Music while drowning: German Expressionist Poems* (with Stephen Watts), 2003

*The Lariat and other writings* by Jaime de Angulo, 2009

*The Alchemist's Mind: a book of narrative prose by poets*, 2012

# SPIRITUAL
# LETTERS

## David Miller

SPUYTEN DUYVIL
*New York City*

Library of Congress Cataloging-in-Publication Data

Names: Miller, David, 1950- author.
Title: Spiritual letters / David Miller.
Description: New York City : Spuyten Duyvil, [2022]
Identifiers: LCCN 2022030178 | ISBN 9781956005851 (paperback)
Classification: LCC PR9619.3.M47 S65 2022 | DDC 821/.914--dc23
LC record available at https://lccn.loc.gov/2022030178

*For Dodo, with love*

## SPIRITUAL LETTERS

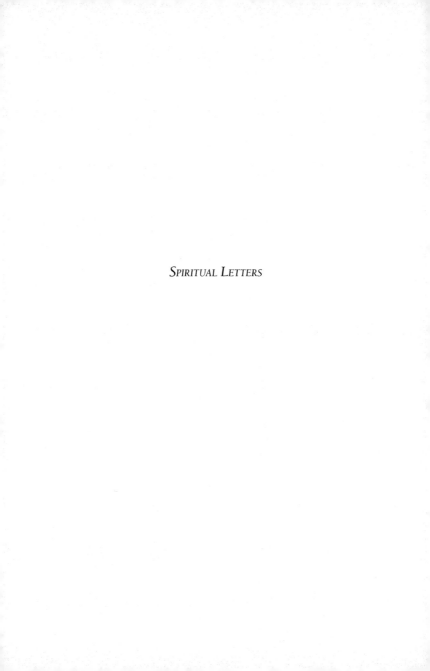

*S*PIRITUAL *L*ETTERS

# Spiritual Letters
## (Series 1)

For an end, a constant ending: images from a life counterpoised with imageless reflections. Smoke rises, spreads over roofs. In the room a sparrow huddles against the wall, near books and china. We discuss the transcendent and the satirical, and find ourselves wondering: a novel? The sheets of paper blacken. Burning animals amongst burning trees haunted the child. You cannot get from A to B by walking a line from one to the other. The girl's eyes habituated to begging touch your lips, burning them. Memory's blasted. He'll keep a record of the epiphany in his breast pocket, if not sewn into the lining of his coat.

The woman has entered through the doorway, a metal cup in her hand; her face, through the thin veil, is that of someone still very young and unwilling to believe in her beauty. A caption reads "Sacraments" and pertains to the act of blessing taking place in the foreground. In front of the underground station a little girl pisses in the gutter, while her mother holds her hand. You leap high in the air; the leap is held through categories of pain. Bruises and welts beneath your clothing. Nights when there has been no one you would call to your aid. I remember a taxicab ride at night in a downpour, when someone got into the cab beside you and all sense of protection failed. The predicament: as if having fallen into it, I found I could do nothing at all. A silence that harms; an absence of writing that calls for an outpouring.

*...letter by letter.* Having no wish to be detained by clever fabrications, stories that might distract. A dark courtyard, a lecture on aesthetics.—And if art is only lies, for the sake of rapture and power? Facing the wall, away from the wind, she struck a match for her cigarette—the flame drawing my look. Feckless, volatile girl; in the dream she began shouting at me as I turned away from her.—Flung across the hospital room by the Holy Ghost, the musician said. A phone-call: the driver survived; he died—the friend I'd stopped seeing. I thought of how he'd insisted on reading poem after poem to me at dinner; I'd looked (but not wanting to) at the spittle ejected upon his lip as he spoke the words. Faces of friends by my bed. Memory's unquenched: her long hair that she tossed around her neck; her hand that reached for mine. *Eye toward eye....* Slow phleboclysis (drop by drop; into the vein).

A white-haired rationalist in a pin-stripe suit, rolling around on the floor; his much-lined face contorted as he cracks jokes about the "hind-parts" of God.—How odd, how *very* funny, he laughs at the idea of a revealing of something that yet remains hidden. The little girl sat looking at the brightly coloured pages of a comic book. The scrub ablaze. A group of children arrived stark naked to hear stories which clustered around the words *poor*, *pure* and *merciful*. Having come to the wall he poses standing on the stones.

.

the words dark
*inescapable*
*an intervention*
*(by something*
*or someone)*
on a stone
by the path

An old man fell down in the street; another man helped him up, comforting him, then suddenly began shouting abuse both at the old man and at passers-by. Pierced; wordless.—Love is the *exceptional* thing, he said; I knew he meant sexual love. You could locate her by her youth as much as her beauty or her violent moods in which she excoriated at length each of your traits. Revealing the cuts on her arms. A fruitless vine. The girls walked past us through the grasses, laughing; we were crouching down, looking at an image of an elephant figured on the stone.—You couldn't mention mythology in that house without feeling remorse. Nothing except for its own sake. Brick and earthen mound, metal plate and token accoutrements: these become an allegory of divine judgment. He was lying in bed with his mouth full of blood when he heard someone at the other end of the room shouting out: That man in the blue pyjamas, I know him! To find himself in a hospital ward with an art critic was bad enough, he thought; but the man started telling him how much he'd admired his last show, and he was helpless in the face of it.

Lost in a once familiar area, wet from the drizzle, I moved toward the lights of a string of late night shops, following behind a small group of teenagers. In the dream, a song with the words *Life can be tough when you get stuck in the butter* played on the café radio, while the waitress' cat rolled around in the butter dish. Children from my own childhood, rows of faces bereft of speech. Rain and street noise; static. A stray description: enclosed by aesthetics, the ideas and beliefs disappeared into a play of sense perceptions. No inbeing, to your eyes; nothing to address save a set of gestures, moves, analogous to your own.—Dear, I said; oh my dear. The drawings on gelatin silver prints were an intervention, he said, provoked by illness. An imagined flight, ghostly and literal. Confronted by silence, the fantasies born of disillusionment are maddened and proliferate further.

A letter written within the shape of a hand. He arrived at the party with his wife, his head covered in bandages. Late in the evening she slowly removed the swathes, seemingly oblivious of the people around them. From the years spent in distant travel, a long series of paintings depicting flowers. Messages disguised as postage stamps. In a dream, the image of the crimson snow plant. He told the woman about a suicide attempt, before realising that she cultivated a flair for lapidation. Momently aware, and removed from shame by her rapture. It was my belief that I had a novel to write; I found myself with a handful of fragments. An absence of explanation. I had thought to speak of struggle but spoke of vigilance instead.

—You can't call any writing that's not concerned with drug-taking contemporary, someone said.— The analogy being a mirror...?—Are you who I think you are? he asked, and mentioned my name.—No, I replied, I'm somebody else. The long process of revision appealed to me with its possibilities of erasure and reversal. A layering of memories and images. A hand touching, a finger travelling along the line of affection. Late; voices loud, in the heat. No form of rhetoric could be adequate to what needs to be said, one to another. Drawn from her face, as we talked: an edge splendent in the obscurity. Unbearable to recall.

They invited me to join them in making art in collaboration, and I set to work enthusiastically. Holes drilled in wood, marks made on paper and canvas, writings arranged in patterns. Nights we spent sitting on the rooftop. The body had been laid out amongst clusters of brooches, pins. A lament for love, *Deep Song*, ends then begins again. He found himself progressively losing interest in the painting he'd once wanted to purchase, as the artist reworked it over several years. Recognition fails. A dream apart from the allure of confusion. A figure of stars seen waking through a glass wall.

A cold night wind. We talked together, upon the road leading from the house to the hills beyond.

> disrupted lines
> in clusters
> erratic shapes
> of tree branches
> how I trusted
> a cynosure
> brief comfort

The artist warned his students that he would mark them harshly for sham, evasion and insincerity. But it's sorrow that's provoked by thraldom.—Only the words of the text, you said, the reflection that appears in the mirror: nothing more. These were taken as realia: the child staring into the oil spread over a polished surface; the shapes that appear to his eyes; the onlookers who see nothing that he sees. For the sake of what one kind of writing fails to disclose, I attempt a writing of a different order; but each occasion's embedded in uncertainty. Gazing—finally—upon the images on a veil formed from blue flame.

Scribbled in the margins of the text: a confession. A girl runs past at the edge of your vision and all else that you see fails. We left the bar at three in the morning, having spent the evening getting drunk with a trauma nurse in a black floppy hat. I walked along the street with the little girl, holding her hand. The dream's a window through which you see the hurt changing her features. It was already morning when I was shifted into the ward. In vain I pulled the sheet over my head. After the crash in which his son was killed and he'd been trapped for hours in the wrecked car, he had gone wandering. Lost; turned away from what had been familiar. Eyes closed, she sang one melancholy song then another, the party at her café table falling silent to listen. The stone's to be inscribed or painted upon, not eaten.

He arrived at the door at five in the morning, with an expectation of some desperate action on your part.— *I'm not angry*, he said in an angry voice when you stood there unharmed. A landscape of reddish hues, hard by the sea. Inscribe in outline a dwelling, a tomb—a city of dwellings and tombs. The bones of a sparrow or mouse beneath the decorations and charms; the charred bones of a small child. As you walk along the littoral, the movements of your gaze *may result in unexpected 'wipes' of colour.* A letter that answers accusations: unsent, it's kept in a cupboard, its eyes open in the dark. You retrace the confidences, too: the beatings her first lover gave her for his pleasure, his rejection of her when she was pregnant by him. Gainsay a concern with persuasion or display, elegance or finesse, as well as the formulas of ruin. Place another sheet alongside the first: move across, reflecting upon, engaging with, in places cancelling. An amateur, I write, rewrite—for the sake of what remains invisible in the showing-forth.

Open the book, flip through the pages: the frog turns into a devouring monster and back into a frog.—Dear (dead) friends, I am writing to you once more. *Dream geometry*, drawn, threaded. If I dream of him lending me books, I am led to that memory of how he would give books to a homeless young man who sat knitting in the town square. In an assemblage: old furniture; cardboard in rolls and sheets cut to shape; used light-bulbs; coverings of gold and silver foil.—A supernal throne, the man said. Chart whatever inversions, transformations you find. A script, cryptic, enigmatic, covers the pages of a notebook, spills over onto the assemblage. He turns away, addressing the absent and the dead.—It is my weakness, he says, that I exult in. Mercy following mercy.

You were walking in the gardens, with the notes beginning to sound. Your life: say it's all there, *as in a piece of arras work*. The old woman stopped the young stranger on the street and asked him to marry her. He stayed and talked with her, then went on his way.—If you wake up and see someone sitting bolt upright, don't worry, it'll be me. An architect who works with shards. One child stops and looks back in greeting, as the others run past. In the dark street, a handkerchief flapping from a door. For loss: these dissonances between the voices, *howling in seconds*, gravely performed. Who would mimic lamentations, mocking them? He was given a coat—to appease the dream in which he killed the man he called *a predacious shit*.—The gold surface was covered with writing, front and back. Contrite in spirit, broken, you cannot continue. Yearning for an old friend, by river, lake or lagoon. Playing improvisations late at night, I fell asleep and woke in the early hours, my clarinet beside me.

Waking to bruises on my right arm one morning, my left arm the next. *It's your ghost—not your immortal spirit—that's careering around, playing havoc. A ghost that doesn't require any death for it to be let loose.* The mules in their panic ran into the plum bushes and were caught fast.—You also allowed the archive to vanish! he said at the end of the objurgation. When she was asked to write about a famous author, my friend said: I could tell you my thoughts about him on a postcard. The artist paints the woman's name on a canvas, a brief phrase about her; he paints a phrase from her writings on another canvas. A large man in shirt sleeves hoses down the steps of the church. Texts on panels adorned the walls. Two small chairs facing the tree.

# Spiritual Letters
## (Series 2)

Everywhere we went, people had moved chairs and even beds out onto the pavement. Sea's redress; a releasing, he said. For your sake, you asked me to remember, speak, dream; what else could I do? The narratives are interrelated—the thread is pulled through one and then into another. Even if the people live remote from each other; or the events take place in different periods. A multitude, or you and I. I was offered wine by a young woman in the dream, and then woke. He had written, What purpose could there be for the memories that I have of those I've loved and who are dead or otherwise lost to me, if we were not to meet again? Saying the words back to him (and writing them) as far as I remember them.

We walked together through dark fields of tall grass. Talking to hear him talk, to follow where his thoughts might take us; talking to ease all the lost years in our friendship. In the quiet, you pointed out the inscriptions on the gilded panels. Remembering: pieces of glass within each iron ring in the column, coloured and worked into relationship. Is it a disquisition that I should write? Again, I draw or paint over the words, leaving some visible, obscuring or cancelling others. The poet lines up his drinks on the table, sufficient to last him through the reading. He sits in the room next door to his listeners; they cup their ears to the wall, straining to catch his words.—*Ill-starred*, she said, the hour in which accidents fall to us and damage follows. In the hospital he imagines a letter that's delivered in spite of disaster; and he makes a likeness, the envelope's triangular stain hinting just barely at storm or flood or wreck. As an image of weeping: *tissues suspended from beneath the table.*—A room set aside for counselling, you said.

...that we may testify, not contrive. Night; a shelter: unseen, unheard.—What I am, is in relation, he said; what I become, in a shared inherence. *In a death, in weakness, inactivity, negation.* You wanted to describe everything, you said. Notebooks held within open hands. Divagations; kisses. We sat on a bench beside the pond, mallards and Canada geese nearby. A chapel on a hill overlooking the ruins of a temple: smoke-darkened ceiling, damaged frescoes. A young girl holds a rabbit, wrapped in the folds of her dress. A darkened room: a scribble of red, hypnagogic; pulsating, glowing, hovering over the pile of letters and photographs. I was pulled under the table where the others already crouched, while ornaments fell from the shaking walls and shattered. Despite every misfortune, the music—an elaboration of individual sounds, an unfolding or drawing-out from an interior—arrives. A night sleeping (trying to sleep) on the deck of the ship, against the engine's beat; waking over and again to wind, cold, sea spray. By the quayside, the street musician flutter-tongues on flute. Children listen to a story told in shadows.

We sat on a stone wall, taking turns drinking ouzo from the bottle's cap, while waiting for the ship to dock. A chair strapped to her back. Sleeping with difficulty; waking with difficulty in the mornings: you asked me to help by telephoning every day. You woke one morning and wrote a postcard to tell me: in the dream you were working on a large painting, surrounded by flying fish.

> alabaster
> in thin sheets
> framework
> of iron
> door posts inscribed
> smeared I can't
> locate again
> occluded
> the juncture
> the black
> diagonals

...walking away from me, abruptly, in the street at night. Jars broken in performance, an image of judgment. And the water—changing colour, what did it become? On the tape, a voice striking off the minutes while the interrogation proceeded. The woman recorded that she'd written an account of her grief and then destroyed the pages.

—Anastasis, they queried; the name of a goddess? False stories were put into play. *Bicycling through the city, with his ears painted red.*—I was seduced, seduced myself, into living through illusion.—What would that mean? I asked. I put little credence in the story that he buried some of his writings in a tin can in a corner of the schoolhouse. Sleeping under mounds of white netting strung over the bed. Night, the shadow of a tree on the pavement—leaves moving in wind. By his own admission: a painter of blue puddles. He wanted to learn ancient Greek so that after his death he could converse with Heraclitus, Socrates and Plato. Each page of the stolen thesis was retrieved from the river, then taken home and ironed. Lines and patterns of dots, in wax on cloth; colour in abeyance. Reflected: you and I together in your room, while you painted. Sitting on the sand near the quay, surrounded by geese. He asked us to look away when he rose from his sickbed and went to the bathroom. When we heard a knock we said: Come in; and the visitor who came in saw us sitting huddled together, our eyes still averted, and left without a word. A gathering-up of stray thoughts by a potlatch thinker, or so it was rumoured. Marble or limestone slab, doorjamb or lintel. Finger or eye tracing what remains, what's shown.

# *Spiritual Letters*
# (Series 3)

Fountains splashed below as I crossed the walkways. A bed, strip-like against the wall. *Hide-and-go-seek.* Moving through level after level of the all but empty building.

> night
> a hand turning
> through a full circle
> hands
> coinciding
> her hand raised
> in reflection

A cloth ready for dyeing, lines etched into the waxed surface. Retelling the story to myself, recalling the details: a face, in lamplight; a shadow traced on the wall…. Earlier, waiting in the doorway… a storm of hail pounding the cobbled alley.

Sitting at a small table on the balcony, drinking wine and writing draft after draft by lamplight. More and more incapacitated, his head snapping backwards in spite of himself, the boy was stranded in the waiting room. Having dropped the heap of leaves, the little girl beseeched her sister and parents to help her pick them up again.—You should try writing a novel, he told me. *Dear is the honie that is lickt out of thornes.* Desire's thrown into confusion; overwhelmed. Full moon above trees in the long window. Stepping down—plunging into water. The stranger he'd been gazing at earlier suddenly came over to speak to him and then fetched a nurse, insisting he should be looked after immediately; her compassion caught him, so unexpected.

To be sung: ...*that the lost might life inherit*.... A sheet draped over the chair. We sat at a table between two banana plants, a pool of water gathering underneath. A banner of flame in the night sky, above the treetops and streetlights. In a shop on the way to her home, she chose a circular mirror for me to purchase; in another shop, fuchsias for herself. I dreamt that the artist—most famously narcissistic of her generation—had died; yet later in the dream I encountered her at a private view. The old woman turns a radio on at the back of the lecture hall, loud static interrupting the discussion. He arrived at my door, his suitcase full of fish bones. On the far wall of the living room, a sheet was draped around the mirror. Between the twin rocks, a reddish light—as if scumbled over the pond's surface.—*A good amulet*, he said, invoking, gathering protection. The small silver hand was engraved with letters, signs.— The motherfuckers won't let me sing, the woman said at her friend's funeral. Around the frame, a pattern of stars, or the names of angels.

The father and mother sat on their front steps, while out in the street their children played a game with a ball. It was my first visit and I had arrived in the early hours, the airport almost deserted; a drunken young cowboy in Stetson, chaps and spurred boots was singing *The Streets of Laredo* at the top of his voice. Pieces of paper, messages, were threaded through the boxes that the boy made after the woman's death. Having chased the cat away, he crouched down, talking gently to the frog in the corner of the room, reassuring it.—Could it have been a scholar in a former life, remiss in religious observances? In the dream there were two houses, the second a mirror image of the first, and it was in this second house, this reflection, that I thought I might live. He was asked if the recurrent black rectangle in his paintings was a symbol of himself. At a table in the cool night air, we were discussing the Greek poet whose grave my friend had visited. Two roosters perched on the wall by the outdoor toilet. *There were bush-fires here... nearby*, my friend wrote; *black ash blowing through the window and settling on the final proofs as I was reading them.*

The house on the mountain, above the temples, had become haunted... but also, he said, *far too draughty to rent*. Homeless men wrapped in blankets, sleeping or sitting hunched over in the pews. A man walked into the hall with a cat on his shoulder. Waking in the night, he looked through the doorway and saw his friend sitting in the other room, writing; waking again, he saw his friend asleep at his desk; and waking a third time, he looked in at his friend writing once more. —Columbaria, he said, for the thoughts and words, attaching, detaching themselves from the rows of spaces.

> *withdrawn*
> the roses
> the drumming
> rigid sync-
> opations
> the door
> of silver
> the faces
> the tears
> *withdrawn*
> the tears
> the gnashing
> of teeth

On the way to the sea we drove past a line of shanty dwellings, dwarfed by the houses that surrounded them. She was afraid that what she'd written was *the wreckage of empty description*. A frenzy: gulls following in the ship's wake out of the harbour.

Heavy rain falling on the table and chairs, the potted plants and flowers, the long grass and boards. Two magpies and a crow, moving back and forth through the leaves of the trees. He received in the mail a map of a city area, without any notations or accompanying letter. Black outlines of tar, rectangular: glistening on the pavement. A fragment of bone in a white cup on the table. He woke in pain, in a strange room; glancing in the bedside mirror, he saw that his face was bruised and streaked with blood. Someone writes on the stones, another taps on them with a stick. When my friend and I visited the old poet, he told us of what he'd seen during the war, what he'd gone through. I was writing a poem in his honour—drafting a second version—when the ringing of the phone woke me. She had hung sheets of black plastic over the shelves, covering all of the books.

—He recognised the handwriting and took it for granted the letter was for him. Picking it up, he saw that it was addressed to someone else and in a language he couldn't understand. Silhouettes on the walls of the room, or held within the book's pages. Wind catchers had been raised from the flat roofs. I was awoken by car horns and the incessant slamming of doors, later by a helicopter overhead. A white shape, too briefly at the window.

> a tent in stone
> or catafalque
> sculpted waves
> a blind man's
>
> -----------------
>
> palm against palm
> the hand inscribed
> the appearances
> moving across

A plank was positioned upright against the wall; next door, where he now slept, a ladder stood in the corner. The television left on in the darkened room. ...*wandering a maze of stone-laid alleys,* he wrote: *one house of black wood pressed tight against another.*

Blue and yellow lights in the dark, as the ship sailed towards the harbour. Searching, he said, *for a benediction.* She had covered the windowpanes with Greek script, white. Looking out at a small courtyard in a downpour. He was unable to rest or to act: if he lay down, he would almost immediately have to get up again, and then lie down once more, only to feel forced to rise and move around yet again. Jumping from the window occurred to him as a release from his distress.—Don't you realise, he said, that I'm the most important avant-garde poet in the world? It was believed that their accomplishments of singing, drawing and reciting were derived from the spirits who possessed them. The bowls, upside down on the floor, were traps, magic inscriptions on their interiors. A large abandoned dovecote had been built into the exterior of the house. Fearing capsize: in a sailboat in a squall. Flowers drawn in dark blue over the poem about flowers, obliterating most of the words.

Disembarking in torrents of rain. Locked out of his flat, wandering or waiting in dark streets, telephoning friends. —...my *intuition*, the mother said; and the little boy asked, Does it tickle when you feel it? I sat on the deck in the cold night wind; he stood at the railings and talked with the Greek priest on his way home. They were both gazing at the island in the distance, and the priest said: Your friend's writing—I would like to read it. A group of singers in red gowns. Driving for miles for solitude, arriving at a crowded beach: what else could we do than talk and argue? He asked his daughter to help him choose which paintings to send through the post as a gift. In flame-light by the sea. Through what occurs, you search for a face, you work with or against each detail, building upon or erasing aspects, images. The child picked up the piece of paper from the floor and began chewing it. In distress: the doorframe a refuge. We looked back at her sitting in the car on top of the hillside, and saw that she was in tears.

Waking to a bright, warm morning in the port, with men washing down cars and motorbikes across the street. A mail-boat on a stamp; an envelope addressed to someone *in the neighbourhood of the spirit*. Despite a heavy cold, I went out in the rain to meet him when he phoned to say that he was lost.—My doctor advised me to take long walks, I told him, with old friends from far away. Birds singing loudly as I made my way to bed. From my friend's flat, I walked past a church and drop-in centre, charity shops and outdoor stalls. The balcony door swings back and forth in the wind. It was only when the service was over, and she was standing with her back to me, that I was able to speak to her; she turned to face me, and wasn't the friend—loved and lost for years—I thought I'd recognised. False apprehensions: a form of constancy. I was staying in a caravan, beside a shack with most of the rooms derelict, wild kittens for company. During her parties she would play recordings of Gregorian chant. When we met for the last time, you told me you'd been working on a series depicting nearby buildings, abandoned or set for demolition.

He sat on a rock in the field, singing to the sheep. Another day, he sang Mahler to the trumpeting elephants in the zoo. As we drove through the gateway, a dog with a crippled back leg came out to meet us. Later we went down to a restaurant by the sea, sharing a meal of fish and octopus and drinking wine. *Fragments of plaster, some with reed impressions, suggested the remains of houses built of plant material*—palm fronds, he thought—*and plaster.* From the street below, the old actress could be seen standing at the mirror framed in lights, preparing for the evening performance. The boy's limbs now affected by the medication, he found that he could move only with difficulty; so his mother helped him to walk the short distance to the hospital. After a long night of drinking his friend returned home, and removed several eggs from the refrigerator for juggling. A single sandal-print impressed in the pavement, rapidly filling with rainwater. On the floor of his bedroom he had arranged his clothes in pile after pile.

Gulls, motionless on posts by the water's edge; one turned its head to look at you when you came near. He walked along the path by the estuary, small boats out in the distance. Waking in distress from a dream of a friend's death. Even the gargoyles defeated him in his attempts at depicting the edifice. It was *a map of heaven*, yet one he couldn't follow. Shadow or stain, unfolding beneath the table. His earliest book, never finished, was entitled *We Shall be Friends in Paradise*. A floor of crystal, *shot with blue and purple, and green.* As the train pulled out, the conductor announced that they would be going on to their destination *without stopping at any intermittent stations.* She had to sit on a tiny, brightly coloured chair to address the children. After her talk, she gave them cherry tomatoes, which most of them spat out. The final, almost empty images. To look, to lose, to meet or be met, to disappear.

*Spiritual Letters*
(Series 4)

We took the path along the cliff, by the ruins of a lighthouse. Waiting for her to arrive, he leaned against the balcony rail for the breeze—drinking wine and gazing at the people in the street. In the dream, water seeped through the ceiling and ran down the walls. She barely acknowledged me—to my sorrow—when I passed her outside the bookshop. Later, after hours, I sat with the staff watching television, while she lay on a couch at the back. My friend and his wife and children all lit tapers at the small shrine.—Here, he said, light a candle for someone you're thinking of. She sang to him over the phone, My home isn't here, my home's in heaven; saying, how sad that is! Stray dogs sat near our table outside the restaurant, watching for scraps. When we left, they followed us through the town and all the way down the hill as far as his house. His friend led him up the steps to a sandal-maker's shop.—He slips one of his poems in with each pair of sandals, he said. Turning to look at her, I saw her turn over in sleep.

She sent me a drawing of a rose, inscribed with my birth date. Sitting in a bar, thinking that you might walk in—without any reason for thinking so. Everything else in the painting—from the landscape to the person's body—was considered background for the depiction of the face. He told me that his favourite book was *The Incoherence of the Incoherence*; I didn't believe him. A rose petal inside the folded sheet. You suggested that I lie back on the floor, and when I did, you leapt on top of me from the couch.—What did you expect, letting yourself look so vulnerable? She recalled the smell of brandy (and the small bottle the woman kept in her handbag), the constant smoking of cigarettes.—I'm heartbroken, you said in the message you left me; my cat has disappeared. Later you found the cat, shut inside one of your trunks. The woman sat on the ledge, dangling her legs and looking pensively after the removal van. *Dear*, you wrote, *how warm and consoled I feel, embraced by your concern, this crucial day of my life.* They came back into the room and found her lying on the wrapped and crated painting.

Glass walls reflecting traffic, other buildings, passers-by. Clouds, birds, paper blown in gusts. The woman walked along the street at night, playing a wooden slide-whistle. Already late, you wanted to stop at the florist's so we could buy chrysanthemums for my friends. A young man stood at the end of the train carriage and delivered a long, apologetic speech about being homeless. He didn't try to collect any money; instead, he rushed past the passengers, and began again in the next carriage. You left after photographing the two drawings; later that day someone took a picture of the artist naked to the waist, in front of the huge drawing of her own eyes. I awoke from a dream in which my friend was knocking on my bedroom door. An open umbrella had been placed upside down and filled with herbs from the field.

There were no images of gods in their house; therefore they were assumed to be godless. Sunlight on olive green water; sheets of paper floating near a small yellow boat. Her fingers traced the words incised on the candle. I took his hand to help him up the steps to the concert hall.— I've been in and out of hospital for months, he said; but I will not miss this performance. Pine needles embedded in the paint. When I looked in the doorway, she was dancing to thirties Swing, *One O'clock Jump*. Through the branches, we saw the blue neon light at the end of the pier, reflected in the dark river.

Trees and stones may have retained some trace of the passing; but he was the sole human witness. In the dream he stood before us, blocking the narrow pathway; a blue iris in his hand. Bright moonlight on the estuary below the hill. I had gone to her place to play music, taking clarinet and bass clarinet. Arriving, I found people with instruments, yet no one playing a note; and when I asked about this, I was ignored or rebuffed.—Come at once, she wrote, for your poor daughter has died; and from this time on she will be happy forever.

> grass clay roofs
> flame melting wax
> light mirrored a voice
> breath a dark cell

He picked up the dead bird in his small hands, thinking he might wish it into living again. His mother startled him, saying: Don't think you can bring it back to life; and he was shocked that she could tell his thoughts. In the square, strings of lights in the trees. Lost in the strange city, we were surprised to see a friend coming towards us; we stopped him and asked if he knew the way to the train station.—I certainly do, he said; I once lived here, in a white van. They shared a kiss before she ascended into the air.—It was a kite to fly in, she said, and it could live on the water.

Ribbon windows and lights reflected in the water; sleet suddenly falling. We sailed under bridges, past tugs and pleasure boats. Books and a carafe held the billowing tablecloth down. Standing together at the party, he told me how he'd used the song of a hermit thrush in one of his clarinet pieces. A little girl wandered over and asked him if he'd like a glass of water. We were reminded to wear something red to the Pentecost service.

> in tears half-light
> a cliff the sea
> steps going up
> and down in sleep
> reflected face
> chiaroscuro

I was woken from a few hours' sleep in my narrow room by a knocking at the door. I'd thought it must be the neighbour's child, and was astonished to find it was a friend from far away. We ate waffles with acacia honey and drank white wine. Shattered glass underfoot on the pavement. A shudder of arrival, boat bumping against pier. She'd written his name and a time on her hand. On another's hand, he saw a small cross in ink.

After climbing the mountain, he arrived at the monastery during a snowstorm, and was given hot gruel by the monks. A child's tent, decorated with cartoon characters, on the balcony. I dreamt I was sitting with a woman on the roof of a tall building; birds were flying overhead, and I became giddy as they swooped lower and lower. You stood at the railings, watching the man in a skiff row past the pier. Tower blocks, barges, cranes, posts, reflected and blurred in the water. Coming home late at night, he saw the dwarf he'd noticed before in the neighbourhood. She was stumbling around drunkenly, cigarette in hand; and he felt ashamed that he failed to offer any help. The spiritual body was said to be of *the fine celestial substance of light as it is native to the stars.* They were enjoined never to cut marks into their bodies because of the dead. Wandering into the unfamiliar temple, he thought he recognised a fellow believer, yet the more they conversed about religious practices, the more puzzled he became. We'd walked down the darkened street towards the café, past the high stone wall with hanging vines, the hill surmounted with trees, the house with a glass brick façade. After hearing us speak his own language, the man at the table across from ours had wine and food sent over, finally joining us for a drink. A swinging door and a bucket of blue paint: how many possibilities were there?—It was a void, she said; a *very interesting* void. The folded sheet of paper was thrown to the floor and stood.

You took me to a terrace overlooking the harbour, the sky darkening with rain clouds. On the doors were carvings of various figures, the faces scratched out. I sat down at a table and ordered a small abstract painting and an omelette. If I learned more of the language, I thought, I could order something different next time.— Don't gesticulate so much, he said as we stood in the parking lot; you might be mistaken for a gang member and get shot by a rival gang. The sign in the library read: Keep the Door Close at All Times. Shelves stacked with books, recordings, boxes of manuscripts.—Oh, she was really sweet, you said, but she was always drunk. Hanging from a board outside the station: a Missing poster, the image so weather-damaged as to be useless. He became convinced that his psychotherapist was a witch; however, she was clearly appalled when he told her. They found numerous shards of black porcelain bowls, some bearing inscriptions. An oil lamp the only light. *The house*, he'd written, *suffers on a journey*.

She was eighteen, she told us, when an elderly woman —once a famous Rembetika singer—tried to pick her up. Standing in front of the large office building, the tramp drunkenly ran his hands over the textured façade, delight in his face. You'd called in the early hours, forgetting the difference in time, and been acutely embarrassed. *I even miss the skirl of starlings in Leicester Square in the evening.* As the taxi turned into the lane, he noticed two teenagers embracing against a tree. Further down, several youths were lounging by a wall; the driver stopped to ask for directions to the guesthouse.

> fallible
> fall in a dance
> eyes the wings
> the dark sky

Old, torn posters in layers, where her shop had been, the building boarded up. Did she write it was a *mending rain*, or *unending rain*? He was helping his neighbour, a poet and retired rancher, to make a door for his front entrance. On the flat roofs: grass growing; pools of water. He said he didn't have another glass, and that I should cup my hands for the wine. When I'd finished playing the solo, she asked if there were any words to the music. To her surprise, I said that the song began *We all believe in one true God....*

It was a necessity, he wrote, that *the whiteness of their nature* should be restored. A blue and red bench between palm trees on the station platform. Waking in the tomb, covered in pus and blood, he remembered fucking his dead wife in his drunkenness. Remorse and sorrow overwhelmed him. He found himself back in the country—the very city—of his birth. After taking a tram a long way, he walked down to the beach; it was so crowded, he had to leap or vault over couples and groups. Turning on a light in the kitchen, I saw in a flash the bulb shatter, fragments flying across the room.— What would you do if you were still composing?— Well, there's a chord in one of my pieces that I think I'd remove. *I would eat rotten apples or dried-up pears if God would place them before me. Where the Word of God is, there is spiritual eating.*—Do you have any plates? she asked.—Why, do you want to break them? After visiting the library, we went on to a shopping centre, then to a park where you persuaded me to join you on a child's slide. During the private view she spat on a handkerchief to clean one of the paintings.

palaces
of light sun
moon a tent
in the sky

--------

palm-leaf book

--------

torch-light or
candlelight
the black black
rectangle

We sat facing the glass wall, talking and drinking whisky, while coyotes howled in the distance. Earlier, we'd startled a roadrunner, skittish and quick, near a neighbour's house. When she was on her deathbed, I asked if I could kiss her forehead and she said yes. A room so small as to disappear. *A flutter or flicker,* he wrote, *could it be that there's nothing else?* He also wrote: *I've written about art, written about art... and always as more than aesthetics could include.* Brocade dress, draped over a chair; white lace curtain at the window. A past lover's face suddenly seen in a crowded post office, where she wasn't; a friend's face glimpsed in the Strand, shortly before his death in a distant country. We gathered in the garden while the minister pressed five nails into the paschal candle, which she then lit. When he asked me for a text, I began to work old drafts and notes into a new piece of writing. Face in memory or in dream: quiddity, exilic. He took a long walk alone, deep into the night. Dark trees, dark ground. *The spiral staircase in this house just reminds me of you,* he wrote to her.—Lollygagging is out of the question, you said. Hurried evacuations, fearful, desperate... with whatever belongings they could throw onto a wheelbarrow or a child's cart or else carry. Through a public garden, then down the riverside path—we opened the gate and walked over the ramp to where the houseboat was moored. Derelict boats in the mud; trees and houses on the other side of the river. As he left the carriage, the drunk suddenly spat in the face of a young woman who sat talking with her friend. The trumpet player stared out of a dark balcony in her dream.

a room
stranded
abandoned

She said she wished to *brush away the knocking on the door.* Visiting a friend once, he looked at a field of grass behind the house and thought: I could spend years drawing this and nothing else…. Of course, it wasn't true. It was said that their letters had been used to make cardboard boxes in Mexico City. In the opening of the story, a detective arrives in Athens from England, following a lead; he stands in a busy street, listening to a blind accordion player…. I failed to write any more; I tried to find the pages again and failed. The cat had died, he told her, and he'd keep it in the fridge until she returned from her holiday.—Gold is difficult…

or doubtful. We'd been instructed to wash our hands before entering the room and after we left. After his wife's death he went through her diaries, crossing out passage after passage. *The only differentiations I could see were between very light and very dark tones, there was no green or blue or what have you. ...towards the end I was hallucinating and all sorts of strange things were occurring.*—He sang that song about footprints showing the way he'd travelled; don't you remember?

He ended up, late at night, drinking in a basement bar with five dwarfs, cast members of a show. You sat on the verandah, out of the afternoon sun, and smoked a cigar, nonchalantly stirring a martini with the arm of your sunglasses.—A strange holiday, she'd remarked, you sitting in the spare office and scribbling. She managed to trick the little Navajo boy into looking into her eyes.—I shouldn't have done that, she said, but he was so sweet—I just couldn't resist. ...*suddenly there was an explosion and ten feet in front of me I saw that a big tree had just been split by lightning. It was especially surprising since it wasn't raining, I hadn't seen any lightning or heard any thunder, it was simply overcast.* Returning to the hotel room late at night, he pulled back the coverlet on his bed and found that the sheets were stained with blood. A blonde wig underneath the opposite seat in the train carriage. On the way to meet my friends for the first time, she asked me to go into a chemist's with her to buy nail polish, and we sat on a bench outside while she painted her nails.—She fell from the window; then the dogs tore her body apart.—No, she was *pushed*. Turning the corner, I came upon a building appalling in its absurd conglomeration of blocks and cylinders and reflecting walls. Along the sides, see-through lifts carried passengers up and down the main structure.

73

Persistently denigrating, a father's words to his small daughter as they walk along the street. The architect made every attempt in his design to prevent students from attaching picture-hooks or nails to their walls. *...the being flitting about there among the shadows and flashes of light belongs to the unreal world.*

       silhouettes
       mirrorings
       waves of silk
       lit glass floor
       consumed she
       disappears
       into dark

*He just didn't write enough music. He painted watercolours for forty years....* Cherry blossom and weeping willow by the lake's edge; birds splashing in the water. A girl sat on the grass, writing sideways in a notebook.—I must phone you to get that chord; I forgot to write it down.—Actually, it was two chords. When it became known that the country was under occupation, he went to the national library to renew his ticket. Sprinkling holy water over places she sensed as troubled; lighting candles for those she saw in dreams and visions as needing her help. She remembered a thousand people by name in her prayers each day. *Some of the copyists were prisoners-of-war or political hostages and worked in chains.* You told me you thought St Paul was a landscape painter, not a tent maker. The church's ceiling, supported by pillars made from ships' masts, had been painted cream, and decorated in grey-blue and gold. Candles, sleeping bags and cushions on the floor. You'd added these words to the drawing: a greeting for Christmas, and an inscription in Greek (which I couldn't decipher). *It was my little cell of solid black.* Messages on slips of paper, thrown into a bowl and burned out in the garden.

# Spiritual Letters
# (Series 5)

The woman twice shouted hello, and I stopped twice in the dark street and turned and replied, Yes?—Wrong man, she said after a pause. She woke from a dream in which her father offered to have sex with her—woke, too, to the memory of his death. In the window of the children's hospital: papier-mâché figures of a cockerel and a mutilated man (one leg cut off at the knee). I turned down a lane past a silent and dark playground, slides and wheels only dimly visible. Met by chance in the street, she called for me to keep up with her as she ran down a flight of stone steps. I called back that I couldn't, as a bus had recently injured my foot. A metal ramp, leading to the long pier illumined by fluorescent light. I sat in the wine bar until three in the morning with an English friend back from Abu Dhabi and an African princess. The princess had held out her hand for me to kiss, but my lips met the long sleeve of her thick white wool cardigan. Branches hanging over the stone wall beside a bus shelter, a wooden bench further along the street. A night of strolling together, talking, waiting, leaving each other and coming back. A white china teapot, left on the edge of the footpath. She quickly had a thousand umbrellas bought and distributed, one for each person, when a sudden downpour interrupted the unveiling of the shrine. Was she really just trying to impress, or, as it was said, putting on airs? I thought she'd said *a lake of stone*, but later realised it was *a lake of snow*.—Let me in, your friend said, having woken you with his unexpected arrival, and make me some lasagne—then I'm back to work on my new masterpiece, which you'll read about in the art journals. He was carried by chair through the streets, with hundreds of helpers bearing his gold streamers.

> the drawings
> through crystals
> frost snow hail
> -----------
> a candle
> the mirror
> *sfumato*

Gazing at his reflection, he mentally undressed himself; he couldn't linger, however, as his next analysand awaited him. While my sister tried out perfumes, I bought candied kumquats in another part of the shop. A girl in her mid-teens—my own age— by accident smeared my coat with her ice cream cone and apologised profusely. Bluish zinc cladding on the rooftops. She had scratched out her own eyes in the graduation photograph.—I won't be making the trip to meet you, I said; I've broken a rib.—Oh, she said, I know how painful that is; I once had several broken ribs... a spinal fracture... and facial lacerations. The architect suffered a fatal heart attack in a station lavatory, his body remaining unidentified for three days. Keeping three separate households, he'd deleted the address in his passport. Looking down from the top of the slope, to the slate roofs dissolving into the sea. Estuarine memories, dreams. As he lay naked in bed, an eagle smashed through the window of his hotel room and fell stunned amongst the glass fragments on the floor. Wrapping it in a towel, he threw the reviving bird back outside, where it flew off. He wrote to me of a lucid dream in which he swam above an underwater town and decided to dive down and explore, even going into some of the houses.

*Yellow flowers, green leaves growing from no visible soil on a low roof across the way.* Though they were staying at the same hotel, she sent her companion a series of postcards. On New Year's eve, we strolled among the crowds by the river, strangers shaking our hands or kissing us. He wrote of her performance that it belonged *more to pyrotechnics than to the art of dance. It is a sort of living fire-works.* Where he stopped the car at a light, a clarinettist was playing wildly and well, so that I wanted to get out and join in. You closed the wooden shutters and secured them each time before we left your apartment. *All in one day you get beautiful sunlight, thunder & lightning, wind & rain. Nights you look up at a clear, starry sky, and far off at no great distance hear thunder.* Shops and cafés; steps and public squares, old houses and fountains; walls with graffiti. At night, we walked so many streets, always....—The bar was so dark you could scarcely see around you, but there was nothing to see anyway—no pool table, no pictures on the walls; the bar staff didn't try to talk to you, just poured drinks: it was my idea of paradise. He listened to his visitors' stories during the day, and to their dream-like stories at night. *Ah, if I die on the boat,* she sang, *throw me into the sea, / So that the black fish and salt water can eat me....*—Are you sure you're all right? he kept asking as we made our way back, drunk, on the bus, and I told him he was being condescending and finally stopped speaking to him. As soon as I entered my doorway, I collapsed to the floor. The monkey-puzzle I'd passed so often: uprooted, gone. The woman with a cane sitting in the train carriage, who looked so like you... could I really no longer tell? *Heartache, heartbreak: you old twin standards.* A few seats away from me, a man repeatedly called someone a bitch over his mobile, before he hung up. When she phoned back, he said: What do I want? I want to destroy your face.—There's a pigeon out in the garden that desperately tries to get into the church.—Perhaps it wants to be saved. *The love we bear to the blessed martyrs causes us,* he wrote, *I know not how, to desire to see in the heavenly kingdom the marks of the wounds which they received for the name of Christ....* Through the streets of the town or village, the funeral portraits were carried in procession with the bodies of the dead. Painted in black: words enjoining the dead to be happy, and a brief farewell. They'd accepted him as a novice in a Carthusian monastery, but he hadn't yet told them about the AIDS. In hospital, dying, the artist referred to the writing of his will as a "career move". *Another night I can't sleep,* he wrote in his diary, *...not even calling you to mind, your eyes, your hands, your* *mouth… yet unable to sleep because of you.* Alone in a small village, far from home—sudden anguish caught him, anguish building on anguish, and none of those he phoned responding to his calls. The group of friends went out together at the same date each year to repaint a small, neglected island church. It would have been impossible to get them to do it at some other time, simply for a filmmaker. *The day we were in the stocks I had this vision: I saw the place, which I had beheld dark before, now luminous; and my brother, with his body very clean and well clad, refreshing himself, and instead of his wound a scar only. I awoke, and I knew he was relieved from his pain.* He'd seen you running, pell-mell, down a crowded street.—I needed to get to a park bench to sit and think, you later explained.

On the way up the mountain to the monastery, we stopped at a café for some wine and listened to Rembetika on the radio. Nearby, at a street vendor's stall, she bought worry beads as a gift for me. He refused to ever return to the city of his youth—the only city where he'd felt at home—because of the atrocities the people had committed in wartime. Standing there in the streaming rain, you drew the attention of every passer-by to the place where a plaque to your favourite writer had once been. Balusters, laths, mitre joints and wainscots from demolished or abandoned buildings, stacked in boxes, on floors, or against walls. A rose window, the glass entirely a single blue. The opening of his exhibition had to be cancelled when the employees of the museum went on strike. Their demonstration caused an enormous traffic jam, and he admitted that he found the event extremely enjoyable—some people, indeed, accused him of arranging it. He wrote to me of his plans to build a labyrinth for children on one of the hills of Jerusalem. To reach the shops to buy bread, mild cheese, butter, sausage and wine, I walked up a steep slope and returned down it, always pausing to look out over the bay. A rock garden, with solar lights in a row; a smaller expanse of pebbles directly behind it. A rippling sheet of blue water beyond the back garden, green hills in the distance; the blue turning to silver, the hills darkening. She hid presents for the little girl behind the trees and in the bushes. After the pub had closed for the afternoon, we wandered around trying to find more to drink and failed.—Manna from heaven! he exclaimed when we found a friend had left a bottle of rum on my doorstep. They hold wreaths of red flowers and glass cups, turning their heads at the sound of a familiar voice. In Reykjavik you bought a music box: to your surprise, raven cries came from it. *Our Lady, who appears in the stains and shadows of the subway.* He phoned from a hotel room in Cairo, leaving a message that he was dying. At his request they removed the altar and pews, and veiled the artworks and windows; robes, chalice and wine all had to be white, and the wafers bleached. As he sat writing, a sudden wind blew the sheet of paper from the table to the other side of the garden. The wooden skeleton of a building, enveloped in flames.

A small distance from the temple ruins we sat for a while and ate figs from a tree. By day or in early evening, children run amongst the jets of water, squealing, splashing, laughing; later, the fountain's still, the children gone. He changed the design for the labyrinth *from a square to a circle and finally to a triangle, the greater part... to be built underground.* Despite the late hour, a few figures could be seen in the elevator capsules, gliding up and down the side of the grandiose building, lit by blue neon. An empty can rattling along the road in a gust of wind. During the long wait for blood samples to be taken, I was curious about the other patients, but only made brief eye contact with anyone. Afterwards I decided to sit and read for a while over coffee—even if the poems happened to be about going blind or dying. *I am overcome with amazement when I hear a voice speaking in the wood, a hand raised to strike, the body bending over, raising itself, sitting down....* A wooden image of the goddess, removed, now lost; miniature statues of young girls and boys, her devotees, arranged in rows. They talked and talked about the problem of painting a white egg on a white tablecloth. Votive offerings, retrieved from the spring: dolls, toys, jewellery boxes, mirrors. To build the Christian basilica, they uncovered and carried off material from the ancient sanctuary, damaged by floods, across the valley. You described it for me: a miniature house, made of iron, placed on the bare floorboards. A tiny iron chair, also mere inches tall, nearby. No stained glass, no Agony in the Garden or Last Judgment: just seven windows divided into small clear panes. On the ceiling, gold flowers arranged in straight lines and circles, and gold rectangles. He got out of bed in the night, feeling ill, and fell on the stairs and lay there helplessly, with no one in earshot, and died. We wandered through the snow in the cemetery until we found the old Cabbalist's grave, surrounded by broken glass. Later that afternoon, in another cemetery, we saw the graves of writers and artists, snow falling faster, heavier. *Darkened windows, candle-light and battery torches, sirens and the army on every corner....*—Where did you think your friends had disappeared to, he asked, when they never called or answered your calls again? The woman still denied knowing about the deportations and deaths, angering him further. *I saw a ladder of tremendous height made of bronze, reaching all the way to the heavens, but it was so narrow that only one person could climb up at a time. To the two sides were fastened all sorts of iron instruments, as swords, lances, hooks, and knives; so that if any one went up carelessly he was in great danger of having his flesh torn....* She dreamt that she was eating curds, and woke with a sweet taste still on her tongue. *I at once told this to my brother, and we realized that we would have to suffer, and that from now on we would no longer have any hope in this life.*

Late one night, he began wandering unfamiliar back streets: and continued on and on, travelling enormous distances, even crossing oceans; though he only ever remembered walking. Far distant family and old friends met him on his way. Suddenly, a flock of ducks flew directly over my head, quacking loudly, as they swooped down towards the lake. Sitting outside a café, we talked about his child: four years old, she still couldn't talk, nor walk—small for her age, she was carried, or wheeled in a pram. They'd arrived at Giza in the evening, going straight to the pyramids from their hotel; but the noise of the crowd, then the bright images, lights and amplified voices made the child scream, over and again. Forced out of art school for his small, highly realistic images of buildings when large abstract paintings were obligatory, he later studied the history of architecture.—I survived my exams with the aid of a water flask filled with vodka, he told me. Printed on your postcard, with a schematic drawing of a person: *I'm lost*. After driving through the desert for a day, we stayed at a Navajo hotel, the only non-Indians there, with stray dogs roaming outside and a scorpion in our bathroom. The following afternoon we reached a lake with snow, water running over rocks, and trees in leaf. A diamond setter in the daytime, he played violin at night in the clubs along Eighth Avenue, amongst other expatriates. This night, the door's left open: for the passer-by, the wanderer, the erring traveller. After she'd taken me on a brief tour of the neighbourhood, we went back to her house, where I met her husband; but something, it struck me, seemed wrong between them. She went out to smoke a small cigar; I took a walk and then a taxi ride, slowly realising how large and strange the city was... and I wondered about leaving. Fountains and pools, even a man-made lake, had been incorporated into the architectural complexes. Stone dragons, red and dark blue railings, trees in blossom. Within the temple, three rooms full of stacked small wooden tablets, recording in Chinese the names of the dead, their districts and villages. *She knew so much of the plants and birds and beasts around her, and loved the beautiful views over the sea of blue forest and real sea beyond....* Falling ill at a friend's, he stayed for a few days to recuperate. One afternoon they took a walk together, with one of his friend's daughters and the family dog: up a muddy hillside, then past frangipanis, ferns, eucalyptus trees.—Sister, let's go in, he said; they'd gone for a walk, and had been drawn by the sight of the basilica's spires. Years later, he could recall the ascension window's blues and reds, but not the cathedral gold windows; what she remembered, he would never know. He was taken aback during a sermon when his minister claimed she'd once glimpsed a ghost. As we left the station, we were caught up in a crowd surging towards the fireworks; even after the display, it was impossible for some while to disentangle ourselves. Two of the bridges had been closed off, and when we eventually reached a third and found it open, we were separated by the crowd and forced to go different ways. *I often wonder if you miss your clarinet. Sometimes I see young people in Bourke Street playing and think of you; there are a lot of buskers in the city these days, sometimes so close together that it is just a meaningless din.* I found myself staying back at the old family home, now my sister's, and sinking into despondency at the windows that were falling in, the front door not locking, and she refusing to do anything to fix them. *Dear adopted sister... thy history would furnish materials for one of the most interesting pernicious novels.* You accused her of bribing a surgeon to operate on you as a child, so that you'd be left with a cleft palate. Doors in the floor and ceiling, or opening onto blank walls; a reservoir of water over a fireplace; a staircase ending at the ceiling. When we were children, we had a cockatoo, a rosella and a crow, as well as dogs, cats and budgerigars. The cockatoo terrified us, and seemed to delight in it, chasing us around the yard while we screamed. Hearing me leave my room during the night, he covered himself in a sheet and hid in a closet to wait for my return. When he heard my footsteps, he opened the closet door, lifted his arms and walked towards me. ...*she is just outside the door raving at me. Unfortunately she is involving other people... she is making me out to be a monster.* Returning from the hospital, she found that her daughter had taken all her cats to a shelter for strays. The journey led through a mountainous region, where a dragon lived near a lake; if it was not propitiated, it would cause storms of snow, hail, wind. His efforts at proselytising were hindered by the interpreter appointed to him, alcoholic and uncooperative. *There were two monastery buildings, but no monks lived in them. If a guest monk attempted to stay, the native people would drive him out with fire.* A hospital famous for its eye clinic: in a place where blind pilgrims once prayed to be cured. You wrote about the quality of the white in her paintings, which she brought back from distant travels: to Japan, Egypt, India, Java, Australia.... But it was her predilection for red—for painting red flowers—that I noticed. ...*then we went on, and soon entered the region of the doum palm. Birds also became more common, we had seen troops of pelicans, ibex, storks, and ducks, and now we had abundance of larks and water-wagtails, and lovely long-tailed green birds almost like parakeets, but smaller.* She'd boiled water in an old black saucepan, and we drank tea together at a table made from a door. Across the street, my neighbours take turns sitting by the window, and smoking; their room's dark, apart from the bright, shifting colours of the TV screen. *Let the country with barbarous customs and smoking blood change into one where the people eat vegetables; and let the state where men kill be transformed into a kingdom where good works are encouraged.* Many of the vagrants he went to interview had never seen anything like his bulky tape recorder and often mistook it for a musical instrument, thinking at first he was a busker. *...he took my hand, and we began to go through rugged and winding places. At last with much breathing hard we came to the amphitheatre, and he led me into the midst of the arena.*—Ah, you extraordinary illusionist! What have you come to show us this time with your occult arts? *Then out came an Egyptian against me, of vicious appearance, together with his seconds, to fight with me. But another beautiful troop of young men declared for me, and anointed me with oil for the combat.* He told his students that there were some things seemingly impossible to write about, such as his recurring dream of a mysterious route by which he travelled to see his mother, after meeting dear, long absent friends again. He would wake elated, and then remember that those he'd found once more in the dream were all dead. *In some cases a laurel crown in gilt, symbolizing their future happy state, has been added to portraits of both men and women....* The composer said that birdsong was "God's language"; he also affirmed the resurrection of the dead. The philosopher praised birdsong for its beauty, nothing more; while his religious philosophy, with its God who was forever in a state of becoming, had no room for any afterlife. *With these Eyes the cathedral's face is on the watch for the candelabra of heaven and the darkness of Lethe.*—Lines from your writing have been appearing in my dreams. *Often when I can't sleep at night I wonder what you are doing, trying to picture you and your pursuits.* Vespers are said here, and sung; Bach is played, jazz, too. *Suffice to say there has been taken out of our limited garden one of the most perfect plants that ever was planted in mutability....* Long after her death, he depicted his granddaughter in his final painting—a little girl amongst the animals of the Peaceable Kingdom, leopard, lion, sheep, wolf and ox. We played music, recited, sang to my mother's memory.—I like your shirt, I said, conscious that I'd never seen him wear one before; he admitted that it was his girlfriend's, worn specially for the occasion. Walking by the lake, the trees illumined from below by yellow lights in the grass, he listened to the calls of the terns, cormorants, teals, mallards and grebes. *Thy rose bush is very pretty and thy geranium will be beautiful.* From the rooftop or windows, *we enjoy every fleeting glimpse of spring growing in the park, or a grey sheet of rain advancing over the trees. For flowers are good both for the living,* he wrote, *and the dead.* Beneath their feet: sun, moon and stars, and the signs of the zodiac, in the mosaic pavement. She wanted to go to the riverside to view the fireworks, and I went along to keep her company. The exploding lights that seemed to fall towards me and the booming noises brought on a panic attack, and I tried to leave; but the display ended, and I was caught in a dense, slowly moving crowd in the near-dark, and kept thinking I'd fall down. He smashed at the door of the synagogue with an axe until they let him in; taking a scroll from the Ark in his arms, he sang an ancient Castilian love song. At midnight, he rose from his bed and walked down to the sea, where he immersed himself according to a ritual. You sat every day by your dying friend's bedside, in accord with his wish. *It was,* you wrote, *a painful, a difficult death.* We were ordered into the sea by the sports master, and I was swept beyond my depth in no time; he called to me to swim back; and I called out that I couldn't, and then went under. I'd gone under three times, into a black tunnel of water, before two of the boys reached me. He collapsed in a tube train and was taken on a stretcher to street level; but he claimed to be all right and attempted to get up, and died of a heart attack. You walked to the hospital in a winter evening's severe wind; and then lost yourself in the mostly deserted corridors, before eventually finding the ward. Your friend was sitting on the side of the bed, and you sat down beside him and listened to his obsessive recital of mistakes and missed opportunities.—*I am praying to God,* he said, *but not to yours: to Osiris, Osiris.* Every evening he prepared a meal, and always insisted, much later, on making a pudding—often after a good deal to drink. He would reject each one after a single taste, and throw it into the garden: for the birds to eat, he'd say. It had been a half-hearted, absurd attempt at suicide, an outburst of adolescent despair in which you'd forced yourself to drink disinfectant as if poison; however, the doctor insisted your mother should have you hospitalised. She asked you what you wanted, and then accordingly told him: No. Having spent the afternoon writing in cafés and searching amongst bookstalls, he headed towards home; reaching it, he realised it was no longer where he resided, but his home of many years ago. Confused, increasingly desperate, he asked passers-by to help him: for he no longer knew at all where he lived. After eating and drinking on the beach with friends at night, he decided, against their advice, to swim along the coast and cast a long string of fishing hooks. He never returned; his corpse was discovered the next morning. A forest of ancient chestnut trees, brooks everywhere, and wild goats gazing intensely at you. He enjoyed the company of sponge divers, the poorest of all—but he was also friends with the captains of the boats. He had to be carried from the ship and taken to an abbey where he was known to the monks, who nursed him until he was strong enough to continue the journey. From the harbour, yellow lights shine in the distance; fishing-tackle hanging from a white T-frame where he stops to rest, and white boats in the water. Muffled voices and faint music from a larger boat, in an otherwise still night. When it began raining, I turned to follow the path back again; the estuary and the island out in the distance were only dimly visible through the rainy mist. When he switched on the kitchen light, something darted across the worktop and ran towards the wall: it turned around, finding itself cornered; and he found himself looking at a field mouse, which sat looking back at him. Another night, he stayed up reading in the lounge and listening to the storm outside; the mouse suddenly scooted across the floor in front of him and dove under the gas fire. Testing for a detached retina, the doctor put drops into my eyes to dilate the pupils. Afterwards, I attempted to walk home, but had to keep to the shadows to avoid being blinded by the sunlight, even then struggling to see, and having to stop. *He could hear the rivers protest as they were soiled by dirt washed into them, and could see blood seeping from the flesh of freshly cut fruits and vegetables.* Late in the evening, heavy rain beats and pours at the windowpanes, while I sit drinking wine. Earlier: a helicopter circling overhead repeatedly; and the sound of breaking glass in the street. *The raft went in out of the bright moonlight to pitch darkness, the roof of the cave so low that it seemed to be touching the top of the mast. Then, in the blackness, the rain and wind struck.*

*Spiritual Letters*
(Series 6)

*I was travelling home by boat from Greece, and found myself one misty day in calm water without any sight of a shore: was the vessel really moving or, as it seemed, at rest?* He accidentally knocked the ostrich egg off the shelf; picking it up, he saw that it was cracked. We were preparing to go on another trip together, but this time we spent days sorting through belongings, packing some, while discarding others—in spite of which, boxes and boxes piled up. Finally, he decided to leave before me, impatient to be on the journey. Under the enormous ceiling, lit by chandeliers and candles, the girl with the scarf over her dark hair turns her head towards you, turns away and turns back again; she stops singing, and smiles. After the memorial service, we visited the cemetery and drank ouzo and poured it over his grave. We went on to a taverna, and exchanged stories about him, surprising each other over and again. He spread linseed oil varnish over the painting's surface with his fingers, removing the excess with the heel and side of the hand. To touch, to kiss: as if the chasm didn't exist. The fire forms itself into a sail in the wind, then a vault, enclosing him. Deported to the labour camp, he was stripped of his priestly garments, shaved of hair and beard. He shared the little bread he had with those who were sick or dying, up until the time he was shot. *Even if while fixing his gaze on the icon, a brother walks from west to east, he will discover that the icon's gaze continuously follows him. And if he returns from east to west, it will likewise not leave him.* The young woman at the back of the bar suddenly breaks into song, her singing clear, vibrant, melismatic: *I once was lost....* He was on the same island where you and your wife and children were staying, though you didn't know until later. Your aunt was with you, too, and she happened to travel back on the ship that carried his body home. Red sandstone cliffs with sculpted, flowing contours, from countless years of heavy rains and strong winds— rain that also washed down the cliffs into a river and turned the water red. It must be a house full of birds, they said when they heard him playing his saxophone ecstatically, late at night in his upstairs room. They said tears streamed not only from her eyes, but also, inexplicably, dripped from her fingers; can I believe this of a painted image? Photographs you took in gardens and parks: philodendron, cabbage rose, lady's mantle, Japanese magnolia.... Rosa alba. Walking across a bridge over the lake, in a light drizzle, I stopped to gaze at the small flocks of birds in the water, and a swan near the bridge dipping its head. A friend wrote to me: *One, a 'gardens' window, commemorates a local gardener and includes a great many of the flowers he grew. It is teeming and medieval in its richness and variety and secret personal significance.* She wandered through gallery after gallery, finally stopping when she came across someone standing absorbed in front of a large abstract painting. Recognising it from a previous life, she said to him: You know, I did that. From the long, horizontal upstairs window, I could see fog drifting across and enveloping the bay. *Eight years of painting and re-painting, building up and scraping back and building up, gluing pieces of wood and bits of jewellery to the surface and painting over them….*—Should I attempt a description?—Stray, she directed.—If you think you know something, you can only appear deluded, bereft of your senses, insane.

—Just to remind you of the wind those days, he wrote, enclosing a photograph of us walking together on the island, his sparse hair standing up, my long hair streaming. A walk in the night: the sky starless, against expectations. Sick of his host's solicitude, he asked for a hammer and nails; and when she brought them, he boarded up his door from the inside and used the window to get in and out. He'd take long walks through the city, and on the way home he would traverse a park, always climbing at least one of the trees and sitting in the top boughs. Tents of black goats' wool, frames of bamboo covered with thatch, structures of mud brick and stone rubble.... I wanted to call it poverty architecture, but knew it was more complicated than that. Water pools. Cupped hands: for simplicity, he said. They broke off the bases of glass cups, decorated with gold leaf, and embedded them in the mortar; the gilt inscriptions and images conveyed good wishes and messages of hope to the dead. Bracelets, earrings, statuettes, bells, lamps and small glass vessels were also fixed in the mortar. Clusters of white roses in a neighbour's front garden. We took refuge from the downpour inside the doorway of a café; the staff allowed us to stay, even though they were closing up, but it seemed the rain would never cease.... The aeroplane she was travelling on flew through a blizzard: one of her fellow passengers suffered a heart-attack; she calmed herself by praying slowly. *The water of the canal flowed backwards. They said, 'Water cannot prove anything.'* Reprimanded, the wooden beams of the study house ceased bending inwards, and began to lift themselves back into place—but stopped before they were completely straight, and stayed that way. She knocked at the door of the synagogue, though it appeared to be deserted; a man came out and spoke with her in Hebrew. Invited inside, she was welcomed by worshippers in festive Shabbath attire, who explained that they were fearful of attacks. Black suit, black hat, and black scarf over his eyes—he stood upright in the boat crossing the water; on another occasion, he dressed in a gold suit and hat and carried a long golden needle when he was ferried across the lagoon. All the walls had to be painted deep red, as he demanded; the windows washed clean of rain streaks; clutter removed from beneath the stair well: all in preparation for his display. — This perfect form, this ideal image, he said.... — As if this finite, shattered and suffering world could admit of perfection. *...the brightness all around us was so great that our house was completely lighted, and as far as we could see all was illuminated with a sheet of fire that nothing could arrest. The wind blew and the night was so extremely cold* *that what little water they could get froze, and... the tide was down, so that they could not get a supply from the river.* She wrote about how odd it seemed *to see depicted in great details the black lace-up leather shoes of nurses and the slightly softened but still harsh lines of iron beds in panels right under barefoot angels.*

I asked the barman for a house of white glass. I wasn't drunk, though I intended to be. —I never promised you a rose window, she said. *Who can undo this tangled and much involved knot?*—You *pay* someone to discuss philosophy with you? he queried, when I told him I'd been arguing with my therapist about Wittgenstein.—It proves I need help. Having come down from the bandstand, the Black South African saxophonist grabbed my shoulder as he walked past.—That's the blues, man, he said.—You've got sort of a whiney personality, his therapist told him.—I see you're going to make a night of it, he commented when I bought two bottles of wine and two boxes of paper tissues to take home by myself. Sutures between my toes and at the side of the foot: blood seeping through the bandages, blood and sweat. Dropping the bedpan, I spilled urine on the floor and was scolded by the nurse, thinking it was on purpose. The fig-tree weeps when its fruit's plucked, stones suffer when struck and broken apart.

> scribble across
> a field a fire
> across a field
> scribble across
> a sky a lake

hallucinating
black lines up
down and across
lines in exile
hallucinating
a sky a lake a field
scribbled a field the sea

—When the door opens, your celestial twin may be standing there. The flowers and leaves of the blood-red angel's trumpet are infused in hot water, or the seeds ground and mixed into maize beer. Having drunk either concoction, you first go into convulsions, then a trance, in which you hallucinate, or have visions.—Ask the oldies at those meetings about black mirrors with a purple tint.—When I stare into the sun, I see things, he said.—You can't do that, it will blind you. ...*I came to regard as true whatever they, in their insanity, said; not because I knew it to be true but simply because I wished it so. Thus it came about that, haltingly and cautiously yet for a long time, I followed men who preferred a shining straw to a living soul.* The orator delights his audience with his elegant speech and pleasant face, yet what he says is merely the same as the others, if more sweetly expressed, and I'd already heard enough of such things. As a young man, he spent his Sundays visiting the catacombs to see the tombs of martyrs and saints. *Heads are found severed from the body, ribs and shoulder blades are broken, bones are often calcined from fire.* A pavement of pavonazzeto, inlaid with flowers of red porphyry and serpentine. *These galleries are about eight feet high and from three to five feet wide, containing on either side several rows of long, low, horizontal recesses, one above another like berths in a ship. In these the dead bodies were placed and the front closed, either by a single marble slab or several great tiles laid in mortar.* An artist depicted Saint Augustine as a baked potato, hot from the oven. But the saint wrote: *I came to Carthage, and a frying-pan full of unholy loves crackled around me.*

After school, he was entering the train station to travel home to South Melbourne when he was stopped by a drunken Scandinavian sailor, who asked him to light his cigarette for him and then stroked his hair with shaking hands. The boy tried to get into a different carriage, walking quickly down the platform when the train arrived, but the sailor followed after and chided him. *During one visit she showed me an antique stereopticon she'd bought at a flea market, complete with several boxes of the glass slides, all very old photos of various oddities and exotica from all over the world. It was dirty and rusty and basically inoperable but I was totally fascinated with it....* We ate breakfast together: bratwurst, boiled eggs and pumpernickel with butter.—I didn't think your friend's wife would look like that, his girlfriend said when he showed her the photographs from his holiday abroad.—Look more closely, he replied; that's not his wife, it's me. He had a remote viewer engaged to try to track his journey, with the viewer in a completely white room somewhere in London and he in an undisclosed, faraway country. While not, he said, having any belief in it, or against it, but intrigued by the idea. As we walked down the street, a van stopped and six policemen climbed out; they forced us against a wall and searched us, allegedly for drugs. When one of them asked my friend what he had under his cap, he said: My brains.—My brother's a professor, and he'd spit on you, the woman at the next table said, apparently outraged by our bookish talk.—You're so rude, she continued, someone should kill you; I think *I'll* kill you. He told me about the exploits of the Ninja, and later bought me a Ninja suit to wear when I appeared with him. *They travelled in disguise to other territories to judge the situation of the enemy, they would... enter enemy castles and set them on fire, and carried out assassinations, arriving in secret.*—What have you been doing recently? I asked.—I've been practising shape shifting. We were taken aback to find that he, with his love of marble, limestone, gilded terra-cotta and brass, glass spheres and gold, had been buried in a cemetery in Old Cairo with a tin can as a marker, flattened and written on with a felt-tip pen. *Men who humble themselves to worship things preserved by human skill commit sin: such are but the cold carving of stone, dry wood, hard metal, or dead bones. Deprive them of your veneration, and, since they are unfeeling, they will be defiled by dogs and crows.* Fragile pyramid, newspaper and wire mesh; branches in leaf pushing through the walls. I wondered about the possibility of a soft pyramid. *For the protection of the head of the mummy... layers of linen and papyrus glued*

*together and stiffened with gesso, moulded and painted in the*
*likeness of the human face, were introduced....* I was shown
a photograph of a woman they claimed was my wife, with
cuts on her face.—It's good to see that we're taking such
a shit off the streets. On his last night in the small village
by the sea he went to a pub and sat reading Keats, across
the room from a group of skinheads. — Did they walk on
water, as it was said?—No, nor did they become invisible.
When the two policewomen arrested me, they called me
by someone else's name, and took me in front of a senior
officer who showed me a photograph of hands that were
supposedly mine.—See, they don't look like mine at all, I
said, but the two women replied that they really did. Until
the end of his life he will keep a painting of *a reclining*
*woman whose face has been ferociously obliterated.* You can
see the little boy's reflection on the side of the car, as he
reaches to touch the door handle. A young woman in a
straw hat and a young man are in the front seats; an older
man—the woman's and the boy's father—sits in the back.
Blood dashed from a bucket over the decaying carcass of
beef, for its colour's sake—for the painting's sake. Large
blue flies gathering around, chased away, gathering again.
Walking along the shore at night, I passed the sea cadet club
where a dance was in full swing, everyone dressed in their
uniforms and some older girls dancing with young male

cadets.—I don't know how you could be an artist, she said, and never visited Norfolk. He has publicly championed the younger man's paintings, writing a monograph on his art... praising him in rapturous, almost delirious, yet apt prose. His daughter will decline an offer of marriage from the artist; while her father will no longer be on speaking terms with him. In the dream a strange animal spat out pieces of manuscript in my face, then, shaking itself, shed or lost its spines. A workman in paint smeared overalls grabbed me by the arm and pulled me back from an oncoming car.— I'll see you tomorrow! he called out as we went separate ways—as if he somehow expected me to be there at the same time every day.—Someone commented that his friend, the mathematician and cartographer, had a mind like a spice merchant's.—A compliment, of course. *...your gaze prompts me to consider how this image of your face is thus portrayed in a sensible fashion since a face could not have been painted without colour and colour does not exist without quantity. Your true face is absolute from every contraction.* He stood gazing at the small boats—white and blue or white and black—in the still, smooth water; the rocks near the shore were clearly visible, but the boats were less distinct the further away in the fog, and the island in the distance a mere spectral smudge.

As I approached the station footbridge, a woman stopped me, asking why I wasn't in school. Did I know her? I wondered; but I kept going, determined to play hooky for the afternoon. I walk through the rooms of my grandmother's house, strangely multiplied... bedroom after bedroom, living-room after living-room... corridor after corridor. In these interiors from fifty years ago, I lose myself, find myself. When the other schoolboys and I entered the carriage, we saw a young woman already sitting there: extremely drunk, smoking a cigarette, swearing and cursing to herself. Some of the boys whispered and tittered; I thought she was wonderful. Black houses, yellow windows... deep blue sky. A jib-door: pause there; wait. A river. A lake. A rose said to be black... really a dark, dark red. The front windows of the house shattered in the storm, shards of glass flying through the rooms, driven by the wind and rain. By the lakeside, an old man sat next to a pelican, stroking its feathers. When a woman approached and tried to touch the bird, it made as if to bite her, then grabbed at her leather handbag with its beak.—How could there be a castle in a tree?—Only in a grove of singing birds, she said. Entering the hothouse, we were both blinded until we removed our glasses. In the semi-darkened room: an envelope of light beneath the chair.

*I'm glad you found your Dad a kindly man,* she wrote, *so different from what your sister calls him, she calls him an old mongrel, and what she calls me I can't bear to write.* He said that the last time he'd seen her, she was running fast along the street.—Maybe the Furies were after her, I said. How well or badly did I pass my time amongst companions, and to what end? His sister always read the final page of a novel first, before turning to the beginning. Many people disappear from our lives; and also, sometimes, they disappear to themselves. Do they miss themselves, as we, sometimes, miss them? Empty tables and chairs, wet with rain, outside the wine bar. An inscription on stone: *I was kidnapped by the sweetness of the celestial kingdom.* It wasn't the saint's eyes but his horse's, sad and tender and beautiful, which caught me: I came close to tears seeing them. *...they heroically endured all that the people* en masse *heaped on them: abuse, blows, dragging, despoiling, stoning, imprisonment, and all that an enraged mob is likely to inflict on their most hated enemies.* The boy riding pillion behind the saint holds aloft a large glass of red wine, which, prior to his rescue, he'd intended for his captor. *They commonly call him The Green—according to their favourite manner of using epithets instead of names. Why he should be called green, however, I cannot tell—unless it is from the colour* *of his horse.*—That boy scouts should emulate St George and slay dragons is beyond question. The old horse continually distracted me with nudges for the sugar cubes I kept, while I attempted to shoo the hens into their coop.—Fuck off, horse! I finally yelled, causing him to walk off in what seemed high dudgeon and me to go after him to reconcile. My friend worked for a while, he told me, in an abattoir; he would sit by a river after his shift, hoping for a breeze, but nothing took away the stench from his nostrils. The snaggle-toothed woman stopped her pacing up and down the waiting room to ask me if I had a bad temper. I lied and said no, and she informed me that she did, and that she'd throw cups, saucers and plates at me, and hit me over the head with a frying-pan. As he walked up the escalator, he made a figure from a long length of string looped around his fingers, as if playing a game of cat's cradle, but when he reached me, he slipped the string over my head.... *A tall hat for the teacher, a hat that bends over, too tall for its own good, a hat fit for the black dog of a teacher, a tall hat and a sign hung around the neck, and a beating, blows and more blows, a whipping, shit in the mouth, boiling water, boiling water and blows, and teeth pulled out with pliers and nails driven into the head, and death, death for the foolish, despised, treacherous teacher.* After the news of the despots' arrest spread through the cities, the streets and squares filled with people, and wine-shops were depleted. She was refused entry to the park because she wasn't accompanied by a child. Lighted window, isolated in black night.

> we set sail
> we drowned
> we set sail
> - - -
> he drowns
> he dreams
> he dreams
> and drowns
> - - -
> dreams equine eyes

He pulled the hair out of his tongue; astonishingly, his mouth filled with blood, which kept on coming, though he spat it out and soaked handkerchiefs with it.—*What a thing would be a history of her Life and sensations,* he wrote, describing as inane the look on the old woman's face; she puffed smoke out of her pipe, while two girls poor as she carried her along on a makeshift litter, or what served for one. Did he hold out his hand, when we ran into each other in a pub, and I refuse it?—I'm a collector of cobalt glass, she said; the shapes of the vessels can attract me as much as the colour. The inscription on the shard read: *oft.* My time was spent unwisely and to no end amongst the smug, the self-regarding, the arrogant, the indifferent.... The elderly poet wrote to say he was shut out of his flat and would I send him a pair of slippers? Alas, I had no way of knowing where to send them, and no way of asking. The shack was swept down the hillside during the heavy rains; afterwards, you spent hours sorting through the debris for what you'd lost... what your friends had given you. Sky: smalt. Cracked and splintered, the pieces stuck together again. From cloud to ground.—Does it fly downwards, does it stride and stalk, does it sink its jagged lines?

> there were glass beads
> glass cups and urns
> the windows
> slabs of glass
>
> - - -
>
> faces appearing
> as images imprinted
> on the windows
> and slate tiles

—I think I'm beginning to see things, he said.—I get the picture, you replied. *Dark's commotion,* or *dusk's commuter...* if indeed I called you either, I'd have to regret it. *Ashes were already falling, not as yet very thickly. I looked round: a dense black cloud was coming up behind us, spreading over the earth like a flood.* I noticed the ladybird's tiny legs kicking helplessly, and scooped it out of the water on a sheet of paper, then set it down in a dry and sheltered spot.

> bird taken ill
> another sings
> and now what colour
>
> - - -
>
> an angel

breaking through
the wall?
punching tear-
ing and the wall
now derelict

She told me that as a little girl she thought of spiders as her friends and would read stories to them. *Did the other children call you Spider Girl?* I wondered, hoping that they didn't. The Persian rugs displayed outside the café drew the eye as surely as the hookah pipes. Was it then or some other time that she mentioned a hankering for hookah-smoking?

> foreshortening
> your face here there here
> foreshadowing
>
> - - - -
>
> *in dark looking out*
> four hours past midnight
> cathedral glass blue
> above the white
> wooden shutters

I shook the old piece of chocolate intended as bait out of the trap and into a rubbish bag; but as I did I noticed the small dark shape had a tail, and realised I had something to rescue and release. – I've made a breakthrough, he told me; I'm no longer afraid of the mouse in my flat.—There's someone here with a strong body odour, she said as we entered the gallery; I replied that I couldn't detect anything.—Yes, she continued, I have a really good sense of smell; my mother and I can both smell snakes. An apple tree in blossom, with a lone squirrel negotiating the branches. The two fox cubs jumped over each other, tussled, exposing their bellies, and ran back and forth in the garden; one found an abandoned yellow plastic toy to play with, and every time it picked it up in its jaws the toy let out a squeak. My philosophy tutor introduced me to her cat, Pascal, and then to her pet rabbit, but without telling me its name (– It's too embarrassing, she said). I had been thinking it might be called Spinoza or Kierkegaard, but she eventually told me it was Bun-bun. Hail beating, crashing, battering against the windows and roofs as I sit in a room upstairs overlooking the garden, writing to a friend; the white stones covering the grass and the long beds of soil. A dog bitten on the face by a rattler survived; a different dog was bit on the leg and died.— Why did he leave his dead dog out in the woods to rot—and what did he really expect his friends to say when they encountered it? The storm hit, as sudden as the rain and wind were violent; he hysterically chased around the rooms of his house arranging buckets and saucepans, with little sense that I could see. I stood there astonished at his panic, as I really thought I'd seen worse in my own country. You claimed that the colour of your eyes had recently changed, and that the brown irises had become tinged with red. But I'd never allowed myself to look closely enough before; and I refrained from doing so now. The lashing rain obscured the streetlamp outside my window. Water dripped from the ceiling while, oblivious, he talked on the phone.— Is there anything I can carry for you, dear one? I know you don't have socks or a pocket watch, but the water is deep, and there must be something I could carry.... When I heard that someone had dropped ten thousand poems from a helicopter, I could easily imagine that she'd been the pilot, as well as one of the poets. No way of asking her, however, as she'd completely stopped speaking to me.—It's the sea that the heart lives on, and the sea is salt; it's salt the heart lives on. A stark ark. Often one by one, and none by none at times. Wind, hail, heavy rain, thundersnow... heart's beat. *Then*, he wrote, *it all stopped: she stopped painting, he stopped living, I couldn't continue writing, you and I stopped*.... Please tell me *no*.

*We had sat down to rest when darkness fell, not the dark of a moonless or cloudy night, but as if the lamp had been put out in a closed room.* The young girl dreamt that she was walking down a stairway with the leader of the country, and that they chatted amiably together and all was well, all was pleasant, despite her grandmother's Jewish name.—Fairies may fool you into thinking they're your natural offspring; but one supposed father woke to the deception and put the alien child, now six, on a bed of burning coals to die. Another changeling was deposited with a human family during a tornado; after he reached adulthood, he built himself a studio and became the town photographer. *A gleam of light returned, but we took this to be a warning of the approaching flames rather than daylight.*

> though my best friend
> he shot at me
> as well as the others
> shooting all around
> I begged him begged and begged
>
> ----
>
> struck struck through
> he was struck down
> struck with a cane
> struck cut beaten

To release what was in his grasp upon death, it proved necessary to break the fingers. Could the words on paper dropped from the sky have been secret messages, telling of disappearances and deaths? Were a thousand and two hundred Jews waiting to converge on Giza and place a Star of David on top of the Great Pyramid? *The intricate lead crystal window above the door crashed into the street and pieces of furniture came flying through doors and windows.*—Separate out, he commanded.— No, I replied. *The subjugated should be left nothing but eyes for weeping.*—Anything, anything whatsoever you wish: anything's possible, everything you desire is permissible.—Can you walk through closed doors and walls, leap from a window high above the ground without injury, fly by your own agency... and what if you could, you who aren't capable of performing an act of compassion? Still in his army uniform, having just returned from being a prisoner-of-war, he stood in the middle, leaning his arms on the others' shoulders; and all three of them trying to look like *bad boys*, cigarettes in their mouths, cocky poses.... And I'd remembered sweat stains under their arms, all three of them, but the photograph gives this the lie. When news of the approaching army reached you, you shut the remaining prisoners in the mess and set the building alight; and those who managed to break out were met with flame-throwers and machine guns. He chose to jump from the ship that had been set ablaze, and swim amongst and past corpses in the freezing water.—You either burn or you swim; but if you decide to swim, you'll be shot at: because you're a Jew. Spark, flame, smoke... skip, trip, stop.

She called out to me from across the street, as I was walking along with a friend, and came over to join us, friendly and eager to talk, as always; turning her head away when she exhaled smoke from her cigarette. When she left us, my friend said, oddly shocked: She's *rough*—you don't *really* know her, do you? Smoke disappears into leaves: sycamore, acanthus.... I was taken aback to see her from the bus, striding down the street at an alarming pace and singing at the top of her voice. It was in the market, the market you and I went to so often: the stranger walked up to us and blessed you, and you accepted this, knowing that however ill she might be, a blessing was still a blessing. I heard that she caught a mouse in her bare hands and that it didn't try to bite her even when caressed; later she broke into a neighbouring house to release it there.—I can understand these people less than the birds in my garden, he said of his patients. We went to the foyer bar together, and he noticed some of the odder regulars— the sad-looking woman, probably homeless, with her head resting on the table, the old man sleeping over his book.... I remarked that I, with my habit of writing there, was probably looked upon as a local eccentric; he responded with horror that he hoped no one would ever think of him that way. *On coming in, he throws off his slippers, sings a hymn loudly and then cries twice (in English), 'My father, my real father!'* Whose hairpin was it in the ashes, supposedly your son's, within the urn? And did you enquire who she had been? A man with a lantern, who leaves his home during a storm at night, illumines his way, despite the winds that blow, and shines his light on the threshold he comes to. *The aboriginal Fire, confined in membranes and in tissues, hides itself in the eyes' pupils; these tissues are pierced throughout with marvellous passages. They keep out the deep water that surrounds the pupil, but they let through the fire, as much of it as is finer.*

> called out to
> you looked everywhere
> peregrinations
> in tears bereft
> in the luminance
> - - -
> a rooftop at night
> drinking wine endeavouring
> to re-create the voice
> enlarged marks
> amplified minutiae

*Four barren hillsides, the bed of a lake, gloomy heat and nothing else:* where he had expected grandeur, there was *an incredible smallness... great humility.* Flashes, flares... fires, fires that would burn and burn....—What if a conflagration could reach even to the stars—what hope would there be for you and me?—*Could* there be such a conflagration? He sang: *How can I ever stand it, just to see those eyes, your eyes? They're shining like two diamonds, two diamonds in the sky.* This place, you thought, appeared to have been visited by fire; *everything seemed burnt—burnt in material and in spirit.*

# Spiritual Letters
## (Series 7)

While the jazz played, a woman made sketches of the musicians in pencil, and someone else in the audience banged on a biscuit tin as a drum until it was beaten out of shape. Drunkenly falling asleep at the dinner table... her face in the mashed potato. Or was it sour cherry soup, as someone told me?

> line after line
> seashells set
> in a plaster wall
> for ears that listen
> mouths murmuring
> in response or ears
> in a wall a wall
> of ears row after
> row
> ears for the mouth
> the mouth the "I"
> speaking or reciting

*The snow begins to fall*, she wrote, *and then falls and falls, faster and faster, heavier and heavier... and I want to die.* Your hand glitters, just for a moment.—The poet! she exclaimed, clearly not remembering my name, although we'd been lovers. And then there ensued, in a small rain which eventually soaked us all the same, some talk, all about her. *I would wake up outside, on the grass, dishevelled, hung over, with stains on my clothes; I would also wake, sometimes, in my own piss, shit or vomit. Students accused me of trying to seduce them while I was drunk, no doubt rightly.* In early light, roofs slick with rain; your ears beginning to bleed. He'd attached long lines of tough red yarn to her cheeks, stitched to the skin, and was pulling on them. I could see it was a performance and a perverse game between them, but it was unbearable to watch, and I cut the strands. A black wall; black, broken shells. A goblet, on fire: forced into flame.

The neighbours threw raw eggs at us from their balcony, while we sat talking in the courtyard.—Don't you realise you could have scarred someone? you shouted angrily. *Schwarzkopf*, the purple leaves so dark that we thought them to be black. Dead of a heroin overdose, he'd turned bright blue by the time he was found. *Of night, lonely, blind-eyed.* We were being held captive, my mother, my friend and I, by a tall, thin, sinister-looking literary academic, in an abandoned flat; he told us that he hated his mother and that his colleagues were arseholes: I drew my own conclusions, and effected an escape. Without even waiting to involve the police, I gathered some friends together and we broke into the flat, fearful of what we'd find: we found it empty. *Your shadow is a squirrel, mine a bobcat.*

> it wasn't you after all
> or anything like you
> but when the figure first
> appeared in the room
> it didn't seem
> an apparition let alone
> sinister
> but then the animals came
> and proliferated

a cat attached itself
to my back with its claws
and I couldn't detach it
yet I did kill its companions

The old man stood in my doorway, with rain pouring down outside, asking if I'd look after his flat, next door to mine, while he was away. It didn't make me uneasy that he had black silk hangings and covers in his bedroom; but on a later occasion he telephoned me while I was staying at a friend's, although I could have sworn I'd never given him the number or mentioned my friend's name. *At the time he entered the asylum, he was very handsome, like a movie star—in fact, he'd acted in films. When he was released, nine years later, he looked like an old witch.*—That kike mentality, he said, that kike spirit exemplified in the Kabbalah... I want to hear no more of it, ever. An old image comes back to me, of black fire on white fire—a writing of fiery black letters on a ground of fiery white. *Half bricks on whole bricks.* The doctor inscribed a cross in red on the patient's record, signifying extermination by lethal gas. *The intricate lead crystal window above the door crashed into the street and pieces of furniture came flying through doors and windows.* A Brownshirt climbed onto the roof, waving the Torah scroll and shouting: 'Wipe your arses on it, Jews!' *The Snake has been liberated. We must crush the Snake's head.* All he could engender in his disciples was despair. But a rival's disciples were brought false elation. *…we were not only shut out of our houses, the baths, and the public square, but they forbade us to be seen in any place whatsoever. For we praise the fish of the living.* An owl flew off into the trees, its eyes orange and black. In the park, two small girls, one white, one black, were on swings and both laughing. *The skies open for you: may you live in peace.* Words inscribed on stone, tile or marble slab, with images of acrobat and gymnast, fisherman and shepherd, martyr and saint. *Nor is the fire ever lulled to sleep,* he wrote, *but it will consume the sea, the mountains, and the woods; God will destroy everything with it, judging every soul.* I took up a conch shell, and blew into it; you took up a ram's horn…. Neither of us ceased from weeping.

As we stood at the gate, looking towards the distant bay, we suddenly heard a stonechat calling.—If we're going to their place for dinner, we need to take our own plates, not to mention knives and forks. A rustle, not of wings but of paper. Burned black. A chair, standing by itself in the room: spectral, abandoned.

> *no end*
> *or beginning*
> *to humility*
> *its foundation*
> *its increase*
> *in the central*
> *nothing*
>
> – – –
> islands
> mountains
> no end
> of islands
> or mountains

*With violence he began to persecute and to defame for heresy the women he had known and had at one time cherished and commended as holy.* We had not long set sail for the island, when a ship caught us up and came alongside, bearing word that we were to be exiled to an even more remote place. And so we changed course….

> bell tolling
> *most simple*
> *most one*
> clear light
> or darkness
> how cold here
> where? remembering
> and to dream
> first one book
> then so many

*Fruit rots, gold-leaf encloses.* Prepare food while you can, eat while you can; then make your way quickly. There was wine, there was a house... there was a lantern, a road... a line, a fork, a break.... *We are aware that someone has passed by.* A sycamore split open, amidst smoke and flames. For now: poverty bread. The saxophonist always wanted to know the lyrics to a song before playing the melody.

> *before your door*
> *I fell down*
> *the wind took it*
> *the blonde colour*
> *of my hair*
> *nights O such nights*
> *now look towards the sea*
> *inviolate*

—As you drink from this goblet, let me see your eyes: lift them to mine.—Well washed! they shouted, amused, as the blood of men and women below in the amphitheatre spurted and streamed. *And with this you asked the man standing by for a ring from his finger; and having dipped it into your wound you gave it back again, that he might be a witness.*

As I passed a schoolgirl standing at a bus-stop, she exclaimed loudly: I'm bored! I'm waiting for my bus and I'm bored!

    eyes staring avidly and blankly
    at bright screens
    appetitive
    ………………..
    …………
    askew
    am I a horse?
    or am I
    a
    boat
    with
    sail?

—*A sublime place, in its smallness, its extreme poverty....*
—*Yes, a poor, humble, desperate little green river.*

a sail
of flame
forms a
vault of
itself
enclos-
ing him

A herring gull drinking from the birdbath in the back garden. Gull shit on the windows in the room where I write. He came over to where I sat in the pub and greeted me; I didn't remember him, but he insisted we knew each other, and gave me his card. He was, I later discovered, widely regarded as "the *enfant terrible* of electrical engineering".—He designed and made a device for an injured bird to rest in, to aid in its recovery. He sacked one of his secretaries because she was overweight. The metal egg span around and around, eventually standing on its end.—They called it a bridge and I guess it was, though it only led from one section of the library stacks to another, not across a road or over water. I was about to leave there once, having finished the evening shift, when I heard someone cry out that she'd been locked in. Conjured lightning, flaring across the sky, sometimes for 135 feet… with false thunder heard for 15 miles. Butterflies electrified, haloed. *The idea that human beings are machines is an example of reason's sleep breeding nightmares out of analogy.* Is it true you would have liked to have taken the white pigeon as your wife? Imagining something so strongly, realistically, that he couldn't distinguish it from an actual thing. *I preferred seeing a child skipping rope in the street, for the sheer pleasure of it, to an artist skipping rope in a gallery as a performance.* A photograph of an unworked stone standing in a studio, oddly placed, nothing more. A gilded sphere containing his ashes. *The transformations of fire are first sea; and of sea the half is earth and the half the lightning flash.*

—He'd collapsed from overdoses before; but when we forced our way into his hotel room, we found him curled up in death, the needle still in his arm. Only twenty-four, he was someone who'd "sung a new song, played skilfully"... one of the most singular and progressive jazz pianists I'd ever encountered. A young man in a blue shirt and blue cardigan leans out of the third storey window, looking down to the street, looking for a long time.... A young couple took it upon themselves to lead the psalm-singing, accompanying themselves on guitar: a pair of strummers, I quickly concluded. *It was cold, and snow was falling... we hid in the straw. Then we heard shouting, and we saw that the forest was on fire.* I was given an old door to lie down upon for a bed, little better than the stone floor, in a room full of people I didn't know: a night without sleep. Ritual washing of feet. Then they ate unleavened bread, drank wine. A strawberry tree in a field. He told me that his wife was in hospital, having had a breakdown and been discovered wandering barefoot and in only a nightgown in the street on a chilly night, trying to gain entrance to a nearby church.—There's a church I know where I'll spend Easter, he said, sleeping on a pew, rather than at home in my bed; I need the solace.—Can you eat this wine, drink this bread?—Only if a storm or strong winds cut out the lights: then a candle-flame moves here, moves there. Displaced. *...he was a great fan of the dithyramb; walking at night through the streets of Vienna, he would suddenly begin to recite Hölderlin with a loud and beautiful voice, or even sing one of his twelve-tone settings.* You were arrested and later shot for publishing Hasidic stories illustrated with your own prints. A door, a room. A man pauses at the threshold. To sing: *tehillim*. Suffused with blue: dark blue, and darker.

Egyptian blue: a curtain of it, closing. Parsley dipped in salt water; bitter herbs; matzot; roasted lamb....

> the sea
> inherits
> ink
> but which?
> blue ink
> or black
> or red

Black or brunette hair, or blonde? *Dusk was falling but it was light, for the earth was covered in snow. I noticed on his writing-table something like a rather large envelope, made of black material and decorated with a big triple cross and the inscription: 'In this sign you shall conquer'.*— Jewesses pretending to be French or Italian connive to corrupt the morals of our youth, acting as whores and governesses and even as teachers; they insinuate themselves into the lives of those in high office as mistresses, swaying opinion through their wiles. *The executioners run through the streets shooting anyone who dares leave the house. They shoot anyone who is near the window.* The two little girls hurry along the road, hand in hand, beneath a threatening sky: the clouds are nothing but viscous smears. There'd been fires, without any doubt: buildings were burned down. *Near some of the burned-out houses there is a strong smell of dead bodies.* When I could get no more sense from him about why he followed such an odious and dangerous leader, he finally said: His hands are so beautiful. *Children cannot walk on their own strength and are loaded into wagons. Mothers, looking on, become insane.*—When, after the war, he returned to the university where he'd been rector and a supporter of the Nazis, a number of the students, including me, wanted to boycott his lecture; but we were also curious to hear him, so we stood at the back of the hall with our backs to him.

...and O
the
language
inherits
dark
also


Bloodied swathes. Within the straight lines, curves and loops of lead: pieces of coloured glass. A man lies in a convalescent bed; a nurse standing beside him; and another man sitting beside her, in a wheelchair. Below us we saw a squadron of planes, strangely innocent-looking in the afternoon sunlight: such a pity, I thought, to bomb them.—Long live death! he bellowed to those in the crowd below.—General, I hate to speak harshly to one who I see is a cripple; but what you've just said is the most repellent nonsense: you are a cripple in more ways than one, and you want our society to be a society of cripples like *you*.


*in darkness*
*I*
*dwell*
*or*
*is it*
*undwelling?*

When I said I wouldn't listen to her bizarre accusations and got up to leave, she threw hot coffee in my face.— Stay! she shouted. *Orthodoxy is I myself.* Or for another: *I am orthodoxy; orthodoxy is what I am.* At college his ambition was to lead a Communist uprising, but he eventually became a sheep farmer in the Brecon Beacons.—My friend, an American woman, went to Maoist China, and it was there that she found herself as a person.—That's bullshit, you replied. *My neighbour is not here, my neighbour is not you.* I've passed him on the street and seen him in the Underground, wearing multi-coloured cardigans; and once I heard him sing 'You Don't Know What Love Is'.

# EPILOGUE

A surge of wind in the trees—leafed branches stirring, swaying and bending: the sound wakes, raises itself in a wash, breaks. I sit down on the small stone ledge, near the bird feeders: listen to the wooden wind chimes.

in
or
at
flux
the
play
and
force
of
it

Water running down... it hits metal and splashes. Oil heated in a pan. Ginger and garlic, ground black pepper of course, but beaten egg first, and boiled rice, red or green peppers, mushrooms, spring onions, then soy sauce to taste, and either prawns or sausage, depending. Finding a home, losing it: torn, thrown, dispersed. An empty room.— The room isn't empty, although no people or animals or even insects are there; it is always imprinted. Wounded window, wounded door. Rain, then hail, sleet, snowstorm: blotting out the horizon line. Only the stones left to see.

Two deer—a hind and her young—appeared in the garden, content to stand or sit in poses as if for lens, inked brush or pen, chewing foliage, even in the rain. For me, they were welcome, though you were apprehensive: rightly so, as later on they ate your roses, lilies and geraniums. As I walked along the arcade, a small horse came up behind me and put its forelegs on the back of my shoulders, licking my neck affectionately. I fell; the horse fell. The hedge sparrow flew at one of the glass walls and hit it; then fell, dazed, to the floor. I gingerly picked it up, feeling the softness of its body in my hands; when I set it down outside, the toes of one of its feet clung tenaciously to my finger. There: a swirl of blood across the grass; the mutilated carcass of a sheep. I threw the staff to the ground, breaking the ceremony, and abjured magic thenceforth. *And sometimes even the best captain loses his balance,* you wrote. Seagulls flew in circles in the darkening sky over a coastal village of white-painted buildings, with hills stretching beyond. *In all faces is seen the Face of faces, veiled, and in a riddle.* He wrote in praise of *the best nurses,* in a poem's dedication: the rest was dream and dreaming's release. He died in hospital; my other friend died in the sea. A necklace or chain thrown into the sky. A skirl. *By the way, you are first watch tonight. Close your eyes—*

*and look at the schooner approaching.* Had you really listened to his music when you called him *a poor fool in the fullest sense of the word? Poor beyond all measure and foolish beyond all measure.*—And that day when you almost drowned, on the school trip to St Kilda Beach?—Yes, I was told to swim, without being asked if I *could* swim, and there was no question of querying the order; but it just seemed like one bad dream amongst others in those years.—Does it really shimmer, sway, surge, break? *...for the direct way to ascend is first to descend.* Spices, seeds, legumes, we used; and leaves, earth, wax, stones; also wool, calico, silk, cotton cloth; and doorframes, and sheets of glass. Snow blocks are placed in rows, forming a circle; then row piled upon row, with gaps filled with wedges of snow; the whole thing slanting towards a ceiling. Resist temptations to pour water on the exterior snow or light a fire inside.

> you could or you could
> not and would it
> be a pity
> steel bronze iron marble

A house made from boxes: wooden for the exterior, cardboard the interior.—It was the connection between poverty and art that concerned me, whatever the problems and contradictions; wanting an art that was pared down and without pomp or pretension or displays of sterile wit, and with common materials its basis. But not impoverished art, inane or trite art, or art for shock's-sake or as mere novelty. The written, the spoken: if a conflict then to no right end. The eye sees, the ear hears: first the lightning, then the thunder. Tap, tap, tap, tap: rain on window panes; and rain on plants in window boxes.—A kiss is a kiss unless it's a concept or a lie. Is a formality a concept? and does a lie always betray? The sky descends to the smallest flower: willingly, graciously.

> stars hill sea enfolded
> imprisoned or else released
> a lamp a table and wine
> window door gate and pathway

Elderberry dye soaks into linen. As the bridesmaid suffered from nosebleeds, her mother had brought along a supply of handkerchiefs in readiness.—Goodbye, the bride said to me, her young cousin, as she broke into tears: would we never meet again, I wondered? *Although it will most likely occur in the distant future, I would happily live to witness an exhibition of everything I have created and still hope to create, if only to arrive at the conclusion: is it anything and does it mean anything?* He told the man who'd gone blind to get down on his knees, and then he pissed into his eyes; and the man could see again.

*Everyone became so wise that eventually they all turned to atheism, including the king. Every now and then, the king's conscience would trouble him because of the wrong turning he'd taken, but then he'd slip back into his lamentable ways again.* They leapt, they tried to fly, but their wings didn't serve their efforts; instead, they plunged into the water below. *And the grandchildren... to now through the gaps in the garden fence see them play, and to know during the night that they breathe in sleep so near.* A building, if a building could be nothing but water: outer and inner walls, all water, and a flooded floor. Children's shouts, cries, yelps, squeals....—Because I possessed charity, I could pass through the ten walls of water, which were like waves standing upright, held up by the winds; and yet not drown. Because of charity, I was able to reach the Princess and remove the ten arrows from her body, and heal her with the melodies I played and sang. *Tears kill the heart, believe...* his voice at first surprisingly high, yet full and rich when required, as well as supple and superbly modulated. Grey lettering for the gravestone? Black. We arranged twigs over the flowers, broken eggshells at the base of the pots. Coming back from the cemetery, we drove by a field of sheep, and you stopped the car and called out 'Hello, sheep! It's Tuesday'; explaining that otherwise they wouldn't know. I responded that the tags on their ears looked oddly like hearing-aids.—Am I a body, no; do I have a body, no; do I have fingers and toes, a head and legs, yes, these are aspects of me; do these aspects constitute a body, no. A body is a dead thing; I'm not a dead thing. Though neglected by the music critics, he wrote: *I have had good luck. These 60 little pieces interest children taking piano lessons.* Reversed. What was here, is now there; black lace is white lace, and white lace black.—Rise up, rise up, the elder said. And the other children rose up and followed.

## Notes:

*I began writing 'Spiritual Letters' in October 1995, and completed the work in late 2016.*

*I gave a talk entitled "Concerning 'Spiritual Letters'" at St James's Church, Piccadilly (London) in May 1998, later printed in 'Poetry Salzburg Review', No. 4, 2003, in which I stated:*

*"'Spiritual Letters' derives much of its inspiration from the Scriptures, especially from tracing certain keywords through the Scriptures using a Biblical concordance. [I stopped using the concordance after Series 4, as I felt that the process had become internalised, to a large extent.] One of the things that directed my approach was the Jewish Kabbalistic tradition, especially the 13th century work known as the 'Zohar' [by Moses de Léon and others]. I'd long been impressed with the 'Zohar's' mystical commentaries and elaboration upon Scripture, and its use of a creative, imaginative mode of interpretation involving independent narrative developments and rich and startling imagery. I was also impressed by the way the 'Zohar' moves far beyond the literal meaning of the Torah, in order to wrench free some more radical meaning.*

"I'd also like to mention two other examples that I found very instructive—the work of two artists from the second half of [the twentieth] century. The first of these, Mathias Goeritz, was a wonderful sculptor, experimental architect and visual poet. (...) I exchanged letters with him over a long period of time, and he was a great encouragement to me, especially when I was still a young poet. Mathias made a series of works called 'Messages'—a powerful series of abstract images, which he developed in response to specific Biblical passages, beginning around 1959 and extending through to at least 1975. This series was quite strongly in my mind when I began writing the 'Letters'.

"The other artist I want to mention is Wallace Berman. Berman was a Californian artist whose major works were created between 1964 and his death in 1976. In particular, he produced a long series of collages using a forerunner of the photocopier called a Verifax machine. These were in part inspired by his interest in Kabbalism, and combined a regular—yet variable—visual framework with a wide range of imagery (using images from popular culture and images derived from spiritual traditions, amongst other things). I was impressed by the way that Berman juxtaposed highly diverse images, as well as by the visual clarity of his work, however complex, and I was also very intrigued by his acknowledged inspiration from Jewish mysticism.

"I wouldn't see any direct influence from Berman on either the images or the way that the writing is structured in the 'Spiritual Letters'. Berman's significance for me was in the way that he provided a powerful example of a thoroughly contemporary art, which took inspiration from a religious or spiritual tradition. My own background is Christian rather than Jewish, but as I've already mentioned, I am also drawn to Jewish mystical sources—so Berman's art seemed instructive and encouraging to me."

"So what I've been concerned with is a poetic form of writing—[mostly] in prose—that's in part determined by associations from specific Scriptural passages. But in common with the 'Zohar', 'Spiritual Letters' uses the Scriptures as "a springboard for the imagination" [Daniel Chanan Matt, Introduction to his translation of the 'Zohar', Paulist Press, 1983.] My writing sets up a relationship of sorts with Scripture and Scriptural commentary, but a very indirect one. (...) Also, my concern is with a writing that investigates and explores its themes and sources, never deriving from any sort of dogmatic position."

*I'd tend to emphasise that, as I said in the talk, 'Spiritual Letters' "exists quite independently and possesses its own integrity and intensity", at the same time as it has a relationship to Scriptural tradition (however indirect).*

*I would like to acknowledge the sources of some brief quotations and paraphrases used in these writings, solely to give credit where credit is due. There is no reason for anyone to read these notes except out of curiosity.*

*In 'Spiritual Letters (Series 1)', the words "…may result in unexpected 'wipes' of colour" are quoted from Philip Smith ("After Harry Smith" in 'American Magus: Harry Smith: A Modern Alchemist', ed. Paola Igliori, Inanout Press, 1996). The phrase "Dream geometry" derives from the title of an animated film by Canadian filmmaker, artist and poet Shelley McIntosh. "…as in a piece of arras work": Thomas De Quincey, writing about the way that music can provoke memory and indeed a sense of one's entire life. (I'm afraid I no longer remember which of his writings this occurs in.)*

*The first text in 'Spiritual Letters (Series 2)' uses a paraphrase from Robert Lax's 'Journal C' (a selection which I made from his journals and which was published by Pendo Verlag in 1990). For anyone interested, the passage occurs* on p. 66, and begins: "i remember the people i loved (who have died) or who've just disappeared...." Bob Lax wrote to me on Dec. 14 1999 (the year before his death) that he was pleased about the paraphrase and that I should feel free to mention 'Journal C' or not, as I saw fit. The quotation "In a death, in weakness, inactivity, negation" is from Rowan Williams and was taken from Mark A McIntosh's 'Mystical Theology: The Integrity of Spirituality and Theology' (Blackwell, 1998). "Bicycling through the city, with his ears painted red" is paraphrased from a biographical note in 'Paul Thek: The wonderful world that almost was' (Witte de With, 1995).

In Series 3, the sentence "Dear is the honie that is lickt out of thornes" is taken from Gerard's 'Herball'. "The motherfuckers won't let me sing" is supposed to have been said by Billie Holiday at Lester Young's funeral, though I don't remember where I heard or read this. "... wandering a maze of stone-laid alleys: one house of black wood pressed tight against another" is from my late friend Will Petersen's 'The Return' (privately printed, 1975). Will's autobiographical writings, as well as his translations and his visual art, remain an inspiration to me. The artist Donald Evans was my source for the phrase "in the neighbourhood of the spirit" (quoted in Willy

*Eisenhart, 'The World of Donald Evans', Harlin Quist, 1980). "Fragments of plaster…": Mark Beech, "Fishing in the 'Ubaid: A Review of Fish-bone Assemblages from Early Prehistoric Coastal Settlements in the Arabian Gulf" (The Journal of Oman Studies, Vol. 12, 2002). "…shot with blue and purple, and green": quoted (from a 10th century Irish source) in Jeffrey Burton Russell, 'A History of Heaven: The Singing Silence' (Princeton University Press, 1997).*

*The fifth text in the third series is dedicated to the memory of Nicholas Zurbrugg, friend and fellow writer. The ninth text is dedicated to my late friend, the painter Lambros Koumantanos. The eleventh is dedicated to the poet Carl Rakosi, who was still alive when the text was written but has since passed away.*

*Series 4: "…the fine celestial substance of light as it is native to the stars" is from Wilhelm Bousset (trans. John E. Steely), quoted in Colleen McDannell and Bernhard Lang, 'Heaven: A History' (Yale UP, 2nd ed., 1988). "I even miss the skirl of starlings…": a letter from a poet friend in Canada, clearly nostalgic for London. "We all believe in one true God…": the Apostles' Creed, which Martin Luther set to music so beautifully. "…the whiteness of their nature": from a Chinese Nestorian inscription, quoted in Richard*

C. Foltz, 'Religions of the Silk Road: Overland Trade and Cultural Exchange from Antiquity to the Fifteenth Century' (St. Martin's Griffin, 1999). (I've drawn upon Foltz's book in a number of instances in both this series and the next.) "I would eat rotten apples...": Martin Luther, quoted in Eric W. Gritsch and Robert W. Jenson, 'Lutheranism: The Theological Movement and Its Confessional Writings' (Fortress Press, 1976). "The only differentiations I could see...": Ian McKeever, in an interview with Matthew Collings, Artscribe, no. 46, May-July 1984. "...suddenly there was an explosion...": John Levy, from an e-letter to the present writer. "...the being flitting about there among the shadows...": Loie Fuller, quoted in Richard Nelson Current and Marcia Ewig Current, 'Loie Fuller: Goddess of Light' (Northeastern University Press, 1997). "He just didn't write enough music": Morton Feldman ("Conversation between Morton Feldman and Walter Zimmerman", which I found at some point on the Internet, but which is now available in 'Morton Feldman says: interviews and lectures 1964-1987', ed. Chris Villars, Hyphen Press, 2006). "Some of the copyists...": Andrew George, in the Introduction to his translation of 'The Epic of Gilgamesh' (Penguin, 2000). "It was my little cell of solid black": Jay DeFeo, quoted in 'Jay DeFeo and The Rose', ed. Jane Green and Leah Levy (University of California Press, 2003). "Come at once, she wrote..." is a paraphrase from a letter by a Roman Egyptian named Thaubas, quoted in Euphrosyne Doxiadis, 'The Mysterious Fayum Portraits: Faces from Ancient Egypt' (Thames & Hudson, 1995). "—It was a kite to fly in..." is paraphrased from Mabel Hubbard Bell (Alexander Graham Bell's wife), if I remember correctly—I don't remember the specific source. "I was woken from a few hours' sleep...": a paraphrase from Lisa Fittko, quoted in Momme Brodersen, 'Walter Benjamin: A Biography', translated by Malcolm R Green and Ingrida Ligers, edited by Martina Derviş(Verso, 1996).

In Series 5, #1,both the sentence beginning "She quickly had a thousand umbrellas bought...", and also the following sentence, were inspired by a passage in Rai Sanyō's "The Biography of Snowflake", translated by Burton Watson ('Anthology of Japanese Literature: Earliest Era to Mid-Nineteenth Century', compiled and edited by Donald Keene, Grove Press, 1955).

In Series 5, #2, "Yellow flowers, green leaves...": Robert Lax, in a letter to the present writer (from March 1994). Marcia Kelly, Bob Lax's niece and executor, kindly gave her blessing to my using this quotation and the following one by Lax. "...more to pyrotechnics than to the art of dance": a critic writing about Loie Fuller, quoted in 'Loie Fuller: Goddess of Light'. "All in one day...": Lax again, from a letter written in February 1995. "Ah, if I die on the boat...": from Gail Holst-Warhaft's translation of an anonymous Rembetika song, associated by many with Sotiria Bellou's great rendition. See Gail Holst (now Gail Holst-Warhaft), 'Road to Rembetika: music of a Greek sub-culture / songs of love, sorrow and hashish' (Denise Harvey, (1975) 1994). "The love we bear to the blessed martyrs...": St Augustine, quoted in McDannell and Lang, 'Heaven: A History'. "The day we were in the stocks...": from 'The Passion (or Martyrdom) of Saints Perpetua and Felicitas' (the title is translated variously). I've used the translation by Rev Alban Butler in this instance, from his book 'The Lives of the Fathers, Martyrs and Other Principal Saints', Vol. 1 (D. & J. Sadlier, 1864).

In series 5, #4, "...from a square to a circle..." is taken from Michael Levin's introduction to 'Mathias Goeritz: architectural sculpture' (Israel Museum, 1980). "Darkened windows...": Momme Broderson, 'Walter Benjamin: A Biography'. "I saw a ladder...": 'Perpetua' again, using Butler's translation for the second sentence and Herbert Musurillo's (from 'The Acts of the Christian Martyrs', Clarendon Press, 1972) for the first. "I at once...": 'Perpetua', in Musurillo's translation.

*With series 5, #5, many more voices have entered into the writing than with any other "letter", though of course it's also the longest of these texts. "She knew so much…": Marianne North, 'Recollections of a Happy Life', abridged by Graham Bateman as 'A Vision of Eden: The Life and Work of Marianne North' (Webb & Bower / Royal Botanical Gardens, 1980). "Dear adopted sister…": Edward Hicks, quoted in Alice Ford, 'Edward Hicks: Painter of the Peaceable Kingdom' (University of Pennsylvania Press, (1952) 1998). "Doors in the floor and ceiling…": paraphrased from "The House that Frank Built" by Dorothy G. Owens, on the website 'Old Spooky or Shangriold Spooky or Shangri-La' (about folk artist/architect James Franklin Butts). "There were two monastery buildings…": quoted in Richard C Foltz, 'Religions of the Silk Road'. I've drawn upon Foltz's book for a few paraphrases in #5, as well. "…then we went on…": Marianne North, 'Recollections of a Happy Life'. "She'd boiled water…": this sentence is paraphrased from a passage in a letter from the poet Andrew Schelling to the present writer. "Let the country…": from a Manichaean text quoted in Foltz's book (I've removed square brackets from "the country"). "…he took my hand…": 'Perpetua', in W.H. Shewring's translation ('The Passion of SS Perpetua and Felicity MM. A new edition and translation…', Sheed & Ward, 1931, modernized by Paul Halsall on* the Internet Medieval Source Book site). "– Ah, you extraordinary illusionist! What have you come to show us…": paraphrased from lines in the film 'Der Golem' by Paul Wegener (1920). "Then out came an Egyptian against me…": 'Perpetua', in the Musurillo and Butler translations (first and second sentence respectively). "In some cases a laurel crown…": A F Shore, 'Portrait Painting from Roman Egypt' (The Trustees of the British Museum, 1962). "With these Eyes…": Hugh of St. Victor, writing about Lincoln Cathedral (quoted in Painton Cowen, 'The Rose Window: Splendour and Symbol', Thames & Hudson, 2005). "Suffice to say…": Edward Hicks, quoted in Alice Ford, 'Edward Hicks: Painter of the Peaceable Kingdom'. (I've changed the spelling of "limmited" in the quotation to "limited".) "Thy rose bush is very pretty…": Sarah Hicks Parry, quoted in Alice Ford's book on Edward Hicks. "…we enjoy every fleeting glimpse…": Ben Sackheim, quoted in a memorial publication (2000) for Ben, who was a friend of mine. "For flowers are good…": Christopher Smart, 'Jubilate Agno', from a website provided by Ray Davis. "He smashed at the door…", and the next sentence, "At midnight he rose…", are paraphrased from passages in Gershom Scholem's 'Kabbalah' (Keter Publishing House, 1988). "I am praying to God…": Nicolas Berdyaev, quoting from a conversation with Vassili Rozanov ('Dream and Reality: An Essay in

*Autobiography', tr. Katharine Lampert, Geoffrey Bles, 1950). "He could hear the rivers protest…": Zsuzsanne Gulácsi, on the prophet Mani ('Manichaean Art in Berlin Collections', Brepols, 2001). "The raft went in…": Ian Fairweather, quoted by Mary Eagle, "The Painter and the Raft", in 'Fairweather', ed. Murray Bail (Art & Australia Books / Queensland Art Gallery, 1994).*

*Series 5, #5 is dedicated to the memory of my dear friends Petros Bourgos, filmmaker and poet, and Michael Thorp, artist, poet and critic.*

*Series 6, #1: "Even if while fixing his gaze...": Nicholas of Cusa, 'On the Vision of God', in 'Selected Spiritual Writings', tr. H. Lawrence Bond, Paulist Press, 1997. There are other derivations from Cusanus here, and elsewhere— he has been an enduring influence, in fact—but they are not always easy to specify. "One, a 'gardens' window...": Vahni Capildeo, writing about St Andrew's and St Peter's Church, Blofield (often called Blofield Church), in Norfolk, in an e-mail letter to the present writer, 5 August 2008. "Eight years of painting and re-painting...": this comes from a text of my own, 'Wild Poignancy', which was published in conjunction with an exhibition of Ian McKeever's in the text + work series, The Gallery at The Arts Institute at Bournemouth, 2003. I've slightly revised the passage* that appears here. The text later appeared in my book *'Reassembling Still: Collected Poems'*, Shearsman Books, 2014.

6, #2: *"The water of the canal..."*: from *"a cautionary Jewish story found in b Baba Mezia 59b"*, quoted by Gavin D'Costa in *'Resurrection Reconsidered'*, ed. G D'Costa, Oneworld Publications, 1996. *"...the brightness all around us..."*: Susan Hicks, quoted in Alice Ford, *'Edward Hicks: Painter of the Peaceable Kingdom'*. *"...to see depicted in great details..."*: Vahni Capildeo, from the same e-letter.

6, #3: *"Who can undo..."*: St Augustine, from the *'Confessions'* (*Confessiones*), quoted in Vernon J Bourke, *'Augustine's Quest of Wisdom: His Life, Thought and Works'*, Magi Books, (1945) 1993.

*"...I came to regard to true..."*: St Augustine, from the same source. *"Heads are found severed..."*: John Foxe (or Fox), *'Actes and Monuments'*, often referred to as *'Fox's Book of Martyrs'*. This can be conveniently found online at the *'Christian Classics Ethereal Library'*, under Fox's Book of Martyrs, ed. William Byron Forbush. *"These galleries are about eight feet high..."*: also from John Foxe. *"I came to Carthage..."*: St Augustine, as above.

6, #4: "During one visit...": Mark Terrill, in an e-mail letter to the present writer, 27 July 2009. (I've incorporated some very slight changes.) The subject here is the painter Jay DeFeo. "They travelled in disguise...": Hanawa Hokinoichi, quoted in Stephen Turnbull, 'Ninja AD 1460-1650', Osprey Publishing, 2003. "Men who humble themselves...": 'The Martyrdom of the Saintly and Blessed Apostle Apollonius, also called Sakkeas', in Herbert Musurillo, 'The Acts of the Christian Martyrs', Clarendon Press, 1972. "Deprive them of your veneration...": 'The Martyrdom of Saints Carpus, Papylus, and Agathonicê' (The Latin Recension), in the same Musurillo book. "For the protection of the head...": A F Shore, 'Portrait Painting from Roman Egypt', The Trustees of the British Museum, 1972. "...a reclining woman whose face has been ferociously obliterated": Pascal Neveux, 'Elie Faure and Chaim Soutine: The Story of an Ill-Fated Friendship", in Norman L Kleeblatt and Kenneth E Silver, eds., 'An Expressionist in Paris: The Paintings of Chaim Soutine', Prestel / The Jewish Museum, 1998. "...your gaze prompts me...": Nicholas of Cusa, 'On the Vision of God'.


6, #5: "I was kidnapped by the sweetness...": a Christian catacomb inscription, quoted in Vincenzo Fiocchi Nicolai, Fabrizio Bisconti and Danilo Mazzoleni, 'The Christian

Catacombs of Rome: History, Decoration, Inscriptions', tr. Cristina Carlo Stella and Lori-Ann Touchette, Schnell & Steiner, 2002. "...they heroically endured...": 'The Martyrs of Lyons', in Musurillo, 'The Acts of the Christian Martyrs'. "They commonly call him The Green...": from Elizabeth Ann Finn, 'Home in the Holyland' (James Nisbet, 1866). I found the quotation (the wording of which I've very slightly changed) in a Wikipedia article on St. George.

6, #6: "– What a thing would be a history...": John Keats, in 'Letters of John Keats', ed. Robert Gittings, OUP, 1970. The letter is to Tom Keats, 3rd-9th July 1818. "Ashes were already falling...": Pliny the Younger,' Selected Letters', ed. G B Allen, Clarendon Press, 1915. I found this on the 'EyeWitness to History' website.

6, #8: "We had sat down to rest...": Pliny the Younger, from the same source. "A gleam of light returned...": this is also from Pliny the Younger. "The intricate lead crystal window...": quoted in Saul Friedlander, 'The Years of Persecution: Nazi Germany and the Jews 1933-1939', Phoenix, 2007. "The subjugated should be left nothing...": Carl von Clausewitz, 'On War'. The quotation (which actually begins "The conquered...") comes from an intertitle in Frank Capra's film 'Here is Germany' (1945).

6,# 9: "On coming in...": Emil Kraepelin, quoted in R D Laing, 'The Divided Self: An Existential Study in Sanity and Madness', Penguin, 1960. "The aboriginal Fire...": Empedocles, adapted (though with only slight changes) from Kathleen Freeman's translation in her book 'Ancilla to the Pre-Socratic Philosophers', Harvard UP, (1948) 1983. "They keep out the deep water...": Empedocles, in John Burnet's translation, from his book 'Early Greek Philosophy', 3rd ed., A & C Black, 1920. "Four barren hillsides...": Pier Paolo Pasolini, 'Seeking Locations in Palestine for the Film 'The Gospel According to St. Matthew' (1965). I've no idea who was responsible for the English language version of this film. "...an incredible smallness...": also from Pasolini, same source. "How can I ever stand it...": adapted from the folk song 'Little Maggie'. This has been recorded by many singers/musicians; my favourite versions are those of Mike Seeger and Barbara Dane, and also the instrumental version by Sandy Bull. "...everything seemed burnt...": another phrase taken from the Pasolini film.


7, #1: "I would wake up outside...": this paraphrases an autobiographical note by John Berryman, if I remember correctly.

7, #2: "Of night, lonely, blind-eyed": Empedocles, translated by Kathleen Freeman in her 'Ancilla to the Pre-Socratic Philosophers', Harvard University Press, 1948. "At the time he entered...": see 'La veritable histoire d'Artaud le Momo' ('The True Story of Artaud the Momo') by Gérard Mordillat and Jerôme Prieur, 1993, especially the interviews with Anie Besnard and Marthe Roberts. "That kike mentality...": paraphrasing Antonin Artaud, 'Letter Against the Kabbala', tr David Rattray in Jack Hirschman, ed, 'Artaud Anthology', 2nd ed., City Lights Books, 1965. "Half bricks on whole bricks": Talmudic reference to the black fiery letters on white fire of Divine poetry. My source here is an online article by Rabbi Avi Weiss, 'Shabbat Forshpeis: A Taste of Torah in Honor of Shabbat', Hebrew Institute of Riverdale Weekly Newsletter, 2002, www.hir.org/a_weekly_gallery/8.16.02-weekly.html. "The intricate lead crystal window..." and the following sentence are quoted, and paraphrased, respectively, from Saul Friedlander, 'The Years of Persecution: Nazi Germany and the Jews 1933-1939'. "...we were not only shut out of our houses...": from one of the martyrdom texts in Herbert Musurillo, 'The Acts of the Christian Martyrs'. "The skies open for you: may you live in peace": from the Christian catacomb inscriptions quoted in Vincenzo Fiocchi Nicolai, Fabrizio Biaconti and Danilo Mazzoleni, 'The Christian Catacombs of Rome:

History, Decoration, Inscriptions'. "Nor is the fire ever lulled to sleep...": adapted from 'The Martyrdom of Saints Carpus, Papylus and Agathonicê' (The Latin Recension), in Musurillo, 'The Acts of the Christian Martyrs'.

7, #3: "no end/ or beginning...": adapted from Peter John Olivi, 'Letter to the Sons of Charles II', in 'Apocalyptic Spirituality', tr. Bernard McGinn, SPCK, 1980. "With violence he began to persecute...": Angelo of Clareno, 'A Letter to the Pope concerning the False Accusations and Calumnies Made by the Franciscans', in 'Apocalyptic Spirituality'.

7, #4: "before your door/ I fell down..." loosely adapted from Judeo-Spanish medieval lyrics, which I found in the notes to La Roza Enflorese's excellent CD 'séfarad', Pavane Records, 2001.

7, #5: "And with this you asked the man standing by...": adapted from 'The Martyrdom of Saints Perpetua and Felicitas' in Musurillo, 'The Acts of the Christian Martyrs'.

7, #7: "A sublime place...": from Pier Paolo Pasolini's 'Seeking Locations in Palestine for the film 'The Gospel According to St Matthew'."

*7, #8:* "The transformations of fire are first sea...": from 'The Fragments of Heracleitus', an anonymous translation and publication from 1976.

*7, #9:* "It was cold, and snow was falling...": quoted in Nechama Tec, 'When Light Pierced the Darkness', OUP, 1986. "...he was a great fan of the dithyramb...": Hermann Heiß, quoted by Herbert Henck in the notes to his CD 'Joseph Matthias Hauer, Klavierwerke', Schott Wergo Music Media, 1997.

*7, #10:* "Dusk was falling but it was light...": quoted in Norman Cohn, 'Warrant for Genocide', Harper & Row, 1966. "Jewesses pretending to be French or Italian...": paraphrased from the notorious 'Protocols of the Elders of Zion', which has been ascribed to various authors... even "the Elders of Zion"! Numerous editions in English have been published over the years, one regrets to say. "The executioners run through the streets...": quoted in Nechama Tec, 'When Light Pierced the Darkness'. "Near some of the burned-out houses...": quoted in Norman Cohn, 'Warrant for Genocide'. "Children cannot walk...": quoted in Nechama Tec, 'When Light Pierced the Darkness'.

*7, #11: The "Long live death!" interchange recalls an actual exchange between General Millán Astray and the philosopher and novelist Miguel de Unamuno. "Orthodoxy is I myself": Nicholas Berdyaev quotes this, not at all approvingly, in his fascinating "essay in autobiography", 'Dream and Reality', tr. Katharine Lampert, Geoffrey Bles, 1950.*

*In the Epilogue, the first text is in memory of David Menzies, poet and friend.*

*In the second text, "In all faces is seen the Face..." is from Nicholas of Cusa, 'The Vision of God', tr Emma Gurney Salter, Cosimo, 2007. "...a poor fool in the fullest sense of the word": Alban Berg, unkindly at the say the least, on Josef Matthias Hauer; quoted by Herbert Henck in the notes to 'Joseph Matthias Hauer, Klavierwerke'. "...for the direct way to ascend is first to descend" comes from one of the Franciscan Spirituals, if I remember correctly. "Although it will most likely occur in the distant future...": H N Werkman, quoted in Alston W Purvis, 'H N Werkman', Yale UP / Laurence King Publishing, 2004.*

*In the third text, I use paraphrases from Rabbi Nachman of Breslov's 'The Story of the Seven Beggars' ("Everyone*

became so wise..." and "—Because I possessed charity...").
*An English translation of this extraordinary story can be found at www.shuvubonim.org/storysb.html (Breslov Institutions, Yeshivat 'Shuvu Bonim'). "And the grandchildren...": paraphrased from Anton Webern, 'Letters to Hildegard Jone and Josef Humplik', ed Josef Polnauer, Universal Edition / Theodore Presser, 1967. "Tears kill the heart, believe": John Dowland, 'I Saw My Lady Weep'. The sheep anecdote comes partly from a letter from Michael Walters in the 'FLS News', c. 2015/16 (I sometimes wish I kept better notes). "I have had good luck...": Josef Matthias Hauer, quoted by Herbert Henck, same source as above. "– Rise up, rise up...": echoing 'The Wife of Usher's Well' (also known as 'Lady Gay').*

*There are also a few other quotations and paraphrases in these texts, which I haven't specified—either because I've forgotten the sources or because, in the case of personal correspondence, I prefer the sources to remain private. I should also admit that some passages that look like quotations actually aren't at all.*

*To reiterate, these notes are purely for acknowledgment, not for elucidation, except perhaps in a very general way. (E.g. it may possibly be helpful to know that Nicholas of*

*Cusa has influenced the thinking behind my writing.) I didn't write these texts with the classroom in mind. On the other hand, I don't mind people knowing that I read books, listen to music, watch films, look at artworks....*

*DM*
*January 2017*

ACKNOWLEDGEMENTS:

These texts were first published in *Across Borders, Bongos of the Lord, Delicate Iron, Dispatches from the Poetry Wars, Fire, First Intensity, Free Verse, Gangway, Golden Handcuffs Review, Hassle, House Organ, Intimacy, kadar koli, Kater Murr's Press, Lamport Court, Long Poem Magazine, Metre, NOON, Oasis, Painted, spoken, Poetry Salzburg Review, Sentence: a Journal of Prose Poetics, Shadow Train, Shearsman, Shuffle Boil, Southfields, Stride, Tears in the Fency, 26, Versal* and *Vértebra: Revista de Artes, Literatura y Crítica* (with translations by Fernando Pérez), as well as in *A Formerly United Kingdom,* compiled by otata, otata's bookshelf (e-book), *Don't Start Me Talking: interviews with contemporary poets,* ed. Tim Allen and Andrew Duncan, Salt Publishing (Cambridge), *A Gathering for Gael Turnbull,* ed. Peter McCarey, Au Quai (Glasgow and Staines, Middlesex), *In the Company of Poets,* ed. John Rety, Hearing Eye (London), *poetry tREnD: Eine englisch-deutsche Anthologie zeitgenössischer Lyrik,* ed. Aprilia Zank (with translations by Judith Königer, Sabine Stiglmayr, Julia Offermann and Anna Hubrich), Lit Verlag (Berlin), *Take Five 06,* ed. John Lucas, Shoestring Press (Nottingham, UK) and the Tony Frazer *webfestschrift.*

Various parts of this book have also appeared in the following limited edition publications: *Spiritual Letters (1-7),* tel-let (Charleston, Illinois); *Spiritual Letters (1-10),* EMH Arts/Eagle Graphics (London), with artwork by Andrew Bick; *Spiritual Letters (1-12),* hawkhaven press (San Francisco); *Spiritual Letters (Series 2, #1-5),* Nyxpress (Sydney), with artwork by Denis Mizzi; *Spiritual Letters*

(*Series 3, #1-7*), Nyxpress, with artwork by Denis Mizzi; *Spiritual Letters (Series 4)*, hawkhaven press, with artwork by Louise Victor; *Spiritual Letters (Series 5)*, Nyxpress. *Spiritual Letters (Series 6, #6)* was published as a broadside by Ed. Il Bagatto (Bagnore, Italy). The final text from this project was published as a broadside from Sloow Tapes (Stekene, Belgium), with artwork by Ken White, under the title 'From *Epilogue*'.

The first two series were published in *Spiritual Letters (I-II) and other writings*, Reality Street Editions (Hastings), and *Spiritual Letters (Series 3)* appeared from Stride Publications in Exeter, while *Spiritual Letters (Series 6)* came out from Shearsman Books (Bristol).

To relieve confusion, the sections that were published by tel-let and EMH Arts/Eagle Graphics, as well as *Spiritual Letters (1-12)* (hawkhaven), were all from the first series of the project—I simply wasn't thinking of it as consisting of separate series at the time.

The largest previous gathering of this work had been *Spiritual Letters (Series 1-5)*, Chax Press (Tucson). In addition, a double CD sound recording of the first five series appeared from LARYNX. And then in 2017, Contraband Books in the UK (now in the Netherlands) published an edition of the entire work.

This edition by Spuyten Duyvil is the first time the entire *Spiritual Letters* has appeared in the US.

Printed in Great Britain
by Amazon